LOUIS XV,
Roi de France.

Édition de Luxe

# MEMOIRS OF A PHYSICIAN

### IN THREE VOLUMES
### VOL. III.

## BY ALEXANDRE DUMAS

WITH ILLUSTRATIONS

BOSTON
ESTES AND LAURIAT
1895

# MEMOIRS OF A PHYSICIAN.

## VOLUME III.

# CONTENTS.

# LIST OF ILLUSTRATIONS.

## Vol. III.

# MEMOIRS OF A PHYSICIAN.

## CHAPTER XCIX.

### THE CONFUSION INCREASES.

MADAME DE BÉARN followed Richelieu's advice literally. Two hours and a half after the duke had left her she was waiting in the ante-chamber at Luciennes, in the company of Monsieur Zamore.

It was some time since she had been seen at Madame Dubarry's, and her presence therefore excited a feeling of curiosity in the countess's boudoir when her name was announced.

Monsieur d'Aiguillon had not lost any time either, and he was plotting with the favourite when Chon entered to request an audience for Madame de Béarn. The duke made a movement to retire, but the countess detained him.

"I would rather you would remain," said she. "In case my old alms-giver comes to ask a loan, you would be most useful to me, for she will ask less."

The duke remained. Madame de Béarn, with a face composed for the occasion, took the chair opposite the countess, which the latter offered to her, and after the first civilities were exchanged,—

"May I ask to what fortunate chance I am indebted for your presence, madame?" said Madame Dubarry.

"Ah, madame," said the old litigant, "a great misfortune."

"What! madame, a misfortune?"

"A piece of news which will deeply afflict his Majesty."

"I am all impatience, madame —"

"The parliament —"

"Oh, ho!" grumbled the Duke d'Aiguillon.

"The Duke d'Aiguillon," said the countess, hastily introducing her guest to her lady visitor, for fear of some unpleasant contretemps. But the old countess was as cunning as all the other courtiers put together, and never caused a misunderstanding, except wittingly, and when the misunderstanding seemed likely to benefit her.

"I know," said she, "all the baseness of these rascals, and their want of respect for merit of high birth."

This compliment, aimed directly at the duke, drew a most graceful bow from him, which the litigant returned with an equally graceful courtesy.

"But," continued she, "it is not the duke alone who is now concerned, but the entire population: the parliament refuse to act."

"Indeed!" exclaimed Madame Dubarry, throwing herself back upon the sofa; "there will be no more justice in France! Well! What change will that produce?"

The duke smiled. As for Madame de Béarn, instead of taking the affair pleasantly, her morose features darkened still more. "It is a great calamity, madame," said she.

"Ah! indeed?" replied the favourite.

"It is evident, madame, that you are happy enough to have no lawsuits."

"Hem!" said D'Aiguillon, to recall the attention of Madame Dubarry, who at last comprehended the insinuation of the litigant.

"Alas, madame," said she, "it is true; you remind me that if I have no lawsuit, you have a very important one."

"Ah, yes, madame, and delay will be ruinous to me."

"Poor lady!"

"Unless, countess, the king takes some decided step."

"Oh, madame, the king is right well inclined to do so; he will exile messieurs the councillors, and all will be right."

"But, madame, that would be an indefinite adjournment."

"Do you see any remedy, then? Will you be kind enough to point it out to us?"

The litigant concealed her face beneath her hood, like Cæsar expiring under his toga.

"There is one remedy, certainly," said D'Aiguillon; "but perhaps his Majesty might shrink from employing it."

"What is it?" asked the plaintiff, with anxiety.

"The ordinary resource of royalty in France, when it is rather embarrassed. It is to hold a bed of justice, and to say, 'I will!' when all the opponents say, 'I will not.'"

"An excellent idea!" exclaimed Madame de Béarn, with enthusiasm.

"But which must not be divulged," replied D'Aiguillon, diplomatically, and with a gesture which Madame de Béarn fully comprehended.

"Oh, madame," said she, instantly, "you who have so much influence with the king, persuade him to say, 'I will have the suit of Madame de Béarn judged.' Besides, you know, it was promised long ago."

Monsieur d'Aiguillon bit his lips, glanced an adieu to Madame Dubarry, and left the boudoir. He had heard the sound of the king's carriage in the courtyard.

"Here is the king!" said Madame Dubarry, rising to dismiss her visitor.

"Oh, madame, why will you not permit me to throw myself at his Majesty's feet?"

"To ask him for a bed of justice?" replied the countess, quickly. "Most willingly! Remain here, madame, since such is your desire."

Scarcely had Madame de Béarn adjusted her head-dress when the king entered.

"Ah," said he, "you have visitors, countess!"

"Madame de Béarn, sire."

"Sire, justice!" exclaimed the old lady, making a most profound reverence.

"Oh!" said Louis XV., in a bantering tone, imperceptible to those who did not know him; "has any one offended you, madame?"

"Sire, I ask for justice."

"Against whom?"

"Against the parliament."

"Ah, good!" said the king, rubbing his hands; "you complain of my parliament. Well, do me the pleasure to bring them to reason. I, too, have to complain of them, and I beg you to grant me justice also," added he, imitating the courtesies of the old countess.

"But, sire, you are the king, — the master."

"The king, — yes; the master, — not always."

"Sire, proclaim your will."

"I do that every evening, madame; and they proclaim theirs every morning. Now, as these two wills are diametrically opposed to each other, it is with us as with the earth and the moon, which are ever running after each other without meeting."

"Sire, your voice is powerful enough to drown all the bawlings of these fellows."

"There you are mistaken. I am not a lawyer, as they are. If I say yes, they say no; it is impossible for us to come to any arrangement. If, when I have said yes, you can find any means to prevent their saying no, I will make an alliance with you."

"Sire, I have the means."

"Let me hear it quickly."

"I will, sire. Hold a bed of justice."

"That is another embarrassment," said the king; "a bed of justice — remember, madame — is almost a revolution."

"It is simply telling these rebellious subjects that you are the master. You know, sire, that when the king proclaims his will in this manner, he alone has a right to speak: no one answers. You say to them, *I will*, and they bow their assent."

"The fact is," said the Countess Dubarry, "the idea is a magnificent one."

"Magnificent it may be, but not good," replied Louis.

"But what a noble spectacle!" resumed Madame Dubarry, with warmth; "the procession, the nobles, the peers, the entire military staff of the king! Then the immense crowd of people; then the bed of justice, composed of five cushions embroidered with golden *fleurs-de-lys*,— it would be a splendid ceremony!"

"You think so?" said the king, rather shaken in his resolution.

"Then the king's magnificent dress, — the cloak lined with ermine, the diamonds in the crown, the golden sceptre, — all the splendour which so well suits an august and noble countenance. Oh, how handsome you would look, sire!"

"It is a long time since we had a bed of justice," said Louis, with affected carelessness.

"Not since your childhood, sire," said Madame de Béarn. "The remembrance of your brilliant beauty on that occasion has remained engraven on the hearts of all."

"And then," added Madame Dubarry, "there would be an excellent opportunity for the chancellor to display his keen and concise eloquence, — to crush these people with his truth, dignity, and power."

"I must wait for the parliament's next misdeed," said Louis; "then I shall see."

"What can you wait for, sire, more outrageous than what they have just committed?"

"Why, what have they done?"

"Do you not know?"

"They have teased Monsieur d'Aiguillon a little, but that is not a hanging offence; although," said the king, looking at Madame Dubarry, "although this dear duke is a friend of mine. Besides, if the parliament has teased the duke a little, I have punished them for their ill-nature by my decree of yesterday or the day before, — I do not remember which. We are now even."

"Well, sire," said Madame Dubarry, with warmth, "Madame de Béarn has just informed us that this morning these black-gowned gentlemen have taken the start of you."

"How so?" said the king, frowning.

"Speak, madame, the king permits it," said the favourite.

"Sire, the councillors have determined not to hold a court of parliament until your Majesty yields to their wishes."

"What say you?" said the king. "You mistake, madame; that would be an act of rebellion, and my parliament dares not revolt, I hope."

"Sire, I assure you —"

"Oh, madame, it is a mere rumour."

"Will your Majesty deign to hear me?"

"Speak, countess."

"Well, my procureur has this morning returned me all the papers relating to my lawsuit; he can no longer plead, since they will no longer judge."

"Mere reports, I tell you, — attempts at intimidation."

But while he spoke, the king paced up and down the boudoir in agitation.

"Sire, will your Majesty believe Monsieur de Richelieu, if you will not believe me? In my presence his papers were returned to him also, and the duke left the house in a rage."

"Some one is tapping at the door," said the king, to change the conversation.

"It is Zamore, sire."

Zamore entered.

"A letter, mistress," said he.

"With your permission, sire," said the countess. "Ah! good heavens!" exclaimed she, suddenly.

"What is the matter?"

"From the chancellor, sire. Monsieur de Maupeou, knowing that your Majesty has deigned to pay me a visit, solicits my intervention to obtain an audience for him."

"What is in the wind now?"

"Show the chancellor in," said Madame Dubarry. The Countess de Béarn rose to take her leave.

"You need not go, madame," said the king. "Good-day, Monsieur de Maupeou. What news?"

"Sire," said the chancellor, bowing, "the parliament embarrassed you; you have no longer a parliament."

"How so? Are they all dead? Have they taken arsenic?"

"Would to Heaven they had! No, sire, they live; but they will not sit any longer, and have sent in their resignations. I have just received them in a mass."

"The counsellors?"

"No, sire, the resignations."

"I told you, sire, that it was a serious matter," said the countess, in a low voice.

"Most serious," replied Louis, impatiently. "Well, chancellor, what have you done?"

"Sire, I have come to receive your Majesty's orders."

"We shall exile these people, Maupeou."

"Sire, they will not judge any better in exile."

"We shall command them to judge. Bah! injunctions are out of date — letters of order likewise — "

"Ah, sire, this time you must be determined."

"Yes, you are right."

"Courage!" said Madame de Béarn, aside to the countess.

"And act the master, after having too often acted only the father," said the countess.

"Chancellor," said the king, slowly, "I know only one remedy; it is serious, but efficacious. I will hold a bed of justice; these people must be made to tremble once for all."

"Ah, sire," exclaimed the chancellor, "that is well spoken; they must bend or break."

"Madame," added the king, addressing Madame de Béarn, "if your suit be not judged, you see it will not be my fault."

"Sire, you are the greatest monarch in the world!"

"Oh, yes!" echoed the countess, Chon, and the chancellor.

"The world does not say so, however," murmured the king.

## CHAPTER C.

### THE BED OF JUSTICE.

THIS famous bed of justice took place with all the ceremonies which royal pride, on the one hand, and the intrigues which drove the master to this step, on the other,
demanded.

The household of the king was placed under arms; an
abundance of short-robed archers, soldiers of the watch,
and police officers were commissioned to protect the lord
chancellor, who, like a general upon the decisive day,
would have to expose his sacred person to secure the
success of the enterprise.

The chancellor was execrated. Of this he was well
aware, and if his vanity made him fear assassination, those
better versed in the sentiments of the public towards him
could, without exaggerating, have predicted some down-
right insults, or at least hootings, as likely to fall to his
share. The same perquisites were promised to Monsieur
d'Aiguillon, who was equally obnoxious to the popular
instincts, improved, perhaps, by parliamentary debates.
The king affected serenity, yet he was not easy. But he
donned with great satisfaction his magnificent robes, and
straightway came to the conclusion that nothing protects
so surely as majesty. He might have added, "and the
love of the people." But this phrase had been so frequently repeated to him at Metz during his illness, that
he imagined he could not repeat it now without being
guilty of plagiarism.

The dauphiness, for whom the sight was a new one, and
who at heart perhaps wished to see it, assumed her

plaintive look, and wore it during the whole way to the ceremony, which disposed public opinion very favourably towards her.

Madame Dubarry was brave; she possessed that confidence which is given by youth and beauty. Besides, had not everything been said that could be said of her? What could be added now? She appeared radiant with beauty, as if the splendour of her august lover had been reflected upon her.

The Duke d'Aiguillon marched boldly among the peers who preceded the king; his noble and impressive countenance betrayed no symptoms of grief or discontent, nor did he bear himself triumphantly. To see him walking thus, none would have guessed that the struggle of the king with his parliament was on his account.

The crowd pointed him out in the crowd, terrible glances were darted at him from the parliament, and that was all. The great hall of the Palais was crammed to overflowing; actors and spectators together made a total of more than three thousand persons.

Outside the Palais the crowd, kept in order by the staves of the officers, and the batons and maces of the archers, gave token of its presence only by that indescribable hum which is not a voice, which articulates nothing, but which nevertheless makes itself heard, and which may justly be called the sound of the popular flood.

The same silence reigned in the great hall, when, the sound of footsteps having ceased, and every one having taken his place, the king, majestic and gloomy, had commanded his chancellor to begin the proceedings.

The parliament knew beforehand what the bed of justice held in reserve for them; they fully understood why they had been convoked. They were to hear the unmitigated expression of the royal will; but they knew the patience, not to say the timidity, of the king, and if they feared, it was rather for the consequences of the bed of justice than for the sitting itself.

The chancellor commenced his address. He was an excellent orator; his exordium was clever, and the amateurs of a demonstrative style found ample scope for study in it. As it proceeded, however, the speech degenerated into a tirade so severe that all the nobility had a smile on their lips, while the parliament felt very ill at ease.

The king, by the mouth of his chancellor, ordered them to cut short the affairs of Brittany, of which he had had enough. He commanded them to be reconciled to the Duke d'Aiguillon, whose services pleased him; and not to interrupt the service of justice, by which means everything should go on as in that happy period of the golden age, when the flowing streams murmured judicial or argumentative discourses, when the trees were loaded with bags of law papers, placed within reach of the lawyers and attorneys, who had the right to pluck them as fruit belonging to them.

These flippancies did not reconcile the parliament to the Lord Chancellor, nor to the Duke d'Aiguillon; but the speech had been made, and all reply was impossible.

The members of the parliament, although scarcely able to contain their vexation, assumed, with that admirable unity which gives so much strength to constituted bodies, a calm and indifferent demeanour, which highly displeased his Majesty and the aristocratic world upon the platform.

The dauphiness turned pale with anger; for the first time she found herself in the presence of popular resistance, and she coldly calculated its power. She had come to this bed of justice with the intention of opposing, at least by her look, the resolution which was about to be adopted there; but gradually she felt herself drawn to make common cause with those of her own caste and race, so that in proportion as the chancellor attacked the parliament more severely, this proud young creature was indignant to find his words so weak. She fancied she could have found words which would have made this assembly start like a troop of oxen under the goad. In short, she found the chancellor too feeble and the parliament too strong.

Louis XV. was a physiognomist, — as all selfish people would be if they were not sometimes idle as well as selfish. He cast a glance around to observe the effect of his will, expressed in words which he thought tolerably eloquent. The paleness and the compressed lips of the dauphiness showed him what was passing in her mind. As a counterpoise, he turned to look at Madame Dubarry; but instead of the victorious smile he hoped to find there, he only saw an anxious desire to attract the king's looks, as if to judge what he thought.

Nothing intimidates weak minds so much as being forestalled by the wills and minds of others. If they find themselves observed by those who have already taken a resolution, they conclude that they have not done enough; that they are about to be, or have been, ridiculous; that people had a right to expect more than they have done.

Then they pass to extremes; the timid man becomes furious, and a sudden manifestation betrays the effect of this reaction produced by fear upon a fear less powerful than itself.

The king had no need to add a single word to those his chancellor had already spoken; it was not according to etiquette, — it was not even necessary. But on this occasion he was possessed of the babbling demon, and, making a sign with his hand, he signified that he intended to speak.

Immediately attention was changed to stupor.

The heads of the members of parliament were all seen to wheel round towards the bed of justice, with the precision of a file of soldiers upon drill; the princes, peers, and military felt uneasy. It was not impossible that after so many excellent things had been said, his most Christian Majesty might add something which, to say the least, would be quite useless. Their respect prevented them from giving any other title to the words which might fall from the royal lips.

Monsieur de Richelieu, who had affected to keep aloof from his nephew, was now seen to approach the most stubborn of the parliamentarians, and exchange a glance of mysterious intelligence. But his glances, which were becoming rebellious, met the penetrating eye of Madame Dubarry. Richelieu possessed, as no one else did, the precious power of transition; he passed easily from the satirical to the admiring tone, and chose the beautiful countess as the point of intersection between these two extremes. He sent a smile of gallantry and congratulation, therefore, to Madame Dubarry in passing, but the latter was not duped by it; the more so that the old marshal, who had commenced a correspondence with the parliament and the opposing princes, was obliged to continue it, that he might not appear what he really was.

What sights there are in a drop of water, — that ocean for an observer! What centuries in a second, — that indescribable eternity! All we have related took place while Louis was preparing to speak, and was opening his lips.

"You have heard," said he, in a firm voice, "what my chancellor has told you of my wishes. Prepare, therefore, to execute them; for such are my intentions, and I shall never change them!"

Louis XV. uttered these last words with the noise and force of a thunderbolt. The whole assembly was literally thunderstruck.

A shudder passed over the parliament, and was quickly communicated like an electric spark to the crowd. A like thrill was felt by the partisans of the king. Surprise and admiration were on every face and in every heart.

The dauphiness involuntarily thanked the king by a lightning glance from her beautiful eyes. Madame Dubarry, electrified, could not refrain from rising, and would have clapped her hands, but for the very natural fear of being stoned as she left the house, or of receiving hundreds of couplets the next morning, each more odious than the other.

Louis could from this moment enjoy his triumph. The parliament bent low, still with the same unanimity. The king rose from his embroidered cushions. Instantly the captain of the guards, the commandant of the household, and all the gentlemen of the king's suite rose. Drums beat, and trumpets sounded outside. The almost silent stir of the people on the arrival was now changed into a deep murmur, which died away in the distance, repressed by the solders and archers.

The king proudly crossed the hall, without seeing anything on his way but humbled foreheads. The Duke d'Aiguillon still preceded his Majesty, without abusing his triumph.

The chancellor, having reached the door of the hall, saw the immense crowd of people extending on all sides, and heard their execrations, which reached his ears notwithstanding the distance. He trembled, and said to the archers, —

"Close around me."

Monsieur de Richelieu bowed low to the Duke d'Aiguillon as he passed, and whispered, —

"These heads are very low, duke; some day or other they will rise devilish high. Take care!"

Madame Dubarry was passing at the moment, accompanied by her brother, the Marchioness de Mirepoix, and several ladies. She heard the marshal's words, and as she was more inclined to repartee than malice, she said,—

"Oh, there is nothing to fear, marshal; did you not hear his Majesty's words? The king, I think, said he would never change."

"Terrible words, indeed, madame," replied the duke, with a smile; "but happily for us, these poor parliament men did not remark that whilst saying he would never change, the king looked at you."

And he finished this compliment with one of those inimitable bows which are no longer seen, even upon the stage.

Madame Dubarry was a woman, and by no means a politician; she only saw the compliment, where D'Aiguillon detected plainly the epigram and the threat. Therefore she replied with a smile, while her ally turned pale and bit his lips with vexation, to see the marshal's anger endure so long.

The effect of the bed of justice was for the moment favourable to the royal cause. But it frequently happens that a great blow only stuns, and it is remarked that after the stunning effect has passed away, the blood circulates with more vigour and purity than before. Such, at least, were the reflections made by a little group of plainly dressed persons, who were stationed as spectators at the corner of the Quai aux Fleurs and the Rue de la Barillerie, on seeing the king, attended by his brillant *cortége*, leave the hall.

They were three in number. Chance had brought them together at this corner, and from thence they seemed to study with interest the impressions of the crowd; and without knowing each other, after once exchanging a few words, they had discussed the sitting even before it was over.

"These passions are well ripened," said one of them, an old man with bright eyes, and a mild and honest expression. "A bed of justice is a great work."

"Yes," replied a young man, smiling bitterly; "yes, if the work realise the title."

"Monsieur," replied the old man, turning round, "I think I should know you, — I fancy I have seen you before."

"On the night of the 31st May. You are not mistaken, Monsieur Rousseau."

"Oh! you are that young surgeon, — my countryman, Monsieur Marat!"

"Yes, monsieur; at your service."

The two men exchanged salutations. The third had not yet spoken. He was also young, eminently handsome, and aristocratic in his appearance, and during the whole cere-

mony had unceasingly observed the crowd.   The young
surgeon moved away the first, and plunged into the densest
masses of the people, who, less grateful than Rousseau,
had already forgotten him, but whose memory he calculated
upon refreshing one day or other.

The other young man waited until he was gone, and
then, addressing Rousseau, —

"Monsieur," said he, "you do not go!"

"Oh! I am too old to venture amongst such a mob."

"In that case," said the unknown, lowering his voice,
"I will see you again this evening in the Rue Plastrière,
Monsieur Rousseau; do not fail."

The philosopher started as if a phantom had risen before
him.   His complexion, always pale, became livid; he made
an effort to reply to this strange appeal, but the man had
already disappeared.

## CHAPTER CI.

### THE INFLUENCE OF THE WORDS OF THE UNKNOWN UPON J. J. ROUSSEAU.

On hearing these singular words spoken by a man whom he did not know, Rousseau, trembling and unhappy, plunged into the crowd; and without remembering that he was old and naturally timid, elbowed his way through it. He soon reached the bridge of Notre-Dame; then, still plunged in his reverie, and muttering to himself, he crossed the quarter of La Grève, which was the shortest way to his own dwelling.

"So," said he to himself, "this secret, which the initiated guard at the peril of their lives, is in possession of the first comer. This is what mysterious associations gain by passing through the popular sieve. A man recognises me, who knows that I shall be his associate, perhaps his accomplice, yonder. Such a state of things is absurd and intolerable."

And while he spoke, Rousseau walked forward quickly — he, usually so cautious, especially since his accident in the Rue Ménil-Montant.

"Thus," continued the philosopher, "I must wish, forsooth, to sound to the bottom these plans of human regeneration which some spirits who boast of the title of 'illuminati' propose to carry out. I was foolish enough to imagine that any good ideas could come from Germany — that land of beer and fog — and may have compromised my name by joining it to those of fools or plotters, whom it will serve as a cloak to shelter their folly. Oh, no; it shall not be thus. No; a flash of lightning has shown me the abyss, and I will not rashly throw myself into it."

And Rousseau paused to take breath, resting upon his cane, and standing motionless for a moment.

"Yet it was a beautiful chimera," pursued the philosopher. "Liberty in the midst of slavery; the future conquered without noise and struggle; the snare mysteriously woven while earth's tyrants slept. It was too beautiful! I was a fool to believe it! I will not be the sport of fears, of suspicions, of shadows, which are unworthy of a free spirit and an independent body."

He had got thus far, and was continuing his progress, when the sight of some of Monsieur de Sartine's agents gazing round with their ubiquitous eyes frightened the free spirit, and gave such an impulse to the independent body, that it plunged into the deepest shadows of the pillars under which it was walking.

From these pillars it was not far to the Rue Plastrière. Rousseau accomplished the distance with the speed of lightning, ascended the stairs to his domicile — breathing like a stag pursued by the hunters — and sank upon a chair, unable to utter a word in answer to all Thérèse's questions.

At last he recovered sufficiently to account for his emotion; it was the walk, the heat, the news of the king's angry remarks at the Bed of Justice, the commotion caused by the popular terror, — a sort of panic, in short, which had spread amongst all who witnessed what had happened.

Thérèse grumblingly replied that all that was no reason for allowing the dinner to cool; and, moreover, that a man ought not to be such a soft, chicken-hearted wretch as to be frightened at the least noise.

Rousseau could make no reply to this last argument, which he himself had so frequently stated in other terms.

Thérèse added that these philosophers, these imaginative people, were all the same; that they always talked very grandly in their writings; they said that they feared nothing; that God and man were very little to them; but, at the slightest barking of the smallest poodle, they cried,

"Help!" — at the least feverishness they exclaimed, "Oh, heavens! I am dead!"

This was one of Thérèse's favourite themes, that which most excited her eloquence, and to which Rousseau, who was naturally timid, found it most difficult to reply. Rousseau, therefore, pursued his own thoughts to the sound of this discordant music, — thoughts which were certainly well worth Thérèse's, notwithstanding the abuse the latter showered so plentifully on him.

"Happiness," said he, "is composed of perfume and music; now, noise and odour are conventional things. Who can prove that the onion smells less sweet than the rose, or the peacock sings less melodiously than the nightingale?"

After which axiom, which might pass for an excellent paradox, they sat down to table.

After dinner, Rousseau did not, as usual, sit down to his harpsichord. He paced up and down the apartment, and stopped a hundred times to look out of the window, apparently studying the physiognomy of the Rue Plastrière. Thérèse was forthwith seized with one of those fits of jealousy which peevish people — that is to say, the least really jealous people in the world — often indulge in for the sake of opposition. For if there is a disagreeable affectation in the world, it is the affectation of a fault; the affectation of virtue may be tolerated.

Thérèse, who held Rousseau's age, complexion, mind, and manners in the utmost contempt — who thought him old, sickly, and ugly — did not fear that any one should run off with her husband; she never dreamed that other women might look upon him with different eyes from herself. But as the torture of jealousy is woman's most dainty punishment, Thérèse sometimes indulged herself in this treat. Seeing Rousseau, therefore, approach the window so frequently, and observing his dreaming and restless air, she said:

"Very good! I understand your agitation — you have just left some one."

Rousseau turned to her with a startled look which served as an additional proof of the truth of her suspicions.

"Some one you wish to see again," she continued.

"What do you say?" asked Rousseau.

"Yes; we make assignations, it seems!"

"Oh!" said Rousseau, comprehending that Thérèse was jealous; "an assignation! You are mad, Thérèse!"

"I know perfectly well that it would be madness in you," said she; "but you are capable of any folly. Go — go, with your *papier-mâché* complexion, your palpitations, and your coughs — go, and make conquests! It is one way of getting on in the world!"

"But, Thérèse, you know there is not a word of truth in what you are saying," said Rousseau, angrily; "let me think in peace."

"You are a libertine," said Thérèse, with the utmost seriousness.

Rousseau reddened as if she had hit the truth, or as if he had received a compliment.

Thérèse forthwith thought herself justified in putting on a terrible countenance, turning the whole household upside down, slamming the doors violently, and playing with Rousseau's tranquillity, — as children with those metal rings which they shut up in a box and shake to make a noise. Rousseau took refuge in his cabinet; this uproar had rather confused his ideas.

He reflected that there would doubtless be some danger in not being present at the mysterious ceremony of which the stranger had spoken at the corner of the Quai.

"If there are punishments for traitors, there will also be punishments for the lukewarm or careless," thought he. "Now I have always remarked that great dangers mean in reality nothing, just like loud threats. The cases in which either are productive of any result are extremely rare; but petty revenges, underhand attacks, mystifications, and other such small coin — these we must be on our guard against. Some day the masonic brothers may repay my contempt by stretching a string across my staircase; I shall stumble over it and break a leg, or the six or eight teeth I have left. Or else they will have a stone ready to fall upon my head when I am passing under a scaffolding; or, better still, there may be some pamphleteer belonging to the fraternity, living quite near me, upon the same floor, perhaps, looking from his windows into my room. That is not impossible, since the réunions take place even in the Rue Plastrière. Well, this wretch will write stupid lampoons on me, which will make me ridiculous all over Paris. Have I not enemies everywhere? "

A moment afterwards Rousseau's thoughts took a different turn.

"Well," said he to himself, "but where is courage? where is honour? Shall I be afraid of myself? Shall I see in my glass only the face of a coward — a slave? No; it shall not be so. If the whole world should combine to ruin me — if the very street should fall upon me — I will go. What pitiable reasoning does fear produce! Since I met this man, I have been continually turning in a circle of absurdities. I doubt every one, and even myself! That is not logical — I know myself, I am not an enthusiast; if I thought I saw wonders in this projected association, it is because there are wonders in it. Who will say I may not be the regenerator of the human race, I, who am sought after, I, whom, on the faith of my writings, the mysterious agents of an unlimited power have eagerly consulted? Shall I retreat when the time has come to follow up my work, to substitute practice for theory? "

Rousseau became animated.

"What can be more beautiful! Ages roll on; the people rise out of their brutishness; step follows step into the darkness, hand follows hand into the shadows; the immense pyramid is raised, upon the summit of which, as its crowning glory, future ages shall place the bust of Rousseau, citizen of Geneva, who risked his liberty, his life, that he might act as he had spoken — that he might be faithful to his motto: ' Vitam impendere vero.' "

Thereupon Rousseau, in a fit of enthusiasm, seated himself at his harpsichord, and exalted his imagination by the
loudest, the most sonorous, and the most warlike melodies
he could call forth from its sounding cavity.

Night closed in.  Thérèse, wearied with her vain endeavours to torment her captive, had fallen asleep upon
her chair.  Rousseau, with beating heart, took his new
coat, as if to go out on a pleasure excursion, glanced for a
moment in the glass at the play of his black eyes, and was
charmed to find that they were sparkling and expressive.

He grasped his knotted stick in his hand, and slipped out
of the room without awakening Thérèse.  But when he
arrived at the foot of the stairs, and had drawn back the
bolt of the street-door, Rousseau paused and looked out, to
assure himself as to the state of the locality.

No carriage was passing; the street, as usual, was full
of idlers gazing at each other, as they do at this day, while
many stopped at the shop windows to ogle the pretty girls.
A new-comer would therefore be quite unnoticed in such a
crowd.  Rousseau plunged into it; he had not far to go.
A ballad-singer, with a cracked violin, was stationed before
the door which had been pointed out to him.  This music,
to which every true Parisian's ear is extremely sensitive,
filled the street with echoes which repeated the last bars
of the air sung by the violin or by the singer himself.
Nothing could be more unfavourable, therefore, to the free
passage along the street than the crowd gathered at this
spot, and the passers-by were obliged to turn either to the
right or left of the group.  Those who turned to the left
took the centre of the street, those to the right brushed
along the side of the house indicated, and *vice versa.*

Rousseau remarked that several of these passers-by disappeared on the way as if they had fallen into some trap.
He concluded that these people had come with the same
purpose as himself, and determined to imitate their
manœuvre.  It was not difficult to accomplish.  Having
stationed himself in the rear of the assembly of listeners,

as if to join their number, he watched the first person whom he saw entering the open alley. More timid than they, probably because he had more to risk, he waited until a particularly favourable opportunity should present itself.

He did not wait long. A cabriolet which drove along the street divided the circle, and caused the two hemispheres to fall back upon the houses on either side. Rousseau thus found himself driven to the very entrance of the passage; he had only to walk on. Our philosopher observed that all the idlers were looking at the cabriolet and had turned their backs on the house; he took advantage of this circumstance, and disappeared in the dark passage.

After advancing a few steps he preceived a lamp, beneath which a man was seated quietly, like a stall-keeper after the day's business was over, and read, or seemed to read, a newspaper. At the sound of Rousseau's footsteps this man raised his head and visibly placed his finger upon his breast, upon which the lamp threw a strong light. Rousseau replied to this symbolic gesture by raising his finger to his lips.

The man then immediately rose, and, pushing open a door at his right hand, which door was so artificially concealed in the wooden panel of which it formed a part as to be wholly invisible, he showed Rousseau a very steep staircase, which descended underground. Rousseau entered, 'and the door closed quickly but noiselessly after him.

The philosopher descended the steps slowly, assisted by his cane. He thought it rather disrespectful that the brothers should cause him, at this, his first interview, to run the risk of breaking his neck or his legs.

But the stair, if steep, was not long. Rousseau counted seventeen steps and then felt as if suddenly plunged into a highly-heated atmosphere.

This moist heat proceeded from the breath of a considerable number of men who were assembled in the low hall

Rousseau remarked that the walls were tapestried with red and white drapery, on which figures of various implements of labour, rather symbolic doubtless than real, were depicted. A single lamp hung from the vaulted ceiling, and threw a gloomy light upon the faces of those present, who were conversing with each other on the wooden benches, and who wore the appearance of honest and respectable citizens.

The floor was neither polished nor carpeted, but was covered with a thick mat of plaited rushes which deadened the sound of the footsteps. Rousseau's entrance, therefore, produced no sensation. No one seemed to have remarked it.

Five minutes previously Rousseau had longed for nothing so much as such an entrance; and yet, when he had entered, he felt annoyed that he had succeeded so well. He saw an unoccupied place on one of the back benches, and installed himself as modestly as possible on this seat, behind all the others.

He counted thirty-three heads in the assembly. A desk placed upon a platform, seemed to wait for a president.

## CHAPTER CII.

### THE HOUSE IN THE RUE PLASTRIÈRE.

Rousseau remarked that the conversation of those present was very cautious and reserved. Many did not open their lips; and scarcely three or four couples exchanged a few words.

Those who did not speak endeavoured even to conceal their faces, which was not difficult — thanks to the great body of shadow cast by the platform of the expected president. The refuge of these last, who seemed to be the timid individuals of the assembly, was behind this platform. But, in return, two or three members of this corporation gave themselves a great deal of trouble to recognise their colleagues. They came and went, talked among themselves, and frequently disappeared through a door before which was drawn a black curtain, ornamented with red flames.

In a short time a bell was rung. A man immediately rose from the end of the bench upon which he was seated, and where he was previously confounded with the other free-masons, and took his place upon the platform.

After making some signs with the hands and fingers, which were repeated by all those present, and adding a last sign more explicit than the others, he declared the sitting commenced.

This man was entirely unknown to Rousseau. Beneath the exterior of a working man in easy circumstances, he concealed great presence of mind, aided by an elocution as flowing as could have been wished for in an orator.

His speech was brief, and to the point. He declared

that the lodge had been assembled to proceed to the election of a new brother.

"You will not be suprised," said he, "that we have assembled you in a place where the usual trials cannot be attempted. These trials have seemed useless to the chiefs; the brother whom we are to receive to-day is one of the lights of contemporary philosophy — a thoughtful spirit who will be devoted to us from conviction, not from fear. One who has discovered all the mysteries of nature and of the human heart cannot be treated in the same manner as the simple mortal from whom we demand the help of his arm, his will, and his gold. In order to have the co-operation of his distinguished mind, of his honest and energetic character, his promise and his assent are sufficient."

The speaker, when he had concluded, looked round to mark the effect of his words.

Upon Rousseau the effect had been magical; the Genevese philosopher was acquainted with the preparatory mysteries of freemasonry, and looked upon them with the repugnance natural to enlightened minds. The concessions, absurd because they were useless, which the chiefs required from the candidates, this simulating fear when every one knew there was nothing to fear, seemed to him to be the acme of puerility and senseless superstition.

Besides this, the timid philosopher, an enemy to all personal exhibitions and manifestations, would have felt most unhappy had he been obliged to serve as a spectacle for people whom he did not know, and who would have certainly mystified him more or less.

To dispense with these trials in his case was therefore more than a satisfaction to him. He knew the strictness with which equality was enforced by the masonic principles, therefore an exception in his favour constituted a triumph.

He was preparing to say some words in reply to the gracious address of the president, when a voice was heard among the audience.

"At least," said this voice, which was sharp and discordant, "since you think yourself obliged to treat in this
princely fashion a man like ourselves, since you dispense
in his case with physical pains, as if the pursuit of liberty
through bodily suffering were not one of our symbols, we
hope you will not confer a precious title upon an unknown
person without having questioned him according to the
usual ritual, and without having received his profession of
faith."

Rousseau turned round to discover the features of the
aggressive person who so rudely jostled his triumphant
car, and with the greatest suprise recognised the young
surgeon whom he had that morning met upon the Quai-
aux-Fleurs. A conviction of his own honesty of purpose,
perhaps also a feeling of disdain for the *precious title*,
prevented him from replying.

"You have heard?" said the president, addressing
Rousseau.

"Perfectly," replied the philosopher, who trembled
slightly at the sound of his voice as it echoed through the
vaulted roof of the dark hall, "and I am the more surprised
at the interpellation when I see from whom it proceeds.
What! A man whose profession it is to combat what is
called physical suffering, and to assist his brethren, who
are common men as well as freemasons, preaches the utility
of physical suffering! He chooses a singular path through
which to lead the creature to happiness, the sick to health."

"We do not here speak of this or that person," replied
the young man warmly; "I am supposed to be unknown to
the candidate, and he to me. I am merely the utterer of
an abstract truth, and I assert that the chief has done
wrong in making an exception in favour of any one. I do
not recognise in him," pointing to Rousseau, "the philosopher, and he must not recognise the surgeon in me.
We shall perhaps walk side by side through life, without a
look or gesture betraying our intimacy, which nevertheless,
thanks to the laws of the association, is more binding than

all vulgar friendships. I repeat, therefore, that if it has been thought well to spare this candidate the usual trials, he ought at least to have the usual questions put to him."

Rousseau made no reply. The president saw depicted on his features disgust at this discussion, and regret at having engaged in the enterprise.

"Brother," said he, authoritatively to the young man, "you will please be silent when the chief speaks, and do not venture on light grounds to blame his actions, which are sovereign here."

"I have a right to speak," replied the young man, more gently.

"To speak, yes; but not to blame. The brother who is about to enter our association is so well known that we have no wish to add to our masonic relations a ridiculous and useless mystery. All the brothers here present know his name, and his name itself is a perfect guarantee. But as he himself, I am certain, loves equality, I request him to answer the question which I shall put to him merely for form:

"What do you seek in this association?"

Rousseau made two steps forward in advance of the crowd, and his dreamy and melancholy eye wandered over the assembly.

"I seek," said he, "that which I do not find — truths, not sophisms. Why should you surround me with poniards which do not wound, with poisons which are only clear water, and with traps under which mattresses are spread? I know the extent of human endurance. I know the vigour of my physical frame. If you were to destroy it, it would not be worth your while to elect me a brother, for when dead I could be of no use to you. Therefore you do not wish to kill me, still less to wound me; and all the doctors in the world would not make me approve of an initiation in the course of which my limbs had been broken. I have served a longer apprenticeship to pain than any of you; I have sounded the body, and probed even to the soul. If I consented to come amongst you when I was *solicited*" —

and he laid particular emphasis on the word — "it was because I thought I might be useful.  I give, therefore; I do not receive.  Alas! before you could do anything to defend me, before you could restore me to liberty were I imprisoned — before you could give me bread if I were starving, or consolation if I were afflicted — before, I repeat, you could do anything — the brother whom you admit to-day, if this gentleman," turning to Marat, "permits it — this brother will have paid the last tribute of nature; for progress is halting, light is slow, and from the grave into which he will be thrown, none of you can raise him."

" You are mistaken, illustrious brother," said a mild and penetrating voice which charmed Rousseau's ear; " there is more than you think in the association into which you are about to enter; there is the whole future destiny of the world.  The future, you are aware, is hope — is science; the future is God, who will give His light to the world, since He has promised to give it, and God cannot lie."

Astonished at this elevated language, Rousseau looked around and recognised the young man who had made the appointment with him in the morning at the Bed of Justice.  This man, who was dressed in black with great neatness, and, above all, with a marked air of distinction in his appearance, was leaning against the side of the platform, and his face, illumined by the lamp, shone in all its beauty, grace, and expressiveness.

" Ah ! " said Rousseau, "science — the bottomless abyss ! *You* speak to me of science, consolation, futurity, hope; another speaks of matter, of rigour, and of violence ; whom shall I believe ?  Shall it be then, in this assembly of brothers, as it is amongst the devouring wolves of the world which stirs above us ?  Wolves and sheep !  Listen to my profession of faith, since you have not read it in my books."

" Your books ! " exclaimed Marat.  " They are sublime — I confess it — but they are Utopias.  You are useful in the same point of view as Pythagoras, Solon, and Cicero the sophist. You point out the good, but it is an artificial, unsubstantial, unattainable good. You are like one who would feed a hungry crowd with air-bubbles, more or less illumined by the sun."

"Have you ever seen," said Rousseau, frowning, "great commotions of nature take place without preparation? Have you seen the birth of a man — that common and yet sublime event? Have you not seen him collect substance and life in the womb of his mother for nine months? Ah! you wish me to regenerate the world with actions. That is not to regenerate, monsieur; it is to revolutionise!"

"Then," retorted the young surgeon, violently, "you do not wish for independence; you do not wish for liberty!"

"On the contrary," replied Rousseau, "independence is my idol — liberty is my goddess. But I wish for a mild and radiant liberty — a liberty which warms and vivifies. I wish for an equality which will connect men by ties of friendship, not by fear. I wish for education, for the instruction of each element of the social body, as the mechanic wishes for harmonious movement — as the cabinet-maker wishes for the perfect exactness, for the closest fitting, in each piece of his work. I repeat it, I wish for that which I have written — progress, concord, devotion."

A smile of disdain flitted over Marat's lips.

"Yes," he said, "rivulets of milk and honey, Elysian fields like Virgil's poetic dreams, which philosophy would make a reality."

Rousseau made no reply. It seemed to him too hard that he should have to defend his moderation — he, whom all Europe called a violent innovator.

He took his seat in silence, after having satisfied his ingenuous and timid mind by appealing for and obtaining the tacit approbation of the person who had just before defended him.

The president rose.

"You have all heard?" said he.

"Yes," replied the entire assembly.

"Does the candidate appear to you worthy of entering the association, and does he comprehend its duties?"

"Yes," replied the assembly again; but this time with a reserve which did not evince much unanimity.

"Take the oath," said the president to Rousseau.

"It would be disagreeable to me," said the philosopher, with some pride, "to displease any members of this association; and I must repeat the words I made use of just now, as they are the expression of my earnest conviction. If I were an orator, I would put them in a more eloquent manner; but my organ of speech is rebellious, and always betrays my thoughts when I ask it for an immediate translation. I wish to say that I can do more for the world and for you out of this assembly, than I could were I strictly to follow your usages. Leave me, therefore, to my work, to my weakness, to my loneliness. I have told you I am descending to the grave; grief, infirmity, and want hurry me on. You cannot delay this great work of nature. Abandon me; I am not made for the society of men; I hate and fly them. Nevertheless, I serve them, because I am a man myself; and in serving them I fancy them better than they are. Now you have my whole thoughts; I shall not say another word."

"Then you refuse to take the oath?" said Marat, with some emotion.

"I refuse positively; I do not wish to join the association. I see too many convincing proofs to assure me that I should be useless to it."

"Brother," said the unknown personage with the conciliatory voice, — "allow me to call you so, for we are brothers, independently of all combinations of the human mind — brother! do not give way to a very natural feeling of irritation; sacrifice your legitimate pride; do for us what is repulsive to yourself. Your advice, your ideas, your presence, are light to our paths. Do not plunge us in the twofold darkness of your absence and your refusal."

"You are in error," said Rousseau; "I take nothing

from you, since I should never have given you more than I have given to the whole world, to the first chance reader, to the first consulter of the journals. If you wish for the name and essence of Rousseau —"

"We do wish for them!" said several voices, politely.

"Then make a collection of my books; place them upon the table of your president; and when you are taking the opinions of the meeting, and my turn to give one comes, open my books — you will find my counsel and my vote there."

Rousseau made a step towards the door.

"Stop one moment!" said the surgeon; "mind is free, and that of the illustrious philosopher more than any other; but it would not be regular to have allowed a stranger even to enter our sanctuary, who, not being bound by any tacit agreement, might, without dishonesty, reveal our mysteries."

Rousseau smiled compassionately.

"You want an oath of secrecy?" said he.

"You have said it."

"I am ready."

"Be good enough to read the formula, venerable brother," said Marat.

The venerable brother read the following form of oath: —

"I swear, in the presence of the Eternal God, the Architect of the Universe, and before my superiors, and the respectable assembly which surrounds me, never to reveal or to make known, or write anything which has happened in my presence, under penalty, in case of indiscretion, of being punished according to the laws of the Great Founder, of my superiors, and the anger of my fathers."

Rousseau had already raised his hand to swear, when the unknown, who had followed the progress of the debate with a sort of authority which no one seemed to dispute, although he was not distinguished from the crowd, approached the president, and whispered some words in his ear.

"True," said the venerable chief, and he added: —

"You are a man, not a brother; you are a man of honour, placed towards us only in the position of a fellow-man. We here abjure, therefore, our distinguishing peculiarity, and ask from you merely your word of honour to forget what has passed between us."

"Like a dream of the morning — I swear it upon my honour," said Rousseau, with emotion.

With these words he retired, and many of the members followed him.

## CHAPTER CIII.

WHEN the members of the second and third orders had gone, seven associates remained in the lodge; they were the seven chiefs.  They recognised each other by means of signs which proved their initiation to a superior degree.

Their first care was to close the doors.  Then their president made himself known by displaying a ring, on which were engraved the mysterious letters, L. P. D.[1]

This president was charged with the most important correspondence of the order.  He was in communication with the six other chiefs, who dwelt in Switzerland, Russia, America, Sweden, Spain, and Italy.

He brought with him some of the most important documents he had received from his colleagues, in order to communicate their contents to the superior circles of initiated brothers, who were above the others but beneath him.

We have already recognised this chief: it was Balsamo.

The most important of the letters contained threatening intelligence; it was from Sweden, and written by Swedenborg.

"Watch the South, brothers," he said; "under its burning rays has been hatched a traitor who will ruin you.

"Watch in Paris, brothers.  The traitor dwells there; he possesses the secrets of the order; a feeling of hatred urges him on.

"A murmuring voice, a rustling flight, whispers the denunciation in my ear.  I see a terrible vengeance coming,

---

[1] Lilia pedibus destrue.

but perhaps it will be too late. In the mean time, brothers, watch! watch! A traitorous tongue, even though it be uninstructed, is sometimes sufficient to overthrow our most skilfully constructed plans."

The brothers looked at each other in mute surprise. The language of the fierce old sage, his prescience, which had acquired an imposing authority from many striking examples, contributed in no small degree to cast a gloom over the meeting at which Balsamo presided. Balsamo himself, who placed implicit faith in Swedenborg's second sight, could not resist the saddening influence which this letter had on the assembly.

"Brothers," said he, "the inspired prophet is rarely deceived. Watch, then, as he bids you. You know now, as I do, that the struggle commences. Let us not be conquered by these ridiculous enemies, whose power we sap in the utmost security. You must not forget that they have mercenary swords at their command. It is a powerful weapon in this world, among those who do not see beyond the limits of our terrestrial life. Brothers, let us distrust these hired traitors."

"These fears seem to me puerile," said a voice; "we gather strength daily, and we are directed by brilliant genius and powerful hands."

Balsamo bowed his thanks for the flattering eulogy.

"Yes; but as our illustrious president has said, treason creeps everywhere," replied a brother, who was no other than the surgeon Marat, promoted, notwithstanding his youth, to a superior grade, in virtue of which he now sat for the first time on a consulting committee. "Remember, brothers, that by doubling the bait, you make a more important capture. If Monsieur de Sartines with a bag of crown-pieces can purchase the revelations of one of our obscurer brothers, the minister, with a million, or with holding out the hope of advancement, may buy over one of our superiors. Now, with us, the obscurer brother knows nothing. At the most he is cognizant of the names of some of his colleagues, and these names signify nothing. Ours is an excellent constitution, but it is an eminently aristocratic one: the inferiors know nothing, can do nothing. They are called together to say or to hear trifles, and yet they contribute their time and their money to increase the solidity of our edifice. Reflect that the workman brings only the stone and the mortar, but without stone and mortar could you build the house? Now, the workman receives a very small salary, but I consider him equal to the architect who plans, creates, and superintends the whole work; and I consider him equal because he is a man, and in the eyes of a philosopher, one man is worth as much as another, seeing that he bears his misfortunes and his fate equally, and because, even more than another man, he is exposed to the fall of a stone or the breaking of a scaffold."

"I must interrupt you, brother," said Balsamo; "you diverge from the question which alone ought to occupy our thoughts. Your failing, brother, is that you are over-zealous, and apt to generalise discussions. Our business in the present occasion is not to decide whether our constitution be good or bad, but to uphold the integrity of that constitution in all its strength. If I wished, however, to discuss the point with you, I would answer, no; the instrument which receives the impulse is not equal to the architect; the brain is not the equal of the arm."

"Suppose Monsieur de Sartines should seize one of our least important brethren," cried Marat, warmly, "would he not send him to rot in the Bastille equally with you or me?"

"Granted; but the misfortune in that case is for the individual only, not for the order, which is with us the all-important point. If, on the contrary, the chief were imprisoned, the whole conspiracy is at an end. When the general is absent, the army loses the battle. Therefore, brother, watch over the safety of the chiefs!"

"Yes; but let them in return watch over ours."

"That is their duty."

"And let their faults be doubly punished."

"Again, brother, you wander from the constitution of the order. Have you forgotten that the oath which binds all the members of the association is the same, and threatens all with the same punishment?"

"The great ones always escape."

"That is not the opinion of the great themselves, brother. Listen to the conclusion of the letter which one of the greatest among us, our prophet Swedenborg, has written. This is what he adds: —

"'The blow will come from one of the mighty ones, one of the mightiest of the order; or, if it comes not directly from him, the fault will be traceable to him. Remember that fire and water may be accomplices; one gives light, the other revelation.

"'Watch, brothers, over all and over each; watch!'"

"Then," said Marat, seizing upon those points in Balsamo's speech and Swedenborg's letter which suited his purpose, "let us repeat the oath which binds us together, and let us pledge ourselves to maintain it in its utmost vigour, whosoever he may be who shall betray us, or be the cause of our betrayal."

Balsamo paused for a moment, and then, rising from his seat, he pronounced the consecrated words, with which our readers are already acquainted, in a slow, solemn, terrible voice: —

"In the name of the crucified Son, I swear to break all the bonds of nature which unite me to father, mother, brother, sister, wife, relation, friend, mistress, king, benefactor, and to any being whatsoever to whom I have promised faith, obedience, gratitude, or service.

"I swear to reveal to the chief, whom I acknowledge according to the statutes of the order, all that I have seen or done, read or guessed, and even to search out and penetrate that which may not of itself be openly present to my eyes.

"I will honour poison, steel, and fire, as a means of ridding the world, by death or idiocy, of the enemies of truth and liberty.

"I subscribe to the law of silence. I consent to die, as if struck by lightning, on the day when I shall have merited this punishment; and I await, without murmuring, the knife which will reach me in whatsoever part of the world I may be."

Then the seven men who composed this solemn assembly repeated the oath, word for word, standing, and with uncovered heads.

When the words of the oath had been repeated by all, —

"We are now guaranteed against treachery," said Balsamo; "let us no longer mingle extraneous matter with our discussion. I have to make my report to the committee of the principal events of the year.

"My summary of the affairs of France may have interest for enlightened and zealous minds like yours; I will commence with it.

"France is situated in the centre of Europe, as the heart in the centre of the body; it lives, and radiates life. It is in its palpitations that we must look for the cause of all the disorder in the general organization.

"I came to France, therefore, and approached Paris as a physician approaches the heart. I listened, I felt, I experimented. When I entered it a year ago, the monarchy harassed it; to-day, vices kill it. I required to hasten the effect of these fatal debauches, and therefore I assisted them.

"An obstacle was in my way; this obstacle was a man, not only the first, but the most powerful man in the state, next to the king.

"He was gifted with some of those qualities which please other men; he was too proud, it is true, but his pride was applied to his works. He knew how to lighten the hardships of the people by making them believe and even feel sometimes that they were a portion of the state;

and by sometimes consulting them on their grievances he raised a standard around which the mass will always rally, —the spirit of nationality.

"He hated the English, the natural enemies of the French; he hated the favourite, the natural enemy of the working classes. Now, if this man had been a usurper; if he had been one of us; if he would have trodden in our path, acted for our ends, —I would have assisted him, I would have kept him in power, I would have upheld him by the resources I am able to create for my *protégés;* for, instead of patching up decayed royalty, he would have assisted us in overthrowing it on the appointed day. But he belonged to the aristocracy; he was· born with a feeling of respect for that first rank to which he could not aspire, for the monarchy, which he dared not attack; he served royalty while despising the king; he did worse, —he acted as a shield to this royalty against which our blows were directed. The parliament and the people, full of respect for this living dyke which opposed itself to any encroachment on the royal prerogative, limited themselves to a moderate resistance, certain as they were of having in him a powerful assistance when the moment should arrive.

"I understood the position; I undertook Monsieur de Choiseul's fall.

"This laborious task, at which for ten years so much hatred and interest had laboured in vain, I commenced and terminated in a few months, by means which it would be useless to reveal to you. By a secret, which constitutes one of my powers, —a power the greater, because it will remain eternally hidden from the eyes of all, and will manifest itself only by its effects, —I overthrew and banished Monsieur de Choiseul, and attached to his overthrow a long train of regret, disappointment, lamentation, and anger.

"You see now that my labour bears its fruit; all France asks for Choiseul, and rises to demand him back, as orphans turn to Heaven when God has taken away their earthly parents.

"The parliament employs the only right it possesses, — inertia; it has ceased to act. In a well-organised body, as a state of the first rank ought to be, the paralysis of any essential organ is fatal. Now the parliament in the social is what the stomach is in the human body. When the parliament ceases to act, the people — the intestines of the state — can work no longer; and, consequently, must cease to pay, and the gold — that is, the blood — will be wanting.

"There will be a struggle, no doubt; but who can combat against the people? Not the army — that daughter of the people — which eats the bread of the labourer, and drinks the wine of the vine-grower. There remain, then, the king's household, the privileged classes, the guards, the Swiss, the musketeers, — in all, scarce five or six thousand men. What can this handful of pygmies do when the nation shall rise like a giant?"

"Let them rise, then, let them rise!" cried several voices.

"Yes, yes; to the work!" exclaimed Marat.

"Young man, I have not yet consulted you," said Balsamo, coldly. "This sedition of the masses," continued he, "this revolt of the weak, become strong by their number, against the powerful single-handed, less thoughtful, less ripened, less experienced minds would arouse immediately, and would succeed with a facility which terrifies me; but I have reflected and studied; I have mixed with the people, and, under their dress, with their perseverance, even their coarseness, I have viewed them so closely that I have made myself, as it were, one of themselves. I know them now; I cannot be deceived in them. They are strong, but ignorant; irritable, but not revengeful. In a word, they are not yet ripe for sedition such as I mean and wish for. They want the instruction which will make them see events in the double light of example and utility; they want the memory of their past experience.

"They resemble those daring young men whom I have

seen in Germany, at the public festivals, eagerly climb a vessel's mast, at the top of which hung a ham and a silver cup. They started at first burning with eagerness, and mounted with surprising rapidity; but when they had almost reached the goal, when they had only to extend the arm to seize their prize, their strength abandoned them, and they slipped to the bottom amid the hootings of the crowd.

"The first time it happened as I told you; the second time they husbanded their strength and their breath; but, taking more time, they failed by their slowness, as they had before failed from too great haste. At last — the third time — they took a middle course between precipitation and delay, and this time they succeeded. This is the plan I propose: efforts — never ceasing efforts — which gradually approach the goal, until the day arrives when infallible success will crown our attempts."

Balsamo ceased, and looked around upon his audience, among whom the passions of youth and inexperience were boiling over.

"Speak, brother," said he to Marat, who was more agitated than the others.

"I will be brief," said he. "Efforts soothe the people when they do not discourage them. Efforts! that is the theory of Monsieur Rousseau, citizen of Geneva, a great poet, but a slow and timid genius, a useless citizen, whom Plato would have driven from his republic! Wait! Ever wait! Since the emancipation of the commons, since the revolt of the *maillotins* — for seven centuries we have waited! Count the generations which have died in the mean time, and then dare to pronounce the fatal word *wait !* as your motto of the future ! Monsieur Rousseau speaks to us of opposition as it was practised in the reign of the Grand Monarque, — as Molière practised it in his comedies, Boileau in his satires, and La Fontaine in his fables, — whispering it in the ears of marchionesses, and prostrating it at the feet of kings. Poor and feeble opposition, which

has not advanced the cause of humanity one jot! Lisping
children recite these hidden theories without understanding them, and go to sleep while they recite. Rabelais also
was a politician in your sense of the word; but at such
politics people laugh, and correct nothing. Have you seen
one single abuse redressed for the last three hundred years?
Enough of poets and theoreticians! Let us have deeds,
not words. We have given France up to the care of
physicians for three hundred years, and it is time now
that surgery should enter in its turn, scalpel and saw in
hand. Society is gangrened; let us stop the gangrene
with the steel. He may wait who rises from his table to
recline upon a couch of roses, from which the ruffled leaves
are blown by the breath of his slaves; for the satisfied
stomach exhales grateful vapours which mount into the
brain, and recreate and vivify it. But hunger, misery,
despair, are not satiated nor consoled with verses, with
sentences and fables. They cry out loudly in their sufferings; deaf indeed must he be who does not hear their
lamentation, accursed he who does not reply to them! A
revolt, even should it be crushed, will enlighten the minds
more than a thousand years of precepts, more than three
centuries of examples. It will enlighten the kings, if it do
not overthrow them. That is much! — that is enough!"

A murmur of admiration rose from several lips.

"Where are our enemies?" pursued Marat. "Above
us! Above us! They guard the doors of the palaces, they
surround the steps of the throne. Upon this throne is
their palladium, which they guard with more care and
with more fear than the Trojans did theirs. This palladium, which makes them all powerful, rich, and insolent,
is royalty. This royalty cannot be reached, save by passing over the bodies of those who guard it, — as one can
only reach the general by overthrowing the battalion by
which he is surrounded. Well! History tells us of many
battalions which have been captured, many generals who
have been overthrown, — from Darius down to King John,
from Regulus down to Duguesclin.

"If we overthrow the guard, we reach the idol. Let us begin by striking down the sentinels; we can afterwards strike down the chief. Let the first attack be on the courtiers, the nobility, the aristocracy; the last will be upon the kings. Count the privileged heads; there are scarcely two hundred thousand. Walk through this beautiful garden called France, with a sharp switch in your hand, and cut down these two hundred thousand heads as Tarquin did the poppies of Latium, and all will be done. There will then be only two powers opposed to each other, — the people, and the kingship. Then let this kingship, the emblem, try to struggle with the people, this giant — and you will see! When dwarfs wish to overthrow a colossus, they commence with the pedestal; when the woodmen wish to cut down the oak, they attack it at the foot. Woodmen! woodmen! seize the hatchet, attack the oak at its roots, and the ancient tree with its proud branches will soon bite the dust!"

"And will crush you like pygmies in its fall, unfortunate wretches that you are!" exclaimed Balsamo, in a voice of thunder. "Ah! you rail against the poets, and you speak in metaphors even more poetical and more imaginative than theirs! Brother! brother!" continued he, addressing Marat, "I tell you, you have quoted these sentences from some romance which you are composing in your garret!"

Marat reddened.

"Do you know what a revolution is?" continued Balsamo. "I have seen two hundred, and can tell you. I have seen that of ancient Egypt, that of Assyria, those of Rome and Greece, and that of the Netherlands. I have seen those of the middle ages, when the nations rushed one against another, — East against West, West against East, — and murdered without knowing why. From the Shepherd Kings to our own time there have been perhaps a hundred revolutions, and yet now you complain of being slaves. Revolutions, then, have done no good. And why? Because those who caused the revolution were all struck with the same vertigo, — they were too hasty. Does God, who presides over the revolutions of the world, as genius presides over the revolutions of men, — does He hasten?

"' Cut down the oak!' you cry. And you do not calculate that the oak, which needs but a second to fall, covers as much ground when it falls as a horse at a gallop would cross in thirty seconds. Now, those who throw down the oak, not having time to avoid the unforeseen fall, would be lost, crushed, killed, beneath its immense trunk. That is what you want, is it not? You will never get that from me. I shall be patient. I carry my fate — yours — the world's — in the hollow of this hand. No one can make me open this hand, full of overwhelming truth, unless I wish to open it. There is thunder in it, I know. Well! the thunderbolt shall remain in it, as if hidden in the murky cloud. Brethren! brethren! descend from these sublime heights, and let us once more walk upon the earth!

"Gentlemen, I tell you plainly, and from my inmost soul, that the time has not yet come. The king who is on the throne is the last reflection of the great monarch whom the people still venerate; and in this fading monarchy there is yet something dazzling enough to outweigh the lightning shafts of your petty anger. This man was born a king and will die a king; his race is insolent, but pure. You can read his origin on his brow, in his gestures, in his words; he will always be king. Overthrow him and the same will happen to him as happened to Charles the First, — his executioners will kneel before him, and the courtiers who accompanied him in his misfortune, like Lord Capel, will kiss the axe which struck off the head of their master.

"Now, gentlemen, you all know that England was too hasty. King Charles the First died upon the scaffold, indeed; but King Charles the Second, his son, died upon the throne.

"Wait, wait, brethren! for the time will soon be propitious. You wish to destroy the lilies. That is our

.motto: 'Lilia pedibus destrue.' But not a single root must leave the flower of Saint Louis the hope of blooming again. You wish to destroy royalty, to destroy royalty forever! You must first weaken her *prestige* as well as her essence. You wish to destroy royalty! Wait till royalty is no longer a sacred office, but merely a trade, — till it is practised in a shop, not in a temple. Now, what is most sacred in royalty — namely, the legitimate transmission of the throne, authorised for centuries by God and the people — is about to be lost forever. Listen, listen! This invincible, this impervious barrier between us nothings and these *quasi* divine creatures, this limit which the people have never dared to cross, and which is called legitimacy, this word, brilliant as a lighted watch-tower, and which until now has saved the royal family from shipwreck, — this word will be extinguished by the breath of a mysterious fatality!

"The dauphiness — called to France to perpetuate the race of kings by the admixture of imperial blood — the dauphiness, married now for a year to the heir of the French crown, — approach, brethren, for I fear to let the sound of my words pass beyond your circle."

"Well?" asked the six chiefs, with anxiety.

"Well, brethren, the dauphiness will never have an heir, or if one be born to her, he will die early!"

A sinister murmur, which would have frozen the monarchs of the world with terror had they heard it, — such deep hatred, such revengeful joy, did it breathe, — escaped like a deadly vapour from the little circle of six heads, which almost touched one another, Balsamo's being bent over them from his rostrum.

"Under these conditions two possibilities are presented for our consideration, both alike advantageous to our cause. The first is, that the dauphiness may be childless, and thus the race become extinct; in that case, our friends would have no wars, no difficulties, no perplexities in the future. That which has happened in France, every time

three brothers have reigned successively, would then be
fulfilled in this race, already doomed by fate; that which
happened to the sons of Philip le Bel, — Louis le Hutin,
Philip le Long, and Charles IV., — who all three reigned
and died without leaving any issue; that which happened
to the three sons of Henri II., — François II., Charles IX.,
and Henri III., — dying without issue, having all of them
reigned.   Like them Monsieur le Dauphin, Monsieur le
Comte de Provence, and Monsieur le Comte d'Artois, will
all three reign, and will all three die childless, as the
others died; it is the law of fate.

"Then, as after Charles IV., the last of the Capetian
kings, came Philip VI., of Valois, of a family collateral
with that of the preceding kings; as after Henri III., the
last of the Valois line, came Henri IV. de Bourbon, of a
collateral family with the preceding kings, — after the
Comte d'Artois, whose name is written in the book of
fate, as the last of the kings of the old line, will come,
perchance, some Cromwell or some William of Orange, a
stranger to the race or to the natural order of succession.

"That is what our first possibility offers us.

"The second is, that Madame la Dauphine may not be
childless.   And that is the trap into which our enemies
will fall, while expecting to see us caught in it ourselves.
Oh! if the dauphiness does not remain childless, if she
should become a mother, then, indeed, would there be
rejoicing at court, and they would all think that royalty
was firmly established.   We, too, may likewise rejoice;
for we shall possess a secret so terrible that no prestige,
no power, no efforts shall withstand the crimes which this
secret shall involve, and the misfortunes which will accrue
to the unhappy queen from this maternity.   For this heir
which she will give to the throne, we will easily prove
illegitimate; for this maternity we shall prove to be
adulterous.   So that, far from the seeming good fortune
which Heaven shall have been thought to have granted
them, in comparison they would have considered barren-

ness a gift from God. This is why I have refrained, gentlemen; this is why I have waited, brothers; for, indeed, I consider it useless to set the passions of the people free to-day; I shall use them to good effect when the right time shall come.

"Now, gentlemen, you know this year's work; you see the progress of our mines. Be assured that we shall only succeed by the genius and the courage of some, who will serve as the eyes and the brain; by the perseverance and labour of others, who will represent the arms; by the faith and the devotion of others again, who will be the heart.

"Above all, remember the necessity of a blind submission which ordains that even your chief must sacrifice himself to the will of the statutes of the order, whenever those statutes require it.

"After this, gentlemen and beloved brothers, I would dissolve the meeting, if there were not still a good act to perform, an evil to point out.

"The great writer who came among us this evening, and who would have been one of us but for the stormy zeal of one of our brothers who alarmed his timid soul, — this great author proved himself in the right before our assembly, and I deplore it as a misfortune that a stranger should be victorious before a majority of brothers who are imperfectly acquainted with our rules, and utterly ignorant of our aim.

"Rousseau, triumphing over the truths of our association with the sophisms of his books, represents a fundamental vice which I would extirpate by steel and fire, if I had not the hope of curing it by persuasion. The self-love of one of our brothers has developed itself most unfortunately; he has given us the worst in the discussion. No similar fact, I trust, will again present itself, or else I shall have recourse to the laws of discipline.

"In the mean time, gentlemen, propagate the faith by gentleness and persuasion. Insinuate it, do not impose it; do not force it into rebellious minds with wedges and blows, as the inquisitors tortured their victims. Remember that we cannot be great until after we have been acknowledged good; and that we cannot be acknowledged good but by appearing better than those who surround us. Remember, too, that among us, the great, the good, the best, are nothing without science, art, and faith; nothing, in short, compared with those whom God has marked with a peculiar stamp, as if giving them an authority to govern over men and rule empires.

"Gentlemen, the meeting is dissolved."

After pronouncing these words Balsamo put on his hat and folded himself in his cloak.

Each of the initiated left in his turn, alone and silently, in order not to awaken suspicion.

## CHAPTER CIV.

### THE BODY AND THE SOUL.

THE last who remained beside the master was Marat, the surgeon. He was very pale, and humbly approached the terrible orator, whose power was unlimited.

"Master," said he, "have I indeed committed a fault?"

"A great one, monsieur," said Balsamo; "and, what is worse, you do not believe that you have committed one."

"Well, yes, I confess that not only do I not believe that I committed a fault, but I think that I spoke as I ought to have done."

"Pride, pride!" muttered Balsamo; "pride — destructive demon! Men combat the fever in the blood of the patient — they dispel the plague from the water and the air; but they let pride strike such deep roots in their hearts that they cannot exterminate it."

"Oh, master!" said Marat, "you have a very despicable opinion of me. Am I indeed so worthless that I cannot count for anything among my fellows? Have I gathered the fruits of my labour so ill that I cannot utter a word without being taxed with ignorance? Am I such a lukewarm adept that my earnestness is suspected? If I had no other good quality, at least I exist through my devotion to the holy cause of the people."

"Monsieur," replied Balsamo, "it is because the principle of good yet struggles in you against the principle of evil, which appears to me likely to carry you away one day, that I will try to correct these defects in you. If I can succeed — if pride has not yet subdued every other sentiment in your breast — I shall succeed in one hour."

"In one hour?" said Marat.

"Yes; will you grant me that time?"

"Certainly."

"Where shall I see you?"

"Master, it is my place to seek you in any place you may choose to point out to your servant."

"Well," said Balsamo, "I will come to your house."

"Mark the promise you are making, master. I live in an attic in the Rue des Cordeliers. An attic, remember!" said Marat, with an affectation of proud simplicity, with a boasting display of poverty, which did not escape Balsamo; "while you —"

"Well, while I?"

"While you, it is said, inhabit a palace."

Balsamo shrugged his shoulders, as a giant who looks down with contempt on the anger of a dwarf.

"Well, even so, monsieur," he replied, "I will come to see you in your garret."

"And when, monsieur?"

"To-morrow."

"At what time?"

"In the morning."

"At daybreak I go to my lecture-room, and from thence to the hospital."

"That is precisely what I want. I would have asked you to take me with you, had you not proposed it."

"But early, remember," said Marat; "I sleep little."

"And I do not sleep at all," replied Balsamo. "At daybreak, then."

"I shall expect you."

Thereupon they separated, for they had reached the door opening on the street, now as dark and solitary as it had been noisy and populous when they entered. Balsamo turned to the left, and rapidly disappeared. Marat followed his example, striding toward the right with his long, meagre limbs.

Balsamo was punctual; the next morning, at six o'clock,

he knocked at Marat's door, which was the centre one of
six, opening on a long corridor which formed the topmost
story of an old house in the Rue des Cordeliers.

It was evident that Marat had made great preparations
to receive his illustrious guest. The small bed of walnut-
tree, and the wooden chest of drawers beside it, shone
bright beneath the sturdy arm of the charwoman, who was
busily engaged scrubbing the decayed furniture.

Marat himself lent a helping hand to the old woman, and
was refreshing the withered flowers which were arranged
in a blue delft pot, and which formed the principal ornament of the attic. He still held a duster underneath his
arm, which showed that he had not touched the flowers
until after having given a rub to the furniture.

As the key was in the door, and as Balsamo had entered
without knocking, he interrupted Marat in his occupation.
Marat, at the sight of the master, blushed much more
deeply than was becoming in a true stoic.

"You see, master," said he, stealthily throwing the tell-
tale cloth behind a curtain, "I am a domestic man, and
assist this good woman. It is from preference that I
choose this task, which is, perhaps, not quite plebeian, but
it is still less aristocratic."

"It is that of a poor young man who loves cleanliness,"
said Balsamo, coldly, "nothing more. Are you ready,
monsieur? You know my moments are precious."

"I have only to slip on my coat, monsieur. Dame
Grivette, my coat! She is my portress, monsieur; my
footman, my cook, my housekeeper, and she costs me one
crown a month."

"Economy is praiseworthy," said Balsamo; "it is the
wealth of the poor, and the wisdom of the rich."

"My hat and cane!" said Marat.

"Stretch out your hand," said Balsamo; "there is your
hat, and no doubt this cane which hangs beside your hat
is yours."

"Oh, I beg your pardon, monsieur; I am quite confused."

"Are you ready?"

"Yes, monsieur. My watch, Dame Grivette!"

Dame Grivette bustled about the room as if in search of something, but did not reply.

"You have no occasion for a watch, monsieur, to go to the lecture-room and the hospital; it will perhaps not be easily found, and that would cause some delay."

"But, monsieur, I attach great value to my watch, which is an excellent one, and which I bought with my savings."

"In your absence, Dame Grivette will look for it," replied Balsamo, with a smile; "and if she searches carefully, it will be found when you return."

"Oh, certainly," said Dame Grivette, "it will be found unless monsieur has left it somewhere else. Nothing is lost here."

"You see," said Balsamo. "Come, monsieur, come!"

Marat did not venture to persist, and followed Balsamo, grumbling.

When they reached the door, Balsamo said: —

"Where shall we go first?"

"To the lecture-room, if you please, master; I have marked a subject which must have died last night of acute meningitis. I want to make some observations on the brain, and I do not wish my colleagues to take it from me."

"Then let us go to the lecture-room, Monsieur Marat."

"Moreover, it is only a few yards from here; the lecture-room is close to the hospital, and I shall only have to go in for a moment; you may even wait for me at the door."

"On the contrary, I wish to accompany you inside, and hear your opinion of this subject."

"When it was alive, monsieur?"

"No, since it has become a corpse."

"Take care," said Marat, smiling; "I may gain a point over you, for I am well acquainted with this part of my profession, and am said to be a skilful anatomist."

"Pride! pride! ever pride!" murmured Balsamo.

"What do you say?" asked Marat.

"I say that we shall see, monsieur," replied Balsamo. "Let us enter."

Marat preceded Balsamo in the narrow alley leading to the lecture-room, which was situated at the extremity of the Rue Hautefeuille. Balsamo followed him unhesitatingly until they reached a long, narrow room, where two corpses, a male and a female, lay stretched upon a marble table.

The woman had died young; the man was old and bald. A soiled sheet was thrown over their bodies, leaving their faces half uncovered.

They were lying side by side upon this cold bed; they who had perhaps never met before in the world, and whose souls, then voyaging in eternity, must, could they have looked down on earth, have been struck with wonderment at the proximity of their mortal remains.

Marat, with a single movement, raised and threw aside the coarse linen which covered the two bodies, whom death had thus made equal before the anatomist's scalpel.

"Is not the sight of the dead repugnant to your feelings?" asked Marat, in his usual boasting manner.

"It makes me sad," replied Balsamo.

"Want of custom," said Marat. "I, who see this sight daily, feel neither sadness nor disgust. We practitioners live with the dead, and do not interrupt any of the functions of our existence on their account."

"It is a sad privilege of your profession, monsieur."

"Besides," added Marat, "why should I be sad, or feel disgust? In the first case, reflection forbids it; in the second, custom."

"Explain your ideas," said Balsamo; "I do not understand you clearly. Reflection first."

"Well, why should I be afraid? Why should I fear an inert mass, — a statue of flesh instead of stone, marble, or granite?"

"In short, you think there is nothing in a corpse."

".Nothing — absolutely nothing."

"Do you believe that?"

"I am sure of it."

"But in the living body."

"There is motion," said Marat, proudly.

"And the soul? — you do not speak of it, monsieur."

"I have never found it in the bodies which I have dissected."

"Because you have only dissected corpses."

"Oh, no, monsieur!   I have frequently operated upon living bodies."

"And you have found nothing more in them than in the corpses?"

"Yes, I have found pain.   Do you call pain the soul?"

"Then you do not believe in it?"

"In what?"

"In the soul?"

"I believe in it, because I am at liberty to call it motion if I wish."

"That is well.   You believe in the soul; that is all I asked.   I am glad you believe in it."

"One moment, master.   Let us understand each other, and above all, let us not exaggerate," said Marat, with his serpent smile.   "We practitioners are rather disposed to materialism."

"These bodies are very cold," said Balsamo, dreamily, "and this woman was very beautiful."

"Why, yes."

"A lovely soul would have been suitable in this lovely body."

"Ah! there is the mistake in Him who created her.   A beautiful scabbard, but a vile sword.   This corpse, master, is that of a wretched woman who had just left Saint Lazarus, when she died of cerebral inflammation in the Hotel-Dieu.   Her history is long, and tolerably scandalous.   If you call the motive-power which impelled this creature soul you wrong our souls, which must be of the same essence, since they are derived from the same source." 

"Her soul should have been cured," said Balsamo; "it was lost for want of the only Physician who is indispensable, — the Physician of the Soul."

"Alas, master, that is another of your theories. Medicine is only for the body," replied Marat, with a bitter smile. "Now you have a word on your lips which Molière has often employed in his comedies, and it is this word which makes you smile."

"No," said Balsamo, "you mistake; you cannot guess why I smile. What we concluded just now was, that these corpses are void, was it not?"

"And insensible," added Marat, raising the young woman's head, and letting it fall noisily upon the marble, while the body neither moved nor shuddered.

"Very well," said Balsamo; "let us now go to the hospital."

"Wait one moment, master, I entreat you, until I have separated from the trunk this head, which I am most anxious to have, as it was the seat of a very curious disease. Will you allow me?"

"Do you ask?" said Balsamo.

Marat opened his case, took from it a bistoury, and picked up in a corner a large wooden mallet stained with blood. Then with a practised hand he made a circular incision which separated all the flesh and the muscles of the neck, and having thus reached the bone, he slipped his bistoury between the juncture of the vertebral column, and struck a sharp blow upon it with the mallet.

The head rolled upon the table, and from the table upon the floor; Marat was obliged to seize it with his damp hands. Balsamo turned away, not to give too much joy to the triumphant operator.

"One day," said Marat, who thought he had hit the master in a weak point, — "one day some philanthropist will occupy himself with the details of death as others do of life, and will invent a machine which shall sever a head at a single blow, and cause instantaneous annihilation, which no other instrument of death does. The wheel, quartering, and hanging, are punishments suitable for savages, but not for civilised people. An enlightened nation, as France is, should punish, but not revenge. Those who condemn to the wheel, who hang or quarter, revenge themselves upon the criminal by inflicting pain before punishing him by death, which, in my opinion, is too much by half."

"And in mine also, monsieur. But what kind of an instrument do you mean?"

"I can fancy a machine cold and impassible as the law itself. The man who is charged with fulfilling the last office is moved at the sight of his fellow-man, and sometimes strikes badly, as it happened to the Duke of Monmouth and to Chalais. This could not be the case with a machine, — with two arms of oak wielding a cutlass, for instance."

"And do you believe, monsieur, that because the knife would pass with the rapidity of lightning between the base of the occiput and the trapezoid muscles, that death would be instantaneous, and the pain momentary?"

"Certainly; death would be instantaneous, for the iron would sever the nerves which cause motion at a blow. The pain would be momentary, for the blade would separate the brain, which is the seat of the feelings, from the heart, which is the centre of life."

"Monsieur," said Balsamo, "the punishment of decapitation exists in Germany."

"Yes, but by the sword; and, as I said before, a man's hand may tremble."

"Such a machine exists in Italy; an arm of oak wields it. It is called the *mannaja*."

"Well?"

"Well, monsieur, I have seen criminals, decapitated by the executioner, raise their headless bodies from the bench on which they were seated, and stagger five or six paces off where they fell. I have picked up heads which had rolled to the foot of the mannaja, as that head you are holding by the hair has just rolled from the marble table; and on pronouncing in their ears the name by which those persons had been called, I have seen the eyes open again and turn in their orbit, in their endeavours to see who had called them back again to earth."

"A nervous movement — nothing else."

"Are the nerves not the organs of sensibility ?"

"What do you conclude from that, monsieur ?"

"I conclude that it would be better, instead of inventing a machine which kills to punish, that man should seek a means of punishing without killing. The society which will invent this means will assuredly be the best and the most enlightened of societies."

"Utopias again! always Utopias!" said Marat.

"Perhaps you are right," said Balsamo; "time will show. But did you not speak of the hospital? Let us go!"

"Come, then," said Marat; and he tied the woman's head in his pocket-handkerchief, carefully knotting the four corners. "Now I am sure, at least," said he, as he left the hall, "that my comrades will only have my leavings."

They took the way to the Hôtel-Dieu, — the dreamer and the practician side by side.

"You have cut off this head very coolly and very skilfully, monsieur," said Balsamo; "do you feel less emotion when you operate upon the living than the dead? Does the sight of suffering affect you more than that of immobility? Have you more pity for living bodies than for corpses ?"

"No; that would be as great a fault as for the executioner to be moved. You may kill a man by cutting his thigh unskilfully, just as well as by severing the head from the body. A good surgeon operates with his hand, not with his heart; though he knows well at the same time, in his heart, that for one moment of suffering he gives years of life and health. That is the fair side of our profession, master."

"Yes, monsieur; but in the living bodies you meet with the soul, I hope."

"Yes, if you will agree with me that the soul is motion, or sensibility. Yes, certainly, I meet with it; and it is very troublesome, too; for it kills far more patients than any scalpel."

They had by this time arrived at the threshold of the Hôtel-Dieu, and now entered the hospital. Guided by Marat, who still carried his ominous burden, Balsamo penetrated to the hall where the operations were performed, in which the head-surgeon and the students were assembled. The attendant had just brought in a young man who had been run over the preceding week by a heavy carriage, the wheel of which had crushed his foot. A hasty operation, performed upon the limb when benumbed by pain, had not been sufficient; the inflammation had rapidly extended, and the amputation of the leg had now become urgent.

The unfortunate man, stretched upon his bed of anguish, looked with a horror which would have melted tigers at the band of eager students who were watching for the moment of his martyrdom, perhaps of his death, that they might study the science of life, — that marvellous phenomenon behind which lies the gloomy phenomenon of death.

He seemed to implore a pitying look, a smile, or a word of encouragement from each of the students and attendants, but the beatings of his heart were responded to only by indifference, his beseeching looks with glances of iron. A surviving emotion of pride kept him silent. He reserved all his strength for the cries which pain would soon wring from him. But when he felt the heavy hand of the attendant upon his shoulder, when the arms of the assistants twined around him like the serpents of Laocoön, when he heard the operator's voice cry, "Courage!" the unfortunate man ventured to break the silence, and asked in a plaintive voice: —

"Shall I suffer much?"

"Oh, no, make your mind easy," replied Marat, with a hypocritical smile, which was affectionate to the patient, but ironical to Balsamo.

Marat saw that Balsamo had understood him; he approached and whispered: —

"It is a dreadful operation. The bone is full of cracks and fearfully sensitive. He will die, not of the wound, but of the pain. That is what the soul does for this poor man."

"Then why do you operate ? Why do you not let him die in peace ? "

"Because it is the surgeon's duty to attempt a cure, even when the cure seems impossible."

"And you say he will suffer ? "

"Fearfully."

"And that his soul is the cause ? "

"His soul, which has too much sympathy with the body."

"Then, why not operate upon the soul ? Perhaps the tranquillity of the one would cause the cure of the other."

"I have done so," said Marat, while the attendants continued to bind the patient.

"You have prepared his soul ? "

"Yes."

"How so ? "

"As one always does, by words. I spoke to his soul, his intelligence, his sensibility, — to that organ which caused the Greek philosopher to exclaim, 'Pain, thou art no evil,' — the language suitable for it. I said to him, 'You will not suffer.' That is the only remedy hitherto known as regards the soul, — falsehood ! Why is this she-devil of a soul connected with the body ? When I cut off this head just now, the body said nothing, yet the operation was a serious one. But motion had ceased, sensibility was extinguished, the soul had fled, as you spiritualists say. This is the reason why the head I severed said nothing, why the body which I mutilated allowed me to do

so; while this body, which is yet inhabited by a soul, — for
a short time indeed, but still inhabited, — will cry out fearfully.  Stop your ears well, master, you who are moved by
this union of body and soul, which will always destroy your
theory until you succeed in isolating the body from the
soul."

"And you believe we shall never arrive at this isolation ? "

"Try," said Marat, "this is an excellent opportunity."

"Well, yes, you are right," said Balsamo ; "the opportunity is a good one, and I will make the attempt."

"Yes, try."

"I will."

"How so ? "

"This young man interests me ; he shall not suffer."

"You are an illustrious chief," said Marat, "but you are
not the Almighty, and you cannot prevent this wretch from
suffering."

"If he were not to feel the pain, do you think he would
recover ? "

"His recovery would be more probable, but not certain."

Balsamo cast an inexpressible look of triumph upon
Marat, and placing himself before the young patient, whose
frightened eyes, already dilated with the anguish of terror,
met his, —

"Sleep," said he, not alone with his lips, but with his
look, with his will, with all the heat of his blood, all the
vital energy of his body.

The head-surgeon was just commencing to feel the injured leg, and to point out the aggravated nature of the
case to his students ; but, at Balsamo's command, the
young man, who had raised himself upon his seat, oscillated
for a moment in the arms of his attendants, his head
drooped, and his eyes closed.

"He is ill," said Marat.

"No, monsieur."

"But do you not see that he loses consciousness ? "

"He is sleeping."

"What! he sleeps?"

"Yes."

Every one turned to look at the strange physician, whom they took for a madman. An incredulous smile hovered on Marat's lips.

"Is it usual for people to talk whilst in a swoon?" asked Balsamo.

"No."

"Well! question him, — he will reply."

"Hallo! young man!" cried Marat.

"You need not speak so loud," said Balsamo; "speak in your usual voice."

"Tell us what is the matter with you."

"I was ordered to sleep, and I do sleep," replied the patient.

His voice was perfectly calm, and formed a strange contrast to that they had heard a few moments before.

All the attendants looked at each other.

"Now," said Balsamo, "release him."

"That is impossible," said the head-surgeon; "the slightest movement will spoil the operation.

"He will not stir."

"Who can assure me of that?"

"I, and he also; ask him."

"Can you be left untied, my friend?"

"Yes."

"And will you promise not to move?"

"I will promise it, if you command me."

"I command it."

"Faith! monsieur, you speak so positively that I am tempted to make the trial."

"Do so, monsieur; and fear nothing."

"Untie him."

The assistants obeyed.

Balsamo advanced to the bedside.

"From this moment," said he, "do not stir until I order you."

A carved statue upon a tombstone could not have been more motionless than the patient, upon this injunction.

"Now operate, monsieur," said Balsamo; "the patient is quite ready."

The surgeon took his bistoury; but when upon the point of using it, he hesitated.

"Cut, monsieur, cut!" said Balsamo, with the air of an inspired prophet.

And the surgeon, yielding — like Marat, like the patient, like every one present — to the irresistible influence of Balsamo's words, raised the knife. The sound of the knife passing through the flesh was heard, but the patient never stirred, nor even uttered a sigh.

"From what country do you come, my friend?" asked Balsamo.

"I am a Breton, monsieur," replied the patient, smiling.

"And you love your country?"

"Oh! monsieur, it is so beautiful."

In the mean time the surgeon was making the circular incisions in the flesh, by means of which, in amputations, the bone is laid bare.

"You quitted it when young?" asked Balsamo.

"At ten years of age, monsieur."

The incisions were made, — the surgeon placed the saw on the bone.

"My friend," said Balsamo, "sing me that song which the salt-makers of Batz chant as they return to their homes after the day's work is over. I can only remember the first line: —

"'My salt covered o'er with its mantle of foam.'"

The saw was now severing the bone; but at Balsamo's command the patient smiled, and commenced, in a low, melodious, ecstatic voice, like a lover or like a poet, the following verses: —

" ' My salt covered o'er with its mantle of foam,
  The lake of pure azure that mirrors my home,
  My stove where the peats ever cheerfully burn,
  And the honeyed wheat-cake which awaits my return, —

" ' The wife of my bosom, my silver-haired sire,
  My urchins who sport round the clear evening fire —
  And there, where the wild flowers, in brightest of bloom,
  Their fragrance diffuse round my loved mother's tomb, —

" ' Blest, blest be ye all ! — Now the day's task is o'er,
  And I stand once again at my own cottage door ;
  And richly will love my brief absence repay,
  And the calm joys of eve the rude toils of the day.' "

The leg fell upon the bed while the patient was still
singing.

## CHAPTER CV.

### BODY AND SOUL.

EVERY one looked with astonishment at the patient, with admiration at the surgeon.  Some said both were mad. Marat communicated this opinion to Balsamo in a whisper.

"Terror has made the poor devil lose his senses," said he; "that is why he feels no pain."

"I think not," replied Balsamo; "and far from having lost his senses, I am sure that if I asked him he could tell us the day of his death, if he is to die, or the period of his convalescence, if he is to recover."

Marat was almost inclined to adopt the general opinion, — that Balsamo was as mad as his patient.  In the mean time, however, the surgeon was tying up the arteries, from which spouted streams of blood.

Balsamo drew a small phial from his pocket, poured a few drops of the liquid it contained upon a little ball of lint, and begged the chief surgeon to apply the lint to the arteries.  The latter obeyed with a certain feeling of curiosity.  He was one of the most celebrated practitioners of that period, — a man truly enamoured of his profession, who repudiated none of its mysteries, and for whom chance was but the makeshift of doubt.

He applied the lint to the artery, which quivered, bubbled, and then only allowed the blood to escape drop by drop. He could now tie up the artery with the greatest facility.

This time Balsamo obtained an undoubted triumph, and all present asked him where he had studied, and of what school he was.

"I am a German physician of the school of Göttingen,"
replied he, "and I have made this discovery you have just
witnessed. However, gentlemen and fellow-practitioners,
I wish this discovery to remain a secret for the present, as
I have a wholesome terror of the stake, and the parliament
of Paris might perhaps resume their functions once more
for the pleasure of condemning a sorcerer to be burned."

The chief surgeon was still plunged in a reverie. Marat
also seemed thoughtful, but he was the first to break the
silence.

"You said just now," said he, "that if you were to question this man about the result of this operation he would
reply truly, though the result is still veiled in futurity."

"I assert it again," replied Balsamo.

"Well, let us have the proof."

"What is this poor fellow's name?"

"Havard," replied Marat.

Balsamo turned to the patient, whose lips were yet murmuring the last words of the plaintive air.

"Well, my friend," asked he, "what do you augur from
the state of this poor Havard?"

"What do I augur from his state?" replied the patient;
"stay, I must return from Brittany, where I was, to the
Hôtel-Dieu, where he is."

"Just so; enter, look at him, and tell me the truth respecting him."

"Oh! he is very ill; his leg has been cut off."

"Indeed?" said Balsamo. "And has the operation been
successful?"

"Exceedingly so; but —"

The patient's face darkened.

"But what?" asked Balsamo.

"But," resumed the patient, "he has a terrible trial to
pass through. The fever —"

"When will it commence?"

"At seven o'clock this evening."

All the spectators looked at each other.

" And this fever ? " asked Balsamo.

" Oh ! it will make him very ill; but he will recover from the first attack."

" Are you sure ? "

" Oh, yes ! "

" Then, after this first attack, will he be saved ? "

" Alas ! no," said the wounded man, sighing.

" Will the fever return, then ? "

" Oh, yes ! and more severely than before.  Poor Havard ! poor Havard ! " he continued ; " he has a wife and several children."   And his eyes filled with tears.

" Must his wife be a widow, then, and his children orphans ? " asked Balsamo.

" Wait ! wait ! "

He clasped his hands.

" No, no," he exclaimed, his features lighting up with an expression of sublime faith; " no, his wife and children have prayed, and their prayers have found favour in the sight of God ! "

" Then he will recover ? "

" Yes."

" You hear, gentlemen," said Balsamo, " he will recover."

" Ask him in how many days," said Marat.

" In how many days, do you say ? "

" Yes ; you said he could indicate the phases and the duration of his convalescence."

" I ask nothing better than to question him on the subject."

" Well, then, question him now."

" And when do you think Havard will recover ? " said Balsamo.

" Oh ! his cure will take a long time, — a month, six weeks, two months.  He entered this hospital five days ago, and he will leave it two months and fourteen days after having entered."

" And he will leave it cured ? "

" Yes."

"But," said Marat, "unable to work, and consequently to maintain his wife and children."

Havard again clasped his hands.

" Oh! God is good; God will provide for him!"

"And how will God provide for him?" asked Marat. " As I am in the way of hearing something new to-day, I might as well hear that."

" God has sent to his bedside a charitable man who has taken pity upon him, and who has said to himself, 'Poor Havard shall not want.'"

The spectators were amazed; Balsamo smiled.

" Ha! this is in truth a strange scene," said the chief surgeon, at the same time taking the patient's hand, feeling his chest and forehead; "this man is dreaming."

" Do you think so?" said Balsamo.

Then, darting upon the sick man a look of authority and energy: —

" Awake, Havard!" said he.

The young man opened his eyes with some difficulty, and gazed with profound surprise upon all these spectators, who had so soon laid aside their threatening character, and assumed an inoffensive one towards him.

" Well," said he, sadly, "have you not operated yet? Are you going to make me suffer still more?"

Balsamo replied hastily. He feared the invalid's emotion. But there was no need for such haste; the surprise of all the spectators was so great that none would have anticipated him.

" My friend," said he, "be calm. The head-surgeon has operated upon your leg in such a manner as to satisfy all the requirements of your position. It seems, my poor fellow, that you are not very strong-minded, for you fainted at the first incision."

" Oh! so much the better," said the Breton, smilingly; " I felt nothing, and my sleep was even sweet and refreshing. What happiness, — my leg will not be cut off!"

But just at that moment the poor man looked down, and

saw the bed full of blood, and his amputated leg lying near him. He uttered a scream, and this time fainted in reality.

"Now question him," said Balsamo, coldly, to Marat; "you will see if he replies."

Then, taking the head-surgeon aside, while the nurses carried the poor young man back to his bed, —

"Monsieur," said Balsamo, "you heard what your poor patient said ? "

"Yes, monsieur, that he would recover."

"He said something else; he said that God would take pity upon him, and would send him wherewithal to support his wife and children."

"Well ? "

"Well, monsieur, he told the truth on this point, as on the others. Only you must undertake to be the charitable medium of affording him this assistance. Here is a diamond, worth about twenty thousand francs; when the poor man is cured, sell it and give him the proceeds. In the meantime, since the soul, as your pupil, Monsieur Marat, said very truly, has a great influence upon the body, tell Havard as soon as he is restored to consciousness that his future comfort and that of his children is secured."

"But, monsieur," said the surgeon, hesitating to take the ring which Balsamo offered him, "if he should not recover ? "

"He will recover."

"Then allow me, at least, to give you a receipt."

"Monsieur ! "

"That is the only condition upon which I can receive a jewel of such value."

"Do as you think right, monsieur."

"Your name, if you please ? "

"The Count de Fenix."

The surgeon passed into the adjoining apartment, while Marat, overwhelmed, confounded, but still struggling against the evidence of his senses, approached Balsamo.

In five minutes the surgeon returned, holding in his hand the following receipt, which he gave Balsamo : —

I have received from the Count de Fenix a diamond, which he affirms to be worth twenty thousand francs, the price of which is to be given to the man Havard when he leaves the Hôtel-Dieu.

This 15th of September, 1771.

GUILLOTIN, M. D.

Balsamo bowed to the doctor, took the receipt, and left the room, followed by Marat.

"You are forgetting your head," said Balsamo, for whom the wandering of the young student's thoughts was a great triumph.

"Ah! true," said he.

And he again picked up his dismal burden. When they emerged into the street, both walked forward very quickly without uttering a word; then having reached the Rue des Cordeliers, they ascended the steep stairs which led to the attic.

Marat, who had not forgotten the disappearance of his watch, stopped before the lodge of the portress, if the den which she inhabited deserved that name, and asked for Dame Grivette.

A thin, stunted, miserable-looking child, about seven years old, replied in a whining voice: —

"Mamma is gone out; she said that when you came home I was to give you this letter."

"No, no, my little friend," said Marat; "tell her to bring it me herself."

"Yes, monsieur."

And Marat and Balsamo proceeded on their way.

"Ah!" said Marat, pointing out a chair to Balsamo, and falling upon a stool himself, "I see the master has some noble secrets."

"Perhaps I have penetrated farther than most men into the confidence of nature and into the works of God," replied Balsamo.

"Oh!" said Marat, "how science proves man's omnipotence, and makes us proud to be a man!"

"True; and a physician, you should have added."

"Therefore, I am proud of you, master," said Marat.

"And yet," replied Balsamo, smiling, "I am but a poor physician of souls."

"Oh! do not speak of that monsieur, — you, who stopped the patient's bleeding by material means."

"I thought my best cure was that of having prevented him from suffering. True, you assured me he was mad."

"He was so for a moment, certainly."

"What do you call madness? Is it not an abstraction of the soul?"

"Or of the mind," said Marat.

"We will not discuss the point. The soul serves me as a term for what I mean. When the object is found, it matters little how you call it."

"There is where we differ, monsieur; you pretend you have found the thing and seek only the name; I maintain that you seek both the object and the name."

"We shall return to that immediately. You said, then, that madness was a temporary abstraction of the mind?"

"Certainly."

"Involuntary, is it not?"

"Yes; I have seen a madman at Bicêtre, who bit the iron bars of his cell, crying out all the time, ' Cook, your pheasants are very tender, but they are badly dressed.' "

"But you admit, at least, that this madness passes over the mind like a cloud, and that when it has passed, the mind resumes its former brightness?"

"That scarcely ever happens."

"Yet you saw our patient recover his senses perfectly after his insane dream."

"I saw it, but I did not understand what I saw. It is an exceptional case, — one of those strange events which the Israelites called miracles."

"No, monsieur," said Balsamo; "it is simply the abstraction of the soul, the twofold isolation of spirit and matter, — matter, that inert thing, dust, which will return to dust; and soul, the divine spark which was enclosed for a short period in that dark lantern called the body, and which, being the child of heaven, will return to heaven after the body has sunk to earth."

"Then you abstracted the soul momentarily from the body?"

"Yes, monsieur; I commanded it to quit the miserable abode which it occupied; I raised it from the abyss of suffering in which pain had bound it, and transported it into pure and heavenly regions. What then remained for the surgeon? The same that remained for your dissecting-knife, when you severed that head you are carrying from the dead body,—nothing but inert flesh, matter, clay."

"And in whose name did you command the soul?"

"In His name who created all the souls by His breath, the souls of the world, of men, — in the name of God."

"Then," said Marat, "you deny free will?"

"I!" said Balsamo; "on the contrary, what am I doing at this moment? I show you, on the one hand, free will; on the other, abstraction. I show you a dying man a prey to excruciating pain; this man has a stoical soul, he anticipates the operation, he asks for it, he bears it, but he suffers. That is free will. But when I approach the dying man, — I, the ambassador of God, the prophet, the apostle, — and taking pity upon this man who is my fellow-creature, I abstract, by the powers which the Lord has given me, the soul from the suffering body, this blind, inert, insensible body becomes a spectacle which the soul contemplates with a pitying eye from the height of its celestial sphere. Did you not hear Havard, when speaking of himself, say, 'This poor Havard'? He did not say 'myself.' It was because this soul had, in truth, no longer any connection with the body, — it was already winging its way to heaven."

"But, by this way of reckoning, man is nothing," said Marat, "and I can no longer say to the tyrant, 'You have power over my body, but none over my soul.'"

"Ah! now you pass from truth to sophism; I have already told you, monsieur, it is your failing. God lends the soul to the body, it is true; but it is no less true that during the time the soul animates this body, there is a union between the two; an influence of one over the other; a supremacy of matter over mind, or mind over matter, according as, for some purpose hidden from us, God permits either the body or the soul to be the ruling power. But it is no less true that the soul which animates the beggar is as pure as that which reigns in the bosom of the king. That is the dogma which you, an apostle of equality, ought to preach. Prove the equality of the spiritual essences in these two cases, since you can establish it by the aid of all that is most sacred in the eyes of men, — by holy books and traditions, by science and faith. Of what importance is the equality of matter? With physical equality you are only men; but spiritual equality makes you gods. Just now, this poor, wounded man, this ignorant child of the people, told you things concerning his illness which none amongst the doctors would have ventured to pronounce. How was that? It was because his soul, temporarily freed from earthly ties, floated above this world, and saw from on high a mystery which our opaqueness of vision hides from us."

Marat turned his dead head back and forward upon the table, seeking a reply which he could not find. "Yes," muttered he, at last, "yes; there is something supernatural in all this."

"Perfectly natural, on the contrary, monsieur. Cease to call supernatural what has its origin in the functions and destiny of the soul. These functions are natural, although perhaps not known."

"But though unknown to us, master, these functions cannot surely be a mystery to you. The horse, unknown to the Peruvians, was yet perfectly familiar to the Spaniards, who had tamed him."

"It would be presumptuous in me to say ' I know.' I am more humble, monsieur; I say, ' I believe.' "

"Well, what do you believe?"

"I believe that the first, the most powerful, of all laws, is the law of progress. I believe that God has created nothing without having a beneficent design in view; only, as the duration of this world is uncalculated and incalculable, the progress is slow. Our planet, according to the Scriptures, was sixty centuries old when printing came like some vast lighthouse to illuminate the past and the future. With the advent of printing, obscurity and forgetfulness vanished. Printing is the memory of the world. Well, Gutenberg invented printing, and my confidence returned."

"Ah!" said Marat, ironically, "you will, perhaps, be able at last to read men's hearts."

"Why not?"

"Then you will open that little window in men's breasts which the ancients so much desired to see?"

"There is no need for that, monsieur. I shall separate the soul from the body; and the soul — the pure, immaculate daughter of God — will reveal to me all the turpitudes of the mortal covering it is condemned to animate."

"Can you reveal material secrets?"

"Why not?"

"Can you tell me, for instance, who has stolen my watch?"

"You lower science to a base level, monsieur. But, no matter; God's greatness is proved as much by a grain of sand as by the mountain, — by the flesh-worm as by the elephant. Yes, I will tell you who has stolen your watch."

Just then a timid knock was heard at the door; it was Marat's servant, who had returned, and who came, according to the young surgeon's order, to bring the letter.

## CHAPTER CVI.

### MARAT'S PORTRESS.

THE door opened, and Dame Grivette entered. This woman, whom we have not before taken the trouble to sketch, because she was one of those characters whom the painter keeps in the background, so long as he has no occasion for them, — this woman now advances in the moving picture of this history, and demands her place in the immense picture we have undertaken to unroll before the eyes of our readers, in which, if our genius equalled our good-will, we would introduce all classes of men, from the beggar to the king, from Caliban to Ariel.

We shall now, therefore, attempt to delineate Dame Grivette, who steps forth out of the shade, and advances towards us.

She was a tall, withered creature, from thirty to five-and-thirty years of age, with dark, sallow complexion, and blue eyes encircled with black rings, — the fearful type of that decline, that wasting away, which is produced in densely populated towns by poverty, bad air, and every sort of degradation, mental as well as bodily, amongst those creatures whom God created so beautiful, and who would otherwise have become magnificent in their perfect development, as all living denizens of earth, air, and sky are when man has not made their life one long punishment, — when he has not tortured their limbs with chains and their stomachs with hunger, or with food almost as fatal.

Thus Marat's portress would have been a beautiful woman, if from her fifteenth year she had not dwelt in a den without air or light; if the fire of her natural instincts, fed by this oven-like heat, or by the icy cold, had not ceaselessly burned. She had long, thin hands, which the needle of the sempstress had furrowed with little cuts, which the suds of the wash-house had cracked and softened, which the burning coals of the kitchen had roasted and tanned; but in spite of all, hands which, by their form, that indelible trace of the divine mould, would have been called royal, if, instead of being blistered by the broom, they had wielded the sceptre. So true is it that this poor human body is only the outward sign of our profession.

But in this woman, the mind, which rose superior to the body, and which consequently had resisted external circumstances better, kept watch like a lamp; it illumined, as it were, the body by a reflected light, and at times a ray of beauty, youth, intelligence, and love was seen to glance from her dulled and stupid eyes, — a ray of all the finest feelings of the human heart.

Balsamo gazed attentively at the woman, or rather at this singular nature, which had from the first struck his observing eye.

The portress entered holding the letter in her hand, and in a soft, insinuating voice, like that of an old woman — for women condemned to poverty are old at thirty — said:

"Monsieur Marat, here is the letter you asked for."

"It was not the letter I wanted," said Marat; "I wished to see you."

"Well, here I am at your service, Monsieur Marat" (Dame Grivette made a curtsey); "what do you want with me?"

"You know very well what I want. I wish to know something about my watch."

"Ah, *dame!* I can't tell what has become of it. I saw it all day yesterday hanging from the nail over the mantel-piece."

"You mistake; all day yesterday it was in my fob; but when I went out at six o'clock in the evening, I put it under the candlestick, because I was going among a crowd, and I feared it might be stolen."

"If you put it under the candlestick, it must be there yet."

And with feigned simplicity, which she was far from suspecting to be so transparent, she raised the very candlestick, of the pair which ornamented the mantelpiece, under which Marat had concealed his watch.

"Yes, that is the candlestick, sure enough," said the young man; "but where is the watch?"

"No; I see it is no longer there. Perhaps you did not put it there, Monsieur Marat."

"But when I tell you I did?"

"Look for it carefully."

"Oh, I have looked carefully enough," said Marat, with an angry glance.

"Then you have lost it."

"But I tell you that yesterday I put it under that candlestick myself."

"Then some one must have entered," said Dame Grivette; "you see so many people, so many strangers."

"All an excuse!" cried Marat, more and more enraged. "You know very well that no one has been here since yesterday. No, no; my watch is gone where the silver top of my last cane went, where the little silver spoon you know of is gone to, and my knife with the six blades. I am robbed, Dame Grivette! I have borne much, but I shall not tolerate this; so take notice."

"But, monsieur," said Dame Grivette, "do you mean to accuse me?"

"You ought to take care of my effects."

"I have not the only key."

"You are the portress."

"You give me a crown a month, and you expect to be as well served as if you had ten domestics."

"I do not care about being badly served; but I do care whether I am robbed or not."

"Monsieur, I am an honest woman."

"Yes, an honest woman whom I shall give in charge to the police, if my watch is not found in an hour."

"To the police?"

"Yes."

"To the police, — an honest woman like me?"

"An honest woman, do you say?  Honest! that's good."

"Yes; and of whom nothing bad can be said; do you hear that?"

"Come, come! enough of this, Dame Grivette."

"Ah! I thought that you suspected me, when you went out."

"I have suspected you ever since the top of my cane disappeared."

"Well, Monsieur Marat, I will tell you something, in my turn."

"What will you tell me?"

"While you were away I have consulted my neighbours."

"Your neighbours! — for what purpose?"

"Respecting your suspicions."

"I had said nothing of them to you at the time."

"But I saw them plainly."

"And the neighbours?  I am curious to know what they said."

"They said that if you suspect me, and have even gone so far as to impart your suspicions to another person, you must pursue the affair to the end."

"Well?"

"That is to say you must prove that the watch has been taken."

"It has been taken, since it was there and is now gone."

"Yes; but taken by me — taken by me; do you understand?  Oh! justice requires proofs; your word will not be sufficient, Monsieur Marat; you are no more than one of ourselves, Monsieur Marat."

Balsamo, calm as ever, looked on during this scene; he saw that though Marat's conviction was not altered, he had, nevertheless, lowered his tone.

"Therefore," continued the portress, "if you do not render justice to my probity, if you do not make some reparation to my character, it is I who will send for the police, as our landlord just now advised me to do."

Marat bit his lips; he knew there was a real danger in this. The landlord was an old, rich, retired merchant; he lived on the third story, and the scandal-mongers of the quarter did not hesitate to assert that, some ten years before, he had not been indifferent to the charms of the portress, who was then kitchen-maid to his wife.

Now, Marat attended mysterious meetings. Marat was a young man of not very settled habits, besides being addicted to concealment, and suspected by the police; and, for all these reasons, he was not anxious to have an affair with the commissary, seeing that it might tend to place him in the hands of Monsieur de Sartines, who liked much to read the papers of young men such as Marat, and to send the authors of such noble writings to houses of meditation, — such as Vincennes, the Bastille, Charenton, and Bicêtre.

Marat, therefore, lowered his tone; but, in proportion as he did so, the portress raised hers. The result was that this nervous and hysterical woman raged like a flame which suddenly meets with a current of fresh air.

Oaths, cries, tears, — she employed all in turn; it was a regular tempest.

Then Balsamo judged that the time had come for him to interfere. He advanced towards the woman, and looking at her with an ominous and fiery glance, he stretched two fingers towards her, uttering, not so much with his lips as with his eyes, his thought, his whole will, a word which Marat could not hear.

Immediately Dame Grivette became silent, tottered, and, losing her equilibrium, staggered backwards, her eyes fearfully dilated, and fell upon the bed without uttering a word.

After a short interval her eyes closed and opened again, but this time the pupils could not be seen; her tongue moved convulsively, but her body was perfectly motion-less, and yet her hands trembled as if shaken by fever.

"Ha!" said Marat,—"like the wounded man in the hospital!"

"Yes."

"Then she is asleep?"

"Silence!" said Balsamo.

Then, addressing Marat,—

"Monsieur," said he, "the moment has now come when all your incredulity must cease. Pick up that letter which this woman was bringing you, and which she dropped when she fell."

Marat obeyed.

"Well?" he asked.

"Wait!"

And taking the letter from Marat's hands,—

"You know from whom this letter comes?" asked Balsamo of the somnambulist.

"No, monsieur," she replied.

Balsamo held the sealed letter close to the woman. "Read it to Monsieur Marat, who wishes to know the contents."

"She cannot read," said Marat.

"Yes, but you can read?"

"Of course."

"Well, read it, and she will read it after you in proportion as the words are engraven upon your mind."

Marat broke the seal of the letter and read it, while Dame Grivette, standing, and trembling beneath the all-powerful will of Balsamo, repeated, word for word, as Marat read them to himself, the following words: —

My dear Hippocrates, — Apelles has just finished his portrait; he has sold it for fifty francs, and these fifty francs are to be eaten to-day at the tavern in the Rue Saint Jacques. Will you come?

P. S. — It is understood that part is to be drunk.

Your friend,

L. David.

It was word for word what was written.

Marat let the paper fall from his hand.

"Well," said Balsamo, "you see that Dame Grivette also has a soul, and that this soul wakes while she sleeps."

"And a strange soul," said Marat; "a soul which can read when the body cannot."

"Because the soul knows everything ; because the soul can reproduce by reflection. Try to make her read this when she is awake, — that is to say, when the body has wrapped the soul in its shadow, — and you will see."

Marat was dumb; his whole material philosophy rebelled within him, but he could not find a reply.

"Now," continued Balsamo, "we shall pass on to what interests you most, — that is to say, to what has become of your watch. Dame Grivette," said he, turning to her, "who has taken Monsieur Marat's watch?"

The somnambulist made a violent gesture of denial.

"I do not know," said she.

"You know perfectly well," persisted Balsamo, "and you shall tell me."

Then, with a more decided exertion of his will, —

"Who has taken Monsieur Marat's watch? — speak!"

"Dame Grivette has not stolen Monsieur Marat's watch. Why does Monsieur Marat believe she has?"

"If it is not she who has taken it, tell me who has?"

"I do not know."

"You see," said Marat; "conscience is an impenetrable refuge."

"Well, since you have only this last doubt," said Balsamo, "you shall be convinced."

Then, turning again to the portress, —

"Tell me who took the watch; I insist upon it."

"Come, come," said Marat, "do not ask an impossibility!"

"You heard?" said Balsamo; "I have said you must tell me."

Then, beneath the pressure of this imperious command, the unhappy woman began to wring her hands and arms as if she were mad; a shudder like that of an epileptic fit ran through her whole body; her mouth was distorted with a hideous expression of terror and weakness; she threw herself back, rigid as if she were in a painful convulsion, and fell upon the bed.

"No, no," said she; "I would rather die!"

"Well," said Balsamo, with a burst of anger which made the fire flash from his eyes, "you shall die if necessary, but you shall speak. Your silence and your obstinacy are sufficient indications for me; but for an incredulous person we must have irrefragable proofs. Speak!—I will it: who has taken the watch?"

The nervous excitement was at its height; all the strength and power of the somnambulist struggled against Balsamo's will; inarticulate cries escaped from her lips, which were stained with a reddish foam.

"She will fall into an epileptic fit," said Marat.

"Fear nothing; it is the demon of falsehood who is in her, and who refuses to come out."

Then, turning towards the woman, and throwing in her face as much fluid as his hands could contain:

"Speak!" said he; "who has taken the watch?"

"Dame Grivette," replied the somnambulist, in an almost inaudible voice.

"When did she take it?"

"Yesterday evening."

"Where was it?"

"Underneath the candlestick."

"What has she done with it?"

"She has taken it to the Rue St. Jacques."

"Where in the Rue St. Jacques?"

"To No. 29."

"Which story?"

"The fifth."

"To whom did she give it?"

"To a shoemaker's apprentice."

"What is his name?"

"Simon."

"What is this man to her?"

The woman was silent.

"What is this man to her?"

The somnambulist was again silent.

"What is this man to her?" repeated Balsamo.

The same silence.

Balsamo extended towards her his hand, impregnated with the fluid, and the unfortunate woman, overwhelmed by this terrible attack, had only strength to murmur:

" Her lover."

Marat uttered an exclamation of astonishment.

"Silence!" said Balsamo; "allow conscience to speak."

Then, continuing to address the woman, who was trembling all over, and bathed in perspiration:

"And who advised Dame Grivette to steal the watch?" asked he.

"No one.  She raised the candlestick by accident, she saw the watch, and the demon tempted her."

"Did she do it from want?"

"No; for she did not sell the watch."

"She gave it away, then?"

"Yes."

"To Simon?"

The somnambulist made a violent effort.

"To Simon," said she.

Then she covered her face with her hands, and burst into a flood of tears.

Balsamo glanced at Marat, who, with gaping mouth, disordered hair, and dilated eyes, was gazing at the fearful spectacle.

"Well, monsieur!" said he; "you see, at last, the struggle between the body and the soul; you see conscience forced to yield, even in a redoubt which it had believed impregnable.  Do you confess now that God has forgotten nothing in this world, and that He is in everything?  Then deny no longer that there is a conscience;

deny no longer that there is a soul; deny no longer the unknown, young man! Above all, do not deny faith, which is power supreme; and since you are ambitious, Monsieur Marat, study; speak little, think much, and do not judge your superiors lightly. Adieu; my words have opened a vast field before you; cultivate this field, which contains hidden treasures. Adieu! Happy will you be if you can conquer the demon of incredulity which is in you, as I have conquered the demon of falsehood which was in this woman."

And with these words, which caused the blush of shame to tinge the young man's cheeks, he left the room.

Marat did not even think of taking leave of him. But after his first stupor was over, he perceived that Dame Grivette was still sleeping. This sleep struck terror to his soul. Marat would rather have seen a corpse upon his bed, even if Monsieur de Sartines should interpret the fact after his own fashion.

He gazed on this lifeless form, these turned-up eyes, these palpitations, and he felt afraid. His fear increased when the living corpse rose, advanced towards him, took his hand, and said:

"Come with me, Monsieur Marat."

" Where to? "

"To the Rue St. Jacques."

" Why? "

"Come, come; he commands me to take you."

Marat, who had fallen upon a chair, rose.

Then Dame Grivette, still asleep, opened the door, and descended the stairs with the stealthy pace of a cat, scarcely touching the steps.

Marat followed, fearing every moment that she would fall, and in falling break her neck.

Having reached the foot of the stairs, she crossed the threshold and entered the street, still followed by the young man, whom she led in this manner to the house and the garret she had pointed out.

She knocked at the door; Marat felt his heart beat so violently that he thought it must be audible.

A man was in the garret; he opened the door. In this man Marat recognised a workman of from five-and-twenty to thirty years of age, whom he had several times seen in the porter's lodge.

Seeing Dame Grivette followed by Marat, he started back.

But the somnambulist walked straight to the bed, and putting her hand under the thin bolster, she drew out the watch, which she gave to Marat, whilst the shoemaker, Simon, pale with terror, dared not utter a word, and watched with alarmed gaze the least movements of this woman, whom he believed to be mad.

Scarcely had her hand touched Marat's, in returning him the watch, than she gave a deep sigh and murmured:

"He awakes me! He awakes me!"

Her nerves relaxed like a cable freed from the capstan, the vital spark again animated her eyes, and finding herself face to face with Marat, her hand in his, and still holding the watch, — that is to say, the irrefragable proof of her crime, — she fell upon the floor of the garret in a deep swoon.

"Does conscience really exist, then?" asked Marat of himself, as he left the room, doubt in his heart and reverie in his eyes.

## CHAPTER CVII.

### THE MAN AND HIS WORKS.

WHILE Marat was employing his time so profitably in philosophising on conscience and a dual existence, another philosopher in the Rue Plastrière was also busy in reconstructing, piece by piece, every part of the preceding evening's adventures, and asking himself if he were or were not a very wicked man. Rousseau, with his elbows leaning upon the table, and his head drooping heavily on his left shoulder, was deep in thought.

His philosophical and political works, "Emilius" and the "Social Contract," were lying open before him.

From time to time, when his reflections required it, he stooped down to turn over the leaves of these books, which he knew by heart.

"Ah! good heavens!" said he, reading a paragraph from "Emilius" upon liberty of conscience, "what incendiary expressions! What philosophy! Just heaven! was there ever in the world a firebrand like me?

"What!" added he, clasping his hands above his head, "have I written such violent outbursts against the throne — the altar of society? I can no longer be surprised if some dark and brooding minds have outstripped my sophisms, and have gone astray in the paths which I have strewed for them with all the flowers of rhetoric. I have acted as the disturber of society!"

He rose from his chair, and paced the room in great agitation.

"I have," continued he, "abused those men in power who exercise tyranny over authors. Fool! barbarian that

I was! Those people are right — a thousand times right! What am I, if not a man dangerous to the state? My words, written to enlighten the masses, — at least, such was the pretext I gave myself, — have become a torch which will set the world on fire. I have sown discourses on the inequality of ranks, projects of universal fraternity, plans of education — and now I reap a harvest of passions so ferocious that they would overturn the whole framework of society, of intestine wars capable of depopulating the world, and of manners so barbarous that they would roll back the civilisation of ten centuries! Oh! I am a great criminal!"

He read once more a page of his "Savoyard Vicar."

"Yes, that is it! *Let us unite to form plans for our happiness.*

"I have written it! *Let us give our virtues the force which others give to their vices.* I have written that also."

And Rousseau became still more agitated and unhappy than before.

"Thus, by my fault," said he, "brothers are united to brothers, and one day or other some of these concealed places of meeting will be invaded by the police; the whole nest of these men, who have sworn to eat one another in case of treachery, will be arrested, and one bolder than the others will take my book from his pocket and will say — ' What do you complain of? We are disciples of Monsieur Rousseau; we are going through a course of philosophy!' Oh! how Voltaire will laugh at that! There is no fear of that courtier's ever getting into such a wasp's nest!"

The idea that Voltaire would ridicule him put the Genevese philosopher into a violent rage.

"I a conspirator!" muttered he; "I must be in my dotage, certainly! Am I not, in truth, a famous conspirator?"

He was at this point when Thérèse entered with the breakfast, but he did not see her. She perceived that he was attentively reading a passage in the "Reveries of a Recluse."

"Very good," said she, placing the hot milk noisily upon the very book; "my peacock is looking at himself in the glass! Monsieur reads his books! Monsieur Rousseau admires himself!"

"Come, Thérèse," said the philosopher, "patience — leave me; I am in no humour for laughing."

"Oh, yes; it is magnificent! is it not?" said she, mockingly. "You are delighted with yourself. What vanity authors have! and how angry they are to see it in us poor women! If I only happen to look in my little mirror, monsieur grumbles, and calls me a coquette."

She proceeded in this strain, making him the most unhappy man in the world, as if Rousseau had not been richly enough endowed by nature in this respect. He drank his milk without steeping his bread; he reflected.

"Very good," said she; "there you are, thinking again. You are going to write another book full of horrible things."

Rousseau shuddered.

"You dream," continued Thérèse, "of your ideal women, and you write books which young girls ought not to read, or else profane works which will be burnt by the hands of the common executioner."

The martyr shuddered again. Thérèse had touched him to the quick.

"No," replied he; "I will write nothing more which can cause an evil thought. On the contrary, I wish to write a book which all honest people will read with transports of joy."

"Oh! oh!" said Thérèse, taking away the cup, "that is impossible; your mind is full of obscene thoughts! Only the other day I heard you read some passage or other, and in it you spoke of women whom you adored. You are a satyr! a magus!"

This word "magus" was one of the most abusive in Thérèse's vocabulary; it always made Rousseau shudder.

"There, there now!" said he; "my dear woman, you will

find that you shall be satisfied. I intend to write that I have found the means of regenerating the world without causing pain to a single individual by the changes which will be effected. Yes, yes; I will mature this project. No revolutions! Great heavens! my good Thérèse, no revolutions!"

"Well, we shall see," said the housekeeper.

"Stay! some one rings."

Thérèse went out, and returned almost immediately with a handsome young man, whom she requested to wait in the outer apartment. Then, rejoining Rousseau, who was already taking notes with his pencil:

"Be quick," said she, "and lock all these infamous things fast. There is some one who wishes to see you."

"Who is it?"

"A nobleman of the court."

"Did he not tell you his name?"

"A good idea; as if I would receive a stranger!"

"Tell it me, then."

"Monsieur de Coigny."

"Monsieur de Coigny!" exclaimed Rousseau; "Monsieur de Coigny, gentleman-in-waiting to the dauphin?"

"It must be the same, — a charming youth, a most amiable young man."

"I will go, Thérèse."

Rousseau gave a glance at himself in the mirror, dusted his coat, wiped his slippers, which were only old shoes, trodden down in the heels by long wear, and entered the dining-room, where the gentleman was waiting.

The latter had not sat down; he was looking, with a sort of curiosity, at the dried plants pasted by Rousseau upon paper, and enclosed in frames of black wood. At the noise Rousseau made in entering, he turned, and bowing most courteously:

"Have I the honour," said he, "of speaking to Monsieur Rousseau?"

"Yes, monsieur," replied the philosopher, in a morose

voice, not unmingled, however, with a kind of admiration for the remarkable beauty and unaffected elegance of the person before him.

Monsieur de Coigny was, in fact, one of the handsomest and most accomplished gentlemen in France. It must have been for him, and such as him, that the costume of that period was invented. It displayed to the greatest advantage the symmetry and beauty of his well-turned leg, his broad shoulders and deep chest; it gave a majestic air to his exquisitely-formed head, and added to the ivory whiteness of his aristocratic hands.

His examination satisfied Rousseau, who, like a true artist, admired the beautiful wherever he met with it.

"Monsieur," said he, "what can I do for you?"

"You have been, perhaps, informed, monsieur," replied the young nobleman, "that I am the Count de Coigny. I may add that I come from madame the dauphiness."

Rousseau reddened and bowed. Thérèse, who was standing in a corner of the dining-room, with her hands in her pockets, gazed with complacent eyes at the handsome messenger of the greatest princess in France.

"Madame wants me; for what purpose?" asked Rousseau. "But take a chair, if you please, monsieur."

Rousseau sat down, and Monsieur de Coigny drew forward a straw-bottomed chair and followed his example.

"Monsieur, here is the fact. The other day, when his Majesty dined at Trianon, he expressed a good deal of admiration for your music, which is indeed charming. His Majesty sang your prettiest airs, and the dauphiness, who is always anxious to please his Majesty in every respect, thought that it might give him pleasure to see one of your comic operas performed in the theatre at Trianon."

Rousseau bowed low.

"I come, therefore, to ask you, from the dauphiness —"

"Oh, monsieur," interrupted Rousseau, "my permission has nothing to do in the matter. My pieces, and the airs belonging to them, are the property of the theatre where they are represented. The permission must therefore be sought from the comedians, and madame will, I am assured, find no obstacles in that quarter. The actors will be too happy to play and sing before his Majesty and the court."

"That is not precisely what I am commissioned to request, monsieur," said Monsieur de Coigny. "Madame the dauphiness wishes to give a more complete and more *recherché* entertainment to his Majesty; he knows all your operas, monsieur."

Another bow from Rousseau.

"And sings them charmingly."

Rousseau bit his lips.

"It is too much honour," stammered he.

"Now," pursued Monsieur de Coigny, "as several ladies of the court are excellent musicians, and sing delightfully, and as several gentlemen also have studied music with some success, whichever of your operas the dauphiness may choose shall be performed by this company of ladies and gentlemen, the principal actors being their royal highnesses."

Rousseau bounded in his chair.

"I assure you, monsieur," said he, "that this is a signal honour conferred upon me, and I beg you will offer my most humble thanks to the dauphiness."

"Oh! that is not all," said Monsieur de Coigny, with a smile.

"Ah!"

"The troupe thus composed is more illustrious, certainly, than that usually employed, but also more inexperienced. The superintendence and the advice of a master are therefore indispensable. The performance ought to be worthy of the august spectator who will occupy the royal box, and also of the illustrious author."

Rousseau rose to bow again. This time the compliment had touched him, and he saluted Monsieur de Coigny most graciously.

"For this purpose, monsieur," continued the gentleman-

in-waiting, " her Royal Highness requests your company
at Trianon, to superintend the general rehearsal of the
work."

" Oh! " said Rousseau, " Madame cannot surely think of
such a thing. I at Trianon ? "

" Well! " said Monsieur de Coigny, with the most natural
air possible.

" Oh! monsieur, you are a man of taste and judgment, you
have more tact than the majority of men; answer me, on
your conscience, is not the idea of Rousseau, the philosopher, the outlaw, the misanthrope, attending at court,
enough to make the whole cabal split their sides with
laughter ? "

" I do not see," replied Monsieur de Coigny, coldly,
" how the laughter and the remarks of that foolish set
which persecutes you should disturb the repose of a gallant
man, and an author who may lay claim to be the first in the
kingdom. If you have this weakness, Monsieur Rousseau,
conceal it carefully; it alone would be sufficient to raise a
laugh at your expense. As to what remarks may be made,
you will confess that those making them had better be
careful on that point, when the pleasure and the wishes of
her Royal Highness the dauphiness, presumptive heiress of
the French kingdom, are in question."

" Certainly," said Rousseau; " certainly."

" Can it be, possibly, a lingering feeling of false shame ? "
said Monsieur de Coigny, smiling. " Because you have
been severe upon kings, do you fear to humanize yourself ?
Ah! Monsieur Rousseau, you have given valuable lessons
to the human race, but I hope you do not hate them. And,
besides, you certainly except the ladies of the blood-royal."

" Monsieur, you are very kind to press me so much ; but
think of my position — I live retired, alone, unhappy."

Thérèse made a grimace.

" Unhappy ! " said she; " he is hard to please ! "

" Whatever effort I may make, there will always be something in my features and manner unpleasing to the eyes of

the king and the princesses, who seek only joy and happiness. What should I do there — what should I say ? ”

“ One would think you distrusted yourself.  But, monsieur, do you not think that he who has written the ‘ Nouvelle Héloïse ’ and the ‘ Confessions,’ must have more talent for speaking and acting than all of us others put together, no matter what position we occupy ? ”

“ I assure you, monsieur, it is impossible.”

“ That word, monsieur, is not known to princes.”

“ And for that very reason, monsieur, I shall remain at home.”

“ Monsieur, you would not inflict the dreadful disappointment of returning vanquished and disgraced to Versailles on me, the venturous messenger who undertook to satisfy her Royal Highness ?   It would be such a blow to me, that I should immediately retire into voluntary exile.   Come, my dear Monsieur Rousseau, grant to me, a man full of the deepest sympathy for your works, this favour — a favour which you would refuse to supplicating kings.”

“ Monsieur, your kindness gains my heart ; your eloquence is irresistible ; and your voice touches me more than I can express.”

“ Will you allow yourself to be persuaded.”

“ No, I cannot — no, decidedly ; my health forbids such a journey.”

“ A journey ! oh, Monsieur Rousseau, what are you thinking of ?   An hour and a quarter in a carriage ! ”

“ Yes ; for you and your prancing horses.”

“ But all the equipages of the court are at your disposal, Monsieur Rousseau.   The dauphiness charged me to tell you that there is an apartment prepared for you at Trianon ; for she is unwilling that you should have to return so late to Paris.   The dauphin, who knows all your works by heart, said, before the whole court, that he would be proud to show the room in his palace where Monsieur Rousseau had slept.”

Thérèse uttered a cry of admiration, not for Rousseau, but for the good prince.

Rousseau could not withstand this last mark of good-will.

"I must surrender," said he, "for never have I been so well attacked."

"Your heart only is vanquished, monsieur," replied De Coigny; "your mind is impregnable."

"I shall go, then, monsieur, in obedience to the wishes of her Royal Highness."

"Oh! monsieur, receive my personal thanks. As regards the dauphiness's, permit me to abstain. She would feel annoyed at being forestalled, as she means to pay them to you in person this evening. Besides, you know, it is the man's part to thank a young and adorable lady who is good enough to make advances to him."

"True, monsieur," replied Rousseau, smiling; "but old men have the privilege of pretty women — they are sought after."

"If you will name your hour, Monsieur Rousseau, I shall send my carriage for you; or, rather, I will come myself to take you up."

"No, thank you, monsieur. I must positively refuse your kind offer. I will go to Trianon, but let me go in whatever manner I may choose. From this moment leave me to myself. I shall come, that is all. Tell me the hour."

"What, monsieur! you will not allow me to introduce you? I know I am not worthy of the honour, and that a name like yours needs no announcement —"

"Monsieur, I am aware that you are more at court than I am anywhere in the world. I do not refuse your offer, therefore, from any motives personal to yourself; but I love my liberty. I wish to go as if I were merely taking a walk, and — in short, that is my ultimatum."

"Monsieur, I bow to your decision, and should be most unwilling to displease you in any particular. The rehearsal commences at six o'clock."

"Very well. At a quarter before six I shall be at Trianon."

"But by what conveyance?"

"That is my affair; these are my horses."

He pointed to his legs, which were still well formed, and displayed with some pretension.

"Five leagues!" said Monsieur de Coigny, alarmed; "you will be knocked up — take care, it will be a fatiguing evening!"

"In that case, I have my carriage and my horses also, — a fraternal carriage, the popular vehicle, which belongs to my neighbour as well as to myself, and which costs only fifteen sous."

"Oh! good heavens! The stage-coach! You make me shudder."

"Its benches, which seem to you so hard, are to me like the Sybarite's couch; to me they seem stuffed with down or strewn with rose-leaves. Adieu, monsieur, till this evening."

Monsieur de Coigny, seeing himself thus dismissed, took his leave after a multitude of thanks, indications more or less precise, and expressions of gratitude for his services.

He descended the dark staircase, accompanied by Rousseau to the landing, and by Thérèse half way down the stairs.

Monsieur de Coigny entered his carriage, which was waiting in the street, and drove back to Versailles, smiling to himself.

Thérèse returned to the apartment, slamming the door with angry violence, which foretold a storm for Rousseau.

## CHAPTER CVIII.

ROUSSEAU'S TOILET.

WHEN Monsieur de Coigny was gone, Rousseau, whose ideas this visit had entirely changed, threw himself into a little arm-chair, with a deep sigh, and said, in a sleepy tone:

"Oh, how tiresome this is! How these people weary me with their persecutions!"

Thérèse caught the last words as she entered, and placing herself before Rousseau:

"How proud we are!" said she.

"I?" asked Rousseau, surprised.

"Yes; you are a vain fellow — a hypocrite!"

"I?"

"Yes, you! you are enchanted to go to court, and you conceal your joy under this feigned indifference."

"Oh! good heavens!" replied Rousseau, shrugging his shoulders, and humiliated at being so truly described.

"Do you not wish to make me believe that it is not a great honour for you to perform for the king the airs you thump here upon your spinet, like a good-for-nothing, as you are?"

Rousseau looked angrily at his wife.

"You are a simpleton," said he; "it is no honour for a man such as I am to appear before a king. To what does this man owe that he is on the throne? To a caprice of nature, which gave him a queen as his mother; but I am worthy of being called before the king to minister to his recreation. It is to my works I owe it, and to the fame acquired by my works."

Thérèse was not a woman to be so easily conquered.

"I wish Monsieur de Sartines heard you talking in this style; he would give you a lodging in Bicêtre, or a cell at Charenton."

"Because this Monsieur de Sartines is a tyrant in the pay of another tyrant, and because man is defenceless against tyrants with the aid of his genius alone. But if Monsieur de Sartines were to persecute me — "

"Well, what then?" asked Thérèse.

"Ah! yes," sighed Rousseau, "yes, I know that would delight my enemies."

"Why have you enemies?" continued Thérèse. "Because you are ill-natured, and because you have attacked every one. Ah, Monsieur de Voltaire knows how to make friends, he does!"

"True," said Rousseau, with an angelic smile.

"But, *dame!* Monsieur de Voltaire is a gentleman, — he is the intimate friend of the King of Prussia; he has horses, he is rich, and lives in his château at Ferney. And all that he owes to his merit. Therefore, when he goes to court, he does not act the disdainful man — he is quite at home there."

"And do you think," said Rousseau, "that I shall not be at home there? Think you that I do not know where all the money that is spent there comes from, or that I am duped by the respect which is paid to the master? Oh! my good woman, who judgest everything falsely, remember, if I act the disdainful, it is because I really feel contempt; remember, that if I despise the pomp of these courtiers, it is because they have stolen their riches."

"Stolen!" said Thérèse, with inexpressible indignation.

"Yes, stolen, from you — from me — from every one. All the gold they have upon their fine clothes should be restored to the poor wretches who want bread. That is the reason why I, who know all these things, go so reluctantly to court."

"I do not say that the people are happy — but the king is always the king."

"Well, I obey him; what more does he want?"

"Ah! you obey because you are afraid. You must not say in my hearing that you go against your will, or that you are a brave man, for if so, I shall reply that you are a hypocrite, and that you are very glad to go."

"I do not fear anything," said Rousseau, superbly.

"Good! Just go and say to the king one quarter of what you have been telling me the last half hour."

"I shall assuredly do so, if my feelings prompt me."

"You?"

"Yes. Have I ever recoiled?"

"Bah! You dare not take a bone from a cat when she is gnawing it, for fear she should scratch you! What would you be if surrounded by guards and swordsmen? Look you, I know you as well as if I were your mother. You will just now go and shave yourself afresh, oil your hair, and make yourself beautiful; you will display your leg to the utmost advantage; you will put on your interesting little winking expression, because your eyes are small and round, and if you opened them naturally, that would be seen, while, when you wink, you make people believe that they are as large as carriage entrances. You will ask me for your silk stockings, you will put on your chocolate-coloured coat with steel buttons, and your beautiful new wig; you will order a coach, and my philosopher will go and be adored by the ladies! And to-morrow — ah! — to-morrow, there will be such ecstatic reveries, such interesting langour! You will come back amorous, you will sigh and write verses, and you will dilute your coffee with your tears. Oh, how well I know you!"

"You are wrong, my dear," said Rousseau. "I tell you I am reluctantly obliged to go to court; I go because, after all, I fear to cause scandal, as every honest citizen should do. Moreover, I am not one of those who refuse to acknowledge the supremacy of one citizen in a republic; but as to making advances, as to brushing my new coat against the gold spangles of these gentlemen of the Œilde-Bœuf — no, no — I shall do nothing of the sort; and if you catch me doing so, laugh at me as much as you please."

"Then you will not dress?" said Thérèse, sarcastically.

"No."

"You will not put on your new wig?"

"No."

"You will not wink with your little eyes?"

"I tell you I shall go like a free man, without affectation and without fear. I shall go to court as if I were going to the theatre; and let the actors like me or not, I care not for them."

"Oh! you will at least trim your beard," said Thérèse; "it is half a foot long!"

"I tell you I shall make no change."

Thérèse burst into so loud and prolonged a laugh that Rousseau was obliged to take refuge in the next room. But the housekeeper had not finished her persecutions; she had them of all colours and kinds.

She opened the cupboard and took out his best coat, his clean linen, and beautifully polished shoes. She spread all these articles out upon the bed and over the chairs in the apartment; but Rousseau did not seem to pay the least attention.

At last Thérèse said:

"Come, it is time you should dress; a court toilet is tedious. You will have barely time to reach Versailles at the appointed hour."

"I have told you, Thérèse, that I shall do very well as I am. It is the same dress in which I present myself every day amongst my fellow-citizens. A king is but a citizen like myself."

"Come, come," said Thérèse, trying to tempt him and bring him to her purpose by artful insinuation; "do not pout, Jacques, and don't be foolish. Here are your clothes. Your razor is ready; I have sent for the barber, in case you have your nervousness to-day."

"Thank you, my dear," replied Rousseau; "I shall only just give myself a brush, and take my shoes, because I cannot go out in slippers."

"Is he going to be firm, I wonder?" thought Thérèse.

She tried to coax him, sometimes by coquetry, sometimes by persuasion, and sometimes by the violence of her raillery; but Rousseau knew her, and saw the snare. He felt that the moment he should give way, he would be unmercifully disgraced and ridiculed by his better-half; he determined, therefore, not to give way, and abstained from looking at the fine clothes, which set off what he termed his natural advantages.

Thérèse watched him. She had only one resource left, — this was the glance which Rousseau never failed to give in the glass before he went out; for the philosopher was neat to an extreme, if there can be an extreme in neatness.

But Rousseau continued to be on his guard, and as he had caught Thérèse's anxious look, he turned his back to the looking-glass. The hour arrived; the philosopher had filled his head with all the disagreeable remarks he could think of to say to the king.

He repeated some scraps of them to himself while he buckled his shoes, then tucked his hat under his arm, seized his cane, and taking advantage of a moment when Thérèse could not see him, he pulled down his coat and his waistcoat with both hands, to smooth the creases.

Thérèse now returned, handed him a handkerchief, which he plunged into his huge pocket, and then accompanied him to the landing-place, saying:

"Come, Jacques, be reasonable; you look quite frightful; you have the air of some false moneyer."

"Adieu!" said Rousseau.

"You look like a thief, monsieur," said Thérèse; "take care!"

"Take care of fire," said Rousseau, "and do not touch my papers."

"You have just the air of a spy, I assure you!" said Thérèse in despair.

Rousseau made no reply; he descended the steps singing, and favoured by the obscurity, he gave his hat a brush with his sleeve, smoothed his shirt-frill with his left hand, and touched up his toilet with a rapid but skilful movement.

Arrived at the foot of the stairs, he boldly confronted the mud of the Rue Plastrière, walking upon tiptoe, and reached the Champs-Elysées, where those honest vehicles which some rather affectedly call *pataches* were stationed, and which, so late as ten years ago, still carried, or rather bundled, from Paris to Versailles those travellers who were obliged to use economy.

# CHAPTER CIX.

### THE SIDE SCENES OF TRIANON.

THE adventures of the journey are of no importance. A
Swiss, an assistant-clerk, a citizen, and an abbé, were, of
course, amongst his travelling companions.

He arrived at half-past five.   The court was already
assembled at Trianon, and the performers were going over
their parts while waiting for the king; for as to the author,
no one thought of him.   Some were aware that Monsieur
Rousseau of Geneva was to come to direct the rehearsal;
but they took no greater interest in seeing Monsieur Rousseau than Monsieur Rameau, or Monsieur Marmontel, or
any other of those singular animals, to a sight of which the
courtiers sometimes treated themselves in their drawing-
rooms or country-houses.

Rousseau was received by the usher-in-waiting, who had
been ordered by Monsieur de Coigny to inform him as soon
as the philosopher should arrive.

This young nobleman hastened with his usual courtesy,
and received Rousseau with the most amiable *empressement*.
But scarcely had he cast his eyes over his person, than he
stared with astonishment, and could not prevent himself
from recommencing the examination.

Rousseau was dusty, pale, and dishevelled, and his paleness rendered conspicuous such a beard as no master of
the ceremonies had ever seen reflected in the mirrors of
Versailles.

Rousseau felt deeply embarrassed under Monsieur de
Coigny's scrutiny, but more embarrassed still when,
approaching the hall of the theatre, he saw the profusion

of splendid dresses, valuable lace, diamonds, and blue ribbons, which, with the gilding of the hall, produced the effect of a bouquet of flowers in an immense basket.

Rousseau felt ill at ease also when he breathed this perfumed atmosphere, so intoxicating for plebeian nerves. Yet he was obliged to proceed, and put a bold face on the matter. Multitudes of eyes were fixed upon him who thus formed a stain, as it were, on the polish of the assembly. Monsieur de Coigny still preceding him led him to the orchestra, where the musicians were awaiting him.

When there, he felt rather relieved, and while his music was being performed, he seriously reflected that the worst danger was past, that the step was taken, and that all the reasoning in the world could now be of no avail.

Already the dauphiness was on the stage, in her costume as Colette; she waited for Colin.

Monsieur de Coigny was changing his dress in his box.

All at once the king entered, surrounded by a crowd of bending heads. Louis smiled, and seemed to be in the best humour possible.

The dauphin seated himself at his right hand, and the Count de Provence, arriving soon after, took his place on the left. On a sign from the king, the fifty persons who composed the assembly, private as it was, took their seats.

"Well, why do you not begin?" asked Louis.

"Sire," said the dauphiness, "the shepherds and shepherdesses are not yet dressed; we are waiting for them."

"They can perform in their usual dresses," said the king.

"No, sire," replied the dauphiness, "for we wish to try the dresses and costumes by candle-light, to be certain of the effect."

"You are right, madame," said the king; "then let us take a stroll."

And Louis rose to make the circuit of the corridor and the stage. Besides, he was rather uneasy at not seeing Madame Dubarry.

When the king had left the box, Rousseau gazed in a melancholy mood and with an aching heart at the empty hall and his own solitary position; it was a singular contrast to the reception he had anticipated.

He had pictured to himself that on his entrance all the groups would separate before him; that the curiosity of the courtiers would be even more importunate and more significative than that of the Parisians; he had feared questions and presentations; and lo! no one paid any attention to him!

He thought that his long beard was not yet long enough, that rags would not have been more remarked than his old clothes; and he applauded himself for not having been so ridiculous as to aim at elegance. But in the bottom of his heart he felt humiliated at being thus reduced to the simple post of leader of the orchestra. Suddenly an officer approached and asked him if he was not Monsieur Rousseau?

"Yes, monsieur," replied he.

"Madame the dauphiness wishes to speak to you, monsieur," said the officer.

Rousseau rose, much agitated.

The dauphiness was waiting for him. She held in her hand the air of Colette: —

"My happiness is gone."

The moment she saw Rousseau, she advanced towards him. The philosopher bowed very humbly, saying to himself, "that his bow was for the woman, not for the . princess."

The dauphiness, on the contrary, was as gracious towards the savage philosopher as she would have been to the most finished gentleman in Europe.

She requested his advice about the inflection she ought to give to the third strophe —

"Colin leaves me."

Rousseau forthwith commenced to develop a theory of
declamation and melody, which, learned as it was, was
interrupted by the noisy arrival of the king and several
courtiers.

Louis entered the room in which the dauphiness was
taking her lesson from the philosopher.  The first impulse
of the king's, when he saw this carelessly-dressed person,
was the same that Monsieur de Coigny had manifested,
only Monsieur de Coigny knew Rousseau, and the king did
not.

He stared, therefore, long and steadily at our freeman,
whilst still receiving the thanks and compliments of the
dauphiness.

This look, stamped with royal authority — this look, not
accustomed to be lowered before any one — produced a
powerful effect upon Rousseau, whose quick eye was timid
and unsteady.

The dauphiness waited until the king had finished his
scrutiny, then, advancing towards Rousseau, she said:

"Will your Majesty allow me to present our author to
you?"

"Your author?" said the king, seeming to consult
memory.

During this short dialogue Rousseau was upon burning
coals.  The king's eye had successively rested upon and
burnt up, like the sun's rays under a powerful lens, the
long beard, the dubious shirt-frill, the dusty garb, and the
old wig of the greatest writer in his kingdom.

The dauphiness took pity on the latter.

"Monsieur Jean Jacques Rousseau, sire," said she, "the
author of the charming opera we are going to execute
before your Majesty."

The king raised his head.

"Ah!" said he, coldly, "Monsieur Rousseau, I greet
you."

And he continued to look at him in such a manner as to
point out all the imperfections of his dress.

Rousseau asked himself how he ought to salute the King of France, without being a courtier, but also without impoliteness, for he confessed that he was in the prince's house.

But while he was making these reflections, the king addressed him with that graceful ease of princes who have said everything when they have uttered an agreeable or a disagreeable remark to the person before them. Rousseau, petrified, had at first stood speechless. All the phrases he had prepared for the tyrant were forgotten.

"Monsieur Rousseau," said the king, still looking at his coat and wig, "you have composed some charming music, which has caused me to pass several very pleasant moments."

Then the king, in a voice which was diametrically opposed to all diapason and melody, commenced singing: —

> "Had I turned a willing ear,
> The gallants of the town to hear,
> Ah! I had found with ease
> Other lovers then to please."

"It is charming!" said the king, when he had finished. Rousseau bowed.

"I do not know if I shall sing it well," said the dauphiness.

Rousseau turned towards the dauphiness to make some remark in reply; but the king had commenced again, and was singing the romance of Colin: —

> "From my hut, obscure and cold,
> Care is absent never ;
> Whether storm, or sun, or cold,
> Suffering, toil, forever."

His Majesty sang frightfully for a musician. Rousseau, half flattered by the monarch's good memory, half wounded by his detestable execution, looked like a monkey nibbling an onion, — crying on one side of his face and laughing on the other.

The dauphiness preserved her composure with that imperturbable self-possession which is only found at court. The king, without the least embarrassment, continued: —

> " If thou 'lt come to cast thy lot
> In thy Colin's humble cot,
> My sweet shepherdess Colette,
> I 'd bid adieu to all regret."

Rousseau felt the colour rising to his face.

"Tell me, Monsieur Rousseau," said the king, "is it true that you sometimes dress in the costume of an Armenian ? "

Rousseau blushed more deeply than before, and his tongue was so glued to his throat that not for a kingdom could he have pronounced a word at this moment.

The king continued to sing, without waiting for a reply : —

> " Ah ! but little, as times go,
> Doth love know
> What he 'd let, òr what he 'd hinder."

"You live in the Rue Plastrière, I believe, Monsieur Rousseau ? " said the king.

Rousseau made a gesture in the affirmative with his head, but that was the *ultima thule* of his strength. Never had he called up so much to his support. The king hummed : —

> " She is a child,
> She is a child."

"It is said that you are on bad terms with Voltaire, Monsieur Rousseau ? "

At this blow, Rousseau lost the little presence of mind he had remaining, and was totally put out of countenance. The king did not seem to have much pity for him, and, continuing his ferocious melomania, he moved off singing, —

> " Come, dance with me beneath the elms;
> Young maidens, come, be merry," —

with orchestral accompaniments which would have killed
Apollo, as the latter killed Marsyas.

Rousseau remained alone in the centre of the room. The
dauphiness had quitted it to finish her toilet.

Rousseau, trembling and confused, regained the corridor;
but on his way he stumbled against a couple dazzling with
diamonds, flowers, and lace, who filled up the entire width
of the corridor, although the young man squeezed his
lovely companion tenderly to his side.

The young woman, with her fluttering laces, her tower-
ing head-dress, her fan, and her perfumes, was radiant as
a star. It was she against whom Rousseau brushed in
passing.

The young man, slender, elegant, and charming, with his
blue ribbon rustling against his English shirt-frill, every
now and then burst into a laugh of most engaging frankness, and then suddenly interrupted it with little confidential whispers, which made the lady laugh in her turn, and
showed that they were on excellent terms.

Rousseau recognised the Countess Dubarry in this beautiful lady, this seducing creature; and the moment he
perceived her, true to his habit of absorbing his whole
thoughts on a single object, he no longer saw her
companion.

The young man with the blue ribbon was no other than
the Count d'Artois, who was merrily toying with his grandfather's favourite.

When Madame Dubarry perceived Rousseau's dark figure, she exclaimed : —

"Ah, good heavens ! "

"What ! " said the Count d'Artois, also looking at the
philosopher ; and already he had stretched out his hand to
make way for his companion.

"Monsieur Rousseau ! " exclaimed Madame Dubarry.

"Rousseau of Geneva ? " said the Count d'Artois, in the
tone of a schoolboy in the holidays.

"Yes, monseigneur," replied the countess.

"Ah! good day, Monsieur Rousseau," said the young fop, seeing Rousseau making a despairing effort to force a passage, — "good day; we are going to hear your music."

"Monseigneur!" stammered Rousseau, seeing the blue ribbon.

"Ah! most charming music!" exclaimed the countess; "and completely in harmony with the heart and mind of the author."

Rousseau raised his head, and his eyes met the burning gaze of the countess.

"Madame!" said he, ill-humoredly.

"I will play Colin, madame," cried the Count d'Artois, "and I entreat that you, Madame la Comtesse, will play Colette."

"With all my heart, monseigneur; but I would never dare — I, who am not an artist — to profane the music of a master."

Rousseau would have given his life to look again at her; but the voice, the tone, the flattery, the beauty, had each planted a baited hook in his heart. He tried to escape.

"Monsieur Rousseau," said the prince, blocking up the passage, "I wish you would teach me the part of Colin."

"I dare not ask Monsieur Rousseau to give me his advice respecting Colette," said the countess, feigning timidity, and thus completing the overthrow of the philosopher.

But yet his eyes inquired why.

"Monsieur Rousseau hates me," said she to the prince, with her enchanting voice.

"You are jesting!" exclaimed the Count d'Artois. "Who could hate you, madame?"

"You see it plainly," replied she.

"Monsieur Rousseau is too great a man, and has written too many noble works, to fly from such a charming woman," said the Count d'Artois.

Rousseau heaved a sigh as if he were ready to give up the ghost, and made his escape through a narrow loophole which the Count d'Artois had imprudently left between himself and the wall.   But Rousseau was not in luck this evening.   He had scarcely proceeded four steps when he met another group, composed of two men, one old, the other young.   The young one wore the blue ribbon; the other, who might be about fifty years of age, was dressed in red, and looked austere and pale.   These two men overheard the merry laugh of the Count d'Artois, who exclaimed loudly : —

" Ah! Monsieur Rousseau, Monsieur Rousseau!   I shall say that the countess put you to flight; and, in truth, no one would believe it."

" Rousseau ! " murmured the two men.

" Stop him, brother ! " said the prince, still laughing; "stop him, Monsieur de Vauguyon ! "

Rousseau now comprehended on what rock his evil star had shipwrecked him.   The Count de Provence and the governor of the royal youths were before him.

The Count de Provence also barred the way.

"Good day, monsieur," said he, with his dry pedantic voice.

Rousseau, almost at his wits' end, bowed, muttering to himself : —

" I shall never get away ! "

" Ah ! I am delighted to have met you," said the prince, with the air of a schoolmaster who finds a pupil in fault.

"More absurd compliments ! " thought Rousseau.  "How insipid these great people are ! "

"I have read your translation of Tacitus, monsieur."

" Ah ! true," thought Rousseau; " this one is a pedant, a scholar."

" Do you  know  that it is  very  difficult to translate Tacitus ? "

" Monseigneur, I said so in a short preface."

" Yes, I know, I know ; you said in it that you had only a slight knowledge of Latin."

" It is true, monseigneur."

" Then, Monsieur Rousseau, why translate Tacitus ? "

" Monseigneur, it improves one's style."

" Ah! Monsieur Rousseau, it was wrong to translate
'imperatoria brevitate' by *a grave and concise discourse.*"

Rousseau, uneasy, consulted his memory.

" Yes," said the young prince, with the confidence of an
old savant who discovers a fault in Saumaise; " yes, you
translated it so. It is in the paragraph where Tacitus
relates that Pison harangued his soldiers."

" Well, monsiegneur ? "

" Well, Monsieur Rousseau, 'imperatoria brevitate'
means *with the conciseness of a general,* or of a man accustomed to command. *With the brevity of command;* that
is the expression, is it not, Monsieur de la Vauguyon ? "

" Yes, monseigneur," replied the governor.

Rousseau made no reply. The prince added : —

" That is an evident mistake, Monsieur Rousseau. Oh! I
will find you another."

Rousseau turned pale.

" Stay, Monsieur Rousseau, there is one in the paragraph
relating to Cecina. It commences thus : 'At in superiore
Germania.' You know he is describing Cecina, and Tacitus
says, 'Cito sermone.' "

" I remember it perfectly, monseigneur."

" You translated that by *speaking well.*"

" Yes, monseigneur, and I thought — "

" 'Cito sermone' means *speaking quickly,* that is to say
*easily.*"

" I said *speaking well.*"

" Then it should have been 'decoro,' or 'ornato,' or
'eleganti sermone'; 'cito' is a picturesque epithet, Monsieur Rousseau. Just as, in portraying the change in
Otho's conduct, Tacitus says, 'Delata voluptate, dissimulata luxuria, cunctaque ad imperii decorem composita."

" I have translated that, *Dismissing luxury and effemi-
nacy to other times, he surprised the world by industriously
applying himself to re-establish the glory of the empire.*"

" Wrong, Monsieur Rousseau, wrong ! In the first place,

you have run the three little phrases into one, which obliges you to translate 'dissimulata luxuria' badly. Then you made a blunder in the last portion of the phrase. Tacitus did not mean that the Emperor Otho applied himself to re-establishing the glory of the empire: he meant to say that, no longer gratifying his passions, and dissimulating his luxurious habits, Otho accommodated all, made all turn — all, you understand, Monsieur Rousseau, that is to say, even his passions and his vices — to the glory of the empire. That is the sense, — it is rather complex; yours, however, is too restricted, is it not, Monsieur de la Vauguyon ? "

"Yes, monseigneur."

Rousseau perspired and panted under this pitiless infliction.

The prince allowed him a moment's breathing time, and then continued : —

"You are much more in your element in philosophy, monsieur."

Rousseau bowed.

"But your 'Emilius' is a dangerous book."

"Dangerous, monseigneur ? "

"Yes, from the quantity of false ideas it will put into the humble citizens' heads ! "

"Monseigneur, as soon as a man is a father, he can enter into the spirit of my book, whether he be the first or the last in the kingdom. To be a father — is — is— "

"Tell me, Monsieur Rousseau," asked the satirical prince, all at once, "your 'Confessions' form a very amusing book. How many children have you had ? "

Rousseau turned pale, staggered, and raised an angry and stupefied glance to his young tormentor's face, the expression of which only increased the malicious humour of the Count de Provence.

It was only malice, for, without waiting for a reply, the prince moved away arm in arm with his preceptor, continuing his commentaries on the works of the man whom he had so cruelly crushed.

Rousseau, left alone, was gradually recovering from his stupefaction, when he heard the first bars of his overture executed by the orchestra.

He proceeded in that direction with a faltering step, and when he had reached his seat he said to himself : —

"Fool! coward! stupid ass that I am! Now only do I find the answer I should have made the cruel little pedant. 'Monseigneur,' I should have said, 'it is not charitable in a young person to torment a poor old man!'"

He had just reached this point, quite content with his phrase, when the dauphiness and Monsieur de Coigny commenced their duet. The preoccupation of the philosopher was disturbed by the suffering of the musician, — the ear was to be tortured after the heart.

## CHAPTER CX.

### THE REHEARSAL.

THE rehearsal once fairly commenced, and the general attention drawn to the stage, Rousseau was no longer remarked, and it was he, on the contrary, who became the observer. He heard court lords who sang completely out of tune in their shepherd's dresses, and saw ladies arrayed in their court dresses coquetting like shepherdesses.

The dauphiness sang correctly, but she was a bad actress; and her voice, moreover, was so weak that she could scarcely be heard. The king, not to intimidate any one, had retired to an obscure box, where he chatted with the ladies. The dauphin prompted the words of the opera, which went off royally badly.

Rousseau determined not to listen, but he felt it very difficult to avoid overhearing what passed. He had one consolation, however, for he had just perceived a charming face among the illustrous figurantes, and the village maiden, who was the possessor of this charming face, had incomparably the most delightful voice of the entire company.

Rousseau's attention became at once completely riveted, and from his position behind his desk he gazed with his whole soul at the charming figurante, and listened with all his ears to drink in the enchanting melody of her voice.

When the dauphiness saw the author so deeply attentive, she felt persuaded, from his smile and his sentimental air, that he was pleased with the execution of his work, and, eager for a compliment, — for she was a woman, — she leaned forward to the desk, saying, —

"Is our performance very bad, Monsieur Rousseau?"

But Rousseau, with lips apart and absent air, did not reply.

"Oh! we have made some blunders," said the dauphiness, "and Monsieur Rousseau dares not tell us! Pray do, Monsieur Rousseau!"

Rousseau's gaze never left the beautiful personage, who on her side did not perceive in the least the attention which she excited.

"Ah!" said the dauphiness, following the direction of our philosopher's eyes, "it is Mademoiselle Taverney who has been in fault!"

Andrée blushed; she saw all eyes directed towards her.

"No! no!" exclaimed Rousseau; "it was not mademoiselle, for mademoiselle sings like an angel!"

Madame Dubarry darted at the philosopher a look keener than a javelin.

The Baron de Taverney, on the contrary, felt his heart bound with joy, and greeted Rousseau with a most enchanting smile.

"Do you think that young girl sings well?" said Madame Dubarry to the king, who was evidently struck by Rousseau's words.

"In a chorus I cannot hear distinctly," said Louis XV.; "it requires a musician to be able to distinguish."

Meanwhile Rousseau was busy in the orchestra directing the chorus: —

> "Colin revient à sa bergère,
> Célébrons un retour si beau."

As he turned to resume his seat, he saw Monsieur de Jussieu bowing to him graciously.

It was no slight pleasure for the Genevese to be seen thus giving laws to the court by a courtier who had wounded him a little by his superiority. He returned his bow most ceremoniously, and continued to gaze at Andrée, who looked even more lovely for the praises she had received.

As the rehearsal proceeded, Madame Dubarry became

furious; twice had she surprised Louis XV.'s attention wandering, distracted by the spectacle before him from the sweet speeches she whispered.

The spectacle in the eyes of the jealous favourite meant Andrée alone, but this did not prevent the dauphiness from receiving many compliments, and being in charmingly gay spirits. Monsieur de Richelieu fluttered around her with the agility of a young man, and succeeded in forming, at the extremity of the stage, a circle of laughers, of which the dauphiness was the centre, and which rendered the Dubarry party extremely uneasy.

"It appears," said he, aloud, "that Mademoiselle de Taverney has a sweet voice."

"Charming!" said the dauphiness; "and had I not been too selfish, I should have allowed her to play Colette; but as it is for my amusement that I undertook the character, I will give it up to no one."

"Oh! Mademoiselle de Taverney would not sing it better than your royal Highness," said Richelieu, "and — "

"Mademoiselle is an excellent musician," said Rousseau, with enthusiasm.

"Excellent!" responded the dauphiness; "and, to confess the truth, it is she who teaches me my part; besides, she dances enchantingly, and I dance very badly."

The effect of this conversation upon the king, upon Madame Dubarry, and the whole crowd of curious newsmongers and envious intriguers, may be imagined. All either tasted the pleasure of inflicting a wound, or received the blow with shame and grief. There were no indifferent spectators, except perhaps Andrée herself.

The dauphiness, incited by Richelieu, ended by making Andrée sing the air: —

> "I have lost my love, —
> Colin leaves me."

The king's head was seen to mark the time with such evident tokens of pleasure, that Madame Dubarry's rouge fell off, from her agitation, in little flakes, as paintings fall to pieces from damp.

Richelieu, more malicious than a woman, enjoyed his revenge. He had drawn near the elder Taverney, and the two old men formed a tableau which might have been taken for Hypocrisy and Corruption sealing a project of union.

Their joy increased the more as Madame Dubarry's features grew by degrees darker and darker. She added the finishing stroke to it by rising angrily, which was contrary to all etiquette, as the king was still seated.

The courtiers, like ants, felt the storm approach, and hastened to seek shelter with the strongest. The dauphiness was more closely surrounded by her own friends, Madame Dubarry was more courted by hers.

By degrees the interest of the rehearsal was diverted from its natural course, and was turned in quite a different direction. Colin and Colette were no more thought of, and many spectators thought that it would soon be Madame Dubarry's turn to sing: —

> " I have lost my love, —
> Colin leaves me."

"Do you mark," whispered Richelieu to Taverney, "your daughter's immense success?"

And he drew him into the corridor, pushing open a glass door, and causing a looker-on, who had been clinging to the framework in order to see into the hall, to fall backwards.

"Plague take the wretch!" grumbled Richelieu, dusting his sleeve, which the rebound of the door had brushed against, and seeming still more angry when he saw that the looker-on was dressed like a workman of the château.

It was, in fact, a workman with a basket of flowers under his arm, who had succeeded in climbing up behind the glass, from which position he commanded a view of the entire salon.

He was pushed back into the corridor, and almost overturned; but, although he himself escaped falling, his basket was upset.

"Ah! I know the rascal," said Taverney, angrily.

"Who is it?" asked the duke.

"What are you doing here, scoundrel?" said Taverney.

Gilbert — for the reader has doubtless already recognised him — replied, haughtily: —

"You see, — I am looking."

"Instead of being at your work?" said Richelieu.

"My work is done," said Gilbert, humbly addressing the duke, without deigning to look at Taverney.

"Am I fated to meet this lazy rascal everywhere?" said Taverney.

"Gently, monsieur," interrupted a voice; "gently. My little Gilbert is a good workman and an industrious botanist."

Taverney turned, and saw Monsieur de Jussieu, who was patting Gilbert on the head. The baron reddened with anger and moved off.

"Valets here!" muttered he.

"Hush!" said Richelieu, "there is Nicole! — look, — up there, at the corner of the door. The little buxom witch! she is not making bad use of her eyes either."

The marshal was correct. Partially concealed behind a score of the domestics of Trianon, Nicole raised her charming head above all the others, and her eyes, dilated with surprise and admiration, seemed to magnify everything she saw.

Gilbert perceived her, and turned another way.

"Come, come!" said the duke to Taverney; "I fancy the king wishes to speak to you. He is looking this way."

And the two friends disappeared in the direction of the royal box.

Madame Dubarry was standing behind the king, and interchanging signs with Monsieur d'Aiguillon, who was also standing, and who did not lose one of his uncle's movements.

Rousseau, now left alone, admired Andrée; he was endeavouring, if we may use the expression, to fall in love with her.

The illustrious actors proceeded to disrobe in their boxes, which Gilbert had decorated with fresh flowers.

Taverney, left alone in the passage by Monsieur de Richelieu, who had gone to rejoin the king, felt his heart alternately chilled and elated. At last the duke returned and placed his finger upon his lips. Taverney turned pale with joy, and advanced to meet his friend, who drew him beneath the royal box. There they overheard the following conversation, which was quite inaudible to the rest of the company. Madame Dubarry was saying to the king: —

"May I expect your Majesty to supper this evening?"

And the king replied: —

"I feel fatigued, countess; excuse me."

At the same moment, the dauphin entered, treading almost on Madame Dubarry's toes, without seeming to see her.

"Sire," said he, "will your Majesty do us the honour of supping with us at Trianon?"

"No, my son; I was just this moment saying to the countess that I feel fatigued. Our young people have made me giddy; I shall sup alone."

The dauphin bowed and retired. Madame Dubarry curtseyed almost to the ground, and, trembling with rage, left the box. When she was gone, the king made a sign to the Duke de Richelieu.

"Duke," said he, "I wish to speak to you about an affair which concerns you."

"Sire — "

"I am not satisfied. I wish you to explain. Stay, I shall sup alone; you will keep me company."

And the king looked at Taverney.

"You know this gentleman, I think, duke?"

"Monsieur de Taverney? Yes, sire."

"Ah! the father of the charming singer?"

"Yes, sire."

"Listen, duke!"

And the king stooped to whisper in Richelieu's ears. Taverney clenched his hands till the nails entered the flesh, to avoid showing any emotion. Immediately afterwards Richelieu brushed past Taverney, and said: —

"Follow me without appearing so to do."

"Whither?" asked Taverney, in the same tone.

"No matter; follow me."

The duke moved away. Taverney followed him at a little distance to the king's apartment. The duke entered; Taverney waited in the anteroom.

# CHAPTER CXI.

### THE CASKET.

Monsieur de Taverney had not to wait long. Richelieu, having asked the king's valet for something his Majesty had left upon his dressing-table, soon returned, carrying something the nature of which the baron could not distinguish, on account of the covering of silk which enveloped it.

But the marshal soon relieved his friend from all anxiety. Drawing him into a corner of the gallery, —

"Baron," said he, as soon as he saw that they were alone, "you have at times seemed to doubt my friendship for you?"

"Never since our reconciliation," replied Taverney.

"At least, you doubted your own good fortune and that of your children?"

"Oh! as for that — yes."

"Well, you were wrong. Your children's fortune and your own is made with a rapidity which might make you giddy."

"Bah!" said Taverney, who suspected part of the truth, but who, as he was not quite certain, took care to guard against mistakes, "by what means do my children so easily make their fortune?"

"Monsieur Philip is already a captain, with a company paid for by the king."

"It is true, — I owe that to you."

"By no means. Then we shall have Mademoiselle de Taverney a marchioness, perhaps."

"Come, come!" exclaimed Taverney; "how! — my daughter!"

"Listen, Taverney! the king has great taste; and beauty, grace, and virtue, when accompanied by talent, delight his Majesty. Now, Mademoiselle de Taverney unites all these qualities in a very high degree; the king is therefore delighted with Mademoiselle de Taverney."

"Duke," replied Taverney, assuming an air of dignity at which the marshal could scarcely repress a smile, "duke, what do you mean by 'delighted'?"

Richelieu did not like airs, and replied drily:

"Baron, I am not a great linguist; I am not even well versed in orthography. I have always thought that 'delighted' signified 'content beyond measure.' If you are grieved beyond measure to see the king pleased with the beauty, the talent, the merit of your children, you have only to say so. I am about to return to his Majesty."

And Richelieu turned on his heel and made a pirouette with truly juvenile grace.

"You misunderstand me, duke," exclaimed the baron, stopping him. "*Ventre bleu!* how hasty you are!"

"Why did you say that you were not satisfied?"

"I did not say so."

"You asked for explanations of the king's pleasure. Plague take the fool!"

"But, duke, I did not breathe a syllable of that. I am most certainly content."

"Ah! *you* — well, who will be displeased? Your daughter?"

"Oh! oh!"

"My dear friend, you have brought up your daughter like a savage, as you are."

"My dear friend, the young lady educated herself; you may easily imagine that I could not possibly trouble myself with any such matter. I had enough to do to support life in my den at Taverney. Virtue in her has sprung up spontaneously."

"And yet people say that country folks know how to pull up weeds! In short, your daughter is a prude."

"You mistake; she is a dove."

Richelieu made a grimace. "Well," said he, "the poor child must only look out for a good husband, for opportunities of making a fortune happen rarely with this defect."

Taverney looked uneasily at the duke.

"Fortunately for her," continued he, "the king is so desperately in love with the Dubarry, that he will never think seriously of another."

Taverney's alarm was changed to anguish.

"Therefore," continued Richelieu, "you and your daughter may make your minds easy. I will state the necessary objections to his Majesty, and the king will never bestow another thought on the matter."

"But objections to what? — good heavens!" exclaimed Taverney, turning pale, and holding his friend's arm.

"To his making a little present to Mademoiselle Andrée, my dear baron."

"A little present! What is it?" asked the baron, brimful of hope and avarice.

"Oh! a mere trifle," said Richelieu carelessly, and he took a casket from its silken covering.

"A casket!"

"A mere trifle, — a necklace worth a few millions of francs, which his Majesty, flattered at hearing her sing his favourite air, wished to present to the fair singer. It is the usual custom. But if your daughter is proud, we will say no more about it."

"Duke, you must not think of it, — that would be to offend the king!"

"Of course it would; but is it not the attribute of virtue always to offend some person, or some thing?"

"But, duke, consider, — the child is not so unreasonable."

"That is to say, it is you, and not your child, who speaks?"

"Oh! I know so well what she will do and say."

"The Chinese are a very fortunate nation," said Richelieu.

"Why?" asked Taverney, astonished.

"Because they have so many rivers and canals in the country."

"Duke, you turn the conversation, — do not drive me to despair; speak to me."

"I am speaking to you, baron, and am not changing the conversation at all."

"Then why do you speak of China? What have its rivers to do with my daughter?"

"A great deal. The Chinese, I repeat, have the happiness of being able to drown their daughters when they are too virtuous, and no one can forbid it."

"Come, duke, you must be just. Suppose you had a daughter yourself."

"*Pardieu!* I have one; and if any one were to tell me that she is too virtuous it would be very ill-natured of him, — that's all."

"In short, you would like her better otherwise, would you not?"

"Oh! for my part, I don't meddle with my children after they are eight years old."

"Listen to me, at least. If the king were to commission me to offer a necklace to your daughter, and if your daughter were to complain to you?"

"Oh, my dear monsieur, there is no comparison. I have always lived at court, you have lived like a North American Indian; there is no similarity. What you call virtue, I think folly. Remember, for the future, that nothing is more ill-bred than to say to people, ' What would you do in this or that case?' And besides, your comparisons are erroneous, my friend. It is not true that I am about to present a necklace to your daughter."

"You said so."

"I said nothing of the sort. I said that the king had directed me to bring him a casket for Mademoiselle de

Taverney, whose voice had pleased him; but I did not say that his Majesty had charged me to give it to her."

"Then, in truth," said the baron, in despair, "I know not what to think. I do not understand a single word, — you speak in enigmas. Why give this necklace, if it is not to be given? Why do you take charge of it, if not to deliver it?"

Richelieu uttered an exclamation as if he had seen a spider.

"Ah!" said he; "pouah! — pouah! — the Huron! the ugly animal!"

"Who?"

"You, my good friend, — you, my trusty comrade, — you seem as if you had fallen from the clouds, baron!"

"I am at my wits' end."

"No, you never had any. When a king makes a lady a present, and when he charges Monsieur de Richelieu with the commission, the present is noble and the commission well executed, — remember that. I do not deliver caskets, my dear sir, — that was Monsieur Lebel's office. Did you know Monsieur Lebel?"

"What is your office, then?"

"My friend," said Richelieu, tapping Taverney on the shoulder, and accompanying this amicable gesture by a sardonic smile, "when I have to do with such paragons of virtue as Mademoiselle Andrée, I am the most moral man in the world. When I approach a dove, as you call your daughter, I do not display the talons of the hawk. When I am deputed to wait on a young lady, I speak to her father. I speak to you, therefore, Taverney, and give you the casket to present to your daughter. Well, are you willing?" — And he offered the casket. "Or do you decline?" — And he drew it back.

"Oh! say at once," exclaimed the baron, "say at once that I am commissioned by his Majesty to deliver the present! If so, it assumes quite a correct and paternal character, — it is, so to speak, purified from —"

"Purified! Why, you must have suspected his Majesty of evil intentions!" said Richelieu, seriously. "Now, you cannot have dared to do that?"

"Heaven forbid! But the world, — that is to say, my daughter —"

Richelieu shrugged his shoulders.

"Will you take it? — yes, or no?" asked he.

Taverney rapidly held out his hand.

"You are certain it is moral?" said he to the duke, with a smile, the counterpart of that which the duke had just addressed to him.

"Do you not think it pure morality, baron," said the marshal, "to make the father, who, as you have just said, purifies everything, an intermediate party between the king's delight and your daughter's charms? Let Monsieur Rousseau, of Geneva, who was hovering about here just now, be the judge; he would say that Joseph of happy memory was impure compared to me."

Richelieu pronounced these few words with a calmness — an abrupt haughtiness — a precision — which silenced Taverney's objections, and assisted to make him believe that he ought to be convinced. He seized his illustrious friend's hand, therefore, and pressing it, —

"Thanks to your delicacy," said he, "my daughter can accept this present."

"The source and origin of the good fortune to which I alluded at the commencement of our tiresome discussion on virtue."

"Thanks, dear duke; most hearty thanks!"

"One word more. Conceal this favour carefully from the Dubarrys. It might make Madame Dubarry leave the king and take flight."

"And the king would be displeased?"

"I don't know, but the countess would not thank us. As for me, I should be lost! Be discreet, therefore —"

"Do not fear. But at least present my most humble thanks to the king."

"And your daughter's, — I shall not fail. But you have
not yet reached the limits of the favours bestowed upon
you. It is you who are to thank the king, my dear sir;
his Majesty invites you to sup with him this evening."

"Me ?"

"You, Taverney. We shall be a select party. His
Majesty, you, and myself. We will talk of your daughter's
virtue. Adieu, Taverney, I see Dubarry with Monsieur
d'Aiguillon. We must not be perceived together."

And, agile as a page, he disappeared at the farther end
of the gallery, leaving Taverney gazing at his casket, like
a Saxon child who awakens and finds the Christmas gifts
which have been placed in his hands while he slept.

## CHAPTER CXII.

### KING LOUIS XV.'S PETIT SOUPER.

THE marshal found the king in the little salon whither several of the courtiers had followed him, preferring rather to lose their supper than to allow the wandering glance of their sovereign to fall on any others than themselves. But Louis XV. seemed to have something else to do this evening than to look at these gentlemen. He dismissed every one, saying that he did not intend to sup, or that, if he did, it would be alone. All the guests having thus received their dismissal, and fearing to displease the dauphin if they were not present at the fête which he was to give at the close of the rehearsal, instantly flew off like a cloud of parasite pigeons, and winged their way to him whom they were permitted to see, ready to assert that they had deserted his Majesty's drawing-room for him.

Louis XV., whom they left so rapidly, was far from bestowing a thought on them. At another time, the littleness of all this swarm of courtiers would have excited a smile, but on this occasion it awoke no sentiment in the monarch's breast, — a monarch so sarcastic that he spared neither bodily nor mental defect in his best friends, always supposing that Louis XV. ever had a friend.

No; at that moment Louis XV. concentrated his entire attention on a carriage which was drawn up opposite the door of the offices of Trianon, the coachman seeming to wait only for the step which should announce the owner's presence in the gilded vehicle to urge on his horses. The carriage was Madame Dubarry's, and was lighted by

torches. Zamore, seated beside the coachman, was swing-
ing his legs backwards and forwards like a child at play.

At last, Madame Dubarry, who had no doubt delayed
in the corridors in the hope of receiving some message from
the king, appeared, supported on Monsieur d'Aiguillon's
arm. Her anger, or at least her disappointment, was apparent in the rapidity of her gait. She affected too much
resolution not to have lost her presence of mind.

After Madame Dubarry followed Jean, looking gloomy
in the extreme, and absently crushing his hat beneath his
arm. He had not been present at the representation, the
dauphin having forgotten to invite him; but he had stolen
into the anteroom somewhat after the fashion of a lackey,
and stood pensive as Hippolytus, with his shirt-frill falling
over his vest embroidered with silver and red flowers, and
not even looking at his tattered ruffles, which seemed in
harmony with his sad thoughts. Jean had seen his sister
look pale and alarmed, and had concluded from this that
the danger was great. Jean was brave in diplomacy only
when opposed to flesh and blood, never when opposed to
phantoms.

Concealed behind the window-curtain, the king watched
this funereal procession defile before him and engulf themselves in the countess's carriage like a troop of phantoms.
Then, when the door was closed, and the footman had
mounted behind the carriage, the coachman shook the
reins, and the horses started forward at a gallop.

"Oh!" said the king, "without making an attempt to
see me, — to speak to me? the countess is furious!"

And he repeated aloud: —

"Yes, the countess is furious!"

Richelieu, who had just glided into the room like an
expected visitor, caught these last words: —

"Furious, sire! and for what? Because your Majesty
is amused for a moment? Oh! that is not amiable of the
countess."

"Duke," replied Louis XV., "I am not amused; on the

contrary, I am wearied and wish for repose. Music ener-
vates me. If I had listened to the countess, I ought to have
supped at Luciennes; I ought to have eaten, and, above
all, to have drunk. The countess's wines are too strong;
I do not know from what vineyards they come, but they
overpower me. 'Sdeath! I prefer to take my ease here."

"And your Majesty is perfectly in the right," said the
duke.

"Besides, the countess will find amusement elsewhere.
Am I such an amiable companion? She may say so as
much as she likes, but I do not believe her."

"Ah! this time your Majesty is in the wrong," exclaimed
the marshal.

"No, duke; no, in truth. I count my years, and I
reflect."

"Sire, the countess is well aware that she could not possibly have better company, and it is that which makes her
furious."

"In truth, duke, I do not know how you manage. You
still lead the women as if you were twenty. At that age
it is for a man to choose; but at mine, duke — "

"Well, sire?"

"It is for the woman to make her calculations."

The marshal burst into a laugh.

"Well, sire," said he, "that is only an additional reason;
if your Majesty thinks the countess is amused, let us console ourselves as well as we can."

"I do not say she is amused, duke; I only say that she
will, in the end, be driven to seek amusement."

"Ah! sire, I dare not assert that such things have never
happened."

The king rose, much agitated.

"Who waits outside?" inquired he.

"All your suite, sire."

The king reflected for a moment.

"But have you any one there?"

"I have Rafté."

"Very good."

"What shall he do, sire?"

"He must find out if the countess really returned to Luciennes."

"The countess is already gone, I fancy, sire."

"Yes, ostensibly."

"But whither does your Majesty think she is gone?"

"Who can tell? Jealousy makes her frantic, duke."

"Sire, is it not rather your Majesty — ?"

"How? — what?"

"Whom jealousy — "

"Duke!"

"In truth, it would be very humiliating for us all, sire."

"I jealous?" said Louis, with a forced laugh; "are you speaking seriously, duke?"

Richelieu did not, in truth, believe it. It must even be confessed that he was very near the truth in thinking that, on the contrary, the king only wished to know if Madame Dubarry was really at Luciennes, in order to be sure that she would not return to Trianon.

"Then, sire," said he, aloud, "it is understood that I am to send Rafté on a voyage of discovery?"

"Send him, duke."

"In the mean time, what will your Majesty do before supper?"

"Nothing; we shall sup instantly. Have you spoken to the person in question?"

"Yes; he is in your Majesty's antechamber."

"What did he say?"

"He expressed his deep thanks."

"And the daughter?"

"She has not been spoken to yet."

"Duke, Madame Dubarry is jealous, and might readily return."

"Ah! sire, that would be in very bad taste. I think the countess would be incapable of committing such an enormity."

"Duke, she is capable of anything in such moods, especially when hatred is combined with jealousy. She execrates you; I don't know if you were aware of that?"

Richelieu bowed.

"I know she does me that honour, sire."

"She execrates Monsieur de Taverney also."

"If your Majesty would be good enough to reckon, I am sure there is a third person whom she hates even more than me, — even more than the baron."

"Whom?"

" Mademoiselle Andrée."

"Ah!" said the king, "I think that is natural enough."

"Then —"

"Yes, but that does not prevent its being necessary to watch that Madame Dubarry does not cause some scandal this evening."

"On the contrary, it proves the necessity of such a measure."

"Here is the *maître d'hôtel;* hush! give your orders to Rafté, and join me in the dining-room with — you know whom."

Louis rose and passed into the dining-room, while Richelieu made his exit by the opposite door. Five minutes afterwards, he rejoined the king, accompanied by the baron.

The king, in the most gracious manner, bade Taverney good evening. The baron was a man of talent, and replied in that peculiar manner which betokens a person accustomed to good society, and which puts kings and princes instantly at their ease. They sat down to table. Louis XV. was a bad king, but a delightful companion; when he pleased, his conversation was full of attraction for boon companions, talkers, and voluptuaries. The king, in short, had studied life carefully, and from its most agreeable side.

He ate heartily, made his guests drink, and turned the conversation on music.

Richelieu caught the ball at the rebound.

"Sire," says he, "if music makes men agree, as our ballet-master says, and as your Majesty seems to think, will you say as much of women?"

"Oh, duke!" replied the king, "let us not speak of women. From the Trojan war to the present time, women have always exercised an influence the contrary of music. You, especially, have too many quarrels to compound with them to bring such a subject on the tapis. Amongst others, there is one, and that not the least dangerous, with whom you are at daggers drawn."

"The countess, sire! Is that my fault?"

"Of course it is."

"Ah! indeed! Your Majesty, I trust, will explain."

"In two words, and with the greatest pleasure," said the king slyly.

"I am all ears, sire."

"What! she offers you the portfolio of I don't know which department, and you refuse, because, you say, she is not very popular?"

"I?" exclaimed Richelieu, a good deal embarrassed by the turn the conversation was taking.

"*Dame!* the report is quite public," said the king, with that feigned off-hand good-nature which was peculiar to him. "I forget now who told it to me, — most probably the gazette."

"Well, sire," said Richelieu, taking advantage of the freedom which the unusual gaiety of the august host afforded his guests, "I must confess that on this occasion rumours and even the gazettes have reported something not quite so absurd as usual."

"What!" exclaimed Louis XV., "then you have really refused a portfolio, my dear duke?"

Richelieu, it may easily be imagined, was in an awkward position. The king well knew that he had refused nothing; but it was necessary that Taverney should continue to believe what Richelieu had told him. The duke had there-

fore to frame his reply so as to avoid furnishing matter for
amusement to the king, without at the same time incur-
ring the reproach of falsehood, which was already hovering
upon the baron's lips and twinkling in his smile.

"Sire," said Richelieu, "pray let us not speak of effects,
but of the cause.    Whether I have or have not refused a
portfolio is a state secret which your Majesty is not bound
to divulge over the bottle; but the cause for which I
should have refused the portfolio had it been offered to me
is the important point."

"Oh! oh! duke," said the monarch, laughing; "and this
cause is not a state secret?"

"No, sire, and certainly not for your Majesty, who is at
this moment, I beg pardon of the divinity, the most amiable earthly Amphytrion in the universe for my friend the
Baron de Taverney and myself.    I have no secrets, therefore, from my king.    I give my whole soul up to him, for
I do not wish it to be said that the King of France has
not one servant who would tell him the entire truth."

"Let us hear the truth, then, duke," said the king, while
Taverney, fearing that Richelieu might go too far, pinched
up his lips and composed his countenance scrupulously
after the king's.

"Sire, in your dominions there are two powers which a
minister must obey: the first is your will; the second,
that of your Majesty's most intimate friends.    The first
power is irresistible, none dare to rebel against it; the
second is yet more sacred, for it imposes duties of the
heart on whosoever serves you.    It is termed your confidence. To obey it, a minister must have the most devoted
regard for the favourite of the king."

Louis XV. laughed.

"Duke," said he, "that is a very good maxim, and one
I am delighted to hear from your lips; but I dare you to
proclaim it aloud by sound of trumpet upon the Pont
Neuf."

"Oh, I know, sire," said Richelieu, "that the philosophers would be up in arms; but I do not think that their objurgations would matter much to your Majesty or to me. The chief point is that the two preponderating influences in the kingdom be satisfied. Well, the will of a certain person, — I will confess it openly to your Majesty, even should my disgrace, that is my death, be the consequence, — Madame Dubarry's will I could not conform to."

Louis was silent.

"It occurred to me the other day," continued Richelieu, "to look around amongst your Majesty's court, and in truth I saw so many noble girls, so many women of dazzling beauty, that had I been King of France I should have found it almost impossible to choose."

Louis turned to Taverney, who, seeing things take such a favourable turn for him, sat trembling with hope and fear, aiding the marshal's eloquence with eyes and breath, as if he would waft forward the vessel loaded with his fortunes to a safe harbour.

"Come, baron, what is your opinion?" said the king.

"Sire," replied Taverney, with swelling heart, "the duke, as it seems to me, has been discoursing most eloquently, and at the same time with profound discernment, to your Majesty for the last few minutes."

"Then you are of his opinion in what he says of lovely girls?"

"In fact, sire, I think there are indeed very lovely young girls at the French court."

"Then you are of his opinion?"

"Yes, sire."

"And, like him, you advise me to choose among the beauties of the court?"

"I would venture to confess that I am of the marshal's opinion, if I dared to believe that it was also your Majesty's."

There was a short silence, during which the king looked complaisantly at Taverney.  ·

"Gentlemen," said he, "no doubt I would follow your

advice, if I were only thirty years of age. I should have a very natural predilection for it, but I find myself at present rather too old to be credulous."

"Credulous! pray, sire, explain the meaning of the word."

"To be credulous, my dear duke, means to believe. Now, nothing will make me believe certain things."

"What are they?"

"That at my age it would be possible to inspire love."

"Ah, sire," exclaimed Richelieu, "until this moment I thought your Majesty was the most polite gentleman in your dominions, but with deep regret I see that I have been mistaken."

"How so?" asked the king, laughing.

"Because, in that case, I must be old as Methuselah, as I was born in '94. Remember, sire, I am sixteen years older than your Majesty."

This was an adroit piece of flattery on the duke's part. Louis XV. had always admired this man's age, who had outlived so many younger men in his service; for, having this example before him, he might hope to reach the same advanced period.

"Granted," said Louis; "but I hope you no longer have the pretension to be loved for yourself, duke?"

"If I thought so, sire, I would instantly quarrel with two ladies who told me the contrary only this very morning."

"Well, duke," said Louis, "we shall see; Monsieur de Taverney, we shall see; youth rejuvenates, that is very true."

"Yes, yes, sire; and we must not forget that a powerful constitution like your Majesty's always gains and never loses."

"Yet I remember," said Louis, "that my predecessor, when he became old, thought not of such toys as woman's love, but became exceedingly devout."

"Come, come, sire," said Richelieu, "your Majesty knows my great respect for the deceased king, who twice sent me to the Bastille; but that ought not to prevent me from saying that there is a vast difference between the ripe age of Louis XV. and that of Louis XIV. *Diable!* your most Christian Majesty, although honouring fully your title of eldest son of the Church, need not carry asceticism so far as to forget your humanity."

"Faith, no," said Louis. "I may confess it, since neither my doctor nor confessor is present."

"Well, sire, the king, your grandfather, frequently astonished Madame de Maintenon, who was even older than he, by his excess of religious zeal and his innumerable penances. I repeat it, sire; can there be any comparison made between your two Majesties?"

The king this evening was in a good humour. Richelieu's words acted upon him like so many drops of water from the fountain of youth.

Richelieu thought the time had come; he touched Taverney's knee with his.

"Sire," said the latter, "will your Majesty deign to accept my thanks for the magnificent present you have made my daughter?"

"You need not thank me for that, baron," said the king. "Mademoiselle de Taverney pleased me by her modest and ingenuous grace. I wish my daughters had still their households to form; certainly, Mademoiselle Andrée — that is her name, is it not — ?"

"Yes, sire," said Taverney, delighted that the king knew his daughter's Christian name.

"A very pretty name — certainly Mademoiselle Andrée should have been the first upon the list; but every post in my house is filled up. In the mean time, baron, you may reckon upon my protection for your daughter. I think I have heard she has not a rich dowry?"

"Alas! no, sire."

"Well, I will make her marriage my especial care."

Taverney bowed to the ground.

"Then your Majesty must be good enough," said he, "to select a husband; for I confess that, in our confined circumstances — our almost poverty — "

"Yes, yes; rest easy on that point," said Louis; "but she seems very young, — there is no haste."

"The less, sire, that your *protégée* has a horror of marriage."

"Ha!" said Louis, rubbing his hands, and looking at Richelieu. "Well, at all events, Monsieur de Taverney, command me whenever you are at all embarrassed."

Then, rising, the king beckoned the duke, who approached.

"Was the little one satisfied?" asked he.

"With what?"

"With the casket."

"Your Majesty must excuse my speaking low, but the father is listening, and he must not overhear what I have to tell you."

"Bah!"

"No, I assure you, sire."

"Well, speak!"

"Sire, the little one has indeed a horror of marriage; but of one thing I am certain, — namely, that she has not a horror of your Majesty."

Uttering these words in a tone of familiarity which pleased the king from its very frankness, the marshal, with his little pattering steps, hastened to rejoin Taverney, who, from respect, had moved away to the doorway of the gallery.

Both retired by the gardens. It was a lovely evening. Two servants walked before them, holding torches in one hand, and with the other pulling aside the branches of the flowering shrubs. The windows of Trianon were blazing with light, and flitting across them could be discerned a crowd of joyous figures, the honoured guests of the dauphiness.

His Majesty's band gave life and animation to the minuet, for dancing had commenced after supper, and was still kept up with undiminished spirit.

Concealed in a dense thicket of lilac and snowball

shrubs, Gilbert, kneeling upon the ground, was gazing at the movements of the shadows, through the transparent curtains. A thunderbolt cleaving the earth at his feet would scarcely have distracted the attention of the gazer, so much was he entranced by the lovely forms he was following with his eyes through all the mazes of the dance. Nevertheless, when Richelieu and Taverney passed, and brushed against the thicket in which this night-bird was concealed, the sound of their voices, and, above all, a certain word, made Gilbert raise his head; for this word was an all important one for him.

The marshal, leaning upon his friend's arm, and bending down to his ear, was saying, —

"Everything well weighed and considered, baron, — it is a hard thing to tell you, — but you must at once send your daughter to a convent."

"Why so?" asked the baron.

"Because I would wager," replied the marshal, "that the king is madly in love with Mademoiselle de Taverney."

At these words Gilbert started and turned paler than the flaky snowberries which, at his abrupt movement, showered down upon his head and shoulders.

## CHAPTER CXIII.

### PRESENTIMENTS.

THE next day, as the clock at Trianon was striking twelve, Nicole's voice was heard calling Andrée, who had not yet left her apartment: —

"Mademoiselle, mademoiselle, here is Monsieur Philip!"

The exclamation came from the bottom of the stairs.

Andrée, at once surprised and delighted, drew her muslin robe closely over her neck and shoulders, and hastened to meet the young man, who was in fact dismounting in the court-yard of Trianon, and inquiring from the servants at what time he could see his sister.

Andrée therefore opened the door in person, and found herself face to face with Philip, whom the officious Nicole had run to summon from the court-yard, and was accompanying up the stairs.

The young girl threw her arms round her brother's neck, and they entered Andrée's apartments together, followed by Nicole.

It was then that Andrée for the first time remarked that Philip was more serious than usual, — that his smile was not free from sadness, — that he wore his elegant uniform with the most scrupulous neatness, and that he held a travelling cloak over his arm.

"What is the matter, Philip?" asked she, with the instinct of tender affection, of which a look is a sufficient revelation.

"My sister," said Philip, "this morning I received an order to join my regiment."

"And you are going?"

"I must."

"Oh!" said Andrée; and with this plaintive exclamation all her courage, and almost all her strength, seemed to desert her.

And although this departure was a very natural occurrence, and one which she might have foreseen, yet she felt so overpowered by the announcement that she was obliged to lean for support on her brother's arm.

"Good heavens!" asked Philip, astonished, "does this departure afflict you so much, Andrée? You know, in a a soldier's life, it is a most commonplace event."

"Yes, yes; it is in truth common," murmured the young girl. "And whither do you go, brother?"

"My garrison is at Rheims. You see, I have not a very long journey to undertake. But it is probable that from thence the regiment will return to Strasbourg."

"Alas!" said Andrée; "and when do you set out?"

"The order commands me to start immediately."

"You have come to bid me good-bye, then?"

"Yes, sister."

"A farewell!"

"Have you anything particular to say to me, Andrée?" asked Philip, fearing that this extreme dejection might have some other cause than his departure.

Andrée understood that these words were meant to call her attention to Nicole, who, astonished at Andrée's extreme grief, was gazing at this scene with much surprise; for, in fact, the departure of an officer to his garrison was not a catastrophe to cause such a flood of tears.

Andrée, therefore, saw at the same instant Philip's feelings and Nicole's surprise. She took up a mantle, threw it over her shoulders, and, leading her brother to the staircase, —

"Come," said she, "as far as the park gates, Philip. I will accompany you through the covered alley. I have, in truth, many things to tell you, brother."

These words were equivalent to a dismissal for Nicole,

who returned to her mistress's chamber, while the latter descended the staircase with Philip.

Andrée led the way to the passage which still even at the present day opens from the chapel into the garden; but although Philip's look anxiously questioned her, she remained for a long time silent, leaning upon his arm, and supporting her head upon his shoulder.

But at last her heart was too full; her features were overspread with a death-like paleness, a deep sigh escaped her lips, and tears rushed from her eyes.

" My dear sister, — my sweet Andrée! " exclaimed Philip, " in the name of Heaven what is the matter ? "

" My friend, — my only friend! " said Andrée, " you depart, — you leave me alone in this great world, which I entered but yesterday, and yet you ask me why I weep? Ah! remember, Philip, I lost my mother at my birth; it is dreadful to acknowledge it, but I have never had a father. All my little griefs, all my little secrets, I could confide to you alone. Who smiled upon me ? Who caressed me ? Who rocked me in my cradle ? It was you. Who has protected me since I grew up ? You. Who taught me that God's creatures were not cast into the world only to suffer ? You, Philip, — you alone. For since the hour of my birth I have loved no one in the world but you, and no one but you has loved me in return. Oh! Philip, Philip," continued Andrée, sadly, " you turn away your head, and I can read your thoughts. You think I am young, — that I am beautiful, — and that I am wrong not to trust to the future and to love. And yet you see, alas! Philip, it is not enough to be young and handsome, for no one thinks of me.

" You will say the dauphiness is kind, and she is so. She is all perfection; at least, she seems so in my eyes, and I look upon her as a divinity. But it is exactly because she holds this exalted situation that I can feel only respect for her, and not affection. Yet, Philip, affection is necessary for my heart, which if always thrust back on it-

self must at last break. My father, — I tell you nothing
new, Philip, — my father is not only no protector or friend,
but I cannot even look at him without feeling terror. Yes,
yes, I fear him, Philip, and still more now, since you are
leaving me.

"You will ask, why should I fear him? I know not.
Do not the birds of the air and the flocks of the field feel
and dread the approaching storm? You will say they
are endowed with instinct; but why will you deny the instinct of misfortune to our immortal souls? For some
time past everything has prospered with our family; I
know it well. You are a captain; I am in the household,
and almost in the intimacy, of the dauphiness; my father,
it is said, supped last night almost *tête-à-tête* with the
king. Well, Philip, I repeat it, even should you think me
mad, all this alarms me more than our peaceful poverty
and obscurity at Taverney."

"And yet, dear sister," said Philip, sadly, "you were
alone there also; I was not with you there to console you."

"Yes, but at least I was alone, — alone with the memories of childhood. It seemed to me as if the house where
my mother lived and breathed her last would give me, if
I may so speak, a protecting care; all there was peaceful,
gentle, affectionate. I could see you depart with calmness,
and welcome you back with joy. But whether you departed
or returned, my heart was not all with you; it was attached
also to that dear house, to my gardens, to my flowers, to
the whole scene of which formerly you were but a part.
Now you are all to me, Philip, and when you leave me I
am indeed alone."

"And yet, Andreé, you have now a protector far more
powerful than I am."

"True."

"A happy future before you."

"Who can tell?"

"Why do you doubt it?"

"I do not know."

"This is ingratitude towards God, my sister."

"Oh, no, thank Heaven! I am not ungrateful to God. Morning and evening I offer up thanks to Him; but it seems to me as if, instead of receiving my prayers with grace, every time I bend the knee a voice from on high whispers to my heart, 'Take care, young girl, take care!'"

"But against what are you to guard? Answer me. I will admit that a danger threatens you. Have you any presentiment of the nature of this misfortune? Do you know how to act so as best to confront it, or how to avoid it?"

"I know nothing, Philip, except that my life seems to hang by a thread, that nothing will look bright to me from the moment of your departure. In a word, it seems as if during my sleep I had been placed on the declivity of a precipice too steep to allow me to arrest my progress when roused to a sense of my danger; that I see the abyss, and yet am dragged down; and that, you being far away, and your helping hand no longer ready to support me, I shall be dashed down and crushed in the fall."

"Dear sister! my sweet Andrée!" said Philip, agitated in spite of himself by the expression of deep and unaffected terror in her voice and manner, "you exaggerate the extent of an affection for which I feel deeply grateful. Yes, you will lose your friend, but only for a time; I shall not be so far distant but that you can send for me if necessity should arise. Besides, remember that, except chimerical fears, nothing threatens you."

Andrée placed herself in her brother's way.

"Then, Philip," said she, "how does it happen that you, who are a man, and gifted with so much more strength, are at this moment as sad as I am? Tell me, my brother, how do you explain that?"

"Easily, dear sister," said Philip, arresting Andrée's steps, for she had again moved forwards on ceasing to speak. "We are not only brother and sister by blood, but in heart and affection; therefore we have lived in an intimate communion of thoughts and feelings, which, especially since our arrival in Paris, has become to me a delightful necessity. I break this chain, my sweet love, or rather it is broken by others, and I feel the blow in my inmost heart. I am sad, but only for the moment, Andrée. I can look beyond our separation; I do not believe in any misfortune, except in that of not seeing you for some months, perhaps for a year. I am resigned, and do not say ' Farewell,' but rather, ' We shall soon meet again.' "

In spite of these consolatory words, Andrée could only reply by sobs and tears.  ·

"Dearest sister," exclaimed Philip, grieved at this dejection, which seemed so incomprehensible to him, "dearest sister, you have not told me all,—you hide something from me. In Heaven's name, speak!"

And he took her in his arms, pressing her to his heart, and gazing earnestly in her eyes.

"I!" said she. "No, no, Philip, I assure you solemnly. You know all the most secret recesses of my heart are open before you."

"Well, then, Andrée, for pity's sake, take courage; do not grieve me so."

"You are right," said she, " and I am mad. Listen: I never had a strong mind, as you, Philip, know better than any one; I have always been a timid, dreaming, melancholy creature. But I have no right to make so tenderly beloved a brother a sharer in my fears, above all when he labours to give me courage, and proves to me that I am wrong to be alarmed. You are right, Philip; it is true, everything here is conducive to my happiness. Forgive me, Philip! You see, I dry my tears,—I weep no longer, —I smile, Philip,—I do not say ' Adieu,' but rather, ' We shall soon meet again.' "

And the young maiden tenderly embraced her brother, hiding her head on his shoulder to conceal from his view a tear which still dimmed her eye, and which dropped like a pearl upon the golden epaulette of the young officer.

Philip gazed upon her with that infinite tenderness which partakes at the same time of a father's and a brother's affection.

"Andrée," said he, "I love to see you bear yourself thus bravely. Be of good courage; I must go, but the courier shall bring you a letter every week. And every week let me receive one from you in return."

"Yes, Philip," said Andrée; "yes, it will be my only happiness. But you have informed my father, have you not?"

"Of what?"

"Of your departure."

"Dear sister, it was the baron himself who brought me the minister's order this morning. Monsieur de Taverney is not like you, Andrée, and it seems will easily part with me. He appeared pleased at the thought of my departure, and in fact he was right. Here I can never get forward, while there many occasions may present themselves."

"My father is glad to see you go?" murmured Andrée. "Are you not mistaken, Philip?"

"He has you," replied Philip, eluding the question; "that is a consolation for him, sister."

"Do you think so, Philip? He never sees me."

"My sister, he bade me tell you that this very day, after my departure, he would come to Trianon. Believe me, he loves you; only it is after his own fashion."

"What is the matter now, Philip? you seem embarrassed."

"Dearest Andrée, I heard the clock strike; what hour is it?"

"A quarter to one."

"Well, dear sister, I seem embarrassed because I ought to have been on the road an hour ago, and here we are at the gate where my horse is waiting. Therefore —"

Andreé assumed a calm demeanour, and taking her brother's hand, —

"Therefore," said she, in a voice too firm to be entirely natural, "therefore, brother, adieu!"

Philip gave her one last embrace.

"To meet soon again," said he; "remember your promise."

"What promise?"

"One letter a week, at least."

"Oh! do you think it necessary to ask it?"

She required a violent effort to pronounce these last words. The poor girl's voice was scarcely audible.

Philip waved his hand in token of adieu, and walked quickly towards the gate. Andrée followed his retreating form with her eyes, holding in her breath in the endeavour to repress her sighs. Philip bounded lightly on horseback, shouted a last farewell from the other side of the gate, and was gone. Andrée remained standing motionless till he was out of sight, then she turned, darted like a wounded fawn amongst the shady trees, perceived a bench, and had only strength sufficient to reach it, and to sink on it powerless and almost lifeless. Then, heaving a deep and heart-rending sigh, she exclaimed, —

"Oh, my God! do not leave me quite alone upon earth!"

She buried her face in her hands, while the big tears she did not seek to restrain made their way through her slender fingers. At this instant a slight rustling was heard amidst the shrubs behind her. Andrée thought she heard a sigh; she turned, alarmed; a melancholy form stood before her.

It was Gilbert.

## CHAPTER CXIV.

GILBERT'S ROMANCE.

As pale, as despairing as Andrée, Gilbert stood downcast before her.  At the sight of a man, and of a stranger, for such he seemed at first sight through the thick veil of tears which obscured her gaze, Andrée hastily dried her eyes, as if the proud young girl would have blushed to be seen weeping.  She made an effort to compose herself, and restored calmness to her marble features, only an instant before agitated with the shudder of despair.  Gilbert was much longer in regaining his calmness, and his features still wore an expression of grief when Mademoiselle de Taverney, looking up, at last recognised him.

"Oh, Monsieur Gilbert again!" said Andrée, with that trifling tone which she affected to assume whenever chance brought her in contact with the young man.

Gilbert made no reply; his feelings were still too deeply moved.  The grief which had shaken Andrée's frame to the centre had violently agitated his own.  It was Andrée, therefore, who again broke the silence, wishing to have the last word with this apparition.

"But what is the matter, Monsieur Gilbert?" inquired she.  "Why do you gaze at me in that woe-begone manner? Something must grieve you.  May I ask what it is?"

"Do you wish to know?" ·asked Gilbert, mournfully, for he felt the irony concealed beneath this appearance of interest.

"Yes."

"Well, what grieves me, mademoiselle, is to see you suffer," replied Gilbert.

"And who told you that I am suffering?"

"I see it."

"You mistake, monsieur; I am not suffering," said Andrée, passing her handkerchief over her face.

Gilbert felt the storm rising, but he resolved to turn it aside by humility.

"I entreat your pardon, mademoiselle," said he; "but the reason I spoke was that I heard your sobs."

"Ah! you were listening; better and better!"

"Mademoiselle, it was by accident," stammered Gilbert, for he felt that he was telling a falsehood.

"Accident! I regret exceedingly, Monsieur Gilbert, that chance should have brought you here. But even so, may I ask in what manner these sobs which you heard me utter grieved you? Pray inform me."

"I cannot bear to see a woman weep," said Gilbert, in a tone which highly displeased Andrée.

"Am I, then, a *woman* in Monsieur Gilbert's eyes?" replied the haughty young girl. "I sue for no one's sympathy, but Monsieur Gilbert's still less than any other's."

"Mademoiselle," said Gilbert, sadly, "you do wrong to taunt me thus. I saw you sad, and I felt grieved. I heard you say that, now Monsieur Philip was gone, you would be alone in the world. Never, mademoiselle! for I am beside you, and never did a heart beat more devoted to you. I repeat it, Mademoiselle de Taverney cannot be alone in the world while my head can think, my heart beat, or my arm retains its strength."

While he spoke these words, Gilbert was indeed a model of manly elegance and beauty, although he pronounced them with all the humility which the most sincere respect commanded.

But it was fated that everything which the young man did should displease Andrée, should offend her, and urge her to offensive retorts, — as if his very respect were an insult, and his prayers a provocation. At first she attempted to rise, that she might second her harsh words with as harsh gestures; but a nervous shudder retained her on her seat. Besides, she reflected that, if she were standing, she could be seen from a distance, and seen talking to Gilbert. She therefore remained seated; for she was determined, once for all, to crush the importunate insect before her under foot, and replied, —

"I thought I had already informed you, Monsieur Gilbert, that you are highly displeasing to me, that your voice annoys me, that your philosophical speeches disgust me. Then why, when you know this, do you still persist in addressing me?"

"Mademoiselle," replied Gilbert, pale, but self-possessed, "an honest-hearted woman is never disgusted by sympathy. An honest man is the equal of every human being; and I, whom you maltreat so cruelly, deserve more than any other, perhaps, the sympathy which I regret to perceive you do not feel for me."

At this word *sympathy*, thus twice repeated, Andrée opened her large eyes to their utmost extent, and fixed them impertinently upon Gilbert.

"Sympathy!" said she; "sympathy between you and me, Monsieur Gilbert! In truth, I was deceived in my opinion of you. I took you for insolent, and I find you are even less than that, — you are only a madman."

"I am neither insolent nor mad," said Gilbert, with an apparent calm which it must have caused his proud disposition much to assume. "No, mademoiselle; nature has made me your equal, and chance has made you my debtor."

"Chance again!" said Andrée, sarcastically.

"Perhaps I should have said Providence. I never intended to have spoken to you of this, but your insults refresh my memory."

"*I* your debtor, monsieur? Your *debtor*, I think you said? Explain yourself."

"I should be ashamed to find you ungrateful, mademoiselle. God, who has made you so beautiful, has given

you, to compensate for your beauty, sufficient defects without that."

This time Andrée rose.

"Stay! pardon me!" said Gilbert; "at times you irritate
me too much also, and then I forget for a moment the
interest with which you inspire me."

Andrée burst into a fit of laughter so prolonged that it
was calculated to rouse Gilbert's anger to the utmost; but,
to her great surprise, Gilbert did not take fire.  He folded
his arms on his breast, retained the same hostile and determined expression in his fiery glance, and patiently awaited
the end of this insulting laugh.

When she had finished, —

"Mademoiselle," said Gilbert coldly, "will you condescend to answer one question?  Do you respect your
father?"

"You take the liberty of catechising me, it seems,
Monsieur Gilbert?" replied the young girl, with sovereign
hauteur.

"Yes, you respect your father," continued Gilbert; "and
it is not on account of his good qualities or his virtues,
but simply because he gave you life.  A father, unfortunately, — and you must know it, mademoiselle, — a father
is respected only in one relation, but still it gives him a
claim.  Even more: for this sole benefit," — and Gilbert,
in his turn, felt himself animated by an emotion of scornful
pity, — "you are bound to love your benefactor.  Well,
mademoiselle, this being established as a principle, why
do you insult me? why do you scorn me? why do you hate
him who did not indeed give you life, but who saved it?"

"You!" exclaimed Andrée; "you saved my life?"

"Ah! you did not even dream of that," said Gilbert,
"or rather you have forgotten it.  That is very natural;
it occurred nearly a year ago.  Well, mademoiselle, I
must only, therefore, inform you of it, or recall it to your
memory.  Yes, I saved your life at the risk of my own."

"At least, Monsieur Gilbert," said Andrée, deadly pale,

"you will do me the favour of telling me when and where?"

"The day, mademoiselle, when a hundred thousand persons, crushed one against the other, fleeing from the fiery horses, and the sabres which thinned the crowd, left a long train of dead and dying upon the Place Louis XV."

"Ah! the 30th of May?"

"Yes, mademoiselle."

Andrée seated herself, and her features again assumed a pitiless smile.

"And on that day, you say, you sacrificed your life to save mine, Monsieur Gilbert?"

"I have already told you so."

"Then you are the Baron Balsamo. I beg your pardon, I was not aware of the fact."

"No, I am not the Baron Balsamo," replied Gilbert, with flashing eye and quivering lip; "I am the poor child of the people, — Gilbert, who has the folly, the madness, the misfortune, to love you; who, because he loved you like a madman, like a fool, like a sot, followed you into the crowd; who, separated from you for a moment, recognised you by the piercing shriek you uttered when you lost your footing; who, forcing his way to you, shielded you with his arms until twenty thousand arms, pressing against his, broke their strength; who threw himself upon the stone wall against which you were about to be crushed, to afford you the softer repose of his corpse; and, perceiving among the crowd that strange man who seemed to govern his fellow-men, and whose name you have just pronounced, collected all his strength, all his energy, and raised you in his exhausted arms that this man might see you, seize hold of you, and save you! — Gilbert, who, in yielding you up to a more fortunate protector than himself, retained nothing but a shred of your dress, which he pressed to his lips! And it was time, for already the blood was rushing to his heart, to his temples, to his brain. The rolling tide of executioners and victims swept over him, and buried him beneath its waves, while you ascended aloft from its abyss to a haven of safety!"

Gilbert, in these hurried words, had shown himself as he was, — uncultivated, simple, almost sublime, in his resolution as in his love. Notwithstanding her contempt, Andrée could not refrain from gazing at him with astonishment. For a moment he believed that his narrative had been as irresistible as truth, — as love. But poor Gilbert did not take into his calculations incredulity, that demon prompted by hatred. Andrée, who hated Gilbert, did not allow herself to be moved by any of the forcible arguments of her despised lover.

She did not reply immediately, but looked at Gilbert, while something like a struggle took place in her mind. The young man, therefore, ill at ease during this freezing silence, felt himself obliged to add, as a sort of peroration, —

"And now, mademoiselle, do not detest me as you did formerly, for now it would not only be injustice, but ingratitude, to do so. I said so before, and I now repeat it."

At these words Andrée raised her haughty brow, and in the most indifferent and cutting tone, she asked, —

"How long, Monsieur Gilbert, did you remain under Monsieur Rousseau's tutelage?"

"Mademoiselle," said Gilbert, ingenuously, "I think about three months, without reckoning the few days of my illness, which was caused by the accident on the 30th of May."

"You misunderstand me," said she; "I did not ask you whether you had been ill or not, or what accidents you may have received. They add an artistic finish to your story, but otherwise they are of no importance to me. I merely wished to tell you, that, having resided only three months with the illustrious author, you have profited well by his lessons, and that the pupil at his first essay composes romances almost worthy of his master."

Gilbert had listened with calmness, believing that Andrée

was about to reply seriously to his impassioned narration; but at this stroke of cutting irony, he fell from the summit of his buoyant hopes to the dust.

"A romance!" murmured he, indignantly; "you treat what I have told you as a romance!"

"Yes, monsieur," said Andrée, "a romance — I repeat the word; only you did not force me to read it — for that I have to thank you. I deeply regret that, unfortunately, I am not able to repay its full value; but I should make the attempt in vain — the romance is invaluable."

"And this is your reply?" stammered Gilbert, a pang darting through his heart, and his eyes becoming dim from emotion.

"I do not reply at all, monsieur," said Andrée, pushing him aside to allow her room to pass on.

The fact was, that Nicole had at that moment made her appearance at the end of the alley, calling her mistress, while still a considerable distance off, in order not to interrupt this interview too suddenly, ignorant as she was as to whom Andrée's companion might be, for she had not recognised Gilbert through the foliage. But as she approached she saw the young man, recognised him, and stood astounded; she then repented not having made a détour, in order to overhear what Gilbert had to say to Mademoiselle de Taverney. The latter addressed her in a softened voice, as if to mark more strongly to Gilbert the haughtiness with which she had spoken to him.

"Well, child," said she, "what is the matter?"

"The Baron de Taverney and the Duke de Richelieu have come to present their respects to mademoiselle," replied Nicole.

"Where are they?"

"In mademoiselle's apartments."

"Come, then."

And Andrée moved away. Nicole followed, not without throwing, as she passed, a sarcastic glance back at Gilbert, who, livid with agitation, and almost frantic with rage,

shook his clenched hand in the direction of his departing
enemy, and, grinding his teeth, muttered, —

"Oh! creature without heart, without soul! I saved
your life; I concentrated all my affection on you; I extinguished every feeling which might offend your purity, for
in my madness I looked upon you as some superior being,
— the inhabitant of a higher sphere! Now that I have
seen you more nearly, I find you are no more than a woman
— and I am a man! But one day or other, Andrée de
Taverney, I shall be revenged!"

He rushed from the spot, bounding through the thickest
of the shrubs like a young wolf wounded by the hunter,
who turns and shows his sharp teeth and his bloodshot
eyeballs.

## CHAPTER CXV.

### FATHER AND DAUGHTER.

WHEN she reached the opposite extremity of the alley, Andrée saw her father and the marshal walking up and down before the vestibule, waiting for her. The two friends seemed in high spirits, and as they stood with their arms interlaced, presented the most perfect representation of Orestes and Pylades the court had ever witnessed. As Andrée approached, the two old men seemed still more joyous, and remarked to each other on her radiant beauty, heightened by her walk, and by the emotion she had previously undergone.

The marshal saluted Andrée as he would have done a declared Madame Pompadour. This distinction did not escape Taverney, who was delighted at it, but it surprised Andrée, from its mixture of respect and gallantry; for the cunning courtier could express as many shades of meaning in a bow as Covielle could French phrases by a single Turkish word.

Andrée returned the marshal's salutation, made one equally ceremonious to her father, and then, with fascinating grace, she invited both to follow her to her apartment.

The marshal admired the exquisite neatness which was the only ornament of the furniture and architecture of this retreat. With a few flowers and a little white muslin, Andrée had made her rather gloomy chamber, not a palace, indeed, but a temple.

The duke seated himself upon an arm-chair covered with green chintz, beneath a Chinese cornucopia, from which drooped bunches of perfumed acacia and maple, mingled with iris and Bengal roses.

Taverney occupied a similar chair; and Andrée sank upon a folding-stool, her arm resting on a harpsichord also ornamented with flowers, arranged in a large Dresden vase.

"Mademoiselle," said the marshal, "I come as the bearer, on the part of his Majesty, of the compliments which your charming voice and your musical talents drew from every auditor of yesterday's rehearsal. His Majesty feared to arouse jealousy by praising you too openly at the time, and he therefore charged me to express to you the pleasure you have caused him."

Andrée blushed, and her blush made her so lovely that the marshal proceeded as if speaking on his own account.

"The king has assured me," said he, "that he never saw any one at his court who united to such a high degree the gifts of mind and the charms of personal beauty."

"You forget those of the heart," said Taverney, with a gush of affection; "Andrée is the best of daughters."

The marshal thought for a moment that his old friend was about to weep. Admiring deeply this display of paternal sensibility, he exclaimed,—

"The heart! alas, my dear friend! you alone can judge of the tenderness of which mademoiselle's heart is capable. Were I only five-and-twenty years of age, I would lay my life and my fortune at her feet!"

Andrée did not know how to receive coolly the full fire of a courtier's homage; she could only murmur some almost inaudible words.

"Mademoiselle," continued he, "the king requests you will accept a slight testimony of his satisfaction, and he has charged the baron, your father, to transmit it to you. What reply shall I make to his Majesty from you?"

"Monsieur," replied Andrée, animated by no feeling but that respect which is due to a monarch from all his subjects, "assure his Majesty of my deep gratitude; tell him that he honours me too highly by deigning to think of me, and that I am not worthy the attention of so powerful a monarch."

Richelieu seemed in raptures at this reply, which Andrée pronounced with a firm voice, and without hesitation.   He took her hand, kissed it respectfully, and devouring her with his eyes, —

"A royal hand," said he, "a fairy foot,— mind, purity, resolution!   Ah, baron, what a treasure!   It is not a daughter whom you have — it is a queen!"

With these words he retired, leaving Taverney alone with Andrée, his heart swelling with pride and hope.

Whoever had seen this advocate of antiquated theories, this sceptic, this scoffer, inhaling with delight the air of favouritism in its most disreputable channel, would have said that God had blinded at the same moment both his intellect and heart.   Taverney alone might have replied, with reference to this change, —

"It is not I who have changed — it is the times."

He remained, then, seated beside Andrée, and could not help feeling somewhat embarrassed; for the young girl, with her air of unconquerable serenity, and her clear, limpid, unfathomable look, seemed as if she would penetrate his most secret thoughts.

"Did not Monsieur de Richelieu, monsieur, say that his Majesty had entrusted you with a testimony of his satisfaction?   May I ask what it is?"

"Ah!" thought Taverney, "she is curious — so much the better!   I could not have expected it.   So much the better!"

He drew the casket, which the marshal had given him the evening before, slowly from his pocket, just as a kind papa produces a paper of sweetmeats or a toy, which the children have devoured with their eyes before their hands can reach them.

"Here it is," said he.

"Ah! jewels!" said Andrée.

"Are they to your taste?"

It was a set of pearls of great value.   Twelve immense diamonds connected together the rows of pearls, while a

diamond clasp, earrings, and a tiara of the same precious
material, made the present worth at least thirty thousand
crowns.

"Good heavens, father!" exclaimed Andrée.

"Well?"

"It is too handsome. The king has made some mistake.
I should be ashamed to wear that. I have no dresses suitable to the splendour of these diamonds."

"Oh! complain of it, I beg!" said Taverney, ironically.

"You do not understand me, monsieur. I regret that I
cannot wear these jewels, because they are too beautiful."

"The king, who gives the casket, mademoiselle, is generous enough to add the dresses."

"But, monsieur, this is goodness on the king's part —"

"Do you not think I have deserved it by my services?"

"Ah! pardon me, monsieur; that is true," said Andrée,
drooping her head, but not quite convinced.

After a moment's reflection, she closed the casket.

"I shall not wear these diamonds," said she.

"And why not?" said Taverney, uneasily.

"Because, my dear father, you and my brother are in
want of necessaries, and this superfluity offends my eyes
when I think of your embarrassments."

Taverney smiled and pressed her hand.

"Oh!" said he, "do not think of that, my daughter.
The king has done more for me than for you. We are in
favour, my dear child. It would neither be respectful as a
subject, nor grateful as a woman, to appear before his
majesty without the present he has made you."

"I shall obey, monsieur."

"Yes, but you must obey as if it gave you pleasure to do
so. These ornaments seem not to be to your taste."

"I am no judge of diamonds, monsieur."

"Learn, then, that the pearls alone are worth fifty thousand francs."

Andrée clasped her hands.

"Monsieur," said she, "it is most strange that his
Majesty should make me such a present; reflect!"

"I do not understand you, mademoiselle," replied Taverney, drily.

"If I wear these jewels, I assure you, monsieur, every one will be greatly surprised."

"Why?" asked Taverney in the same tone, and with a cold and imperious glance which made Andrée lower her eyes.

"I feel a scruple."

"Mademoiselle, you must confess that it is strange you should entertain scruples, when even I, your father, feel none. Give me your young modest girls for seeing evil and finding it out, however closely hidden it is, and when none other had remarked it! None like maidenly and simple girls for making old grenadiers like myself blush!"

Andrée hid her blushing face in her lovely white hands.

"Oh! my brother," she murmured to herself, "why are you already so far from me?"

Did Taverney hear these words, or did he guess their purport with that wonderful perspicacity which we know he possessed? We cannot tell, but he immediately changed his tone, and, taking Andrée's hand in his, —

"Come, my child," said he, "is not your father your friend?"

A heavenly smile chased the shadow from Andrée's brow.

"Shall I not be here to love you — to advise you? Are you not proud to contribute to my happiness and that of your brother?"

"Oh, yes!" said Andrée.

The baron fixed a caressing look upon his daughter.

"Well!" said he, "you shall be, as Monsieur de Richelieu said just now, the Queen of Taverney. The king has distinguished you, and the dauphiness also," added he, hastily. "In your intimacy with these two august personages, you will found our future fortunes by making them happy. The friend of the dauphiness, and — of the king! What a glorious career! You have superior talents and unrivalled beauty, a pure and healthy mind untainted by avarice and ambition. Oh! my child, what a part you might play ! Do you remember the maiden who soothed the last moments of Charles VI. ? Her name is cherished in France. Do you remember Agnes Sorel, who restored the honour of the French crown ? All good Frenchmen respect her memory. Andrée, you will be the support of the old age of our glorious monarch. He will cherish you as his daughter, and you will reign in France by the divine right of beauty, courage, and fidelity ! "

Andrée opened her eyes wide with astonishment. The baron resumed, without giving her time to reflect.

" With a single look you will drive away these wretched creatures who dishonour the throne ; your presence will purify the court. To your generous influence the nobility of the kingdom will owe the return of pure morals, politeness, and real gallantry. My daughter, you may be, you must be, the regenerating star of your country, and a crown of glory to your name."

" But," said Andrée, all bewildered, " what must I do to effect all this ? "

The baron reflected for a moment.

" Andrée," said he, " I have often told you that in this world you must force men to be virtuous by making them love virtue. Sullen, melancholy, sermonising virtue makes even those fly who wish most to approach her. Lend to your virtue all the allurements of coquetry, — I had almost said of vice. It is an easy task for a talented and high-minded girl such as you are. Make yourself so lovely that the court shall talk only of you ; make yourself so agreeable to the king that he cannot do without you. Be so reserved and discreet towards all, except his Majesty, that people will soon attribute to you all that power which you cannot fail ultimately to obtain."

" I do not exactly understand your last advice," said Andrée.

" Trust yourself to my guidance — you will fulfil my wishes without understanding them ; the best plan for such a wise and generous creature as you are. But, by-the-bye, to enable you to put in practice my first counsel, I must furnish your purse. Take these hundred louis-d'ors and dress in a manner worthy of the rank to which you belong, since his Majesty has distinguished us."

Taverney gave the hundred louis to his daughter, kissed her hand, and left her.

He returned with rapid steps along the alley by which he had come, so much engrossed in his reflections that he did not perceive Nicole in eager conference with a nobleman at the extremity of the Bosquet des Amours.

## CHAPTER CXVI.

WHAT ALTHOTAS WANTED TO COMPLETE HIS ELIXIR.

THE day subsequent to this conversation, about four o'clock in the afternoon, Balsamo was seated in his cabinet, in the Rue Saint Claude, occupied in reading a letter which Fritz had just brought him. The letter was without signature. He turned it over and over in his hands.

"I know this writing," said he; "large, irregular, slightly tremulous, and full of faults in orthography."

And he read it once more. It ran as follows:

"MONSEIGNEUR, — A person who consulted you some time before the fall of the late ministry, and who had consulted you a long time previously, will wait upon you to-day, in order to have another consultation. Will your numerous occupations permit you to grant this person a quarter of an hour between four and five this evening?"

After reading this for the second or third time, Balsamo fell back into his train of reflection.

"It is not worth while to consult Lorenza for such a trifle," said he; "besides, can I no longer guess myself? The writing is large — a sign of aristocracy; irregular and trembling — a sign of age; full of faults in orthography — it must be a courtier. — Ah! stupid creature that I am! it is the Duke de Richelieu! Most certainly I shall have a half-hour at your service, my lord duke — an hour did I say? — a day! Make my time your own. Are you not, without knowing it, one of my mysterious agents, one of my familiar demons? Do we not both pursue the same task? Do we not both shake the monarchy at the same time — you by making yourself its presiding genius, I by declaring myself its enemy? Come, then, duke, I am ready!"

And Balsamo consulted his watch to see how long he must yet wait for the duke. At that moment a bell sounded in the cornice of the ceiling.

"What can be the matter?" said Balsamo, starting; "Lorenza calls me — she wishes to see me. Can anything unpleasant have happened to her? or is it a return of those fits of passion which I have so often witnessed, and of which I have been at times the victim? Yesterday she was thoughtful, gentle, resigned; she was as I loved to see her. Poor child! I must go to her."

He arranged his dress, glanced at the mirror to see if his hair was not too much in disorder, and proceeded towards the stairs, after having replied to Lorenza's request by a ring similar to her own.

But, according to his invariable custom, Balsamo paused in the apartment adjoining that occupied by the young girl, and turning, with his arms crossed, towards the direction where he supposed her to be, he commanded her to sleep, with that powerful will which recognised no obstacles. Then, as if doubting his own power, or as if he thought it necessary to redouble his precautions, he looked into the apartment through an almost imperceptible crevice in the wood-work.

Lorenza was sleeping upon a couch, to which she had, no doubt, tottered under the influence of her master's will, and had sought a support for her sinking limbs. A painter could not have suggested a more poetic attitude. Panting and subdued beneath the power of the subtle fluid which Balsamo had poured upon her, Lorenza seemed like one of those beautiful Ariadnes of Vanloo, with well-curved breasts and features expressive of fatigue or despair.

Balsamo entered by his usual passage, and stopped for a moment before her to contemplate her sleeping countenance. He then awoke her.

As she opened her eyes, a piercing glance escaped from between the half-closed lids; then, as if to collect her scattered thoughts, she smoothed back her long hair with her hands, dried her lips, moist with slumber, and seemed to reflect anxiously.

Balsamo looked at her with some anxiety. He had been long accustomed to the sudden transition from winning love to outbursts of anger and hatred; but this appearance, to which he was entirely unused — the calmness with which Lorenza on this occasion received him, instead of giving way to a burst of hatred — announced something more serious, perhaps, than he had yet witnessed.

Lorenza sat up on the couch, and fixing her deep, soft eyes upon Balsamo, she said, —

"Pray be good enough to take a seat beside me."

Balsamo started at the sound of her voice, expressing as it did such unusual mildness.

"Beside you!" said he. "You know, my Lorenza, that I have but one wish — to pass my life at your feet."

"Monsieur," replied Lorenza, in the same tone, "I pray you be seated, although, indeed, I have not much to say to you; but, short as it is, I shall say it better, I think, if you are seated."

"Now, as ever, my beloved Lorenza, I shall do as you wish."

And he took a chair near Lorenza, who was still seated upon the couch.

"Monsieur," said she fixing her heavenly eyes upon Balsamo, "I have summoned you to request from you a favour."

"Oh! my Lorenza," exclaimed Balsamo, more and more delighted, "anything you wish! speak — you shall have everything!"

"I wish for only one; but I warn you that I wish for this one most ardently."

"Speak, Lorenza, speak! — should it cost my fortune, or half my life."

"It will cost you nothing, monsieur, but a moment of your time," replied the young girl.

Balsamo, enchanted with the turn the conversation was taking, was already tasking his fertile imagination to supply a list of those wishes which Lorenza was likely to form, and, above all, those which he could satisfy. "She will, perhaps," thought he, "ask for a servant or a companion. Well, even this immense sacrifice — for it would compromise my secret and my friends — I will make, for the poor child is, in truth, very unhappy in her solitude."

"Speak quickly, my Lorenza," said he aloud, with a smile full of love.

"Monsieur," said she, "you are aware that I am pining away with melancholy and weariness."

Balsamo sighed, and bent his head in token of assent.

"My youth," continued Lorenza, "is wasted; my days are one long sigh — my nights a continual terror. I am growing old in solitude and anguish."

"Your life is what you have made it, Lorenza," said Balsamo; "it is not my fault that this life which you have made so sad is not one to make a queen envious."

"Be it so. Therefore it is I, you see, who have recourse to you in my distress."

"Thanks, Lorenza."

"You are a good Christian, you have sometimes told me, although —"

"Although you think me lost to heaven, you would say. I complete your thought, Lorenza."

"Suppose nothing except what I tell you, monsieur; and pray do not conjecture thus groundlessly."

"Proceed, then."

"Well, instead of leaving me plunged in this despair and wrath, grant me, since I am of no service to you —"

She stopped to glance at Balsamo, but he had regained his command over himself, and she only saw a cold look and contracted brow bent upon her.

She became animated as she met his almost threatening eye.

"Grant me," continued she, "not liberty, — for I know that some mysterious secret, or rather, your will, which seems all-powerful to me, condemns me to perpetual captivity, — but at least to see human faces, to hear other voices than yours; permit me, in short, to go out, to walk, to take exercise."

"I had foreseen this request, Lorenza," said Balsamo, taking her hand; "and you know that long since your wish has been also my own."

"Well, then!" exclaimed Lorenza.

"But," resumed Balsamo, "you have yourself prevented it. Like a madman that I was — and every man who loves is such — I allowed you to penetrate into some of my secrets, both of science and politics. You know that Althotas has discovered the philosopher's stone, and seeks the elixir of life; you know that I and my companions conspire against the monarchies of this world. The first of these secrets would cause me to be burnt as a sorcerer; the other would be sufficient to condemn me to be broken on the wheel for high treason. Besides, you have threatened me, Lorenza, — you have told me that you would try every means to regain your liberty; and this liberty once regained, that the first use you would make of it would be to denounce me to Monsieur de Sartines. Did you not say so?"

"What can you expect? At times I lash myself to fury, and then I am half mad."

"Are you calm and sensible now, Lorenza? and can we converse quietly together?"

"I hope so."

"If I grant you the liberty you desire, shall I find in you a devoted and submissive wife — a faithful and gentle companion? You know, Lorenza, this is my most ardent wish."

The young girl was silent.

"In one word — will you love me?" asked Balsamo, with a sigh.

"I am unwilling to promise what I cannot perform," said Lorenza; "neither love nor hatred depends upon ourselves. I hope that God, in return for your good actions, will permit my hatred towards you to take flight, and love to return."

"Unfortunately, Lorenza, such a promise is not a sufficient guarantee that I may trust you. I require a positive, sacred oath, to break which would be a sacrilege, — an oath which binds you in this world as in the next, which would bring with it your death in this world and your damnation in that which is to come."

Lorenza was silent.

"Will you take this oath?"

Lorenza hid her face in her hands, and her breast heaved under the influence of contending emotions.

"Take this oath, Lorenza, as I shall dictate it in the solemn terms in which I shall clothe it, and you shall be free."

"What must I swear, monsieur?"

"Swear that you will never, under any pretext, betray what has come to your knowledge relative to the secrets of Althotas."

"Yes, I will swear it."

"Swear that you will never divulge what you know of our political meetings."

"I will swear that also."

"With the oath and in the form which I shall dictate?"

"Yes. Is that all?"

"No; swear — and this is the principal one, Lorenza; for the other matters would only endanger my life, whilst upon the one I am about to name depends my entire happiness — swear that you will never, either at the instigation of another's will, or in obedience to your own, leave me, Lorenza. Swear this, and you are free."

The young girl started as if cold steel had pierced her heart.

"And in what form must the oath be taken?"

"We will enter a church together, and communicate at the same altar. You will swear on the host never to betray anything relating to Althotas or my companions. You will swear never to leave me. We will then divide the host in two, and each will take the half, you swearing before God that you will never betray me, and I that I will ever do my utmost to make you happy."

"No!" said Lorenza; "such an oath is a sacrilege."

"An oath, Lorenza, is never a sacrilege," replied Balsamo, sadly, "but when you make it with the intention of not keeping it."

"I will not take this oath," said Lorenza; "I should fear to peril my soul."

"It is not — I repeat it — in taking an oath that you peril your soul; it is in breaking it."

"I cannot do it."

"Then learn patience, Lorenza," said Balsamo, without anger, but with the deepest sadness.

Lorenza's brow darkened like an overshadowed plain when a cloud passes between it and the sun.

"Ah! you refuse?" said she.

"Not so, Lorenza; it is you who refuse."

A nervous movement indicated all the impatience the young girl felt at these words.

"Listen, Lorenza!" said Balsamo. "This is what I will do for you, and, believe me, it is much."

"Speak!" said the young girl, with a bitter smile. "Let me see how far your generosity will extend."

"God, chance, or fate — call it what you will, Lorenza — has united us in an indissoluble bond; do not attempt to break this bond in this life, for death alone can accomplish that."

"Proceed; I know that," said Lorenza, impatiently.

"Well, in one week, Lorenza — whatever it may cost me, and however great the sacrifice I make — in eight days you shall have a companion."

"Where?" asked she.

"Here."

"Here!" she exclaimed, "behind these bars — behind these inexorable doors, these iron doors — a fellow-prisoner! Oh, you cannot mean it, monsieur; that is not what I ask!"

"Lorenza, it is all that I can grant."

The young girl made a more vehement gesture of impatience.

"My sweetest girl," resumed Balsamo, mildly, "reflect a little; with a companion you will more easily support the weight of this necessary misfortune."

"You mistake, monsieur. Until now I have grieved only for myself, not for others. This trial only was wanting, and I see that you wish to make me undergo it. Yes, you will immure beside me a victim like myself; I shall see her grow thinner and paler, and pine away with grief, even as I do; I shall see her dash herself, as I do, against these walls, that hateful door, which I examine twenty times each day to see where it opens to give you egress; and when my companion, your victim, has, like me, wounded her hands against the marble blocks in her endeavours to disjoin them; when, like me, she has worn out her eyelids with her tears; when she is dead as I am, in soul and mind, and you have two corpses in place of one, you will say, in your hateful benevolence: ' These two young creatures amuse themselves; they keep each other company; they are happy!' Oh! no, no, no! a thousand times no!"

And she passionately stamped her foot upon the ground, while Balsamo endeavoured in vain to calm her.

"Come, Lorenza," said he, "I entreat you to show a little more mildness and calmness. Let us reason on the matter."

"He asks me to be calm, to be gentle, to reason! The executioner tells the victim whom he is torturing to be gentle, and the innocent martyr to be calm!"

"Yes, Lorenza; I ask you to be gentle and calm, for your anger cannot change our destiny; it only embitters it. Accept what I offer you, Lorenza; I will give you a companion who will hug her chains, since they have procured for her your friendship. You shall not see a sad and tearful face, such as you fear, but smiles and gaiety which will smooth your brow. Come, dearest Lorenza, accept what I offer; for I swear to you that I cannot offer you more."

"That means that you will place near me a hireling, to whom you will say: 'I give you in charge a poor, insane creature, who imagines herself ill and about to die; soothe her, share her confinement, attend to her comforts, and I will recompense you when she is no more.'"

"Oh, Lorenza! Lorenza!"

"No, that is not it; I am mistaken," continued Lorenza, with bitter irony; "I guess badly. But what can you expect? I am so ignorant, I know so little of the world. You will say to the woman: 'Watch over the madwoman, she is dangerous; report all her actions, all her thoughts, to me. Watch over her waking and sleeping.' And you will give her as much gold as she requires, for gold costs you nothing — you make it!"

"Lorenza, you wander; in the name of heaven, Lorenza, read my heart better! In giving you a companion, my beloved, I compromise such mighty interests that you would tremble for me if you did not hate me. In giving you a companion, I endanger my safety, my liberty, my very life, and, notwithstanding, I risk all to save you a little weariness."

"Weariness!" exclaimed Lorenza, with a wild and frantic laugh which made Balsamo shudder. "He calls it weariness!"

"Well, suffering. Yes, you are right, Lorenza; they are poignant sufferings. I repeat, Lorenza, have patience; a day will come when all your sufferings will cease; a day will come when you shall be free and happy."

" Will you permit me to retire to a convent and take the vows? "

" To a convent? "

" I will pray — first for you, and then for myself. I shall be closely confined, indeed, but I shall at least have a garden, air, space. I shall have a cemetery to walk in, and can seek beforehand among the tombs for the place of my repose. I shall have companions who grieve for their own sorrows, and not for mine. Permit me to retire to a convent, and I will take any vows you wish. A convent, Balsamo ! I implore you on my knees to grant this request ! "

" Lorenza ! Lorenza ! we cannot part. Mark me well — we are indissolubly connected in this world ! Ask for nothing which exceeds the limits of this house."

Balsamo pronounced these last words in so calm and determined a tone, that Lorenza did not even repeat the request.

" Then you refuse me? " said she, dejectedly.

" I cannot grant it."

" Is what you say irrevocable? "

" It is."

" Well, I have something else, then, to ask," said she, with a smile.

" Oh ! my good Lorenza, ever smile thus — only smile upon me, and you will compel me to do all you wish !"

" Oh, yes, I shall make you do all that I wish, provided I do everything that pleases you. Well, be it so; I will be as reasonable as possible."

" Speak, Lorenza, speak ! "

" Just now you said : ' One day, Lorenza, your sufferings shall cease — one day you shall be free and happy.' "

" Oh, yes, I said so; and I swear before heaven that I await that day as impatiently as yourself."

" Well, this day may arrive immediately, Balsamo," said the young Italian, with a caressing smile, which her husband had hitherto only seen in her sleep. " I am weary, very weary — you can understand my feelings; I am so young, and have already suffered so much! Well, my friend — for you say you are my friend — listen to me; grant me this happy day immediately."

"I hear you," said Balsamo, inexpressibly agitated.

"I end my appeal by the request I should have made at the commencement, Acharat."

The young girl shuddered.

"Speak, my beloved!"

"Well, I have often remarked, when you made experiments on some unfortunate animal, and when you told me that these experiments were necessary to the cause of humanity —I have often remarked that you possessed the secret of inflicting death, sometimes by a drop of poison, sometimes by an opened vein; that this death was calm, rapid as lightning, and that these unfortunate and innocent creatures, condemned as I am to the miseries of captivity, were instantly liberated by death, the first blessing they had received since their birth. Well — "

She stopped and turned pale.

"Well, my Lorenza?" repeated Balsamo.

"Well, what you sometimes do to these unfortunate animals for the interest of science, do now to me in the name of humanity. Do it for a friend, who will bless you with her whole heart, who will kiss your hands with the deepest gratitude, if you grant her what she asks. Do it, Balsamo, for me, who kneel here at your feet, who promise you with my last sigh more love and happiness than you have aroused in me during my whole life! — for me, Balsamo, who promise you a frank and beaming smile as I quit this earth. By the soul of your mother! by the sufferings of our blessed Lord! by all that is holy, and solemn, and sacred in the world of the living and of the dead! I implore you, kill me! kill me!"

"Lorenza!" exclaimed Balsamo, taking her in his arms as she rose after uttering these last words; "Lorenza, you are delirious. Kill you! You! my love! my life!"

Lorenza disengaged herself by a violent effort from Balsamo's grasp, and fell on her knees.

"I will never rise," said she, "until you have granted my request. Kill me without a shock, without violence, without pain; grant me this favour, since you say you love me; send me to sleep, as you have often done; only take away the awaking,— it is despair!"

"Lorenza, my beloved!" said Balsamo. "Oh, God! do you not see how you torture my heart? What! you are really so unhappy, then? Come, my Lorenza, rise; do not give way to despair. Alas! do you hate me, then, so very much?"

"I hate slavery, constraint, solitude; and as you make me a slave, unhappy and solitary — well, yes! I hate you!"

"But I love you too dearly to see you die, Lorenza. You shall not die, therefore; I will effect the most diffi-cult cure I have yet undertaken, my Lorenza, — I will make you love life!"

"No, no, that is impossible; you have made me long for death."

"Lorenza, for pity's sake! — I promise that soon — "

"Life or death!" exclaimed the young woman, becoming more and more excited. "This is the decisive day; will you give me life, — that is to say, liberty? will you give me death, — that is to say, repose?"

"Life, my Lorenza, life!"

"Then that is liberty."

Balsamo was silent.

"If not, death; a gentle death — by a draught, a needle's point — death during sleep! Repose! repose! repose!"

"Life and patience, Lorenza!"

Lorenza burst into a terrible laugh, and making a spring backwards, drew from her bosom a knife, with a blade so fine and sharp that it glittered in her hand like a flash of lightning.

Balsamo uttered a cry, but it was too late. When he

rushed forward and reached the hand, the weapon had already fulfilled its task, and had fallen on Lorenza's bleeding breast. Balsamo had been dazzled by the flash —he was blinded by the sight of blood.

In his turn he uttered a terrible cry, and seized Lorenza round the waist, meeting in midway her arm raised to deal a second blow, and receiving the weapon in his undefended hand. Lorenza, with a mighty effort, drew the weapon away, and the sharp blade glided through Balsamo's fingers. The blood streamed from his mutilated hand.

Then, instead of continuing the struggle, Balsamo extended his bleeding hand towards the young woman, and said, with a voice of irresistible command: "Sleep, Lorenza, sleep!—I will it."

But on this occasion the irritation was such that the obedience was not as prompt as usual.

"No, no!" murmured Lorenza, tottering, and attempting to strike again. "No, I will not sleep!"

"Sleep, I tell you!" said Balsamo, a second time, advancing a step towards her; "sleep, I command it!"

This time the power of Balsamo's will was so great that all resistance was in vain. Lorenza heaved a sigh, let the knife fall from her hand, and sank back upon the cushions.

Her eyes still remained open, but their threatening glare gradually died away, and finally they closed; her stiffened neck drooped; her head fell upon her shoulder like that of a wounded bird; a nervous shudder passed through her frame,—Lorenza was asleep.

Balsamo hastily opened her robe, and examined the wound, which seemed slight, although the blood flowed from it in abundance.

He then pressed the lion's eye, the spring started, and the back of the fireplace opened; then unfastening the counter-poise, which made the trap-door of Althotas's chamber descend, he leaped upon it and mounted to the old man's laboratory.

"Ah! it is you, Acharat," said the latter, who was still

seated in his arm-chair; "you are aware that in a week I shall be a hundred years old; you are aware that before that time I must have the blood of a child or of an unmarried female."

But Balsamo heard him not; he hastened to the cupboard in which the magic balsams were kept, seized one of the phials of which he had often proved the efficacy, again mounted upon the trap, stamped his foot, and descended to the lower apartment.

Althotas rolled his arm-chair to the mouth of the trap with the intention of seizing him by his dress.

"Do you hear, wretch?" said he, "do you hear? If in a week I have not a child or an unmarried woman to complete my elixir, I am a dead man!"

Balsamo turned; the old man's eyes seemed to glare in the midst of his unearthly and motionless features, as if they alone were alive.

"Yes, yes," replied Balsamo; "yes, be calm; you shall have what you want."

Then, letting go the spring, the trap mounted again, fitting like an ornament in the ceiling of the room.

After which he rushed into Lorenza's apartment, which he had just reached when Fritz's bell rang.

"Monsieur de Richelieu!" muttered Balsamo; "oh! duke and peer as he is, he must wait."

## CHAPTER CXVII.

### MONSIEUR DE RICHELIEU'S TWO DROPS OF WATER.

MONSIEUR DE RICHELIEU left the house in the Rue Saint Claude at half-past four. What his errand with Balsamo was will explain itself in the sequel.

Monsieur de Taverney had dined with his daughter, as the dauphiness had given her leave to absent herself on this day in order that she might receive her father.

They were at dessert, when Monsieur de Richelieu, ever the bearer of good news, made his appearance to announce to his friend that the king had said that he would give not merely a company to Philip, but a regiment. Taverney was exuberant in his expressions of joy, and Andrée warmly thanked the marshal.

The conversation took a turn which may be easily imagined after what had passed; Richelieu spoke of nothing but the king, Andrée of nothing but her brother, and Taverney of nothing but Andrée. The latter announced in the course of conversation that she was set at liberty from her attendance on the dauphiness; that her royal highness was receiving a visit from two German princes, her relations; and that in order to pass a few hours of liberty with them which might remind her of the court of Vienna, Marie Antoinette had dismissed all her attendants, even her lady of honour; which had so deeply shocked Madame de Noailles that she had gone to lay her grievances at the king's feet.

Taverney was, he said, delighted at this, since he had thus an opportunity of conversing with Andrée about many things relating to their fortune and name. This observation made Richelieu propose to retire, in order to leave the father and daughter quite alone; but Mademoiselle de Taverney would not permit it, so he remained.

Richelieu was in a vein of moralizing: he painted most eloquently the degradation into which the French nobility had fallen, forced as they were to submit to the ignominious yoke of these favourites of chance, these contraband queens, instead of the favourites of the olden times, who were almost as noble as their august lovers — women who reigned over the sovereign by their beauty and their love, and over his subjects by their birth, their strength of mind, and their loyal and pure patriotism.

Andrée was surprised at the close analogy between Richelieu's words and those she had heard from the Baron de Taverney a few days previously.

Richelieu then launched into a theory of virtue, so spiritual, so pagan, so French, that Andrée was obliged to confess that she was not at all virtuous according to Monsieur de Richelieu's theories, and that true virtue, as the marshal understood it, was the virtue of Madame Chateauroux, Mademoiselle de La Valliere, and Mademoiselle Fosseuse.

From argument to argument, from proof to proof, Richelieu at last became so clear that Andrée no longer understood a word of what he said. On this footing the conversation continued until about seven o'clock in the evening, when the marshal rose, being obliged, as he said, to pay his court to the king at Versailles.

In passing through the apartment to take his hat, he met Nicole, who had always something to do wherever Monsieur de Richelieu was.

" My girl," said he, tapping her on the shoulder, " you shall see me out. I want you to carry a bouquet which Madame de Noailles cut for me in her garden, and which she commissioned me to present to the Countess d'Egmont."

Nicole curtseyed like the peasant girls in Monsieur Rousseau's comic operas, whereupon the marshal took leave of father and daughter, exchanged a significant glance with Taverney, made a youthful bow to Andrée, and retired.

With the reader's permission, we will leave the baron and Andrée conversing about the fresh mark of favour conferred on Philip, and follow the marshal. By this means we shall know what was his errand at the Rue Saint Claude, where he arrived at such a fearful moment.

Moreover, the baron's arguments surpassed the moralizing of even his friend, the marshal, and might indeed shock the ears of those less pure than Andrée. Such people might perhaps partly understand his vile insinuations.

Richelieu descended the stairs resting on Nicole's shoulder, and as soon as they were in the garden he stopped, and looking her in the face said : —

" Ah! little one, so we have a lover ? "

" I! monseigneur! " exclaimed Nicole, blushing crimson, and retreating a step backwards.

" Oh! perhaps you are not called Nicole Legay ? "

" Yes, monseigneur."

" Well, Nicole Legay has a lover."

" Oh ! indeed ! "

" Yes, faith, a certain well-looking rascal, whom she used to meet in the Rue Coq-Héron, and who has followed her to Versailles."

" Monseigneur, I swear — "

" A sort of exempt, called — shall I tell you, child, how Mademoiselle Legay's lover is called ? "  .

Nicole's last hope was that the marshal was ignorant of the name of the happy mortal.

" Oh! yes, monseigneur, tell me, since you have made a beginning."

" Who is called Monsieur Beausire," repeated the marshal, " and who in truth does not belie his name."

Nicole clasped her hands with an affectation of prudery which did not in the least impose on Richelieu.

" It seems," said he, " we make appointments with him

at Trianon. *Peste!* in a royal château! that is a serious matter. One may be discharged for these freaks, my sweet one, and Monsieur de Sartines sends all young ladies who are discharged from the royal château to the Salpétrière."

Nicole began to be uneasy.

"Monseigneur," said she, "I swear to you that if Monsieur Beausire boasts of being my lover, he is a fool and a villain, for indeed I am innocent."

"I shall not contradict you," said Richelieu; "but have you made appointments with him or not?"

"Monseigneur, a rendezvous is no proof of — "

"Have you or have you not? Answer me."

" Monseigneur — "

" You have. Very well; I do not blame you, my dear child. Besides, I like pretty girls who display their charms, and I have always assisted them in so doing to the utmost of my power. Only, as your friend and protector, I warn you."

"But have I been seen, then?" asked Nicole.

"It seems so, since I am aware of it."

" Monseigneur," said Nicole resolutely, "I have not been seen; it is impossible!"

" As to that, I know nothing; but the report is very prevalent, and must tend to fasten attention on your mistress. Now, you must be aware that being more the friend of the Taverneys than of the Legays, it is my duty to give the baron a hint."

"Oh! monseigneur!" exclaimed Nicole, terrified at the turn the conversation was taking, " you will ruin me. Although innocent, I shall be discharged on the mere suspicion."

"In that case, my poor child, you shall be discharged at all events; for even now some evil-minded person or other, having taken offence at these rendezvous, innocent though they be, has informed Madame de Noailles of them."

" Madame de Noailles! good heavens!"

" Yes ; you see the danger is urgent."

Nicole clasped her hands in despair.

" It is unfortunate, I am aware," said Richelieu; "but what the deuce can you do?"

"And you, who said just now you were my protector — you, who have proved yourself to be such — can you no longer protect me?" asked Nicole, with a wheedling cunning worthy of a woman of thirty.

" Yes *pardieu!* I can protect you."

" Well, monseigneur?"

" Yes, but I will not."

" Oh! monseigneur."

" Yes ; you are pretty, I know that, and your beautiful eyes are telling me all sorts of things; but I have lately become rather blind, my poor Nicole, and I no longer understand the language of lovely eyes. Once I would have offered you an asylum in my pavilion of Hanover, but those days are over."

"Yet you once before received me there," said Nicole, angrily.

" Ah! that is ungrateful in you, Nicole, to reproach me with having taken you there, when I did so to render you a service; for confess that without Monsieur Rafté's assistance, who made you a charming brunette, you would never have entered Trianon, which, after all, perhaps, would have been better than to be dismissed from it now. But why the devil did you give a rendezvous to Monsieur Beausire, and at the very gate of the stables, too?"

" So you know that also?" said Nicole, who saw that she must change her tactics, and place herself at the marshal's discretion.

" *Parbleu!* you see I know it; and Madame de Noailles too. This very evening you have another appointment."

" That is true, monseigneur; but on my faith I shall not go."

" Of course, you are warned; but Monsieur Beausire is not warned, and he will be seized. Then, as he will not like of course to be taken for a thief and be hanged, or for a spy and be whipped, he will prefer to say — especially as there is no disgrace in confessing it — ' Unhand me ! I am the lover of the pretty Nicole.' "

" Monseigneur, I will send to warn him."

" Impossible, my poor child! by whom could you send ? By him who betrayed you, perhaps ? "

" Alas ! that is true," said Nicole, feigning despair.

" What a becoming thing remorse is ! " exclaimed Richelieu.

Nicole covered her face with her hands, taking care, however, to leave space enough between her fingers to allow her to observe every look and gesture of Richelieu.

" You are really adorable ! " said the duke, whom none of these little tricks could escape ; " why am I not fifty years younger ? No matter. *Parbleu!* Nicole, I will bring you out of the scrape."

" Oh, monseigneur ! if you do that, my gratitude — "

" I don't want it, Nicole. On the contrary, I shall give you most disinterested assistance."

" Oh! how good of you, monseigneur ; I thank you from the bottom of my heart."

" Do not thank me yet ; as yet you know nothing. *Diable!* wait till you hear more."

" I will submit to anything, provided Mademoiselle Andrée does not dismiss me."

" Ah ! then you wish very much to remain at Trianon ? "

" Very, monseigneur."

" Well, Nicole, in the very first place, get rid of this feeling."

" But why so, if I am not discovered, monseigneur ? "

" Whether you are discovered or not, you must leave Trianon."

" Oh! why ? "

" I shall tell you ; because if Madame de Noailles has found you out, no one, not even the king, could save you."

" Ah! if I could only see the king."

"In the second place, even if you are not found out, I myself should be the means of dismissing you."

"You ?"

"Immediately."

"In truth, monseigneur, I do not understand you."

"It is as I have had the honour of telling you."

"And that is your protection, is it ?"

"If you do not wish for it, there is yet time; you have only to say the word, Nicole."

"Oh, yes! monseigneur, on the contrary I do wish for it."

"And I will grant it."

"Well ?"

"Well, this is what I will do for you. Hark ye !"

"Speak, monseigneur."

"Instead of getting you discharged, and perhaps imprisoned, I will make you rich and free."

"Rich and free ?"

"Yes."

"And what must I do in order to be rich and free ?"

"Almost nothing."

"But what — "

"What I am about to tell you."

"Is it difficult ?"

"Mere child's play."

"Then," said Nicole, "there is something to do ?"

"Ah, *dame !* you know the motto of this world of ours, Nicole — *nothing for nothing !*"

"And that which I have to do, is it for myself or for you ?"

The duke looked at Nicole.

"*Tudieu !*" said he, "the little masker, how cunning she is !"

"Well, finish, monseigneur."

"Well! it is for yourself," replied he, boldly.

"Ah!" said Nicole, who, perceiving that the marshal had need of her services, already feared him no longer, while her ingenious brain was busily endeavouring to discover the truth amid the windings which, from habit, her companion always used; "what shall I have to do for myself, monseigneur ? "

"This: Monsieur Beausire comes at half-past seven, does he not ? "

"Yes, monseigneur, that is his hour."

"It is now ten minutes past seven."

"That is also true."

"If I say the word he will be arrested."

"Yes, but you will not say it."

"No. You will go to him, and tell him — but in the first place, Nicole, do you love this young man ? "

"Why, I have given him a rendezvous."

"That is no reason you may wish to marry him. Women take such strange caprices."

Nicole burst into a loud laugh.

"Marry him ! " said she. "Ha ! ha ! ha ! "

Richelieu was astounded: he had not, even at court, met many women of this stamp.

"Well," said he, " so be it. You do not wish to marry him; but in that case you love him. So much the better."

"Agreed ! I love Monsieur Beausire. Let us take that for granted, monseigneur, and proceed ! "

"*Peste!* what strides you make ! "

"Of course. You may readily imagine that I am anxious to know what remains for me to do."

"In the first place, since you love him, you must fly with him."

"*Dame!* if you wish it particularly, I suppose I must."

"Oh ! I wish nothing about it — not so fast, little one."

Nicole saw that she was going too far, and that as yet she had neither the secret nor the money of her cunning opponent. She stooped, therefore, only to rise again afterwards.

"Monseigneur," said she, " I await your orders."

"Well ! you must go to Monsieur Beausire and say to him: 'We are discovered; but I have a protector who will save you from Saint Lazarus, and me from the Salpêtrière. Let us fly.' "

Nicole looked at Richelieu.

" Fly ? " repeated she.

Richelieu understood her cunning and expressive look.

" *Parbleu!* " said he, " of course, I shall pay the expenses."

Nicole asked for no farther explanation. It was plain that she must know all, since she was to be paid.

The marshal saw what an important point Nicole had gained, and hastened to say all he had to say, just as a gambler is eager to pay when he has lost, in order to have the disagreeable task of paying over.

" Do you know what you are thinking of, Nicole ? " said he.

" Faith, no," replied the girl : " but I suppose you, monseigneur, who know so many things, can guess it."

" Nicole," he replied, " you were reflecting that if you fled, your mistress might require you during the night, and not finding you, might give the alarm, which would expose you to the risk of being overtaken and seized."

" No," said Nicole, " I was not thinking of that, because, after all, monseigneur, I think I would prefer remaining here."

" But if Monsieur Beausire is taken ? "

" Well, I cannot help it."

" But if he confess ? "

" Let him confess."

" Ah ! " said Richelieu, beginning to be uneasy, " but in that case you are lost."

" No ; for Mademoiselle Andrée is kindness itself, and as she loves me at heart, she will speak to the king for me ; so, even if Monsieur de Beausire is punished, I shall not share his punishment."

The marshal bit his lip.

" Nicole," said he, " I tell you you are a fool. Mademoiselle Andrée is not on such good terms with the king, and I will have you arrested immediately if you do not listen to me as I wish. Do you hear, you little viper ? "

"Oh! monseigneur, my ears do not serve me so ill.  I hear you, but I form my own conclusions."

"Good.  Then you will go at once and arrange your plan of flight with Monsieur Beausire."

"But how?  Do you imagine, monseigneur, that I shall expose myself to the risk of flight, when you tell me yourself that mademoiselle might awake, might ask for me, give the alarm, and a great deal more which I know not, but which you, monseigneur, who are a man of experience, must have foreseen?"

Richelieu bit his lip again, but this time more deeply than he had done before.

"Well, minion, if I have thought of these consequences, I have also thought of how to avoid them."

"And how will you manage to prevent mademoiselle from calling me?"

"By preventing her awaking."

"Bah! she awakes ten times during the night."

"Then she has the same malady that I have?" said Richelieu, calmly.

"The same that you have?" said Nicole, laughing.

"Yes.  I also awake ten times every night, only I have a remedy for this sleeplessness.  She must use the same remedy, or if not, you will do it for her."

"What do you mean, monseigneur?"

"What does your mistress take in the evening before she goes to bed?"

"What does she take?"

"Yes, it is the fashion now to drink something in the evening.  Some take orangeade or lemonade, others take *eau-de-Melisse*, others—"

"Mademoiselle drinks only a glass of pure water in the evening before going to bed; sometimes sweetened and flavoured with orange-water, if her nerves are weak."

"Ah, excellent!" said Richelieu, "just as I do myself.  My remedy will suit her admirably."

"How so?"

"I pour one drop of a certain liquid in my beverage, and I then never wake all night."

Nicole tasked her brain to discover to what end the marshal's diplomacy tended.

"You do not answer?" said he.

"I was just thinking that mademoiselle has not your cordial."

"I will give you some."

"Ah!" thought Nicole, seeing at last a ray of light through the darkness.

"You must put two drops of it in your mistress's glass — neither more nor less, remember — and she will sleep soundly, so that she will not call you, and consequently you will gain time."

"Oh! if that is all, it is very simple."

"You will give her the two drops?"

"Certainly."

"You promise me?"

"I presume it is for my own interest to do so; besides, I will lock the door so carefully — "

"By no means," said Richelieu, hastily. "That is exactly what you must not do; on the contrary, you must leave her room door open."

"Ah!" exclaimed Nicole, with suppressed joy. She now understood all. Richelieu saw it plainly. "Is that all?" inquired she.

"Absolutely all. Now you may go and tell your exempt to pack up his trunks."

"Unfortunately, monsieur, it would be useless to tell him to fill his purse."

"You know that is my affair."

"Yes, I remember your lordship was kind enough to say — "

"Come, Nicole, how much do you want?"

"For what?"

"For pouring in the two drops of water."

"For that, nothing, monseigneur, since you assure me I

do so for my own interest; it would not be just that you should pay me for attending to my own interest.    But for leaving mademoiselle's door open — ah! for that, I warn you, I must have a good round sum."

"At one word, how much?"

"I must have twenty thousand francs, monseigneur."

Richelieu started.

"Nicole," said he, with a sigh, "you will make some figure in the world."

"I ought to do so, monseigneur, for I begin to believe now that I shall attract attention.    But with your twenty thousand francs we shall smooth difficulties."

"Go and warn Monsieur Beausire, Nicole; and when you return I will give you the money."

"Monseigneur, Monsieur Beausire is very incredulous, and he will not believe what I tell him unless I can give him proofs."

Richelieu pulled out a handful of banknotes from his pocket.

"Here is something on account," said he; "in this purse there are a hundred double louis."

"Monseigneur will settle the account in full and give me the balance, then, when I have spoken to Monsieur Beausire?"

"No, *pardieu!* I will settle it on the spot.    You are a careful girl, Nicole; it will bring you luck."

And Richelieu handed her the promised sum, partly in banknotes, and partly in louis-d'or and half-louis.

"There!" said he, "is that right?"

"I think so," said Nicole; "and now, monseigneur, I want only the principal thing."

"The cordial?"

"Yes; of course monseigneur has a bottle?"

"I have my own, which I always carry about with me."

Nicole smiled.

"And then," said she, "Trianon is locked every night, and I have not a key."

"But I have one, as first gentleman of the chamber."

"Ah, indeed!"

"Here it is."

"How fortunate all this is!" said Nicole; "it is one succession of miracles! And now, monseigneur, adieu!"

"How! adieu?"

"Certainly. I shall not see monseigneur again, as I shall go as soon as mademioselle is asleep."

"Quite right. Adieu then, Nicole!"

And Nicole, laughing in her sleeve, disappeared in the increasing darkness.

"I shall still succeed," said Richelieu. "But, in truth, it would seem that I am getting old, and fortune is turning against me. I have been outwitted by this little one. But what matters it, if I return the blow?"

# CHAPTER CXVIII.

## THE FLIGHT.

NICOLE was a conscientious girl. She had received Monsieur de Richelieu's money, and received it in advance too, and she felt anxious to prove herself worthy of this confidence by earning her pay. She ran, therefore, as quickly as possible to the gate, where she arrived at forty minutes past seven, instead of at half-past. Now, Monsieur Beausire, who, being accustomed to military discipline, was a punctual man, had been waiting there for ten minutes. About ten minutes before, too, Monsieur de Taverney had left his daughter, and Andrée was consequently alone. Now, being alone, the young girl had closed the blinds.

Gilbert, as usual, was gazing eagerly at Andrée from his attic, but it would have been difficult to say if his eyes sparkled with love or hatred. When the blinds were closed Gilbert could see nothing. Consequently he looked in another direction, and, while looking, he perceived Monsieur Beausire's plume, and recognised the exempt, who was walking up and down, whistling an air to kill time while he was waiting.

In about ten minutes — that is to say, at forty minutes past seven — Nicole made her appearance. She exchanged a few words with Monsieur Beausire, who made a gesture with his head as a sign that he understood her perfectly, and disappeared by the shady alley leading to the Little Trianon. Nicole, light as a bird, returned in the direction she had come.

"Oh, oh!" thought Gilbert; "monsieur the exempt and

mademoiselle the *femme-de-chambre* have something to do or to say which they fear to have witnessed! Very good!"

Gilbert no longer felt any curiosity with respect to Nicole's movements, but actuated by the idea that the young girl was his natural enemy, he merely sought to collect a mass of proofs against her morality, with which proofs he might successfully repulse any attack, should she attempt one against him. And as he knew the campaign might begin at any moment, like a prudent soldier he collected his munitions of war.

A rendezvous with a man, in the very grounds of Trianon, was one of the weapons which a cunning enemy such as Gilbert could not neglect, especially when it was imprudently placed under his very eyes. Gilbert consequently wished to have the testimony of his ears as well as that of his eyes, and to catch some fatally compromising phrase which would completely floor Nicole at the first onset. He quickly descended from his attic, therefore, hastened along the lobby, and gained the garden by the chapel stairs. Once in the garden, he had nothing to fear, for he knew all its hiding-places, as a fox knows his cover. He glided beneath the linden-trees, then along the espalier, until he reached a small thicket situated about twenty paces from the spot where he calculated upon seeing Nicole.

As he had foreseen, Nicole was there. Scarcely had he installed himself in the thicket when a strange noise reached his ears; it was the chink of gold upon stone,— that metallic sound of which nothing, except the reality, can give a correct idea.

Like a serpent, Gilbert glided along to a raised terrace, out-topped by a hedge of lilacs, which at that season (early in May) diffused their perfume around, and showered down their flowers upon the passers who took the shady alley on their way from the Great to the Little Trianon.

Having reached this retreat, Gilbert, whose eyes were accustomed to pierce the darkness, saw Nicole emptying the purse which Monsieur de Richelieu had given her, upon a stone on the inner side of the gate, and prudently placed out of Monsieur Beausire's reach.

The large louis-d'or showered from it in bright profusion, while Monsieur Beausire, with sparkling eye and trembling hand, looked at Nicole and her louis-d'or as if he could not comprehend how the one should possess the other.

Nicole spoke first.

"You have more than once, my dear Monsieur Beausire," said she, "proposed to elope with me."

"And even to marry you," exclaimed the enthusiastic exempt.

"Oh! my dear monsieur, that is a matter of course; just now, flight is the most important point. Can we fly in two hours?"

"In ten minutes, if you like."

"No; I have something to do first, which will occupy me two hours."

"In two hours, as in ten minutes, I shall be at your orders, dearest."

"Very well. Take these fifty louis."

Nicole counted the fifty louis, and handed them through the gate to Monsieur Beausire, who, without counting them, stuffed them into his waistcoat pocket.

"And in an hour and a half," continued she, "be here with a carriage."

"But —" objected Beausire.

"Oh, if you do not wish, forget what has passed between us, and give me back my fifty louis."

"I do not shrink, dearest Nicole; but I fear the result."

"For whom?"

"For you."

"For me?"

"Yes; the fifty louis once vanished, and vanished they will soon be, you will complain; you will regret Trianon; you will —"

"Oh, how thoughtful you are, Monsieur Beausire! But fear nothing; I am not one of those women who are easily made miserable. Have no scruples on that score; when the fifty louis are gone, we shall see."

And she shook the purse which contained the other fifty. Beausire's eyes were absolutely phosphorescent.

"I would charge through a blazing furnace for your sake!" exclaimed he.

"Oh, content you; I shall not require so much from you, monsieur. Then it is agreed you will be here with the chaise in an hour and a half, and in two hours we shall fly?"

"Agreed!" exclaimed Beausire, seizing Nicole's hand, and drawing it through the gate to kiss it.

"Hush!" said Nicole, "are you mad?"

"No; I am in love."

"Hum!" muttered Nicole.

"Do you not believe me, sweetheart?"

"Yes, yes, I believe you — above all, be sure to have good horses."

"Oh, yes."

And they separated.

But a moment afterwards Beausire returned quite alarmed.

"Hist!" whispered he.

"Well, what is it?" asked Nicole, already some distance off, and putting her hand to her mouth, so as to convey her voice farther.

"And the gate?" asked Beausire, "will you creep under it?"

"How stupid he is!" murmured Nicole, who at this moment was not ten paces distant from Gilbert. Then she added in a louder tone, —

"I have the key."

Beausire uttered a prolonged "oh!" of admiration, and this time took to his heels for good and all. Nicole hastened back with drooping head and nimble step to her mistress.

Gilbert, now left sole master of the field, put the following four questions to himself: —

"Why does Nicole fly with Beausire, when she does not love him?

"How does Nicole come to possess such a large sum of money?

"Why has Nicole the key of the gate?

"Why does Nicole return to Andrée, when she might go at once?"

Gilbert found an answer to the second question, but to the others he could find none.

Thus checked at the commencement, his natural curiosity and his acquired distrust were so much excited that he determined to remain in the cold, beneath the dew-covered trees, to await the end of this scene, of which he had witnessed the commencement.

Andrée had conveyed her father to the barriers of the Great Trianon, and was returning alone and pensive, when Nicole appeared issuing from the alley leading to the famous gate where she had been concerting her measures with Monsieur Beausire.

Nicole stopped on perceiving her mistress, and, upon a sign which Andrée made to her, she followed her to her apartment.

It was now about half-past eight in the evening. The night had closed in earlier than usual; for a huge cloud, sweeping from south to north, had overspread the whole sky, and all around, as far as the eye could reach over the lofty forest of Versailles, the gloomy shroud was gradually enveloping in its folds the stars, a short time before sparkling in the azure dome. A light breeze swept along the ground, breathing warmly on the drooping flowers, which bent their heads as if imploring heaven to send them rain or dew.

The threatening aspect of the sky did not hasten Andrée's steps; on the contrary, melancholy and thoughtful, the young girl seemed to ascend each step leading to her room with regret, and she paused at every window as she passed to gaze at the sky, so much in harmony with her saddened mood, and thus to delay her return to her own little retreat.

Nicole, impatient, angry, fearing that some whim might detain her mistress beyond the uusal hour, grumbled and muttered, as servants never fail to do when their masters are imprudent enough to satisfy their own caprices at the expense of those of their domestics.

At last Andrée reached the door of her chamber, and sank rather than seated herself upon a couch, gently ordering Nicole to leave the window, which looked upon the court, half open.

Nicole obeyed; then, returning to her mistress with that affectionate air which the flatterer could so easily assume, she said, —

"I fear mademoiselle feels ill this evening; her eyes are red and swollen, yet bright. I think that mademoiselle is in great need of repose."

"Do you think so?" asked Andrée, who had scarcely listened.

And she carelessly placed her feet upon a cushion of tapestry work.

Nicole took this as an order to undress her mistress, and commenced to unfasten the ribbons and flowers of her head-dress, — a species of edifice which the most skilful could not unbuild in less than a quarter of an hour. While she was thus employed, Andrée did not utter a word, and Nicole, thus left to follow her own wishes, hastened the business, without disturbing Andrée, whose preoccupation was so great that she permitted Nicole to pull out her hair with impunity.

When the night toilet was finished, Andrée gave her orders for the morrow. In the morning some books were to be fetched from Versailles which Philip had left there for his sister, and the tuner was to be ordered to attend to put the harpsichord in proper order.

Nicole replied, that if she were not called during the night, she would rise early, and would have both these commissions executed before her young lady was awake.

"To-morrow, also, I will write to Philip," said Andrée, speaking to herself; "that will console me a little."

"Come what will," thought Nicole, "I shall not carry the letter."

And at this reflection the girl, who was not quite lost yet, began to think, in saddened mood, that she was about, for the first time, to leave that excellent mistress under whose care her mind and heart had been awakened. The thought of Andrée was linked in her mind with so many other recollections, that to touch it was to stir the whole chain which carried her back to the first days of infancy.

Whilst these two young creatures, so different in their character and their condition, were thus reflecting beside each other, without any connection existing between their thoughts, time was rapidly flying, and Andrée's little time-piece, which was always in advance of the great clock of Trianon, struck nine.

Beausire would be at the appointed place, and Nicole had but half an hour to join her lover.

She finished her task as quickly as possible, not without uttering some sighs, which Andrée did not even notice; she folded a night-shawl around her mistress, and as Andrée still sat immovable, with her eyes fixed on the ceiling, she drew Richelieu's phial from her bosom, put two pieces of sugar into a goblet, added the water necessary to melt it, and without hesitation, and by the resolute force of her will, so strong in one so young, she poured two drops of the fluid from the phial into the water, which immediately became turbid, then changed to a slight opal tint, which soon died away.

"Mademoiselle," said Nicole, "your glass of water is prepared, your clothes are folded, the night-lamp is lighted.

You know I must rise very early to-morrow morning; may I go to bed now? "

"Yes," replied Andrée, absently.

Nicole curtseyed, heaved a last sigh, which, like the others, was unnoticed, and closed behind her the glass door leading to the anteroom. But instead of retiring into her little cell adjoining the corridor, and lighted from Andrée's anteroom, she softly took to flight, leaving the door of the corridor ajar, so that Richelieu's instructions were scrupulously followed.

Then, not to arouse the attention of the neighbours, she descended the stairs on tiptoe, bounded down the outer steps, and ran quickly to join Monsieur Beausire at the gate.

Gilbert had not quitted his post; he had heard Nicole say that she would return in two hours, and he waited. But as it was now ten minutes past the hour, he began to fear that she would not return.

All at once he saw her running as if some one were pursuing her.

Nicole approached the gate, passed the key through the bars to Beausire, who opened it, rushed out, and the gate closed with a dull, grating noise. The key was then thrown among the grass in the ditch, near the spot where Gilbert was stationed; he heard it fall with a dead sound, and marked the place where it had dropped.

Nicole and Beausire in the mean time gained ground; Gilbert heard them move away, and soon he could distinguish, not the noise of a carriage, as Nicole had required, but the pawing of a horse, which, after some moment's delay,—occupied, doubtless, by Nicole in recrimination, who had wished to depart, like a duchess, in her carriage, —changed to the clattering of his iron-shod feet on the pavement, and at last died away in the distance.

Gilbert breathed freely; he was free, free from Nicole, —that is to say, from his enemy. Andrée was henceforth alone.

Perhaps, when Nicole fled, she had forgotten the key, and left it in the door; perhaps he could enter Andrée's room. This thought aroused in the young man a frenzy of hope and fear, of curiosity and desire.

He took the contrary direction from the one Nicole was pursuing, and hurried towards the offices of Trianon.

## CHAPTER CXIX.

### DOUBLE SIGHT.

WHEN Andrée was alone she gradually recovered from the mental torpor into which she had fallen, and while Nicole was flying *en croupe* behind Monsieur Beausire, she knelt down and offered up a fervent prayer for Philip, the only being in the world she loved with a true and deep attachment; and while she prayed, her trust in God assumed new strength and inspired her with fresh courage.

The prayers which Andrée offered were not composed of a succession of words strung one to the other; they were a kind of heavenly ecstasy, during which her soul rose to her God and mingled with His spirit.

In these impassioned supplications of the mind, freed from earthly concerns, there was no alloy of self. Andreé in some degree abandoned all thoughts of herself, — like a shipwrecked mariner who has lost hope, and who prays only for his wife and his children, soon to become orphans. This inward grief had sprung up in Andrée's bosom since her brother's departure, but it was not entirely without another cause. Like her prayer, it was composed of two distinct elements, one of which was quite inexplicable to her.

It was, as it were, a presentiment, the perceptible approach of some impending misfortune; it was a sensation resembling that of the shooting of a cicatrised wound. The acute pain is over, but the remembrance survives, and reminds the sufferer of the calamity, as the wound itself had previously done. She did not even attempt to explain her feelings to herself. Devoted heart and soul to Philip, she centred in her beloved brother every thought and every affection of her heart.

Then she rose, took a book from her modestly furnished library, placed the light within reach of her hand, and stretched herself on a couch. The book she had chosen, or rather upon which she had accidentally placed her hand, was a dictionary of botany. It may readily be imagined that this book was not calculated to absorb her attention, but rather to lull it to rest. Gradually drowsiness weighed down her eyelids, and a filmy veil obscured her vision. For a moment the young girl struggled against sleep; twice or thrice she collected her scattered thoughts, which soon escaped again from her control; then, raising her head to blow out the candle, she perceived the glass of water prepared by Nicole, stretched out her hand and took the glass, stirred the sugar with the spoon, and, already half asleep, she approached the glass to her lips.

All at once, just as her lips were already touching the beverage, a strange emotion made her hand tremble, a moist and burning weight fell on her brow, and Andrée recognised with terror, by the current of the fluid which rushed through her nerves, that supernatural attack of mysterious sensations which had several times already triumphed over her strength and overpowered her mind. She had only time to place the glass upon the plate, when instantly, without a murmur, but with a sigh which escaped from her half-open lips, she lost the use of voice, sight, and reason, and, seized with a death-like torpor, fell back, as if struck by lightning, upon her bed. But this sort of annihilation was but the momentary transition to another state of existence. For an instant she seemed perfectly lifeless, and her eyes seemed to be closed in the slumber of death; but all at once she rose, opened her eyes, which stared with a fearful fixity of gaze, and, like a marble statue descending from its tomb, she once more stood upon the floor. There was no longer room for doubt. Andrée was sunk in that marvellous sleep which had several times already suspended her vital functions.

She crossed the chamber, opened the glass door, and entered the corridor, with the fixed and rigid attitude of breathing marble. She reached the stairs, descended step by step without hesitation and without haste, and emerged upon the portico. Just as Andrée placed her foot upon the topmost step to descend, Gilbert reached the lowest on his way to his attic. Seeing this white and solemn figure advancing as if to meet him, he recoiled before her, and, still retreating as she advanced, he concealed himself in a clump of shrubs. It was thus, he recollected, that he had already seen Andrée de Taverney at the château of Taverney.

Andrée passed close by him, even touched him, but saw him not. The young man, thunderstruck, speechless with surprise, sank to the ground on one knee. His limbs refused to support him, — he was afraid.

Not knowing to what cause to attribute this strange excursion, he followed her with his eyes; but his reason was confounded, his blood beat impetuously against his temples, and he was in a state more closely bordering on madness than the coolness and circumspection necessary for an observer.

He remained, therefore, crouching on the grass among the leaves, watching as he had never ceased to do since this fatal attachment had entered his heart. All at once the mystery was explained; Andrée was neither mad nor bewildered, as he had for a moment supposed, — Andrée was, with this sepulchral step, going to a rendezvous. A gleam of lightning now furrowed the sky, and by its blue and livid light Gilbert saw a man concealed beneath the sombre avenue of linden-trees, and, notwithstanding the rapidity of the flash, he had recognised the pale face and disordered garments of the man, relieved against the dark background.

Andrée advanced towards this man, whose arm was extended as if to draw her towards him.

, A sensation like the branding of a red-hot iron rushed

through Gilbert's heart; he raised himself upon his knees to see more clearly. At that moment another flash of lightning illumined the sky.

Glibert recognised Balsamo, covered with dust and perspiration; Balsamo, who by some mysterious means had succeeded in entering Trianon, and thus drew Andrée towards him as invincibly, as fatally, as the serpent fascinates its prey.

When two paces from him, Andrée stopped. Balsamo took her hand; her whole frame shuddered.

"Do you see?" he asked.

"Yes," replied Andrée; "but in summoning me so suddenly you have nearly killed me."

"Pardon, pardon!" replied Balsamo; "but my brain reels. I am beside myself! I am nearly mad! I shall kill myself!"

"You are indeed suffering," said Andrée, conscious of Balsamo's feelings by the contact of his hand.

"Yes, yes," replied Balsamo, "I suffer, and I come to you for consolation. You alone can save me."

"Question me."

"Once more, do you see?"

"Oh! perfectly."

"Will you follow me to my house? Can you do so?"

"I can, if you will conduct me there in thought."

"Come!"

"Ah!" said Andrée, "we are entering Paris, we follow the boulevard, we plunge into a street lighted by a single lamp."

"Yes, that is it. Enter! enter!"

"We are in an antechamber. There is a staircase to the right, but you draw me toward the wall — the wall opens — steps appear —"

"Ascend!" exclaimed Balsamo, "that is our way."

"Ah! we are in a sleeping-chamber; there are lions' skins, arms. Stay, the back of the fireplace opens."

"Pass through; where are you?"

"In a strange sort of room, without any outlet, and the windows of which are barred.   Oh! how disordered everything in the room appears!"

"But empty — it is empty, is it not?"

"Yes, empty."

"Can you see the person who inhabited it?"

"Yes, if you give me something which has touched her, which comes from her, or which belongs to her."

"Hold! there is some hair."

Andrée took the hair and placed it on her heart.

"Oh! I recognise her," said she; "I have already seen this woman.   She was flying towards Paris."

"Yes, yes; can you tell me what she has been doing during the last two hours, and how she escaped?"

"Wait a moment; yes: she is reclining upon a sofa; her breast is half bared, and she has a wound on one side."

"Look, Andrée, look! do not lose sight of her."

"She was asleep — she awakes — she looks around — she takes a handkerchief and climbs upon a chair.   She ties the handkerchief to the bars of the window — oh! God!"

"Is she really determined to die?"

"Oh, yes! she is resolute.   But this sort of death terrifies her.   She leaves the handkerchief tied to the bars — she descends — ah! poor woman!"

"What?"

"Oh! how she weeps! how she suffers, and wrings her hands!   She searches for a corner of the wall against which to dash her head!"

"Oh! my God! my God!" murmured Balsamo.

"She rushes towards the chimney-piece! It represents two marble lions; she will dash out her brains against the lions!"

"What then? look, Andrée, look — it is my will!"

"She stops."

Balsamo breathed again.

"She looks —"

"What does she look at?" asked Balsamo.

"She has perceived some blood upon the lion's eye."

"Oh, heavens!"

"Yes, blood, and yet she did not strike herself against it. Oh! strange! the blood is not hers, it is yours."

"Mine?" asked Balsamo, frantic with excitement.

"Yes, yours. You had cut your finger with a knife, with a poniard, and had touched the lion's eye with your bleeding hand. I see you."

"True, true. But how does she escape?"

"Stay, I see her examining the blood; she reflects; then she places her finger where you had placed yours. Ah! the lion's eye gives way, — a spring acts, — the chimney-board flies open!"

"Oh! imprudent, wretched fool that I am! I have betrayed myself!"

Andrée was silent.

"And she leaves the room?" asked Balsamo; "she escapes?"

"Oh! you must forgive the poor woman. She was very miserable."

"Where is she? whither does she fly? Follow her, Andrée, it is my will."

"She stops for a moment in the chamber of furs and armour; a cupboard is open; a casket, usually locked in this cupboard, is upon the table; she recognises the box; she takes it."

"What does the box contain?"

"Your papers, I think."

"Describe it."

"It is covered with blue velvet, and studded with brass nails, has clasps of silver, and a silver lock."

"Oh!" exclaimed Balsamo, stamping with anger; "it is she, then, who has taken the casket!"

"Yes. She descends the stairs leading into the anteroom, opens the door, draws back the chain of the street door, and goes out."

"Is it late?"

" It must be late, for it is dark."

" So much the better; she must have fled shortly before
my return, and I shall perhaps have time to overtake her.
Follow her, Andrée! follow her!"

" Once outside the house, she runs as if she were mad;
she reaches the boulevard; she hastens on withont
pausing."

" In which direction ? "

" Towards the Bastille."

" You see her yet ? "

" Yes ; she looks like a mad-woman; she jostles against
the passers-by; she stops; she endeavours to discover where
she is; she inquires."

" What does she say ?   Listen, Andrée, listen; in Heav-
en's name, do not lose a syllable!   You said she inquired ? "

" Yes, from a man dressed in black."

" What does she ask ? "

" She wishes to know the address of the lieutenant of
police."

" Oh! then it was not a vain threat.   Does the person
give it her ? "

" Yes."

" What does she do ? "

" She retraces her steps, and turns down a winding
street.   She crosses a large square."

" The Place Royale, — it is the direct way.   Can you
read her intention ? "

" Follow her quickly ! hasten ! she goes to betray you !
If she arrives before you and sees Monsieur de Sartines,
you are lost!"

Balsamo uttered a terrible cry, plunged into the thicket,
rushed through a little door, which a shadowy apparition
opened and closed after him, and leaped with one bound on
his faithful Djerid, who was pawing the ground at the little
gate.   Urged on at once by voice and spur, he darted like
an arrow towards Paris, and soon nothing was heard but
the clattering of his hoofs on the paved causeway.

As for Andrée, she remained standing there, cold, mute, and pale. Then, as if Balsamo had borne away with him life and strength, she tottered, drooped, and fell. Balsamo, in his eagerness to follow Lorenza, had forgotten to awaken her.

Andrée did not sink, as we have said, all at once, but gradually, in the manner we will attempt to describe.

Alone, abandoned, overpowered with that deathlike coldness which succeeds any violent nervous shock, Andrée began to tremble and totter like one suffering from the commencement of an epileptic fit.

Gilbert had never moved,— rigid, immovable, leaning forward and devouring her with his gaze. But, as it may readily be imagined, Gilbert, entirely ignorant of magnetic phenomena, dreamed neither of sleep nor of suffered violence; he had heard nothing, or almost nothing, of her dialogue with Balsamo. But for the second time, at Trianon as at Taverney, Andrée had appeared to obey the summons of this man, who had acquired such a strange and terrible power over her. To Gilbert, therefore, everything resolved itself in this: Mademoiselle Andrée has, if not a lover, at least a man whom she loves, and to whom she grants a rendezvous at night.

The dialogue which had taken place between Andrée and Balsamo, although sustained in a low voice, had all the appearance of a quarrel. Balsamo, excited, flying, frantic, seemed like a lover in despair; Andrée, left alone, mute and motionless, like the fair one he had abandoned.

It was at this moment that he saw the young girl totter, wring her hands, and sink slowly to the ground. Then she uttered twice or thrice a groan so deep, that her oppressed heart seemed torn by the effort. She endeavoured, or rather nature endeavoured, to throw back the overpowering mass of fluid which, during the magnetic sleep, had endowed her with that double sight which we have seen, in the preceding pages, produce such strange phenomena.

But nature was overpowered; Andrée could not succeed

in throwing off the remains of that mysterious will which Balsamo had forgotten to withdraw; she could not loose the marvellous, inexplicable ties which had bound her hand and foot; and by dint of struggling, she fell into those convulsions which in the olden time the Pythoness suffered upon her tripod, before the crowd of religious questioners who swarmed around the peristyle of the temple. Andrée lost her equilibrium, and, uttering a heart-rending groan, fell to the ground as if she had been struck by the flash which at that moment furrowed the vault of heaven.

But she had not yet touched the earth when Gilbert, strong and agile as a panther, darted towards her, seized her in his arms, and, without being conscious that he carried a burden, bore her back into the chamber which she had left to obey Balsamo's summons, and in which the candle was yet burning beside the disarranged couch.

Gilbert found all the doors open, as Andreé had left them. As he entered, he stumbled against the sofa, and placed on it the cold and inanimate form of the young girl. As her lifeless body rested in his arms, a fever seized him, his nerves trembled, his blood boiled; yet his first impulse was pure and chaste. The most pressing matter was to recall this beautiful statue to life; he looked round for the carafe, in order to sprinkle some drops of water in Andrée's face.

But just as his trembling hand was stretched forth to grasp the thin neck of the crystal ewer, it seemed to him that a firm but light step sounded on the stairs leading to Andrée's chamber.

It could not be Nicole, for Nicole had fled with Monsieur Beausire; it could not be Balsamo, for Balsamo was spurring with lightning haste to Paris. It could therefore only be a stranger.

Gilbert, if discovered, was lost. Andrée was to him like one of those princesses of Spain, whom a subject may not touch, even to save their life.

All these ideas rushed like a whirlwind through Gilbert's mind in less time than we can relate them. He could not calculate the exact distance of the footstep, which every moment approached still nearer, for the storm which raged without dulled every other sound; but, gifted with extraordinary coolness and foresight, the young man felt that that was no place for him, and that the most important matter was to coneal himself from sight.

He hastily blew out the candle which illumined the apartment, and entered the closet which served as Nicole's sleeping-chamber. From this hiding-place he could see through the glass door into Andrée's apartment, and also into the antechamber.

In this antechamber a night-lamp was burning upon a little console table. Gilbert had at first thought of extinguishing it as he had done the candle, but he had no time; the step echoed upon the corridor, a repressed breathing was heard, the figure of a man appeared upon the threshold, glided timidly into the antechamber, and closed the door and bolted it.

Gilbert had only time to hasten into Nicole's closet, and to draw the glass door after him.

He held his breath, pressed his face against the stained glass panes, and listened eagerly.

The storm still howled wildly outside, large raindrops beat against the windows of Andrée's apartment and those of the corridor, where a casement, accidentally left open, creaked upon its hinges, and every now and then, dashed back by the wind which rushed into the corridor, struck noisily against its frame.

But the war of the elements, terrible as it was, produced no effect on Gilbert; his whole soul was concentrated in his gaze, which was riveted upon this man. He crossed the antechamber, passed not two paces distant from Gilbert, and unhesitatingly entered the principal apartment.

As he advanced, he jostled with his arm against the candle upon the table. The candle fell, and Gilbert heard the crystal socket break in falling on the marble table. Then the man called twice, in a subdued voice, —

"Nicole! Nicole!"

"What! Nicole!" thought Gilbert, in his hiding-place. "Why does this man call Nicole instead of Andrée?"

But as no voice replied to his, the man lifted the candle from the floor, and proceeded on tiptoe to light it at the night-lamp in the antechamber. It was then that Gilbert riveted his whole attention upon this strange nocturnal visitor; he gazed as if his vision could have pierced the wall. All at once he trembled, and, even in his hiding-place, recoiled a step backwards.

By the light of these two flames combined, Gilbert, trembling and half dead with affright, recognised in this man who held the candle in his hands — the king!

Then all was explained: Nicole's flight, the money she had given Beausire, the door left upen, the interviews between Richelieu and Taverney, and the whole of that dark and mysterious intrigue of which the young girl was the centre.

Then Gilbert understood why the king had summoned Nicole; she was the instrument of the crime, the complaisant Judas, who had sold and delivered up her mistress.

But at the thought of what the king was going to do in this room, before his very eyes, the blood rushed madly through his brain, and dimmed his sight.

He wished to cry out: but fear — that unreasoning, capricious, overwhelming sentiment inspired by this man, still full of prowess, the King of France — tied Gilbert's tongue. Moreover, Louis had entered the room, a candle in his hand.

Scarcely had he entered, when he perceived Andrée, in a muslin dressing-gown, which, falling back as she lay on the couch, revealed her form; her head leaned against the back of the sofa, one leg lay on the couch, the other, white and rounded, rested gracefully on the carpet. The king smiled at this sight, — a cynical smile, illuminated by the candle; but as soon as it appeared on the king's face, another equally cynical was reflected from Andrée's lips. Louis XV. murmured some amorous expressions, or so Gilbert interpreted them, placed his light on the table, glancing hastily around the room, knelt before the young girl, and kissed her hand.

Gilbert felt the cold perspiration standing on his forehead. Andrée did not move. The king, perceiving how cold her hand was, took it in his own to warm it, and, encircling her form with his other arm, he leaned forward to whisper words of love in her ear, — such as are sometimes murmured in young girls' ears while they sleep.

At this moment his face was so near Andrée's that it almost touched it.

Gilbert felt in his pocket, and breathed a sigh of relief on feeling his pruning knife there.

Her face was as icy as her hand.

The king arose, his eyes wandered to Andreé's foot, white and small as Cinderella's. The king held it closely between his hands. The foot was cold as a marble statue.

Gilbert, as he feasted his eyes on all this beauty, felt as if the king was robbing him of what belonged to him, and ground his teeth, opening the knife, which up to this time he had held shut in his hand.

But already the king had left Andrée's foot, as he had her hand and her face, and bewildered at this young girl's slumber, which he had at first mistaken for coquetry, he tried to find why her feet, her face, and her hands should be so icy cold, and put his hand to her heart to see if it were really beating.

He drew aside Andrée's robe, exposed her maiden breast, cautiously, yet in a cynical mood, endeavouring to find out why she should be white and cold as alabaster.

Gilbert glided half through the door, knife in hand, with set teeth, determined, should the king proceed farther, to stab him on the spot, and then kill himself.

Suddenly a fearful peal of thunder shook all the furniture, even the sofa on which Andrée reposed, and before which Louis XV. was kneeling. A livid, sulphurous flash of lightning shot toward Andrée, and enveloped her whole body with its light, throwing so peculiar a hue upon her features, that Louis XV., frightened by her pallor, her immobility, and her silence, drew back, murmuring, —

"Truly, this girl is dead!"

At the same time, the idea of having embraced a corpse froze the blood in the king's veins. He snatched up the candle, looked again towards Andrée by its flickering light, and seeing her blue lips, her swollen and discoloured eyes, her dishevelled hair, her chest, where not a breath could be perceived, he cried aloud, let his candle fall, and reeled like a drunken man into the antechamber, where he knocked helplessly against the walls, as he stumbled along in his flight. Then his steps were heard rushing down the staircase, then on the ground in the garden; but were soon lost in the howling of the wind that was coursing through the long walks and shady groves of Trianon.

Then Gilbert, knife in hand, emerged, silent and solemn, from his hiding-place. He advanced to the threshold of Andrée's room, and contemplated for some moments the young girl, still buried in deep slumber.

All this time the candle was burning on the carpet where it lay, illuminating the dainty foot and the pure limb of this beautiful corpse.

Gilbert softly closed his knife, his face gradually assuming a determined expression, as he listened carefully at the door by which the king went out.

He listened a long minute; then, like the king, he closed the door and bolted it; then he blew out the light in the antechamber; then, with the same deliberation, with the same dark fire in his eyes, he re-entered Andrée's room and placed his foot on the candle, which was dripping over the carpet.

A sudden darkness obscured the fatal smile that hovered on his lips.

"Andrée! Andrée!" murmured he, "I promised you that the third time you should fall into my arms you would not escape as you did the two other times. Andrée! Andrée! to the terrible romance which you accused me of inventing there shall be a terrible end!"

And with open arms he went straight to the sofa where Andrée was lying, still cold, immovable, and void of all sensations.

## CHAPTER CXX.

### THE WILL.

WE have seen Balsamo depart. Djerid bore him on with the speed of lightning, whilst the rider, pale with terror and impatience, bent forward over the flowing mane, breathing with half-opened lips the air which the crest of the noble steed cleft, as the rapid prow of the vessel cuts the waves.

Behind him houses and trees disappeared, like fantastic visions. He scarcely perceived, as he passed, the clumsy wagon groaning on its axle-tree, while its five huge horses started with affright at the approach of this living meteor, which they could not imagine to belong to the same race as themselves.

Balsamo proceeded at this rate for a league, with whirling brain, sparkling eyes, and panting breath. Horse and rider had traversed Versailles in a few seconds. The startled inhabitants who happened to be in the streets had seen a long train of sparks flash past them, — nothing more. A second league was passed in like manner. Djerid had accomplished the distance in little more than a quarter of an hour, and yet this quarter of an hour had seemed to his rider a century. All at once a thought darted through his brain; he pulled up suddenly, throwing the noble courser back upon his haunches, while his fore-feet ploughed the ground.

Horse and rider breathed for a moment. Drawing a long breath Balsamo raised his head. Then wiping the perspiration from his forehead, while his nostrils dilated in the breeze of night, he murmured, —

"Oh! madman that you are, neither the rapidity of your steed nor the ardour of your desire will ever equal the instantaneous effect of thunder or the rapidity of the electric flash, and yet it is that which you require to avert the danger impending over you! You require the rapid effect, the instantaneous, the all-powerful shock, which will paralyse the feet whose activity you fear, the tongue whose speech destroys you. You require, at this distance, the victorious sleep which restores to you the possession of the slave who has broken her chain. Oh! if she should ever again be in my power!"

And Balsamo ground his teeth with a despairing gesture.

"Oh! you do well to wish, Balsamo, you do well to fly!" exclaimed he; "Lorenza has already arrived; she is about to speak; she has perhaps already spoken. Oh! wretched woman! no punishment can be terrible enough for you.

"Let me try," continued Balsamo, frowning, his eyes fixed, and his chin resting on his hand, "let me try. Either science is a dream or a fact — it is either impotent or powerful; let me try. Lorenza! Lorenza! it is my will that you sleep, wheresoever you may be, Lorenza, sleep — sleep, it is my will! I reckon upon your obedience!

"Oh! no, no!" murmured he, despairingly; "no, I utter a falsehood. I do not believe — I dare not reckon upon it — and yet the will is all. Oh, I will it with my whole soul, with all the strength of my being! Cleave the air, my potent will; traverse all the current of opposing or indifferent wills; pass through walls in thy course like a bullet from a gun; follow her wherever she is; go — strike — destroy! Lorenza! Lorenza! it is my will that you sleep! — be dumb at my command!"

And for some moments he concentrated his thoughts upon this aim, imprinting it on his brain as if to lend it more speed in its flight towards Paris. Then after this mysterious operation — to which, doubtless, all the divine atoms animated by God, the master and lord of all things, assisted — Balsamo, once more setting his teeth hard and clenching his hands, gave the reins to Djerid, but this time without using either the knee or the spurs. It seemed as if Balsamo wished to convince himself.

The noble steed paced gently onwards in obedience to the tacit permission of his master, placing his hoof gently upon the pavement with that light and noiseless step peculiar to his race. During this brief interval, which to a superficial observer would have seemed entirely lost, Balsamo was arranging a complete plan of defence; he concluded it just as Djerid entered the streets of Sèvres, Arrived opposite the park gates, he stopped and looked round as if expecting some one. Almost immediately a man emerged from beneath a carriage entrance, and advanced towards him.

"Is that you, Fritz?" asked Balsamo.

"Yes, master."

"Have you made inquiries?"

"Yes."

"Is Madame Dubarry in Paris or at Luciennes?"

"She is in Paris."

Balsamo raised his eyes to heaven with a triumphant look.

"How did you come?"

"On Sultan."

"Where is he?"

In the court-yard of this inn."

"Ready saddled?"

"Quite ready."

"Very well, be prepared to follow me."

Fritz hastened to bring out Sultan. He was a horse of that strong, willing German race, who grumble a little at forced marches, but who nevertheless go as long as they have breath in their lungs, or while there is a spur at their master's heel. Fritz returned to Balsamo, who was writing by the light of a street lantern.

"Return to Paris," said he, "and manage by some means to give this note to Madame Dubarry in person. You have

half an hour for this purpose; after which you will return
to the Rue Saint Claude, where you will wait for Madame
Lorenza, who cannot fail to return soon. You will let her
pass without any observation and without offering any
opposition. Go, and remember, above all, that in half
an hour your commission must be executed."

"It is well," said Fritz, "it shall be done."

As he gave this confident reply to Balsamo, he attacked
Sultan with whip and spur, and the good steed started
off, astonished at this unusual aggression, and neighing
piteously.

Balsamo, by degrees, resumed his composure, and took
the road to Paris, which he entered three quarters of an
hour afterwards, his features almost unruffled, and his look
calm but pensive.

Balsamo was right. However swift Djerid, the neighing
son of the desert, might be, his speed was powerless, and
thought alone could hope to overtake Lorenza in her flight
from prison.

From the Rue Saint Claude she had gained the boulevard, and turning to the right she soon saw the walls of
the Bastille rise before her; but Lorenza, constantly a
prisoner, was entirely ignorant of Paris. Moreover, her
first aim was to escape from that accursed house in which
she saw only a dungeon; vengeance was a secondary
consideration.

She had just entered the Faubourg Saint Antoine, hastening onward with bewildered steps, when she was accosted
by a young man who had been following her for some
moments with astonishment.

In fact, Lorenza, an Italian girl from the neighbourhood
of Rome, having almost always lived a secluded life, far
from all knowledge of the fashions and customs of the
age, was dressed more like an Oriental than a European
lady; that is, in flowing and sumptuous robes, very un-
like the charming dolls of that time, confined, like wasps,
in long tight waists, rustling with silk and muslin, under

which it was almost useless to seek a body, their utmost ambition being to appear immaterial.

Lorenza had only adopted, from the French costume of that period, the shoes with heels two inches high, — that strange looking invention which stiffened the foot, displayed the beauty of the ankle, and which rendered it impossible for the Arethusas of that rather mythological age to fly from the pursuit of their Alpheuses.

The Alpheus who pursued our Arethusa easily overtook her, therefore. He had seen her lovely ankles peeping from beneath her petticoats of satin and lace, her unpowdered hair, and her dark eyes sparkling with a strange fire from under a mantilla thrown over her head and neck, and he imagined he saw in Lorenza a lady disguised for a masquerade, or for a rendezvous, and proceeding on foot, for want of a coach, to some little house of the faubourg.

He approached her, therefore, and, walking beside her, hat in hand, —

"Good heavens! madame," said he, "you cannot go far in this costume, and with these shoes which retard your progress. Will you accept my arm until we find a coach, and allow me the honour of accompanying you to your destination?"

Lorenza turned her head abruptly, gazed with her dark, expressive eyes at the man who thus made her an offer which to many ladies would have appeared an impertinent one, and, stopping, —

"Yes," said she, "most willingly."

The young man gallantly offered his arm.

"Whither are we going, madame?" asked he.

"To the hotel of the lieutenant of police."

The young man started.

"To Monsieur de Sartines?" he inquired.

"I do not know if his name be Monsieur de Sartines or not; I wish to speak to whoever is lieutenant of police."

The young man began to reflect. A young and handsome woman wandering alone in the streets of Paris at eight o'clock in the evening, in a strange costume, holding a box under her arm, and inquiring for the hotel of the lieutenant of police, while she was going in the contrary direction, seemed suspicious.

"Ah, *diable!*" said he, "the hotel of the lieutenant of police is not in this direction at all."

"Where is it, then?"

"In the Faubourg St. Germain."

"And how must I go to the Faubourg St. Germain?"

"This way, madame," replied the young man, calm, but always polite; "and if you wish, we can take the first coach we meet —"

"Oh, yes, a coach; you are right."

The young man conducted Lorenza back to the boulevard, and, having met a hackney-coach, he hailed it. The coachman answered his summons.

"Where to, madame?" asked he.

"To the hotel of Monsieur de Sartines," said the young man.

And with a last effort of politeness, or rather of astonishment, having opened the coach-door, he bowed to Lorenza, and, after assisting her to get in, gazed at her departing form as we do in a dream or vision.

The coachman, full of respect for the dreadful name, gave his horse the whip, and drove rapidly in the direction indicated.

It was while Lorenza was thus crossing the Place Royale that Andrée, in her magnetic sleep, had seen and heard her, and denounced her to Balsamo. In twenty minutes Lorenza was at the door of the hotel.

"Must I wait for you, my fair lady?" asked the coachman.

"Yes," replied Lorenza, mechanically.

And, stepping lightly from the coach, she disappeared beneath the portal of the splendid hotel.

## CHAPTER CXXI.

THE moment Lorenza entered the court-yard, she found herself surrounded by a crowd of soldiers and officers. She addressed the *garde française* who stood nearest to her, and begged him to conduct her to the lieutenant of police. The guardsman handed her over to the porter, who, seeing a beautiful stranger, richly dressed, and holding a magnificent coffer under her arm, thought that the visit might prove not to be an unimportant one, and preceded her up the grand staircase to an antechamber, where every comer could, after the sagacious scrutiny of the porter, be admitted to present an explanation, an accusation, or a request to Monsieur de Sartines, at any hour of the day or night.

It is needless to say that the first two classes of visitors were more favourably received than the last.

Lorenza, when questioned by the usher, only replied, — "Are you Monsieur de Sartines?"

The usher was profoundly astonished that any one could mistake his black dress and steel chain for the embroidered coat and flowing wig of the lieutenant of police; but as no lieutenant is ever angry at being called captain, as he marked the foreign accent of the lady, and as her firm and steady gaze was not that of a lunatic, he felt convinced that the fair visitor had something important in the coffer which she held so carefully and so securely under her arm.

But as Monsieur de Sartines was a prudent and suspicious man, as traps had been laid for him with baits not less enticing than that of the beautiful Italian, there was good watch kept around him, and Lorenza had to undergo the investigation, the questioning, and the suspicions of half a dozen secretaries and valets. The result of all these questions and replies was, that Monsieur de Sartines had not yet returned, and that Lorenza must wait.

Then the young woman sunk into a moody silence, and her eyes wandered over the bare walls of the vast ante-chamber.

At last the ringing of a bell was heard; a carriage rolled into the court-yard, and a second usher entered and announced to Lorenza that Monsieur de Sartines was waiting for her.

Lorenza rose, and crossed two halls full of people with suspicious-looking faces, and dresses still more strange than her own. At last she was introduced into a large cabinet of an octagon form, lighted by a number of wax candles.

A man of from fifty to fifty-five years of age, enveloped in a dressing-gown, his head surmounted by a wig profusely powdered and curled, was seated at work before a lofty piece of furniture, the upper part of which, somewhat resembling in form a cupboard, was closed with two doors of looking-glass, in which the person seated could, without moving, see any one who entered the room, and could examine their features before they had time to compose them in harmony with his own.

The lower part of this article of furniture formed a secretaire. A number of rosewood drawers composed the front, each of which closed by the combination of some letters of the alphabet. Monsieur de Sartines kept in them his papers, and the ciphers which no one in his lifetime could read, since the drawers opened for him alone, and which none could have deciphered after his death, unless in some drawer still more secret than the others he had found the key to the cipher.

This secretaire, or rather this cupboard, contained, behind the glasses of the upper part, twelve drawers, also closed by an invisible mechanism. This piece of furniture, constructed expressly by the regent to contain his chemical or political secrets, had been given by that prince to Dubois, and left by Dubois to Monsieur Dombreval, lieutenant of police. It was from the latter that Monsieur de Sartines had inherited the press and the secret. However, Monsieur de Sartines had not consented to use it until after the death of the donor, and even then he had had all the arrangements of the locks altered.

This piece of furniture had some reputation in the world, and shut too closely, people said, for Monsieur de Sartines only to keep his wigs in it.

The grumblers, and their name was legion at this period, said that, if it were possible to read through the panels of this secretaire, there would most certainly have been discovered, in one of its drawers, the famous treaty by virtue of which Louis XV. speculated in grain, through the intervention of his devoted agent, Monsieur de Sartines.

The lieutenant of police therefore saw reflected in the glass the pale, serious face of Lorenza, as she advanced towards him with the coffer still beneath her arm. In the centre of the apartment the young girl stopped. Her costume, her figure, and the strangeness of her proceedings, struck the lieutenant.

"Who are you?" asked he, without turning round, but looking at her in the glass. "What do you want with me?"

"Am I in the presence of Monsieur de Sartines, lieutenant of police?" replied Lorenza.

"Yes," replied he, abruptly.

"Who will assure me of that?"

Monsieur de Sartines turned round.

"Will it be a proof that I am the man you seek," said he, "if I send you to prison?"

Lorenza made no reply; she merely looked around the room with that indescribable dignity peculiar to the women of Italy, and seemed to seek the chair which Monsieur de Sartines did not offer her.

He was vanquished by this look, for Monsieur the Count d'Alby de Sartines was a remarkably well-bred man.

"Be seated," said he, sharply.

Lorenza drew a chair forward and sat down.

"Speak quickly," said the magistrate.  "Come, let me know what you want!"

"Monsieur," said Lorenza, "I come to place myself under your protection."

Monsieur de Sartines looked at her with the sarcastic look peculiar to him.

"Ah! ah!" said he.

"Monsieur," continued Lorenza, "I have been carried off from my family, and have, by a false marriage, fallen into the power of a man who for the last three years has oppressed me and made my life miserable."

Monsieur de Sartines looked with admiration upon this noble countenance, and felt touched and charmed by this voice, so soft that it seemed more like a strain of music.

" From what country do you come ? "  he asked.

"I am a Roman."

" What is your name ? "

" Lorenza."

" Lorenza what ? "

" Lorenza Feliciani."

" I do not know that family.  Are you a demoiselle ? "

Demoiselle at this period meant a lady of quality.  In our days a lady thinks herself noble enough when she is married, and only wishes thenceforth to be called madame.

" I am a demoiselle," replied Lorenza.

" Well ?   What do you demand ? "

" I demand justice against this man who has stolen and incarcerated me."

" That is no affair of mine," said the lieutenant of police; "are you his wife ? "

" He says so, at least."

" How ! — says ! "

"Yes, but I do not remember anything of it, as the marriage was contracted whilst I slept."

"Peste! you sleep soundly."

"What do you say?"

"I say that it is not in my province. Apply to a procureur and commence an action; I do not like to meddle in family matters."

Upon which Monsieur de Sartines waved his hand with a gesture which meant, "Begone!" Lorenza did not move.

"Well?" asked Monsieur de Sartines, astonished.

"I have not done yet," said she; "and if I come to you, you must understand that it is not to complain of a trifling matter, but to revenge myself. I have told you that the women of my country revenge themselves, but never complain."

"That is another affair," said Monsieur de Sartine; "but speak quickly, fair lady, for my time is precious."

"I told you that I came to you to ask for your protection; shall I have it?"

"Protection against whom?"

"Against the man upon whom I wish to revenge myself."

"Is he powerful?"

"More powerful than a king."

"Come, explain, my dear madame. Why should I protect you against a man who is, in your opinion, more powerful than a king, an act which is perhaps a crime? If you wish to be revenged on this man, revenge yourself. That is nothing to me; only, if you commit a crime, I shall have to arrest you, after which we shall see — that is the routine."

"No, monsieur," said Lorenza, "no, you will not have me arrested, for my vengeance is of the greatest utility to you, to the king, and to France. I shall revenge myself by revealing this man's secrets.

"Oh ho! he has secrets?" said Monsieur de Sartines, beginning to feel interested in spite of himself.

"Mighty secrets, monsieur."

"Of what kind ? "

"Political ones."

"Mention them."

"But in that case, will you protect me ? "

"What sort of protection do you require ? " said the magistrate, with a cold smile ; "gold or affection ? "

"I only ask permission, monsieur, to retire to a convent and to live there concealed and unknown. I ask that this convent may become my tomb, but that this tomb may never be violated by any one in the world."

"Ah !" said the magistrate, "that is not a very exacting demand. You shall have the convent. Speak."

"Then I have your word, monsieur ? "

"I think I said so."

"Then," said Lorenza, "take this coffer ; it contains mysteries which will make you tremble for the safety of the king and his dominions."

"Then you know these mysteries ? "

"Only partially — but I know they exist."

"And that they are important ? "

"That they are terrible."

"Political secrets, you say ? "

"Have you never heard that there existed a secret society ? "

"Ah! the freemasons ? "

"The invisibles."

"Yes, but I do not believe it."

"When you have opened this coffer you will believe."

"Ah !" said Monsieur de Sartines, eagerly, "let me see."

And he took the coffer from Lorenza's hands. But suddenly, after a moment's reflection, he placed it upon the desk.

"No," said he, with an air of suspicion ; "open the coffer yourself."

"But I have not the key."

"How ! — you have not the key ? You bring me a coffer

which contains the safety of a kingdom, and you forget the key ? "

" Is it so very difficult, then, to open a lock ? "

" No, not when one knows it." Then, after a moment's pause, he added : " We have in this place keys for all kinds of locks ; you shall have a bunch " (and he looked fixedly at Lorenza), " and you shall open it yourself."

" Give it me," said Lorenza, without the slightest hesitation.

Monsieur de Sartines held out a bunch of little keys of all kinds to the young girl. She took them ; Monsieur de Sartines touched her hand, — it was cold as marble.

" But why," said he, " did you not bring the key of the coffer ? "

" Because the master of the coffer never lets it out of his possession."

" And who is the master of the coffer, — this man who is more powerful than a king ? "

" What he is, no one can say. The Almighty alone knows how long he has lived ; the deeds he accomplishes none see but God."

" But his name — his name ? "

" I have known him change it ten times."

" Well, that by which you generally address him ? "

" Acharat."

" And he lives — "

" Rue Saint — "

Suddenly Lorenza started, shuddered, and let the coffer, which she held in the one hand, and the keys which she held in the other, fall to the ground. She made an effort to reply, her lips were distorted convulsively ; she raised her hands to her throat, as if the words she was about to utter had suffocated her ; then, tossing her trembling arms aloft, she fell her whole length upon the carpet of the study, unable to utter a single word.

" Poor girl ! " murmured Monsieur de Sartines, " what the deuce is the matter with her ? She is really very pretty.   Ah! there is some jealousy at work in this project of revenge."

He rang the bell hastily, and in the mean time raised the young girl in his arms, who, with staring eyes and motionless lips, seemed already dead, and disconnected with this lower world.   Two valets entered.

"Carry this young lady carefully into the adjoining apartment," said he; "endeavour to revive her, but above all use no violence.   Go."

The valets obeyed, and carried Lorenza out.

## CHAPTER CXXII.

### THE COFFER.

WHEN he was alone, Monsieur de Sartines turned the coffer round and round with the air of a man who can appreciate the value of a discovery. Then he stretched out his hands and picked up the bundle of keys which had fallen from Lorenza's hands.

He tried them all; none would fit.

He took several similar bunches from his drawer.

These bunches contained keys of all dimensions; keys of all sorts of articles, coffers included, — common keys, and microscopic keys. Monsieur de Sartines might be said to possess a pattern of every key known.

He tried twenty, fifty, a hundred: not one would even turn round. The magistrate concluded, therefore, that the lock was only a feigned one, and that consequently his keys were only counterfeit keys.

He then took a small chisel and a little hammer from the same drawer, and with his white hand buried in an ample frill of Mechlin lace he burst open the lock, the faithful guardian of the coffer.

A bundle of papers appeared, instead of the destructive machine he had feared to find there, or instead of poisons which should diffuse a fatal odour around, and deprive France of its most useful magistrate.

The first words which met the magistrate's eye were the following, written in a handwriting which was evidently feigned.

"Master it is time to abandon the name of Balsamo."

There was no signature, but merely the three letters : — L. P. D.

"Ha!" said he, twitching the curls of his wig, "if I do not know the writing, I think I know the name. Balsamo — let me see — I must search the B's."

He opened one of his twenty-four drawers, and took from it a list, arranged in alphabetical order, written in a fine handwriting full of abbreviations, and containing three or four hundred names, preceded, followed, and accompanied by flaming notes.

"Oh ho!" said he, "there is a long article on this Balsamo."

And he read the whole page with unequivocal signs of dissatisfaction. Then he replaced the list in the drawer, and continued the examination of the coffer.

He had not proceeded far before his brow assumed a darker hue, and soon he came to a note full of names and ciphers.

This paper seemed important; it was much worn at the edges, and filled with pencil marks. Monsieur de Sartines rang the bell; a servant appeared.

"The assistance of the chancery clerk," said he, " immediately. Let him come through the reception-rooms from the office to save time."

The valet retired. Two minutes afterwards, a clerk with a pen in his hand, his hat under one arm, a large register under the other, and wearing sleeves of black serge over his coat sleeves, appeared on the threshold of the study. Monsieur de Sartines perceived his entrance in the mirror before him, and handed him the paper over his shoulder.

"Decipher this," said he.

"Yes, monsieur," replied the clerk.

This decipherer of riddles was a little thin man, with pinched lips, eyebrows contracted by study, pale features, and head pointed both at top and bottom, a narrow chin, a receding forehead, projecting cheek-bones, hollow and dull eyes, which often sparkled with intelligence.

Monsieur de Sartines called him La Fouine.

"Sit down," said the magistrate to him, on seeing him

rather embarrassed by his note-book, his code of ciphers,
his paper, and his pen.

La Fouine modestly took his seat upon the corner of a
stool, approached his knees together, and began to write
upon them, turning over his dictionary and searching his
memory with an impassible countenance.   In five minutes,
he had written : —

§

" An order to assemble three thousand brothers in Paris.

§

" An order to form three circles and six lodges.

§

" An order to form a guard for the Grand Copht, and to contrive
four dwellings for him, one in a royal household.

§

" An order to place five hundred thousand francs at his disposal
for a police.

§

" An order to enroll the flower of literature and philosophy
moving in the first Parisian circles.

§

" An order to hire or to gain over the magistracy, and particularly
to make sure of the lieutenant of police, by corruption, violence, or
cunning."

Here La Fouine stopped for a moment, not that the poor
man was reflecting, — he took care not to do that, it would
have been a crime, — but because his page was filled, and
the ink yet wet, so he was obliged to wait for its drying
before he could proceed.

Monsieur de Sartines, becoming impatient, snatched the
paper from his hands and read it.

At the last paragraph, such an expression of fear was
painted on his face, that he turned a deeper pale at seeing
himself change colour in the mirror of his cupboard.

He did not return the paper to his clerk, but handed him
a fresh sheet.   The clerk once more commenced to write

in proportion as he deciphered, which he did with a facility terrifying for all writers in cipher.

This time Monsieur de Sartines read over his shoulder : —

§

" To drop the name of Balsamo, which is already too well known in Paris, and to take that of the Count de Fe — "

A large blot of ink concealed the rest of the word.

While Monsieur de Sartines was endeavouring to make out the last syllable which would complete the name, a bell was rung outside, and a valet, entering, announced, —

" The Count de Fenix."

Monsieur de Sartines uttered a cry, and at the risk of demolishing the harmonious edifice of his wig, he clasped his hands above his head, and hastened to dismiss his clerk by a secret door.

Then resuming his place before the desk, he said to the valet, —

" Introduce him."

A few seconds afterwards, Monsieur de Sartines perceived in his glass the marked profile of the count, which he had already seen at court, on the day of Madame Dubarry's presentation.

Balsamo entered without any hesitation whatever.

Monsieur de Sartines rose, bowed coldly to the count, and crossing one leg over the other, he seated himself ceremoniously in his arm-chair.

At the first glance the magistrate had divined the cause and the aim of this visit.

At the first glance also Balsamo had perceived the opened box, half emptied upon Monsieur de Sartines' desk. His look, however hasty, at the coffer, did not escape the lieutenant of police.

" To what chance do I owe the honour of your presence, monsieur ? " asked Monsieur de Sartines.

" Monsieur," replied Balsamo, with a most affable smile, " I have had the honour of being presented to all the sovereigns, ministers, and ambassadors of Europe, but I have not found any one to present me to you; I have therefore come to introduce myself."

"In truth, monsieur," replied the lieutenant of police, "you arrive most opportunely, for I feel convinced that, had you not come of yourself, I should have had the honour of sending for you."

"Ah! indeed!" said Balsamo. "What a coincidence!"

Monsieur de Sartines inclined his head with a sarcastic smile.

"Shall I be so fortunate as to be of any use to you?" asked Balsamo.

And these words were uttered without a shadow of emotion or of uneasiness clouding his smiling features.

"You have travelled much, monsieur?" asked the lieutenant of police.

"A great deal, monsieur."

"Ah!"

"You wish for some geographical information, perhaps? A man of your capacity does not confine his observations to France alone. He surveys Europe, — the world."

"Geographical is not exactly the word, count. Moral would be more correct.

"Have no scruples, I beg; one is as welcome as the other. I am wholly at your service."

"Well, count, picture to yourself that I am in search of a most dangerous man, — a man who, on my word, is a complete atheist."

"Oh!"

"A conspirator."

"Oh!"

"A forger."

"Oh!"

"A debauchee, a false coiner, a quack, a charlatan, the chief of a society, — a man whose history I have in my books, in this box that you see here, — everywhere indeed."

"Ah! yes, I comprehend," said Balsamo; "you have the history, but not the man."

" No."

" Diable ! The latter seems to me the most important point."

" Of course ; but you shall see we are not far from having him. Certainly Proteus had not more forms, nor Jupiter more names, than this mysterious traveller. Acharat in Egypt, — Balsamo in Italy — Somini in Sardinia — the Marquis Danna in Malta — the Marquis Pellegrini in Corsica — and lastly, the Count de — ? "

" Count de — ? " added Balsamo.

" The last name I could not decipher perfectly, sir. But I am sure you will be able to assist me, will you not ? For there is no doubt you must have met this man during your travels in each of the countries I have just now named."

" Enlighten me a little, I entreat," said Balsamo, quietly.

" Ah ! I understand : you wish for a description of his person, do you not, count ? "

" Yes, monsieur, if you please."

" Well ! " said Monsieur de Sartines, fixing a glance which he intended to be inquisitorial upon Balsamo, " he is a man of your age, of your size, of your figure. He is sometimes a great lord, scattering money on all sides — sometimes a charlatan, searching into the secrets of nature — sometimes a gloomy member of some mysterious brotherhood which meets by night, and swears 'Death to kings and the overthrow of all thrones.'"

" Oh ! " said Balsamo, " that is very vague."

" How vague ? "

" If you knew how many men I have seen who resemble this description."

" Indeed ! "

" Of course ; and you must be a little more precise if you wish me to assist you. In the first place, do you know in which country he prefers to live ? "

" He dwells in all."

" But at present, for instance ? "

" At present he is in France."

"And what is his errand in France ? "

"He directs an immense conspiracy."

"Ah! that is indeed some clue; and if you know what conspiracy he directs, you probably hold the thread by which to catch your man."

"I am just of your opinion."

"Well! if you think so, why in that case do you ask my advice ?  It is useless."

"Ah! but I am not yet decided."

"On what point ? "

"Whether I shall arrest him or not."

"I do not understand the *not*, Mr. Lieutenant of Police, for if he conspires — "

"Yes ; but if he is partially defended by some name or some title ! "

"Ah! I understand.  But what name ? — what title? You must tell me that before I can assist you in your search, monsieur."

"Why, monsieur, I have told you that I know the name under which he conceals himself, but — "

"But you do not know the one which he openly uses, — is that it ? "

"Yes, otherwise —"

"Otherwise you would arrest him."

"Instantly."

"Well, my dear Monsieur de Sartines, it is very fortunate, as you said just now, that I arrived at this moment, for I will do you the service you require."

"You ? "

"Yes."

"You will tell me his name ? "

"Yes."

"His public name ? "

"Yes."

"Then you know him ? "

"Perfectly well."

"And what is his name ? " asked Monsieur de Sartines, expecting some falsehood.

"The Count de Fenix."

"What! the name by which you were announced?"

"The same."

"Your name?"

"My name."

"Then this Acharat — this Somini — this Marquis Danna — this Marquis Pellegrini — this Joseph Balsamo — is you?"

"Yes," said Balsamo, quietly; "is myself."

It was a minute before Monsieur de Sartines could recover from the vertigo which this frank avowal caused him.

"You see I had guessed as much," said he. "I knew you. I knew that Joseph Balsamo and the Count de Fenix were the same."

"Ah!" said Balsamo, "you are a great minister — I confess it."

"And you are most imprudent," said the magistrate, advancing towards the bell.

"Imprudent? — why?"

"Because I am going to have you arrested."

"What say you?" replied Balsamo, stepping between the magistrate and the bell. "You are going to arrest me?"

"*Pardieu!* what can you do to prevent me, may I ask?"

"You ask me?"

"Yes."

"My dear lieutenant of police, I will blow your brains out."

And Balsamo drew from his pocket a charming little pistol, mounted in silver gilt — which, from its appearance, might have been chased by Benvenuto Cellini — and calmly levelled it at the forehead of Monsieur de Sartines, who turned pale and sunk into an arm-chair.

"There," said Balsamo, drawing another chair close to that occupied by the lieutenant of police, and sitting down; "now that we are comfortably seated, we can chat a little."

## CHAPTER CXXIII.

### CONVERSATION.

MONSIEUR DE SARTINES took a moment or two to recover from his rather severe alarm. He had seen the threatening muzzle of the pistol presented before his very eyes; he had even felt the cold metal of the barrel upon his forehead. At last he recovered.

"Monsieur," said he; "you have an advantage over me. Knowing what sort of a man I had to deal with, I did not take the precautions usually adopted against common malefactors."

"Oh! monsieur," replied Balsamo, "now you are getting angry and use injurious expressions. Do you not see how unjust you are? I come to do you a service."

Monsieur de Sartines moved uneasily.

"Yes, monsieur, to serve you," resumed Balsamo, "and therefore you misunderstand my intentions; you speak to me of conspirators at the very time when I come to denounce a conspiracy to you."

But Balsamo talked in vain. Monsieur de Sartines did not at that moment pay any great attention to the words of his dangerous visitor, and the word "conspiracy," which on other occasions would have been sufficient to make him bound from his seat, scarcely caused him to prick up his ears.

"Since you know so well who I am, monsieur, you are aware of my mission in France. Sent by his Majesty the great Frederick, I am more or less secretly the ambassador of his Prussian Majesty. Now, by ambassador is understood an inquirer; in my quality of inquirer I am ignorant of nothing that happens, and a subject upon which I am particularly well informed is the monopoly of grain."

However unpretendingly Balsamo uttered these last words, they nevertheless produced more effect upon the lieutenant of police than all the others, for they made him attentive. He slowly raised his head.

"What is this affair about corn ?" said he, affecting as much assurance as Balsamo himself had displayed at the commencement of the interview. "Be good enough, in your turn, to instruct me, monsieur."

"Willingly, monsieur," said Balsamo. "This is the whole matter — "

"I am all attention."

"Oh ! you do not need to tell me that. Some very clever speculators have persuaded his Majesty the King of France that he ought to construct granaries for his people in case of scarcity. These granaries therefore have been constructed. Whilst they were doing it, they thought it as well to make them large. Nothing was spared, neither stone nor brick, and they were made very large."

"Well?"

"Well, they had then to be filled. Empty granaries were useless, therefore they were filled."

"Well, monsieur," said Monsieur de Sartines, not seeing very clearly as yet what Balsamo was driving at.

"Well, you may readily conceive that to fill these very large granaries, a great quantity of grain was required. Is that not evident?"

"Yes."

"To continue, then. A large quantity of grain withdrawn from circulation is one way of starving the people; for, mark this: any amount taken from the circulation is equivalent to a failure in the production. A thousand sacks of corn more in the granary are a thousand sacks of corn less in the market-place. If you only multiply these thousand sacks by ten, the corn will rise considerably."

Monsieur de Sartines was seized with an irritating cough.

Balsamo paused, and waited quietly till the cough was gone.

"You see, then," continued he, as soon as the lieutenant of police would permit him, "you see that the speculator in these granaries is enriched by the amount of the rise in value. Is that clear to you?"

"Perfectly clear, monsieur," said Monsieur de Sartines; "but, as far as I can understand, it seems that you have the presumption to denounce to me a conspiracy or a crime of which his Majesty is the author?"

"Exactly," said Balsamo; "you understand me perfectly."

"That is a bold step, monsieur, and I confess that I am rather curious to see how his Majesty will take your accusation; I fear much the result will be precisely the same that I proposed to myself on looking over the papers in this box before your arrival. Take care, monsieur; your destination in either case will be the Bastille."

"Ah! now you do not understand me at all."

"How so?"

"Good heavens! how incorrect an opinion you form of me, and how deeply you wrong me, monsieur, in taking me for a fool! What! you imagine I intend to attack the king — I, an ambassador, an inquirer! Why, that would be the work of a simpleton! Listen to the end, pray." .

Monsieur de Sartines bowed.

"The persons who have discovered this conspiracy against the French people — (forgive me for taking up your valuable time, monsieur, but you will see directly that it is not lost) — they who have discovered this conspiracy against the French people are economists, laborious and precise men, who, by their careful investigation of this underhand game, have discovered that the king does not play alone. They know well that his Majesty keeps an exact register of the rate of corn in the different markets; they know that his Majesty rubs his hands with glee when the rise has produced him eight or ten thousand crowns; but they know also that beside his Majesty there stands a man whose position facilitates the sales, a man who naturally, thanks to certain functions (he is a functionary, you must know), superintends the purchases, the arrivals, the packing — a man, in short, who manages for the king. Now these economists — these microscopic observers, as I call them — will not attack the king, for of course they are not mad; but they will attack, my dear monsieur, the man, the functionary, the agent, who thus plots for his Majesty."

Monsieur de Sartines endeavoured in vain to restore the equilibrium of his wig.

"Now," continued Balsamo, "I am coming to the point. Just as you, who have a police, knew that I was the Count de Fenix, so I know that you are Monsieur de Sartines."

"Well, what then?" said the embarrassed magistrate.

"Yes, I am Monsieur de Sartines. What a discovery!"

"Ah! but cannot you understand that this Monsieur de Sartines is precisely the man of the price list, of the underhand dealings, of the stowing away — he who, either with or without the king's cognisance, traffics with the food of twenty-seven millions of French people, whom his office requires him to feed on the best possible terms? Now just imagine the effect of such a discovery. You are not much beloved by the people; the king is not a very considerate man: as soon as the cries of the famishing millions demand your head, the king — to avert all suspicion of connivance with you, if there is connivance, or if there is no connivance, to do justice — will cause you to be hung upon a gibbet, like Enguerrand de Marigny. Do you recollect Enguerrand?"

"Imperfectly," said Monsieur de Sartines, turning very pale; "and it is a proof of very bad taste, I think, monsieur, to talk of gibbets to a man of my rank."

"Oh! if I alluded to it," replied Balsamo, "it was because I think I see poor Enguerrand still before me. I assure you he was a perfect gentleman, from Normandy, of a very ancient family and a noble descent. He was chamberlain of France, captain of the Louvre, comptroller of finance and of buildings; he was Count of Longueville, which county is more considerable than yours of Alby! Well, monsieur, I saw him hung upon the gallows of Montfaucon, which he had himself constructed! Thank God, it was not a crime to have said to him before the catastrophe, ' Enguerrand, my dear Enguerrand, take care! — you are dipping into the finances to an extent that Charles of Valois will never pardon.' He would not listen to me, monsieur, and unfortunately he perished. Alas! if you knew how many prefects of police I have seen, from Pontius Pilate down to Monsieur Bertin de Belille, Count de Bourdeilhes, Lord of Brantome, your predecessor, who first introduced the lantern and prohibited the scales."

Monsieur de Sartines rose, and endeavoured in vain to conceal the agitation which preyed upon him.

"Well," said he, "you can accuse me if you like. Of what importance is the testimony of a man such as you, who has no influence or connections?"

"Take care, monsieur," said Balsamo; "frequently those who seem to have no connections are connected far and wide; and when I shall write the history of these corn speculations to my correspondent Frederick, who you know is a philosopher; when Frederick shall hasten to communicate the affair, with his comments upon it, to Monsieur Arouet de Voltaire; when the latter, with his pen, whose reputation at least I hope you know, shall have metamorphosed it into a little comic tale in the style of ' L'homme aux quarante Ecus; ' when Monsieur d'Alembert, that excellent geometrician, shall have calculated that the corn withdrawn from the public consumption by you •might have fed a hundred millions of men for two or three years; when Helvetius shall have shown that the price of this corn, converted into crowns of six livres and piled up, would touch the moon, or, into bank-notes fastened together, would reach to St. Petersburg; when this calculation shall have inspired Monsieur de la Harpe to write

a bad drama, Diderot a family conversation, and Monsieur Jean Jacques Rousseau, of Geneva, who has a tolerably sharp bite when he chooses, a terrible paraphrase of this conversation, with his own commentaries; when Monsieur Caron de Beaumarchais — may Heaven preserve you from treading on his toes! — shall have written a memoir, Monsieur Grimm a little letter, Monsieur de Holbach a thundering attack, Monsieur de Marmontel an amiable moral tale in which he will kill you by defending you badly; when you shall be spoken of in the Café de la Régence, the Palais Royal, at Audinot's, at the king's dancers' (kept up, as you know, by Monsieur Nicolet) — ah! Count d'Alby, you will be in a much worse case than poor Enguerrand de Marigny (whom you would not hear me mention) when he stood under the gallows, for he asserted his innocence, and that with so much earnestness that, on my word of honour, I believed him when he told me so."

At these words Monsieur de Sartines, no longer paying any heed to decorum, took off his wig and wiped his bald pate, which was bathed in perspiration.

"Well," said he, "so be it. But all that will not prevent me in the least. Ruin me if you can; you have your proofs, I have mine. Keep your secret, I shall keep the coffer."

"Oh, monsieur," said Balsamo, "that is another error into which I am surprised that a man of your talents should fall; this coffer —"

"Well, what of it?"

"You will not keep."

"Oh!" exclaimed Monsieur de Sartines, with a sarcastic smile, "true; I had forgotten that the Count de Fenix is a gentleman of the highway, who rifles travellers with the strong hand; I forgot your pistol, because you have replaced it in your pocket. Excuse me, monseigneur ambassador."

"But, good heavens! why speak of pistols, Monsieur de Sartines? You surely do not believe that I mean to carry off the coffer by main force; that when on the stairs I may hear your bell ring, and your voice cry, 'Stop thief!' Oh, no! When I say that you will not keep this coffer, I mean that you will restore it to me willingly and without constraint."

"What! I?" exclaimed the magistrate, placing his clenched hand upon the disputed object with so much weight that he nearly broke it.

"Yes, you."

"Oh! very well, monsieur, mock away; but as to taking this coffer, I tell you you shall only have it with my life. And have I not risked my life a thousand times? Do I not owe it, to the last drop, to the service of his Majesty? Kill me — you can do so! but the noise will summon my avengers, and I shall have voice enough left to convict you of all your crimes. Ah! give you back this coffer!" added he, with a bitter smile; "all hell should not wrest it from me!"

"And therefore, I shall not employ the intervention of the subterranean powers; I shall be satisfied with that of the person who is just now knocking at the gate of your court-yard."

And, in fact, just at that moment three blows struck with an air of command were heard outside.

"And whose carriage," continued Balsamo, "is just now entering the court."

"It seems, then, that it is some friend of yours who is coming to honour me with a visit?"

"As you say — a friend of mine."

"And I shall hand this coffer to him."

"Yes, my dear Monsieur de Sartines, you will give it to him."

The lieutenant of police had not finished his gesture of lofty disdain, when a valet opened the door hastily, and announced that Madame Dubarry wished for an interview.

Monsieur de Sartines started, and looked in stupefied

amazement at Balsamo, who required all his self-command to avoid laughing in the face of the honourable magistrate.

Close behind the valet appeared a lady who seemed to have no need of permission to enter. It was the beautiful countess, whose flowing and perfumed skirts gently rustled as they brushed past the doorway of the cabinet.

"You, madame! you!" exclaimed Monsieur de Sartines, who, in the instinct of terror, had seized the open coffer in both hands, and clasped it to his breast.

"Good-day, Sartines," said the countess, with her gayest smile; then, turning to Balsamo, "good-day, dear count," added she, and she gave her hand to the latter, who familiarly bent over the white fingers, and pressed his lips where the royal lips had so often rested.

In this movement Balsamo managed to whisper a few words aside to the countess, which Sartines could not hear.

"Ah! precisely," exclaimed the countess, "there is my coffer."

"Your coffer!" stammered Monsieur de Sartines.

"Of course, my coffer — oh! you have opened it; I see — you do not observe much ceremony!"

"But, madame —"

"Oh, it is delightful! The idea occurred to me at once that some one had stolen this coffer, and then I said to myself, 'I must go to Sartines, he will find it for me.' You did not wait till I asked you; you found it beforehand — a thousand thanks!"

"And as you see," said Balsamo, "monsieur has even opened it."

"Yes, really; who could have thought it! It is odious conduct of you, Sartines!"

"Madame, notwithstanding all the respect I have for you," said the lieutenant of police, "I fear that you are imposed upon."

"Imposed, monsieur!" said Balsamo; "do you perchance mean that word for me?"

"I know what I know," replied Monsieur de Sartines.

"And I know nothing," whispered Madame Dubarry, in a low voice to Balsamo. "Come, tell me what is the matter, my dear count! You have claimed the fulfilment of the promise I made you, to grant the first favour you should ask. I keep my word like a woman of honour, and here I am. Tell me what must I do for you?"

"Madame," replied Balsamo, aloud, "you confided the care of this coffer and everything it contains to me a few days ago."

"Of course," answered Madame Dubarry, replying by a look to the count's appealing glance.

"Of course!" exclaimed Monsieur de Sartines; "you say of course, madame?"

"Yes; madame pronounced the words loud enough for you to hear them, I should think."

"A box which contains perhaps ten conspiracies!"

"Ah! Monsieur de Sartines, you are aware that that word is rather an unfortunate one for you; do not repeat it. Madame asks for her box again; give it her — that is all."

"Do you ask me for it, madame?" said Monsieur de Sartines, trembling with anger.

"Yes, my dear magistrate."

"But learn, at least —"

Balsamo looked at the countess.

"You can tell me nothing I do not know," said Madame Dubarry. "Give me the coffer; you may believe I did not come for nothing!"

"But in the name of Heaven, madame! — in the name of his Majesty's safety!"

Balsamo made an impatient gesture.

"The coffer, monsieur!" said the countess, abruptly; "the coffer — yes or no! Reflect well before you refuse."

"As you please, madame!" said Monsieur de Sartines, humbly.

And he handed the coffer, in which Balsamo had already

replaced all the papers scattered over the desk, to the countess.

Madame Dubarry turned towards the latter with a charming smile.

"Count," said she, "will you carry this coffer to my carriage for me, and give me your hand through all these antechambers, thronged with villainous-looking faces which I do not like to confront alone? Thanks, Sartines."

And Balsamo was already advancing towards the door with his protectress, when he saw Monsieur de Sartines moving towards the bell.

"Countess," said Balsamo, stopping his enemy with a look, "be good enough to tell Monsieur de Sartines, who is quite enraged with me for having claimed this box — be good enough to tell him how much grieved you would be if any misfortune were to happen to me through the agency of the lieutenant of police, and how displeased you would be with him."

The countess smiled on Balsamo.

"You hear what the count says, my dear Sartines? — well, it is the simple truth. The count is an excellent friend of mine, and I should be dreadfully angry with you if you displeased him in any way whatsoever. Adieu, Sartines!" And placing her hand in Balsamo's, who carried the coffer, Madame Dubarry left the study of the lieutenant of police.

Monsieur de Sartines saw them depart without displaying that fury which Balsamo expected him to manifest.

"Go!" said the conquered magistrate; "go — you have the box, but I have the woman!"

And to compensate himself for his disappointment, he rang loud enough to break all the bells in the house.

## CHAPTER CXXIV.

### SARTINES BEGINS TO THINK BALSAMO A SORCERER.

AT the violent ringing of Monsieur de Sartine's bell, an usher entered.

"Well," asked the magistrate, "this woman?"

"What woman, monseigneur?"

"The woman who fainted here just now, and whom I confided to your care."

"Monseigneur, she is quite well," replied the usher.

"Very good; bring her to me."

"Where shall I find her, monseigneur?"

"What do you mean? In that room, of course."

"But she is not there, monseigneur."

"Not there! Then where is she?"

"I do not know."

"She is gone?"

"Yes."

"Alone?"

"Yes."

"But she could not stand."

"Monseigneur, it is true that for some moments she remained in a swoon; but five minutes after the Count de Fenix entered monseigneur's study, she awoke from this strange fit, which neither essences nor salts affected in the least. Then she opened her eyes, rose, and breathed, seemingly with an air of satisfaction."

"Well, what then?"

"She proceeded towards the door; and as monseigneur had not ordered that she should be detained, she was allowed to depart."

"Gone!" cried Monsieur de Sartines. "Ah! wretch that you are! I shall send you all to rot at Bicetre! Quick, quick! send me my head-clerk!"

The usher retired hastily to obey the order he had received.

"The wretch is a sorcerer!" muttered the unfortunate magistrate. "I am lieutenant of police to the king, but he is lieutenant of police to the devil!"

The reader has, no doubt, understood what Monsieur de Sartines could not explain to himself. Immediately after the incident of the pistol, and whilst the lieutenant of police was endeavouring to regain his equanimity, Balsamo, profiting by the momentary respite, had turned successively to the four cardinal points, quite sure of finding Lorenza in one of them, and had ordered her to rise, to go out, and to return by the way she had come, to the Rue St. Claude.

The moment this wish had been formed in Balsamo's mind, a magnetic current was established between him and the young woman, and the latter, obeying the order she had received by intuition, rose and retired, without any one opposing her departure.

Monsieur de Sartines that same evening took to his bed, and caused himself to be bled. The revulsion had been too strong for him to bear with impunity; and the doctor assured him that a quarter of an hour more would have brought on an attack of apoplexy.

Meanwhile, Balsamo had accompanied the countess to her carriage, and had attempted to take his leave of her; but she was not a woman to let him go thus, without knowing, or at least without endeavouring to discover, the solution of the strange event which had taken place before her. She begged the count to enter her carriage. The count obeyed, and a groom led Djerid behind.

"You see now, count," said she, "whether I am true or not, and whether, when I have called a man my friend, I spoke with the lips merely, or my heart. I was just setting out for Luciennes, where the king had said he would pay me a visit to-morrow morning; but your letter arrived, and I left everything for you. Many would have been frightened at the words conspiracies and conspirators which Monsieur de Sartines threw in your teeth; but I looked at your countenance before I acted, and did as you wished me."

"Madame," replied Balsamo, "you have amply repaid the slight service I was able to render you; but with me nothing is lost — you will find that I can be grateful. Do not imagine, however, that I am a criminal, — a conspirator, as Monsieur de Sartines said. That worthy magistrate had received, from some person who betrayed me, this coffer, containing some chemical and hermetical secrets — which I shall share with you, that you may preserve your immortal, your splendid beauty, and your dazzling youth. Now, seeing the ciphers of my receipt, this excellent Monsieur de Sartines called the chancery clerk to assist him, who, in order not to be found wanting, interpreted them after his own fashion. I think I have already told you, madame, that the profession is not yet entirely freed from the dangers which were attendant on it in the Middle Ages. Only young and intelligent minds like yours favour it. In short, madame, you have saved me from a great embarrassment; I thank you for it, and shall prove my gratitude."

"But what would he have done with you if I had not come to your assistance?"

"To annoy King Frederick, whom his Majesty hates, he would have imprisoned me in Vincennes or the Bastille. I should have escaped from it, I know — thanks to my receipt for melting stone with a breath — but I should have lost my coffer, which contains, as I have had the honour of telling you, many curious and invaluable secrets, wrested by a lucky chance from eternal darkness."

"Ah, count! you at once delight and reassure me. Then you promise me a philtre to make me young again?"

"Yes."

" And when will you give it me?"

"Oh! you need be in no hurry; you may ask for it twenty years hence, beautiful countess. In the meantime, I think you do not wish to become quite a child again."

"You are, in truth, a charming man. One question more and I will let you go, for you seem in haste."

" Speak, countess."

" You said that some one had betrayed you. Is it a man or a woman?"

" A woman."

" Ah, ah, count! love affairs."

" Alas! yes; prompted by an almost frantic jealousy, which has produced the pleasant effect you have seen. It is a woman who, not daring to stab me with a knife, because she knows I cannot be killed, wants to imprison and ruin me."

" What! ruin you?"

"She endeavoured to do so, at least."

" Count, I will stop here," said the countess, laughing. "Is it the liquid silver which courses through your veins that gives you that immortality which makes people betray you instead of killing you? Shall I set you down here, or drive you to your own house? Come, choose!"

" No, madame, I cannot allow you to inconvenience yourself on my account. I have my horse, Djerid."

" Ah! that wonderful animal which, it is said, outstrips the wind?"

" He seems to please you, madame."

" He is, in truth, a magnificent steed."

" Allow me to offer him to you, on the condition that you alone ride him."

" Oh! no, thank you; I do not ride on horseback; or, at least, I am a very timid horsewoman. I am as much obliged to you, however, as if I accepted your offer. Adieu! my dear count; do not forget my philtre. In ten years."

"I said twenty."

"Count, you know the proverb: ' a bird in the hand — ' and if you could even give it me in five years, there is no knowing what may happen."

"Whenever you please, countess; are you not aware that I am entirely at your command?"

"Only one word more, count."

"I am all attention, madame."

"It proves that I have great confidence in you to speak of it."

Balsamo, who had already alighted from the carriage, suppressed his impatience, and approached the countess.

"It is reported everywhere," continued Madame Dubarry, "that the king is rather taken with this little Taverney."

"Ah, madame," said Balsamo, "is it possible?"

"A very great partiality, it is said. You must tell me if it is true. Count, do not deceive me; I beseech you to treat me as a friend. Tell me the truth, count."

"Madame," replied Balsamo, "I will do more; I will promise you that Mademoiselle Andrée shall never be anything to the king."

"And why not?" cried Madame Dubarry.

"Because I will it so," said Balsamo.

"Oh!" said Madame Dubarry, incredulously.

"You doubt."

"Is it not allowed?"

"Never doubt the truths of science, madame. You have believed me when I said yes; believe me when I say no."

"But, in short, have you the means — ?"

"Well?"

"Means capable of annihilating the king's will, or conquering his whims?"

Balsamo smiled.

"I create sympathies," said he.

"Yes, I know that."

"You believe it, even."

"I believe it."

"Well, I can create aversions also, and if needful, impossibilities. Therefore, countess, make your mind easy — I am on the watch."

Balsamo uttered all these fragments of sentences with an absence of mind which Madame Dubarry would not have taken as she did for inspiration, had she known the feverish anxiety which Balsamo felt to be with Lorenza as quickly as possible.

"Well, count," said she, "assuredly you are not only my prophet of happiness, but also my guardian angel. Count, mark my words: defend me and I will defend you. Alliance! union!"

"Agreed, madame," replied Balsamo, kissing the countess's hand.

Then closing the door of the carriage, which the countess had stopped upon the Champs Elysées, he mounted his horse, who neighed joyously, and was soon lost to view in the shadows of night.

"To Luciennes!" said the countess, consoled.

This time Balsamo whistled softly, and gently pressed his knees against Djerid's side, who started off at a gallop.

Five minutes afterwards he was in the vestibule of the Rue St. Claude, looking at Fritz.

"Well?" asked he, anxiously.

"Yes, master," replied the domestic, who was accustomed to read his looks.

"She has returned?"

"She is upstairs."

"In which room?"

"In the chamber of furs."

"In what state is she?"

"Oh! very much exhausted. She ran so quickly that although I saw her coming, for I was watching for her, I had scarcely time to hasten to meet her."

"Indeed!"

"Oh! I was quite alarmed. She swept on like a tempest; rushed upstairs without taking breath; and when she entered the room, she fell upon the large black lion's skin. You will find her there."

Balsamo hastily ascended, and found Lorenza where Fritz had said. She was struggling in vain against the first convulsions of a nervous crisis. The fluid had weighed upon her too long already, and forced her to violent efforts. She was in pain, and groaned deeply; it seemed as if a mountain weighed upon her breast, and that she endeavoured with both hands to remove it.

Balsamo looked at her with an eye sparkling with anger, and taking her in his arms, he carried her into her apartment, the mysterious door of which closed behind him.

## CHAPTER CXXV.

### THE ELIXIR OF LIFE.

BALSAMO had just entered Lorenza's apartment, and was preparing to awake her and overwhelm her with all reproaches which his gloomy anger prompted, fully determined to punish her according to the dictates of that anger, when a triple knock upon the ceiling announced that Althotas had watched for his return and wished to speak to him.

Nevertheless Balsamo waited; he was hoping either that he had been mistaken or that the signal had been accidental, when the impatient old man repeated his blows. Balsamo, therefore — fearing, no doubt, to see him descend, as he had already done before, or that Lorenza, awakened by an influence opposed to his own, might acquire the knowledge of some other particulars no less dangerous for him than his political secrets, — Balsamo therefore, after having, if we may so express it, charged Lorenza with a fresh stratum of the electric fluid, left the room to rejoin Althotas.

It was high time: the trap-door was already half-way from the ceiling. Althotas had left his wheeled arm-chair and was seen squatting down upon the movable part of the ceiling which rose and fell. He saw Balsamo leave Lorenza's room.

Squatting down thus, the old man was at once hideous and terrible to behold.

His white face, in those parts which still seemed as if they belonged to a living being, was purple with the violence of his rage. His meagre and bony hands, like those of a human skeleton, trembled and shook; his hollow eyes seemed to vacillate in their deep caverns; and, in a language unknown even to his disciple, he was loading him with the most violent invectives.

Having left his arm-chair to touch the spring, he seemed to live and move only by the aid of his long arms, lean and angular as those of a spider; and issuing, as we have said, from his chamber, inaccessible to all but Balsamo, he was about to descend to the lower apartment. To induce this feeble old man, indolent as he was, to leave his arm-chair (that cleverly constructed machine which spared him all fatigue), and consent to perform one of the actions of common life — to induce him to undergo the care and fatigue of such a change in his usual habits, it must have required no ordinary excitement thus to withdraw him from the ideal life in which he existed, and plunge him into the every-day world.

Balsamo, taken as it were in the fact, seemed at first astonished, then uneasy.

"Ah!" exclaimed Althotas, "there you are, you good-for-nothing, you ingrate! There you are, coward, who desert your master!"

Balsamo called all his patience to his aid, as he invariably did when he spoke to the old man.

"But," replied he quietly, "I think, my friend, you have only just called me."

"Your friend?" exclaimed Althotas; "your friend? you vile human creature! You dare to speak the language of your equals to me! I have been a friend to you, — more than a friend; a father, — a father who has educated, instructed, and enriched you. But you my friend? Oh, no! for you abandon me, — you assassinate me!"

"Come, master, you disturb your bile; you irritate your blood; you will make yourself ill."

"Ill? absurdity! Have I ever been ill, except when you made me a sharer, in spite of myself, in some of the miseries of your impure humankind? Ill! have you forgotten that it is I who heal others?"

"Well, master," replied Balsamo, coldly, "I am here. Let us not lose time in vain."

"Yes, I advise you to remind me of that. Time! time! which you oblige me to economise; me, for whom this element, circumscribed to all the world, should be endless, unlimited! Yes, my time flies — yes, my time is lost — my time, like the time of other people, falls minute by minute into the gulf of eternity, when for me it ought to be eternity itself!"

"Come, master," said Balsamo, with unalterable patience, lowering the trap to the ground as he spoke, placing himself upon it, and causing it to rise again to its place in the room; "come, what is it you want? You say I starve you, but are you not in your forty days of regimen?"

"Yes, yes, doubtless; the work of regeneration commenced thirty-two days ago."

"Then tell me, of what do you complain? I see two or three bottles of rain-water, the only kind you drink, still remaining."

"Of course; but do you imagine I am a silkworm, that I can complete the grand work of renovation of youth and of transformation alone? Do you imagine that, powerless as I am, I can compose alone the elixir of life? Or think you that, reclined on my side, and enervated by cooling drinks, my sole nourishment, I could have presence of mind enough, when left to my own resources and without your assistance, to complete the minute work of my regeneration, in which, as you, ungrateful wretch, well know, I must be aided and supported by a friend?"

"I am here, master — I am here. Answer me now," said Balsamo, replacing the old man in his chair almost in spite of himself, as he would have done a hideous infant; "answer me — you have not been in want of distilled water, for, as I said before, there are three bottles still remaining. This water, as you know, was all collected in the month of May; there are your biscuits of barley and of sesamum, and I myself administered to you the white drops you prescribed."

"Yes, but the elixir! The elixir is not made! You do not remember it, for you were not there — it was your father, your father, who was far more faithful than you are — but at the last fiftieth I had the elixir ready a month beforehand. I had my retreat on Mount Ararat. A Jew provided me with a Christian child, still at its mother's breast, for its weight in gold; I bled it according to the rule; I took the last three drops of its arterial blood, and in an hour my elixir, which only wanted this ingredient, was composed. Therefore, my first regeneration succeeded wonderfully well. My hair and teeth fell out during the convulsions which succeeded the absorption of that wondrous elixir, but they grew again — the latter badly enough, I know, because I neglected the precaution of letting the elixir flow into my throat through a golden conduit. But my hair and my nails grew again in this second youth, and I began again to live as if I were only fifteen. Now I am old again — I am bordering on the extreme limit — and, if the elixir is not ready, if it is not safely enclosed in this bottle, if I do not bestow all possible care upon this work, the science of a century will be annihilated with me, and the admirable, the sublime secret I possess will be lost for man, who, in me and through me, approaches the divinity! Oh! if I fail — if I am mistaken, if I miss it, Acharat — it will be your fault; and take care, for my anger will be terrible — terrible!"

And as he uttered these last words, a livid glare shot from his dying eyeball, and the old man fell into a brief convulsion, which ended in a violent fit of coughing.

Balsamo instantly lavished the most eager attentions on him, and the old man recovered. His complexion had become death-like instead of pale. This feeble attack had weakened his strength so much that one would have thought he was dying.

"Come, master," said Balsamo, "tell me plainly what you want."

"What I want!" said he, looking fixedly at Balsamo.

"Yes."

"What I want is this — "

"Speak ; I hear you, and I will obey, if what you ask is possible."

"Possible! possible!" muttered the old man, contempt-uously. "You know that everything is possible."

"Yes, with time and science."

"Science I have, and I am on the point of conquering time. My dose has succeeded. My strength has almost entirely left me. The white drops have caused the expulsion of all the remaining portion of my former nature. Youth, like the sap of the trees in May, rises under the old bark, and buds, so to speak, through the old wood. You may remark, Acharat, that the symptoms are excellent; my voice is weak, my sight is three-quarters gone; sometimes I feel my mind wander; I have become insensible to the transition from heat to cold. I must therefore hasten to finish my elixir, in order that, on the appointed term of my second fifty years, I may at once pass from a hundred to twenty. The ingredients for the elixir are all made, the conduit is ready; I want nothing but the three drops of blood I told you of."

Balsamo made a gesture of repugnance.

"Very well," said Althotas, "let us abandon the child, since it is so difficult, and since you prefer to shut your-self up the whole day with your mistress, to seeking it for me."

"You know, master, that Lorenza is not my mistress," replied Balsamo.

"Oh! oh! oh!" exclaimed Althotas; "you say that! You think to impose on me as on the mass; you would make me believe in an immaculate creature, and yet you are a man !"

"I swear to you, master, that Lorenza is as pure as an angel; I swear to you, that love, earthly felicity, domestic happiness — I have sacrificed all to my project. For I also have my regenerating work ; only, instead of applying it to myself alone, I shall apply it to all the world."

"Fool! poor fool!" cried Althotas; "I verily believe he is going to speak to me of his cataclysm of fleshworms, his revolutions of ant-hills, when I speak to him of life and eternal youth!"

"Which can only be acquired at the price of a fearful crime — and besides — "

"You doubt, I see you doubt — miserable wretch!"

"No, master; but since you give up the child, tell me what do you want?"

"I must have the first unmarried woman you meet. A woman is the best — I have discovered that, on account of the affinity of the sexes. Find me that, and quickly, for I have only eight days longer."

"Very well, master, I will see — I will search."

Another lightning flash, more terrible than the first, sparkled in the old man's eyes.

"You will see! you will search!" he cried. "Oh! is that your reply? I expected it, and I don't know why I am surprised. And since when, thou worm of the earth, was the creature entitled to speak thus to its master? Ah! you see me powerless, disabled, supplicating, and you are fool enough to think me at your mercy! Yes or no, Acharat? And answer me without embarrassment or falsehood, for I can see and read your heart; for I can judge you, and shall punish you."

"Master," replied Balsamo, "take care; your anger will do you an injury."

"Answer me — answer!"

"I can only say the truth to my master; I will see if I can procure what you desire, without injuring ourselves. I will endeavour to find a man who will sell you what you want; but I will not take the crime upon myself. That is all I can say."

"You are very fastidious!" said Althotas, with a bitter smile.

"It is so, master," said Balsamo.

Althotas made so violent an effort, that with the help of

his two arms resting on the arms of the chair he raised himself to his feet.

" Yes or no ? " said he.

"Master, yes, if I find it ; no, if I do not."

" Then you will expose me to death, wretch ! you will economise three drops of the blood of an insignificant, worth-less creature such as I require, and let a perfect creature such as I am fall into the eternal gulf ! Listen, Acharat !" said the old man, with a smile fearful to behold, " I no longer ask you for anything; I ask absolutely nothing. I shall wait, but if you do not obey, I must serve myself ; if you desert me, I must help myself ! You have heard me — have you not ? Now go ! "

Balsamo, without replying to this threat, prepared every-thing the old man might want. He placed the drinks and the food within his reach, and performed all the services a watchful servant would perform for his master, a devoted son for his father; then, absorbed by a thought very dif-ferent from that which tormented Althotas, he lowered the trap to descend, without remarking that the old man followed him with a sardonic and ominous grin.

Althotas was still grinning like an evil genius when Balsamo stood before the still sleeping Lorenza.

## CHAPTER CXXVI.

### THE STRUGGLE.

BALSAMO stood before her, his heart swelling with mournful thoughts, for the violent ones had vanished.

The scene which had just taken place between himself and Althotas had led him to reflect on the nothingness of all human affairs, and had chased anger from his heart. He remembered the practice of the Greek philosopher who repeated the entire alphabet before listening to the voice of that black divinity, the counsellor of Achilles.

After a moment of mute and cold contemplation before the couch on which Lorenza was lying, —

"I am sad," said he to himself, "but resolved; and I can look my situation fair in the face. Lorenza hates me; Lorenza has threatened to betray me, and has betrayed me. My secret is no longer my own; I have given it into this woman's power, and she casts it to the winds. I am like the fox who has withdrawn from the steel-trap only the bone of his leg, but who has left behind his flesh and his skin, so that the huntsman can say on the morrow, ' The fox has been taken here; I shall know him again, living or dead.'

"And this dreadful misfortune which Althotas cannot comprehend, and which, therefore, I have not even mentioned to him — this misfortune which destroys all my hopes in this country, and consequently in this world, of which France is the soul, I owe to the creature sleeping before me, to this beautiful statue with her entrancing smile. To this tempting angel I owe dishonour and ruin, and shall owe to her captivity, exile, and death.

"Therefore," continued he, becoming more animated,

"the sum of evil has exceeded that of good, and Lorenza is dangerous. Oh! serpent, with thy graceful folds, which nevertheless strangle, with thy golden throat, which is nevertheless full of venom, sleep on, for when thou awakest I shall be obliged to kill thee!"

And with a gloomy smile Balsamo slowly approached the young woman, whose languid eyes were turned towards him as he approached, as the sunflower and volubilis open to the first rays of the rising sun.

"Oh!" said Balsamo, "and yet I must forever close those eyes which now beam so tenderly on me, — those beautiful eyes which are filled with lightning when they no longer sparkle with love."

Lorenza smiled sweetly, and, smiling, she displayed the double row of her pearly teeth.

"But if I kill her who hates me," said Balsamo, wringing his hands, "I shall also kill her who loves me."

And his heart was filled with the deepest grief, strangely mingled with a vague desire.

"No, no," murmured he; "I have sworn in vain; I have threatened in vain; no, I shall never have the courage to kill her. She shall live, but she shall live without being awakened; she shall live this factitious life, which is happiness for her, while the other is despair. Would that I could make her happy! What matters to me the rest? She shall only have one existence, — the one I create, the one during which she loves me, that which she lives at this moment."

And he returned Lorenza's tender look by a look as tender as her own, placing his hand as he did so gently on her head. Lorenza, who seemed to read Balsamo's thoughts as if they were an open book, gave a long sigh, rose gradually with the graceful languor of sleep, and placed her two white arms upon Balsamo's shoulders, who felt her perfumed breath upon his cheek.

"Oh! no, no!" exclaimed Balsamo, passing his hand over his burning forehead and his dazzled eyes; "no, this intoxicating life will make me mad; and with this siren, glory, power, immortality, will all vanish from my thoughts. No, no; she must awake, I must do it.

"Oh!" continued he, "if I awake her, the struggle will begin again. If I awake her, she will kill herself, or she will kill me, or force me to destroy her. Oh, what an abyss!

"Yes, this woman's destiny is written; it stands before me in letters of fire, love, death! Lorenza, Lorenza! thou art doomed to love and to die! Lorenza, Lorenza! I hold thy life and thy love in my hands!"

Instead of a reply, the enchantress rose, advanced towards Balsamo, fell at his feet, and gazed into his eyes with a tender smile. Then she took one of his hands and placed it on her heart.

"Death!" said she in a low voice which whispered from her lips, brilliant as coral when it issues from the caverns of the deep; "death, but love!"

Balsamo retreated two steps, his head thrown back, his hand covering his eyes. Lorenza, breathless, followed him on her knees. "Death!" she repeated, in an intoxicating voice; "death, but love!"

"Oh!" said Balsamo, "it is too much; I have struggled as long as a human being could struggle. Demon, or angel of futurity, whichever thou art, thou must be content. I have long enough sacrificed all the generous passions in my heart to egotism and pride. Oh! no, no; I have no right thus to rebel against the only human feeling which still remains lurking in my heart. I love this woman, I love her; and this passionate love injures her more than the most terrible hatred could do. This love kills her! Oh, coward! oh, ferocious fool that I am! I cannot even compromise with my desires. What! when I breathe my last sigh; when I prepare to appear before God — I, the deceiver, the false prophet; when I throw off my mantle of hypocrisy and artifice before the Sovereign Judge — shall I have not one generous action to confess, not the recollection of a single happiness to console me in the midst of my eternal sufferings?

"Oh! no, no, Lorenza; I know that in loving thee I lose the future; I know that my revealing angel will wing its flight to heaven if I thus change your entire existence and overturn the natural laws of your being. But, Lorenza, you wish it, do you not?"

"My beloved!" she sighed.

"Then you accept the factitious instead of the real life?"

"I ask for it on my knees; I pray for it; I implore it. This life is love and happiness."

"And will it suffice for you when you are my wife, for I love you passionately?"

"Oh, I know it; I can read your heart!"

"And you will never accuse me, before God and men, of having surprised you, of having deceived you?"

"Never! never! before God and men. On the contrary, I shall thank you for having given me your love, the only good, the only pearl, the only diamond in the world!"

"You will never regret your wings, poor dove; for know, that you will never again roam through radiant space for me to seek the ray of light Jehovah once deigned to bestow upon his prophets. When I would know the future, when I would command men, alas! alas! thy voice will not reply. I have had in thee the beloved woman and the helping spirit, I shall only have one of the two now; and yet—"

"Ah, you doubt, you doubt!" cried Lorenza; "I see doubt like a dark stain upon your heart."

"You will always love me, Lorenza?"

"Always! always!"

Balsamo passed his hand over his forehead.

"Well, it shall be so," said he.

"Besides, do I actually need her?" thought he; "is she the only one in the world? While she will make me happy, the other will make me rich and powerful. Andrée has the same clairvoyant power as you; Andrée is young, pure, a maiden, and I do not love her. Yet, in her magnetic sleep, Andrée is as submissive as you, and to me she is the physician's ' *corpus vile*,' which may serve for experiments. She can traverse the realms of the unknown even farther than you. Andrée, you shall be my kingdom, Lorenza, you shall be my love; with Andrée I am powerful, with Lorenza I am happy. From this moment my life is complete, and, except for immortality, I have realised Althotas' fondest dreams. Except for immortality I am equal to the gods."

And raising Lorenza, he folded her in his arms and pressed a kiss upon her forehead — the seal of his promise to love and cherish her till death.

# CHAPTER CXXVII.

## LOVE.

FOR Balsamo another life had commenced, — a life hitherto unknown in his active, troubled, multiplied existence. For three days there had been for him no more anger, no more apprehension, no more jealousy; for three days he had not heard the subject of politics, conspirators, or conspiracies as much as whispered. By Lorenza's side, and he had not left her for an instant, he had forgotten the whole world. This strange, inexplicable love, which, as it were, soared above humanity; this intoxicating and mysterious attachment; this love of a shadow, for he could not conceal from himself that with a word he could change his gentle bride into an implacable enemy; this love, snatched from hatred, thanks to an inexplicable caprice of nature or of science, plunged Balsamo into happiness which bordered on madness.

More than once, during these three days, rousing himself from the opiate torpor of love, Balsamo looked at his ever-smiling, ever-ecstatic companion — for from thenceforth, in the existence he had created for her, she reposed from her factitious life in a sort of ecstasy equally factitious — and when he saw her calm, gentle, happy; when she called him by the most affectionate names, and dreamed aloud her mysterious love, he more than once asked himself if some ruthless demon had not inspired Lorenza with the idea of deceiving him with a falsehood in order to lull his vigilance, and when it was lulled, to escape, and only appear again as the Avenging Eumenides.

In such moments Balsamo doubted of the truth of a

science received by tradition from antiquity, but of which
he had no evidence but examples.     But soon the ever-
springing fountain of her affection reassured him.

"If Lorenza was feigning," argued he with himself, "if
she intended to fly from me, she would seek opportunities
for sending me away, she would invent excuses for occa-
sional solitude; but, far from that, her arms are always
embracing me; her ardent look says to me, 'Do not go
away;' her gentle voice ever whispers, 'Stay!'"

Then Balsamo's confidence in himself and in science
returned.   Why, indeed, should the magic secret, to which
alone he owned his power, have become all at once, and
without any transition, a chimera, fit only to throw to the
winds as a vanished recollection, as the smoke of an extinguished fire?   Never with relation to him had Lorenza
been more lucid, more clear-sighted.   All the thoughts
which sprang up in his mind, all the feelings which made
his heart bound, were instantly reproduced in hers.   It
remained to be seen if this lucidity were not sympathy;
if, beyond himself and the young girl, beyond the circle
which their love had traced, and which their love illuminated with its light, the eyes of her soul, so clear-sighted
before this new era of continued sleep, could yet pierce
the surrounding darkness.

Balsamo dared not make the decisive trial; he hoped
still, and this hope was the resplendent crown of his
happiness.

Sometimes Lorenza said to him, with gentle melancholy,—

"Acharat, you think of another than me, — of a northern
woman, with fair hair and blue eyes.   Acharat! Acharat!
this woman always moves beside me in your thoughts."

Balsamo looked tenderly at Lorenza.

"You see that in me?" said he.

"Oh, yes; as clearly as I read the surface of a mirror."

"Then you know it is not love which makes me think
of that woman," replied Balsamo.   "Read in my heart,
dearest Lorenza!"

"No," replied she, bending her head; "no, I know it well. But yet your thoughts are divided between us two, as in the days when Lorenza Feliciani tormented you — the naughty Lorenza, who sleeps, and whom you will not again awake."

"No, my love, no!" exclaimed Balsamo; "I think only of thee, at least with the heart. Have I not forgotten all, neglected everything — study, politics, work — since our happiness?"

"And you are wrong," said Lorenza, "for I could help you in your work."

"How?"

"Yes; did you not once spend whole hours in your laboratory?"

"Certainly. But I renounce all these vain endeavours; they would be so many hours taken from my life — for during that time I should not see you."

"And why should I not follow you in your labours as in your love? Why should I not make you powerful as I make you happy?"

"Because, my Lorenza, it is true, is beautiful, but she has not studied. God gives beauty and love, but study alone gives science."

"The soul knows everything."

"Then you can really see with the eyes of your soul?"

"Yes."

"And you can guide me in the grand search after the philosopher's stone?"

"I think so."

"Come, then."

And Balsamo, encircling her waist with his arm, led her into his laboratory. The gigantic furnace, which no one had replenished for four days, was extinguished, and the crucibles had grown cold upon their chafing-dishes.

Lorenza looked around on all these strange instruments — the last combinations of expiring alchemy — without surprise; she seemed to know the purpose which each was intended to fulfil.

"You are attempting to make gold?" said she, smiling.

"Yes."

"All these crucibles contain preparations in different stages of progress?"

"All stopped — all lost; but I do not regret it."

"You are right, for your gold would never be anything but coloured mercury; you can render it solid, perhaps, but you cannot transform it."

"But gold can be made?"

"No."

"And yet Daniel of Transylvania sold the receipt for the transmutation of metals to Cosmo the First for twenty thousand ducats."

"Daniel of Transylvania deceived Cosmo the First."

"And yet the Saxon Payken, who was condemned to death by Charles the Second, ransomed his life by changing a leaden ingot into a golden one, from which forty ducats were coined, besides taking as much from the ingot as made a medal, which was struck in honour of the clever alchemist."

"The clever alchemist was nothing but a clever juggler; he merely substituted the golden ingot for the leaden one: nothing more.  Your surest way of making gold, Acharat, is to melt into ingots, as you do already, the riches which your slaves bring you from the four quarters of the world."

Balsamo remained pensive.

"Then the transmutation of metals is impossible?" said he.

"Impossible."

"And the diamond — is it, too, impossible to create?"

"Oh! the diamond is another matter," said Lorenza.

"The diamond can be made, then?"

"Yes; for, to make the diamond, you have not to transmute one body into another; to make the diamond is merely to attempt the simple modification of a known element."

"Then you know the element of which the diamond is formed?"

"To be sure; the diamond is pure carbon crystallised."

Balsamo was almost stunned; a dazzling, unexpected, unheard-of light flashed before his eyes; he covered them with both hands, as if the flame had blinded him.

"Oh, bountiful Creator!" said he, "you give me too much — some danger threatens me! What precious ring must I throw into the sea to appease the jealousy of my fate? Enough, Lorenza, for to-day!"

"Am I not yours? Order, command me!"

"Yes, you are mine. Come, come!"

And he drew her out of the laboratory, crossed the chamber of furs, and, without paying any attention to a light, creaking noise he heard overhead, he once more entered the barred room with Lorenza.

"So you are pleased with your Lorenza, my beloved Balsamo?"

"Oh!" exclaimed he.

"What did you fear, then? Speak — tell me all."

Balsamo clasped his hands, and looked at Lorenza with an expression of such terror, that a spectator, ignorant of what was passing in his heart, would have been totally at a loss to account for it.

"Oh!" murmured he, "and I was near killing this angel — I was near expiring of despair before resolving the problem of being at once powerful and happy! I forgot that the limits of the possible always exceed the horizon traced by the present state of science, and that the majority of truths which have become facts have always, in their infancy, been looked upon as dreams! I thought I knew everything, and I knew nothing!"

The young Italian smiled divinely.

"Lorenza, Lorenza!" continued Balsamo, "the mysterious design of the Creator is, then, accomplished, which makes woman to be born of the substance of the man, and which commands them to have only one heart in common!

Eve is revived for me — an Eve who will not have a thought that is not mine, and whose life hangs by the thread which I hold. It is too much, my God, for a creature to possess! I sink under the weight of Thy gift!"

And he fell upon his knees, gazing with adoration upon the gentle beauty, who smiled on him as no earthly creature can smile.

"Oh, no!" he continued; "no, you shall never leave me more! I shall live in all safety under your look, which can pierce into the future. You will assist me in those laborious researches which you alone, as you have said, can complete, and which one word from you will render easy and successful. You will point me out, since I cannot make gold — gold being a homogeneous substance, a primitive element — you will point me out in what corner of the world the Creator has concealed it; you will tell me where the rich treasures lie which have been swallowed up in the vast depths of the ocean; with your eyes I shall see the pearl grow in the veined shell, and man's thoughts spring up under their gross, earthly covering; with your ears I shall hear the dull sound of the worm beneath the ground, and the footsteps of mine enemy as he approaches! I shall be great as God. Happier than God; for God has no equal or companion in heaven. God is all-powerful, but he is alone in his divine majesty and in his divinity; he shares his omnipotent power with no other being."

And Lorenza still smiled upon him; and as she smiled she replied to his words by affectionate caresses.

"And yet," whispered she, as if she could see each thought which whirled through his restless brain, "and yet you doubt still, Acharat, as you have said, if I can cross the circle of our love — you doubt if I can see into the distance; but you console yourself by thinking that if I cannot see, she can."

"She! Who?"

"The fair-haired beauty. Shall I tell you her name?"

"Yes."

"Stay — Andrée !"

"Ah, yes; you can read my thoughts! Yet a last expiring fear still troubles me. Can you still see through space, though material obstacles intervene?"

"Try me."

"Give me your hand, Lorenza."

The young girl passionately seized Balsamo's hand.

"Can you follow me?"

"Anywhere."

"Come !"

And Balsamo, leaving in thought the Rue St. Claude, drew Lorenza's thoughts along with him.

"Where are we?" asked he.

"We are upon a hill," replied the young Italian.

"Yes, you are right," said Balsamo, trembling with delight. "But what do you see?"

"Before me, to the right, or to the left?"

"Before you."

"I see a long alley, with a wood on one side, a town on the other, and a river which separates them and loses itself in the horizon, after flowing under the walls of a large château."

"That is right, Lorenza. The forest is that of Vesinet; the town, St. Germain; the château is the Château de Maisons. Let us enter the pavilion behind us. What do you see there?"

"Ah! in the first place, in the antechamber, a little negro, fantastically dressed, and employed in eating sugar-plums."

"Yes, Zamore. Proceed, proceed !"

"An empty salon, splendidly furnished; the spaces above the doors painted with goddesses and Cupids."

"The salon is empty, you say?"

"Yes."

"Let us go still further."

"Ah ! we are in a splendid boudoir, lined with blue satin embroidered with flowers of natural colours."

"Is that empty also?"

"No; a lady is reclining upon a sofa."

"What lady? Do you not remember to have seen her before?"

"Yes; it is the Countess Dubarry."

"Right, Lorenza. I shall go frantic with delight! What does the lady do?"

"She is thinking of you, Balsamo."

"Of me?"

"Yes."

"Then you can read her thoughts?"

"Yes; for I repeat she is thinking of you."

"For what purpose?"

"You have made her a promise."

"Yes."

"You promised her that water of beauty which Venus, to revenge herself on Sappho, gave to Phaon."

"Yes, yes; you are right again. And what does she do while thinking?"

"She comes to a decision."

"What decision?"

"She reaches out her hand towards the bell; she rings; another young lady enters."

"Dark or light haired?"

"Dark."

"Tall or short?"

"Little."

"Her sister. Listen to what she says to her."

"She orders the horses to be put to her carriage."

"Where does she wish to go?"

"To come here."

"Are you sure?"

"She is giving the order. Stay!—she is obeyed. I see the horses and the carriage. In two hours she will be here."

Balsamo fell upon his knees.

"Oh!" exclaimed he, "if in two hours she should really be here, I shall have nothing left to ask for on earth!"

"My poor Balsamo! then you still feared?"

"Yes, yes!"

"And why did you fear? Love, which completes the material existence, increases also our mental powers; love, like every generous emotion, brings us nearer to God, and all wisdom comes from God."

"Lorenza, Lorenza, you will drive me mad with joy!"

Balsamo now only waited for another proof to be completely happy; this proof was the arrival of Madame Dubarry.

The two hours of suspense were short. All measure of time had completely ceased for Balsamo.

Suddenly the young girl started, and took Balsamo's hand.

"You are doubting yet," said she, "or you wish to know where she is at this moment."

"Yes," said Balsamo, "you are right."

"Well," replied Lorenza, "she is thundering along the Boulevards at the full speed of her horses; she approaches; she turns into the Rue St. Claude; she stops before the door and knocks."

The apartment in which they were was so retired and so quiet that the noise of the iron knocker could not penetrate its recesses; but Balsamo, raised upon one knee, was anxiously listening.

At this moment two knocks struck by Fritz made him bound to his feet, for the reader will remember that two knocks were the signal of an important visit.

"Oh," said he, "then it is true!"

"Go and convince yourself, Balsamo; but return quickly."

Balsamo advanced towards the fireplace.

"Let me accompany you," said Lorenza, "as far as the door of the staircase."

"Come!"

And they both passed together into the chamber of furs.

"You will not leave this room?"

"No; I will await you here. Oh, do not fear; you know

the Lorenza who loves you is not the Lorenza whom you fear. Besides —"

She stopped and smiled.

"What?" asked Balsamo.

"Can you not read in my soul as I read yours?"

"Alas! no."

"Besides, you can command me to sleep until you return. Command me to remain immovable upon this sofa, and I shall sleep and be motionless."

"Well, my Lorenza, it shall be so. Sleep, and await my return here!"

Lorenza, already struggling with sleep, fell back upon the sofa, murmuring, —

"You will return soon, my Balsamo, will you not?"

Balsamo waved his hand; Lorenza was already asleep; but so beautiful, so pure, with her long, flowing hair, the feverish glow upon her cheeks, her half-opened and swimming eyes, so little like a mortal, that Balsamo turned again, took her hand and kissed her arms and her neck, but dared not kiss her lips.

Two knocks were heard a second time. The lady was becoming impatient, or Fritz feared that his master had not heard him. Balsamo hastened to the door, but as he closed it behind him he fancied he heard a second creaking noise like the former one. He opened the door again, looked round, and saw nothing but Lorenza sleeping, and her breast heaving beneath the magnetic sleep.

Balsamo closed the door and hastened towards the salon, without uneasiness, without fear, without foreboding — all heaven in his heart! But he was mistaken: it was not sleep alone which oppressed Lorenza's bosom and made her breathe so heavily; it was a kind of dream which seemed to belong to the lethargy in which she was plunged, — a lethargy which so nearly resembled death.

Lorenza dreamed, and in the hideous mirror of her gloomy dreams she fancied she saw, through the darkness which commenced to close around her, the oaken ceiling open, and something like a large circular platform descend slowly with a regular, slow, measured movement, accompanied by a disagreeable hissing noise. It seemed to her as if she breathed with difficulty, as if she were almost suffocated by the pressure of this moving circle.

It seemed to her as if, upon this moving trap something moved, — some mis-shapen being like Caliban in "The Tempest;" a monster with a human face; an old man whose eyes and arms alone were living, and who looked at her with his frightful eyes, and stretched his fleshless arms towards her.

And she — she, poor child! — she writhed in vain, without power to escape, without dreaming of the danger which threatened her; she felt nothing but the grasp of two living flesh-hooks seizing upon her white dress, lifting her from her sofa, and placing her upon the trap, which reascended slowly towards the ceiling with the grating noise of iron scraping against iron, and amidst a hideous, mocking laugh from the monster with the human face, who was raising her aloft without shock and without pain.

## CHAPTER CXXVIII.

As Lorenza had foretold, it was Madame Dubarry who had just knocked at the gate.

The beautiful countess had been ushered into the salon. Whilst awaiting Balsamo's arrival, she was looking over that curious Book of Death engraved at Mayence, the plates of which, designed with marvellous skill, show death presiding over all the acts of man's life, — waiting for him at the door of the ball-room after he has pressed the hand of the woman he loves, dragging him to the bottom of the water in which he is bathing, or hiding in the barrel of the gun he carries to the chase. Madame Dubarry was at the plate which represents a beautiful woman daubing her face with rouge, and looking at herself in the glass, when Balsamo opened the door and bowed to her, with the smile of happiness still beaming upon his face.

"Excuse me, madame, for having made you wait; but I had not well calculated the distance, or was ignorant of the speed of your horses. I thought you still at the Place Louis XV."

"What do you mean?" asked the countess. "You knew I was coming, then?"

"Yes, madame; it is about two hours ago since I saw you in your boudoir lined with blue satin, giving orders for your horses to be put to the carriage."

"And you say I was in my blue satin boudoir?"

"Embroidered with flowers coloured after nature. Yes, countess, you were reclining upon a sofa; a pleasing thought passed through your mind; you said to yourself, 'I will go and visit the Count de Fenix;' then you rang the bell."

"And who entered?"

"Your sister, countess; am I right? You requested her to transmit your orders, which were instantly executed."

"Truly, count, you *are* a sorcerer. You really alarm me."

"Oh! have no fear, countess; my sorcery is very harmless."

"And you saw that I was thinking of you?"

"Yes; and even that you thought of me with benevolent intentions."

"Ah! you are right, my dear count; I have the best possible intentions towards you, but confess that you deserve more than intentions — you, who are so kind and so useful, and who seem destined to play in my life the part of tutor, which is the most difficult part I know."

"In truth, madame, you make me very happy. Then I have been of use to you?"

"What! you are a sorcerer, and cannot guess?"

"Allow me, at least, the merit of being modest."

"As you please, my dear count; then I will first speak of what I have done for you."

"I cannot permit it, madame; on the contrary, speak of yourself, I beseech you."

"Well, my dear count, in the first place, give me that talisman which renders one invisible; for on my journey here, rapid as it was, I fancied I recognised one of Monsieur de Richelieu's greys."

"And this grey?"

"Followed my carriage, carrying on his back a courier."

"What do you think of this circumstance? and for what purpose could the duke have caused you to be followed?"

"With the intention of playing me some scurvy trick. Modest as you are, my dear Count de Fenix, you must be aware that Nature has gifted you with personal advantages enough to make a king jealous of my visits to you, or of yours to me."

"Monsieur de Richelieu cannot be dangerous to you in any way, madame," replied Balsamo.

"But he was so, my dear count; he was dangerous before this last event."

Balsamo comprehended that there was a secret concealed beneath these words which Lorenza had not yet revealed to him. He did not therefore venture on the unknown ground, and replied merely by a smile.

"He was indeed," repeated the countess; "and I was nearly falling a victim to a most skilfully constructed plot —a plot in which you also had some share, count."

"I! engaged in a plot against you? Never, madame!"

"Was it not you who gave the Duke de Richelieu the philtre?"

"What philtre?"

"A draught which causes the most ardent love."

"No, madame; Monsieur de Richelieu composes those draughts himself, for he has long known the receipt; I merely gave him a simple narcotic."

"Ah! indeed?"

"Upon my honour!"

"And on what day did Monsieur de Richelieu ask for this narcotic? Remember the date, count; it is of importance."

"Madame, it was last Saturday—the day previous to that on which I had the honour of sending you, through Fritz, the note requesting you to meet me at Monsieur de Sartines."

"The eve of that day!" exclaimed the countess. "The eve of the day on which the king was seen going to the Little Trianon? Oh! now everything is explained."

"Then, if all is explained, you see I only gave the narcotic."

"Yes, the narcotic saved us all."

This time Balsamo waited; he was profoundly ignorant of the subject.

"I am delighted, madame," replied he, "to have been useful to you, even unintentionally."

"Oh! you are always kindness itself. But you can do more for me than you have ever yet done. Oh, doctor! I have been very ill, practically speaking, and even now I can yet scarcely believe in my recovery."

"Madame," said Balsamo, "the doctor, since there is a doctor in the case, always requires the details of the illness he is to cure. Will you give me the exact particulars of what you have experienced? — and if possible, do not forget a single symptom."

"Nothing can be more simple, my dear doctor, or dear sorcerer — whichever you prefer. The eve of the day on which this narcotic was used, his Majesty refused to accompany me to Luciennes. He remained, like a deceiver as he is, at Trianon, pretending fatigue, and yet, as I have since learned, he supped at Trianon with the Duke de Richelieu and the Baron de Taverney."

"Ha!"

"Now you understand. At supper the love-draught was given to the king. He was already captivated by Mademoiselle Andrée. He was not going to see me the next day; therefore the philtre was for that young lady."

"Well, what happened?"

"Oh, that is difficult to discover. The king was seen going in the direction of the offices of Trianon; that is to say, towards Mademoiselle Andrée's rooms."

"I know where she resides; but what happened?"

"Ah! what happened? How fast you go, count. The king cannot be followed without danger, when he wishes his movements to be kept secret."

"But, in short?"

"In short, all I can tell you is, that his Majesty returned to Trianon through a fearful storm, pale, trembling, and feverish — almost on the verge of delirium."

"And you think," said Balsamo, smiling, "that it was not the storm alone which alarmed his Majesty?"

"No, for the valet heard him cry several times, 'Dead, dead, dead!'"

"Oh!" said Balsamo.

"It was the narcotic," continued Madame Dubarry. "Nothing alarms the king so much as death, and next to death, its semblance. He had found Mademoiselle de Taverney sleeping a strange sleep, and must have thought her dead."

"Yes, yes; dead indeed," said Balsamo, who remembered having fled without awakening Andrée; "dead, or at least presenting all the appearance of death. Yes, yes — it must be so. Well, madame, and what then?"

"No one knows what happened during the night, or rather during the first part of the night. The king, on his return, was attacked by a violent fever and a nervous trembling, which did not leave him until the morning, when it occurred to the dauphiness to open the shutters and show his Majesty a lovely morning, with the sun shining upon merry faces. Then all these unknown visions disappeared with the night which had produced them. At noon the king was better, took some broth, and ate a partridge's wing; and in the evening — "

"And in the evening — ?" repeated Balsamo.

"In the evening," continued Madame Dubarry, "his Majesty, who no doubt would not stay at Trianon after his fright, came to see me at Luciennes, where, dear count, I discovered that Monsieur de Richelieu was almost as great a sorcerer as you."

The triumphant countenance and graceful but roguish look of the countess reassured Balsamo as to the power the favourite yet exercised over the king.

"Then you are satisfied with me, madame?" inquired he.

"Delighted, count! and when you spoke of impossibilities you could create, you told the exact truth."

And in token of thanks she gave him her soft, white, perfumed hand, which was not fresh as Lorenza's, but almost as beautiful.

"And now, count, let us speak of yourself."

Balsamo bowed like a man ready to listen.

"If you have preserved me from a great danger," continued Madame Dubarry, "I think I have also saved you from no inconsiderable peril."

"Me!" said Balsamo, concealing his emotion. "I do not require that to feel grateful to you; but yet, be good enough to inform me what — "

"Yes. The coffer in question — "

"Well, madame?"

"Contained a multitude of secret ciphers, which Monsieur de Sartines caused all his clerks to translate. All signed their several translations, executed apart, and all gave the same result. In consequence of this, Monsieur de Sartines arrived at Versailles this morning while I was there, bringing with him all these translations and the dictionary of diplomatic ciphers."

"Ha! — and what did the king say?"

"The king seemed suprised at first, then alarmed. His Majesty easily listens to those who speak to him of danger. Since the stab of Damien's penknife, there is one word which is ever eagerly hearkened to by Louis XV.; it is — *Take care!*"

"Then Monsieur de Sartines accused me of plotting?"

"At first Monsieur de Sartines endeavoured to make me leave the room; but I refused, declaring that as no one was more attached to his Majesty than myself, no one had a right to make me leave him when danger was in question. Monsieur de Sartines insisted, but I resisted, and the king, looking at me in a manner I know well, said:

"'Let her remain, Sartines: I can refuse her nothing to-day.'

"Then you understand, count, that as I was present, Monsieur de Sartines, remembering our adieu, so clearly expressed, feared to displease me by attacking you. He therefore spoke of the evil designs of the King of Prussia towards France; of the disposition prevalent to facilitate the march of rebellion by supernatural means. In a word, he accused a great many people, proving always by the papers he held that these persons were guilty."

"Guilty of what?"

"Of what! Count, dare I disclose secrets of state?"

"Which are our secrets, madame. Oh! you risk nothing. I think it is my interest not to speak."

"Yes, count, I know that Monsieur de Sartines wished to prove that a numerous and powerful sect, composed of bold, skilful, resolute agents, were silently undermining the respect due to the king, by spreading certain reports concerning his Majesty."

"What rumours?"

"Saying, for instance, that his Majesty was accused of starving his people."

"To which the king replied — ?"

"As the king always replies, by a joke."

Balsamo breathed again.

"And what was the joke?" he asked.

"'Since I am accused of starving the people,' said he, 'there is only one reply to make to the accusation — let us feed them.'

"'How so, sire?' said Monsieur de Sartines.

"'I will take the charge of feeding all those who spread this report, and, moreover, will give them safe lodging in my château of the Bastille.'"

A slight shudder passed through Balsamo's limbs, but he retained his smiling countenance.

"What followed?" asked he.

"Then the king seemed to consult me by a smile. 'Sire,' said I, 'I can never believe that those little black characters which Monsieur de Sartines has brought to you mean that you are a bad king.'

"Then the lieutenant of police exclaimed loudly.

"'Any more,' I added, 'than they prove that your clerks can read.'"

"And what did the king say, countess?" asked Balsamo.

"That I might be right, but that Monsieur de Sartines was not wrong."

"Well, and then?"

"Then a great many *lettres-de-cachet* were made out, and I saw that Monsieur de Sartines tried to slip amongst them one for you; but I stood firm, and arrested him by a single word.

"'Monsieur,' I said aloud, and before the king, 'arrest all Paris if you like, — that is your business; but you had better reflect a little before you lay a finger on one of my friends. If not —'

"'Oh ho!' said the king, 'she is getting angry; take care, Sartines.'

"'But, sire, the interest of the kingdom —'

"'Oh! you are not a Sully,' said I, crimson with rage, 'and I am not a Gabrielle.'

"'Madame, they intend to assassinate the king, as Henry IV. was assassinated.'

"For the first time the king turned pale, trembled, and put his hand to his head.

"I feared I was vanquished.

"'Sire,' said I, 'you must let Monsieur de Sartines have his own way; for his clerks have, no doubt, read in these ciphers that I also am conspiring against you.'

"And I left the room.

"But, *dame!* my dear count, it was the morning after the philtre; the king preferred my company to that of Monsieur de Sartines, and ran after me.

"'Ah! for pity's sake, my dear countess,' said he, 'pray do not get angry.'

"'Then send away that horrid man, sire; he smells of dungeons.'

"'Go, Sartines; be off with you!' said the king, shrugging his shoulders.

"'And, for the future, I forbid you not only to visit me, but even to bow to me,' added I.

"At this blow our magistrate became alarmed; he approached me, and humbly kissed my hand.

"'Well,' said he, 'so be it; let us speak no more of it, fair lady. But you will ruin the state. Since you absolutely insist upon it, your *protégé* shall be respected by my agents.'"

Balsamo seemed plunged in a deep reverie.

"Well," said the countess, "so you do not even thank me for having saved you from the pleasure of lodging in the Bastille, which perhaps might have been unjust, but assuredly no less disagreeable on that account?"

Balsamo made no reply. He drew a small phial, filled with a fluid red as blood, from his pocket.

"Hold, madame!" said he; "for the liberty you have procured for me I give you twenty years' additional youth."

The countess slipped the phial into her bosom, and took her leave, joyous and triumphant.

Balsamo still remained thinking.

"They might perhaps have been saved," said he, "but for the coquetry of a woman. This courtesan's little foot dashes them down into the depths of the abyss. Decidedly, God is with us!"

## CHAPTER CXXIX.

### BLOOD.

THE door had no sooner closed upon Madame Dubarry than Balsamo ascended the secret staircase and entered the chamber of furs. This conversation with the countess had been long, and his impatience had two causes.

The first was the desire to see Lorenza; the second, the fear that she might be fatigued, for in the new life he had given her there was no room for weariness of mind. She might be fatigued, inasmuch as she might pass, as she sometimes did, from the magnetic sleep to ecstasy; and to this ecstatic state always succeeded those nervous crises which prostrated Lorenza's strength, if the intervention of the restoring fluid did not restore the necessary equilibrium between the various functions of her being.

Balsamo, therefore, having entered and closed the door, immediately glanced at the couch where he had left Lorenza.

She was no longer there!

Only the fine shawl of cashmere embroidered with golden flowers, which had enveloped her like a scarf, was still lying upon the cushions, as an evidence that she had been in the room, and had been reclining on them.

Balsamo stood motionless, gazing at the empty sofa. Perhaps Lorenza had felt herself incommoded by a strange odour which seemed to have filled the room since he left it; perhaps by a mechanical movement she had usurped some of the functions of actual life, and instinctively changed her place.

Balsamo's first idea was that Lorenza had returned to the laboratory, whither she had accompanied him a short time previously.

He entered the laboratory. At the first glance it seemed empty; but in the shadow of the gigantic furnace, or behind the Oriental tapestry, a woman could easily conceal herself.

He raised the tapestry, therefore; he made the circuit of the furnace; nowhere could he discover even a trace of Lorenza.

There remained only the young girl's chamber, to which she had, no doubt, returned; for this chamber was a prison to her only in her waking state.

He hastened to the chamber, and found the secret door closed. This was no proof that Lorenza had not entered. Nothing was more probable, in fact, than that Lorenza, in her lucid sleep, had remembered the mechanism, and, remembering it, had obeyed the hallucination of a dream barely effaced from her mind. Balsamo pressed the spring.

The chamber was empty, like the laboratory; it did not appear as if Lorenza had even entered it.

Then a heart-rending thought — a thought which, it will be remembered, had already stung his heart — chased away all the suppositions, all the hopes of the happy lover.

Lorenza had been playing a part; she must have feigned to sleep in order to banish all distrust, all uneasiness, all watchfulness, from her husband's mind; and at the first opportunity had fled again, this time with surer precautions, warned as she had been by a first, or rather by two former experiences.

At this idea Balsamo started up and rang for Fritz.

Then, as Fritz, to his impatient mind, seemed to delay, he hastened to meet him, and found him on the secret staircase.

"The signora?" said he.

"Well, master?" said Fritz, seeing by Balsamo's agitation that something extraordinary had taken place.

"Have you seen her?"

"No, master."

"She has not gone?"

"From where?"

"From this house, to be sure!"

"No one has left the house but the countess, behind whom I have just closed the gate."

Balsamo rushed up the stairs again like a madman. Then he fancied that the giddy young creature, so different in her sleep from what she was when waking, had concealed herself in a moment of childish playfulness; that from the corner where she was hid she was now reading his heart, and amusing herself by terrifying him, in order to reassure him afterwards. Then he recommenced a minute search.

Not a nook was omitted, not a cupboard forgotten, not a screen left in its proper place. There was something in this search of Balsamo's like the frantic efforts of a man blinded by passion, alternating with the feeble and tottering gait of a drunkard. He could then only stretch out his arms and cry, "Lorenza! Lorenza!" hoping that the adored creature would rush forth suddenly, and throw herself into his arms with an exclamation of joy.

But silence alone, a gloomy and uninterrupted silence, replied to his extravagant thoughts and mad appeals.

In running wildly about, dashing aside the furniture, shouting to the naked walls, calling Lorenza, staring without seeing any object or forming a single coherent thought, Balsamo passed three minutes — that is to say, three centuries — of agony.

He recovered by degrees from this half insane hallucination, dipped his hand in a vase of iced water, moistened his temples, and, pressing one hand in the other, as if to force himself to be cool, he chased back by his iron will the blood which was beating wildly against his brain, with that fatal, incessant, monotonous movement which indicates life when there is merely motion and silence, but which is a sign of death or madness when it becomes tumultuous and perceptible.

"Come!" said he, "let me reason. Lorenza is not here;

no more false pretences with myself. Lorenza is not here; she must be gone, — yes, gone, quite gone!"

And he looked around once more, and once more shouted her name.

"Gone!" continued he. "In vain Fritz asserts that he has not seen her. She is gone, — gone!

"Two cases present themselves.

"Either he has not seen Lorenza, — and, after all, that is possible, for man is liable to error, — or he has seen her, and has been bribed by her.

"Fritz bribed!

"Why not? In vain does his past fidelity plead against this supposition. If Lorenza, if love, if science, could so deeply deceive and lie, why should the frail nature of a fallible human being not deceive also?

"Oh, I will know all! I will know all! Is there not Mademoiselle de Taverney left? Yes, through Andrée I shall know if Fritz has betrayed me, if Lorenza is false! And this time — oh! this time, as love has proved false, as science has proved an error, as fidelity has become a snare — oh! this time Balsamo will punish without pity, without sparing, like a strong man who revenges himself, who chases pity from his heart, and keeps only pride.

"Let me see: the first step is to leave this as quickly as possible, not to let Fritz suspect anything, and to fly to Trianon."

And Balsamo, seizing his hat, which had rolled on the ground, rushed towards the door.

But all at once he stopped.

"Oh!" said he, "before anything else — my God! poor old man, I had forgotten him — I must see Althotas. During my delirium, during this spasm of forced and unnatural love, I have neglected the unfortunate old man, I have been ungrateful and inhuman!"

And, with the feverishness which now animated all his movements, Balsamo approached the spring which put in motion the trap in the ceiling, and the movable scaffold quickly descended.

Balsamo placed himself upon it, and, aided by the counterpoise, mounted again, still overwhelmed by the anguish of his mind and heart, and without thinking of anything but Lorenza. Scarcely had he attained the level of the floor, when the voice of Althotas struck upon his ear, and roused him from his gloomy reverie.

But, to Balsamo's great astonishment, the old man's first words were not reproaches, as he had expected; he was received with an outburst of simple and natural gaiety.

The pupil looked with an astonished gaze upon his master.

The old man was reclining upon his spring-chair. He breathed noisily and with delight, as if at each inspiration he added a day to his life; his eyes, full of a gloomy fire, but the expression of which was enlivened by the smile upon his lips, were fixed eagerly upon his visitor.

Balsamo summoned up all his strength and collected his ideas in order to conceal his grief from his master, who had so little indulgence for human weaknesses.

During this moment of reflection Balsamo felt a strange oppression weigh upon his breast. No doubt the air was vitiated by being too constantly breathed, for a heavy, dull, close, nauseous odour, like the one he had already felt below, but there in a slighter degree, floated in the air, and, like the vapours which rise from lakes and marshes in autumn at sunrise and sunset, had taken a shape and rested on the windows.

In this dense and acrid atmosphere Balsamo's heart throbbed, his head felt confused, a vertigo seized upon him, and he felt that respiration and strength were fast failing him.

"Master," said he, seeking some object on which to support himself, and endeavouring to dilate his lungs, "master, you cannot live here; there is no air."

"You think so?"

"Oh!"

"Nevertheless, I breathe very well in it," replied Althotas, gaily, "and I live, as you see."

"Master, master," replied Balsamo, growing more and more giddy, "let me open a window! See! it rises from the floor like an exhalation of blood!"

"Of blood! Ah! you think so? Of blood!" cried Althotas, bursting into a laugh.

"Oh, yes, yes; I feel the miasma which is exhaled from a newly killed body; I could weigh it, so heavily does it press upon my brain and heart."

"That is it," said Althotas, with his sardonic laugh; "that is it; I also perceived it. You have a tender heart and a weak brain, Acharat."

"Master," said Balsamo, pointing with his finger at the old man, "master, you have blood upon your hands; master, there is blood upon this table; there is blood everywhere, even in your eyes, which shine like two torches; master, the smell which I breathe, and which makes me giddy, which is suffocating me, is the smell of blood!"

"Well, what then?" said Althotas, quickly; "is this the first time in your life that you have smelt it?"

"No."

"Have you never seen me make experiments? Have you never made any yourself?"

"But human blood!" said Balsamo, pressing his hand upon his burning forehead.

"Ah! you have a subtle sense of smell," said Althotas. "Well, I did not think human blood could be distinguished from that of any other animal."

"Human blood!" muttered Balsamo.

And as he reeled backwards and felt for some projecting point to support him, he perceived with horror a vast copper basin, the shining sides of which reflected the purple colour of the freshly spilled blood.

The enormous vase was half filled.

Balsamo started back, terrified.

"Oh, this blood!" exclaimed he; "whence comes this blood?"

Althotas made no reply, but his watchful glance lost none of the feverish fluctuations and wild terror of Balsamo. Suddenly the latter uttered a fearful groan.

Then, stooping like some wild beast darting upon its prey, he rushed to a corner of the room and picked up from the floor a silken ribbon embroidered with silver, to which was hanging a long tress of black hair.

After this wild, mournful, terrible cry, a deathlike silence reigned for a moment in the old man's apartment. Balsamo slowly raised the ribbon, shuddered as he examined the tresses, which a golden pin fastened to the silk at one end, while, cut off sharply at the other, they seemed like a fringe the extremity of which had been dipped in a wave of blood, the red and sparkling drops of which were still apparent on the margin.

In proportion as Balsamo raised his hand, it, trembled still more.

As he looked more intently at the ribbon, his cheeks grew a deeper livid.

"Whence does this come?" murmured he, in a hollow voice, loud enough, however, for another to hear and to reply to his question.

"That?" asked Althotas.

"Yes, that."

"Well, it is a silken ribbon tying some hair."

"But the hair, — in what is it steeped?"

"You can see, — in blood."

"In what blood?"

"*Parbleu!* in the blood I wanted for my elixir, — in the blood which you refused me, and which, therefore, I was forced to procure for myself."

"But this hair, these tresses, this ribbon, — from whom did you take them? This is not a child's hair."

And who told you it was a child I had killed?" asked Althotas, quietly.

"Did you not want the blood of a child for your elixir?" said Balsamo. "Did you not tell me so?"

"Or of an unmarried female, Acharat, — or of an unmarried female."

And Althotas stretched his long, bony hand from the chair, and took a phial, the contents of which he tasted with delight.

Then, in his most natural tone, and with his most affectionate smile, —

"I have to thank you, Acharat," said he; "you were wise and far-sighted in placing that woman beneath my trap, almost within reach of my hand. Humanity has no cause for complaint. The law has nothing to lay hold upon. He! he! it was not you who gave me the young creature, without whom I should have perished. No! I took her. He! he! — thanks, my dear pupil! thanks, my dear Acharat!"

And he once more put the phial to his lips.

Balsamo let fall the tress of hair which he held; a dreadful light flashed across his mind

Opposite to him was the old man's table, — a large marble slab, always heaped with plants, books, and phials. This table was covered with a long cloth of white damask with dark flowers, on which the lamp of Althotas shed a reddish light, and which displayed an ominous outline which Balsamo had not before remarked. He seized a corner of the cloth and hastily pulled it away.

But instantly his hair stood on end; his gaping mouth could not utter the horrible cry which almost suffocated him.

Under this shroud he had perceived Lorenza's corpse stretched upon this table, her face livid and yet smiling, and her head hanging backwards, as if dragged down by the weight of her long hair.

A large wound gaped underneath the collar-bone, from which not a single drop of blood escaped; her hands were rigid, and her eyes closed beneath their purple eyelids.

"Yes, blood!—the last three drops of an unmarried woman's blood; that is what I wanted," said the old man, putting the phial to his lips for the third time.

"Wretch!" thundered Balsamo, whose cry of despair at last burst from each pore, "die, then! for she was my WIFE, — my wedded wife! You have murdered her in vain! Die in your sin!"

The eyes of Althotas quivered at these words, as if an electric shock had made them dance in their orbits; his pupils were fearfully dilated, his toothless gums chattered, the phial fell from his hand upon the floor and broke into a thousand pieces, whilst he — stupefied, annihilated, struck at once in heart and brain — fell back heavily upon his chair.

Balsamo bent with a sob over Lorenza's body, and, pressing his lips to her blood-stained hair, sank senseless on the ground.

# CHAPTER CXXX.

### DESPAIR.

THE Hours, those mysterious sisters, who cleave the air hand in hand with a flight so slow for the wretched, so rapid for the happy, paused in their onward motion, folding their heavy wings over this chamber loaded with sighs and groans.

Death on one side, agony on the other, and between them despair, — grievous as agony, deep as death.

Balsamo had not uttered a word since the terrible cry which had been wrung from his breast.

Since the terrible revelation which had cast down the ferocious joy of Althotas, Balsamo had not moved.

As for the hideous old man, thus violently thrown back into life such as God grants to man, he seemed as much bewildered in this new element as the bird struck by a leaden bullet and fallen from the skies into a lake, on whose surface it flutters, unable to employ its wings.

The horror expressed in his pale and agonised features revealed the immeasurable extent of his disappointment.

In fact, Althotas no longer even took the trouble to think, since he had seen the goal at which his spirit aimed, and which it thought firm as a rock, vanish like empty vapour.

His deep and silent despair seemed almost like insensibility. To a mind unaccustomed to measure his, it might have seemed an indication of reflection; to Balsamo's, who, however, did not even look upon him, it marked the death-agony of power, of reason, and of life.

Althotas never took his eyes from the broken phial, — the image of the nothingness of his hopes. One would have said he counted the thousand scattered fragments, which, in falling, had diminished his life by so many days; one would have said he wished to drink in with his look the precious fluid which was spilled upon the floor, and which, for a moment, he had believed to be immortality.

At times, also, as if the grief of this disenchantment was too poignant, the old man raised his dull eyes to Balsamo, then from Balsamo his glance wandered to Lorenza's corpse.

He resembled at these moments one of those savage animals which the huntsman finds in the morning caught in the trap by the leg, and which he stirs for a long time with his foot without making them turn their heads, but who, when he pricks them with his hunting-knife, or with the bayonet of his fowling-piece, obliquely raise their bloodshot eyes, throwing on him a look of hatred, vengeance, reproach, and surprise.

"Is it possible," said this look, so expressive even in its agony, "is it credible that so many misfortunes, so many shocks, should overwhelm me, caused by such an insignificant being as the man I see kneeling there a few yards from me, at the feet of such a vulgar object as that dead woman? Is it not a reversion of nature, an overturning of science, a cataclysm of reason, that the gross student should have deceived the skilful master? Is it not monstrous that the grain of sand should have arrested the wheel of the superb chariot, so rapid in its almost unlimited power, in its immortal flight?"

As for Balsamo, — stunned, heart-broken, without voice or motion, almost without life, — no human thought had yet dawned amid the dark vapours of his brain.

Lorenza! his Lorenza! His wife, his idol, doubly precious to him as his revealing angel and his love, — Lorenza, his delight and his glory, the present and the future, his strength and faith, — Lorenza, all he loved, all he wished for, all he desired in this world, — Lorenza was lost to him forever!

He did not weep, he did not groan, he did not even sigh.

He was scarcely surprised at the dreadful misfortune which had befallen him; he was like one of those poor wretches whom an inundation surprises in their bed, in the midst of darkness. They dream that the water gains upon them; they awake; they open their eyes and see a roaring billow breaking over their head, while they have not even time to utter a cry in their passage from life to death.

During three hours Balsamo felt himself buried in the deepest abyss of the tomb. In his overwhelming grief, he looked upon what had happened to him as one of the dark dreams which torment the dead in the eternal silent night of the sepulchre.

For him there no longer existed Althotas, and with him all hatred and revenge had vanished. For him there no longer existed Lorenza, and with her all life, all love, had fled. All was sleep, night, nothingness! Thus the hours glided past, gloomily, silently, heavily, in this chamber where the blood congealed and the lifeless form grew rigid.

Suddenly, amidst the deathlike silence, a bell sounded thrice.

Fritz, doubtless, was aware that his master was with Althotas, for the bell sounded in the room itself.

But although it sounded three times with an insolently strange noise, the sound died away in space.

Balsamo did not raise his head.

In a few moments the same tinkling, only louder this time, sounded again; but, like the first, it could not rouse Balsamo from his torpor.

Then, at a measured interval, but not so far from the second as it had been from the first, the angry bell a third time made the room resound with multiplied echoes of its wailing and impatient sounds.

Balsamo did not start, but slowly raised his head, and interrogated the empty space before him with the cold solemnity of a corpse rising from the tomb. So must Lazarus have looked when Christ's voice called him from the tomb.

The bell never ceased ringing.

At last his increasing energy awoke him to partial consciousness. The unfortunate husband took his hand from the hand of the corpse. All the heat had left his body without passing into his lifeless bride's.

"Some important news or some great danger," muttered Balsamo to himself. "May it prove a great danger!"

And he rose to his feet.

"But why should I reply to this summons?" continued he, aloud, without heeding the gloomy sound of his words echoing beneath the sombre vault of this funereal chamber; "can anything in this world henceforth interest or alarm me?"

Then, as if in reply, the bell struck its iron tongue so rudely against its brazen sides that the clapper broke and fell upon a glass retort, which flew in pieces with a metallic sound, and scattered the fragments upon the floor.

Balsamo resisted no longer; besides, it was important that none, not even Fritz, should come to seek him where he was.

He walked, therefore, with steady step to the spring, pressed it, and placed himself upon the trap, which descended slowly, and deposited him in the chamber of furs.

As he passed the sofa, he brushed against the scarf which had fallen from Lorenza's shoulders when the pitiless old man, impassible as death itself, had carried her off in his arms.

This contact, more living seemingly than Lorenza herself, sent an icy shudder through Balsamo's veins. He took the scarf and kissed it, using it to stifle the cries which burst from his heaving breast.

Then he proceeded to open the door of the staircase.

On the topmost steps stood Fritz, all pale and breathless, holding a torch in one hand, and in the other the cord of the bell, which, in his terror and impatience, he continued to pull convulsively. On seeing his master, he uttered a cry of satisfaction, followed by one of surprise and fear. But Balsamo, ignorant of the cause of this double cry, replied only by a mute interrogation.

Fritz did not speak, but he ventured—he, usually so respectful—to take his master's hand, and led him to the large Venetian mirror that ornamented the mantel-piece at the back of which was the passage into Lorenza's apartment.

"Oh, look, your Excellency!" said he, showing him his own image in the glass.

Balsamo shuddered. Then a smile—one of those deadly smiles which spring from infinite and incurable grief—flitted over his lips. He had understood the cause of Fritz's alarm.

Balsamo had grown twenty years older in an hour. There was no more brightness in his eyes, no more colour in his cheek; an expression of dulness and stupefaction overspread his features; a bloody foam fringed his lips; a large spot of blood stained the whiteness of his cambric shirt.

Balsamo looked at himself in the glass for a moment without being able to recognise himself, then he determinedly fixed his eyes upon the strange person reflected in the mirror.

"Yes, Fritz," said he, "you are right."

Then, remarking the anxious look of his faithful servant,—

"But why did you call me?" inquired he.

"Oh, master, for *them!*"

"For them?"

"Yes."

"Whom do you mean by *them?*"

"Excellency," whispered Fritz, putting his mouth close to his master's ear, "the FIVE MASTERS."

Balsamo shuddered.

"All?" asked he.

"Yes, all."

"And they are here?"

"Here."

"Alone?"

"No; each has an armed servant waiting in the court-yard."

"They came together?"

"Yes, master, together, and they were getting impatient; that is why I rang so many times and so violently."

Balsamo, without even concealing the spot of blood beneath the folds of his frill, without attempting to repair the disorder of his dress, began to descend the stairs, after having asked Fritz if his guests had installed themselves in the salon or in the large study.

"In the salon, Excellency," replied Fritz, following his master.

Then at the foot of the stairs, venturing to stop Balsamo, he asked, —

"Has your Excellency no orders to give me?"

"None, Fritz."

"Excellency —" stammered Fritz.

"Well?" asked Balsamo, with infinite gentleness.

"Will your Excellency go unarmed?"

"Unarmed? yes."

"Even without your sword?"

"And why should I take my sword, Fritz?"

"I do not know," said the faithful servant, casting down his eyes, "but I thought — I believed — I feared —"

"It is well, Fritz; you may go."

Fritz moved away a few steps in obedience to the order he had received, but returned.

"Did you not hear?" asked Balsamo.

"Excellency, I merely wished to tell you that your double-barrelled pistols are in the ebony case upon the gilt stand."

"Go, I tell you!" replied Balsamo.

And he entered the salon.

## CHAPTER CXXXI.

### THE JUDGMENT.

FRITZ was quite right; Balsamo's guests had not entered the Rue Saint-Claude with a pacific display nor with a benevolent exterior.

Five horsemen escorted the travelling carriage in which the Masters had come; five men with a haughty and sombre mien, armed to the teeth, had closed the outer gate and were guarding it whilst appearing to await their masters' return.

A coachman and two footmen on the carriage seat concealed under their overcoats each a small hanger and a musket. It had much more the air of a warlike expedition than a peaceful visit, these people's appearance in the Rue Saint-Claude.

It was for this reason that the nocturnal invasion of these terrible men, the forcible taking possession of the hotel, had inspired the German with an unspeakable terror. He had at first attempted to refuse entrance to the whole party, when he had seen the escort through the wicket, and had suspected them to be armed; but the all-powerful signals they had used, — that irresistible testimony of the right of the new-comers — had left him no option. Scarcely were they masters of the place than the strangers, like skilful generals, posted themselves at each outlet of the house, taking no pains to dissemble their hostile intentions.

The pretended valets in the court-yard and in the passages, the pretended masters in the salon, seemed to Fritz to bode no good ; therefore he had broken the bell.

Balsamo, without displaying any astonishment, without making any preparation, entered the room which Fritz had lighted up in honour of these, as it was his duty to do towards all guests who visited the house.

His five visitors were seated upon chairs around the room, but not one rose when he appeared.

He, as master of the house, having looked at them, bowed politely; then only did they rise and gravely return his salute.

Balsamo took a chair in front of them, without noticing or seeming to notice the strange order of their position. In fact, the five arm-chairs formed a semicircle like to those of the ancient tribunals, with a president, supported by two assessors, and with Balsamo's chair placed in front of that of the president, and occupying the place accorded to the accused in a council or prætorium.

Balsamo did not speak first, as in other circumstances he would have done; he looked around without seeing any object clearly, still affected by a kind of painful drowsiness which had remained after the shock.

"It seems, brother, that you have understood our errand," said the president, or rather he who occupied the centre seat; "yet you delayed to come, and we were already deliberating if we should send to seek you."

"I do not understand your errand," said Balsamo calmly.

"I should not have imagined so, from seeing you take the position and attitude of an accused before us."

"An accused?" stammered Balsamo vacantly, shrugging his shoulders. "I do not understand you."

"We will soon make you understand us. Not a difficult task, if I may believe your pale cheeks, your vacant eyes, and trembling voice. One would think you did not hear."

"Oh, yes, I hear," replied Balsamo, shaking his head, as if to banish the thoughts which oppressed it.

"Do you remember, brother," continued the president, "that in its last communication the superior committee warned you against a treasonable attempt meditated by one of the great ones of the order?"

"Perhaps so — yes — I do not deny it."

" You reply as a disordered and troubled conscience might be expected to do; but rouse yourself, — be not cast down, — reply with that clearness and precision which your terrible position requires. Reply to my questions with the certainty that we are open to conviction, for we have neither prejudice nor hatred in this matter. We are the law; it does not pronounce a verdict until the evidence is heard."

Balsamo made no reply.

" I repeat it, Balsamo, and, my warning once given, let it be to you like the warning which combatants give to each other before commencing their struggle. I will attack you with just but powerful weapons; defend yourself ! "

The assistants, seeing Balsamo's indifference and imperturbable demeanour, looked at each other with astonishment, and then again turned their eyes upon the president.

" You have heard me, Balsamo, have you not ? " repeated the latter.

Balsamo made a sign of the head in the affirmative.

" Like a well-meaning and loyal brother, I have warned you, and given you a hint of the aim of my questionings. You are warned, guard yourself; I am about to commence again.

" After this announcement," continued the president, " the association appointed five of its members to watch in Paris the proceedings of the man who was pointed out to us as a traitor. Now our revelations are not subject to error. We gather them, as you yourself know, either from devoted agents, from the aspect of events, or from infallible symptoms and signs among the mysterious combinations which nature has as yet revealed to us alone. Now one of us had a vision respecting you; we know that he has never been deceived, we were upon our guard, and watched you."

Balsamo listened without giving the least sign of impatience, or even of intelligence. The president continued : —

" It was not an easy task to watch a man such as you.
You enter everywhere ; your mission is to have a footing
wherever our enemies have a residence or any power whatever. You have at your disposal all your natural resources,
which are immense, and which the association intrusts to
you to make its cause triumphant. For a long time we hovered in a sea of doubt when we saw enemies visit you, such
as a Richelieu, a Dubarry, a Rohan. Moreover, at the last
assembly in the Rue Plastrière, you made a long speech full
of clever paradoxes, which led us to imagine that you were
playing a part in flattering and associating with this incor-
rigible race, which it is our duty to exterminate from the
face of the earth. For a long time we respected the mystery of your behaviour, hoping for a happy result ; but at
last the illusion was dispelled."

Balsamo never stirred, and his features were fixed and
motionless, insomuch that the president became impatient.

" Three days ago," said he, " five *lettres-de-cachet* were
issued. They had been demanded from the king by Monsieur de Sartines ; they were filled as soon as signed ; and
the same day were presented to five of our principal agents,
our most faithful and devoted brothers, residing in Paris.
All five were arrested : two were taken to the Bastille,
where they are kept in the most profound secrecy ; two
are at Vincennes, in the *oubliette ;* one in the most noi-
some cell in Bicêtre. Did you know this circumstance ? "

" No," said Balsamo.

" That is strange, after what we know of your relations
with the lofty ones of the kingdom ; but there is something
stranger still."

Balsamo listened.

" To enable Monsieur de Sartines to arrest these five
faithful friends, he must have had the only paper which
contains the names of the victims in his possession. This
paper was sent to you by the supreme council in 1769 ; and
to you it was assigned to receive the new members, and
immediately invest them with the rank which the supreme
council assigned them."

Balsamo expressed by a gesture that he did not recollect the circumstance.

"I shall assist your memory. The five persons in question were represented by five Arabic characters; and these characters, in the paper you received, corresponded with the names and initials of the new brothers."

"Be it so," said Balsamo.

"You acknowledge it?"

"I acknowledge whatever you please."

The president looked at his assessors, as if to order them to take a note of this confession.

"Well," continued he, "on this paper—the only one, remember, which could have compromised the brothers—there was a sixth name. Do you remember it?"

Balsamo made no reply.

"The name was—*the Count de Fenix.*"

"Agreed," said Balsamo.

"Then why—if the names of the five brothers figured in five *lettres-de-cachet*—why was yours respected, caressed, and favourably received at court and in the antechambers of ministers? If our brothers merited prison, you merited it also. What have you to reply?"

"Nothing."

"Ah! I can guess your objection. You may say that the police had by private means discovered the names of the obscurer brethren, but that it was obliged to respect yours as an ambassador and a powerful man. You may even say that they did not suspect this name."

"I shall say nothing."

"Your pride outlives your honour. These names the police could only have discovered by reading the confidential note which the supreme council had sent you; and this is the way it was seen. You kept it in a coffer. Is that true?"

"It is."

"One day a woman left your house carrying the coffer under her arm. She was seen by our agents, and followed to the hotel of the lieutenant of police, in the Faubourg Saint-Germain. We might have arrested the evil at its source; for if we had stopped the woman and taken the coffer from her, everything would have been safe and sure. But we obeyed the rules of our constitution, which command us to respect the secret means by which some members serve the cause, even when these means have the appearance of treason or imprudence."

Balsamo seemed to approve of this assertion, but with a gesture so little marked, that, had it not been for his previous immobility, it would have been unnoticed.

" This woman reached the lieutenant of police," said the president; " she gave him the coffer, and all was discovered. Is this true ? "

" Perfectly true."

The president rose.

" Who was this woman ? " he exclaimed, — " beautiful, impassioned, devotedly attached to you body and soul, tenderly loved by you, — as spiritual, as subtle, as cunning as one of the angels of darkness who assist man to commit evil! Lorenza Feliciani is the woman, Balsamo ! "

Balsamo uttered a groan of despair.

" You are convicted," said the president.

" Have it so," replied Balsamo.

" I have not yet finished. A quarter of an hour after she had entered the hotel of the lieutenant of police, you arrived. She had sown the treason, you came to reap the reward. The obedient servant had taken upon herself the perpetration of the crime, you came to add the finishing stroke to the infamous work. Lorenza departed alone. You renounced her, doubtless, and would not compromise yourself by accompanying her; you left triumphantly along with Madame Dubarry, summoned there to receive from your own lips the information you sold her. You entered the carriage with that harlot, as the boatman entered the boat with the sinner, Mary the Egyptian. You left behind the papers which ruined us with Monsieur de Sartines, but you brought away the coffer which might have ruined you with us. Fortunately we saw you. God's light is with us when we need it most."

Balsamo bowed without speaking.

"I now conclude," added the president. "Two criminals have been pointed out to the order: a woman, your accomplice, who may be innocent perhaps, but who, in point of fact, has injured our cause by revealing one of our secrets; and you, the master, the Great Copht, the enlightened mind, who have had the cowardice to shelter yourself behind this woman, that your treason may be less clearly seen."

Balsamo raised his head, and fixed a look upon the commissioners, burning with all the rage which had smouldered in his breast since the commencement of the interrogation.

"Why do you accuse this woman?" asked he.

"Ah! we know that you will endeavour to defend her; we know that you love her almost to idolatry, — that you prefer her to everything in the world. We know that she is your treasure of science, of happiness, and of fortune; we know that she is more precious to you than all the world beside."

"You know all this?" said Balsamo.

"Yes, we know it; and we shall punish you through her more than through yourself."

"Finish!"

The president rose.

"This is the sentence:

"Joseph Balsamo is a traitor; he has broken his oath; but his knowledge is immense, and he is useful to the order. Balsamo must live for the cause he has betrayed. He belongs to his brothers, though he has cast them off."

"Ha!" said Balsamo, gloomily, almost savagely.

"A perpetual prison will protect the association against any renewal of his treachery, at the same time that it will permit the brothers to gather the knowledge from him which it has a right to expect from all its members.

"As to Lorenza Feliciani, a terrible punishment — "

"Hold!" said Balsamo, with perfect calmness in his voice, "you forget that I did not defend myself. The accused must be heard in his own justification. A word, a single proof, will suffice; wait one moment, and I will bring you the proof I have promised."

The commissaries seemed to deliberate for a moment.

"Ah! you fear lest I should kill myself," said Balsamo with a bitter smile. "If that had been my wish, it would have been already done. There is that in this ring which would kill you all five times over had I opened it. You fear I should escape; let me be guarded if you wish it."

"Go!" said the president.

Balsamo disappeared for about a moment. Then he was heard heavily descending the staircase. He entered, bearing the cold, rigid, and discoloured body of Lorenza upon his shoulder, her white hand hanging to the ground.

"Here is the woman I adored, who was my treasure, my only happiness, my life! — the woman who, as you say, has betrayed you. Here, take her! God did not wait for you to punish, gentlemen!"

And with a movement quick as lightning, he let the corpse glide from his arms, and sent it rolling on the carpet to the feet of the judges, whom her cold hair and the dead and motionless hands touched, to their great horror, while by the light of the lamps they saw the wide gash gaping in her neck, white as a swan's.

"Now pronounce the sentence," added Balsamo.

The horrified judges uttered a cry, and, seized with maddening terror, fled in indescribable confusion. Soon their horses were heard neighing and trampling in the court-yard; the outer gate grated on its hinges; and then silence, the solemn silence of the tomb, returned to seat itself beside despair and death.

## CHAPTER CXXXII.

### DOOM.

WHILE the terrible scene which we have just described was taking place between Balsamo and the Five Masters, nothing apparently had changed in the rest of the house. The old man had seen Balsamo enter his apartment and bear away Lorenza's corpse, and this new demonstration had recalled him to what was passing around him.

But when he saw Balsamo take up the dead body and descend with it into the lower rooms, he fancied it was the last and eternal adieu of this man whose heart he had broken, and fear descended on his soul with an overwhelming force, which, for him who had done all to avoid death, doubled the horror of the grave.

Not knowing for what purpose Balsamo had left him, nor whither he was going, he began to call out: —

" Acharat ! Acharat ! "

It was the name his pupil had borne in childhood, and he hoped it would have retained its influence over the man.

But Balsamo continued to descend. Having touched the ground, he even forgot to make the trap reascend, and disappeared in the corridor.

" Ah ! " cried Althotas, " see what man is, — a blind, ungrateful animal ! Return, Acharat, return ! Ah ! you prefer the ridiculous object called a woman to the perfection of humanity which I represent ! You prefer a fragment of life to immortality ! "

" But no ! " he exclaimed after a moment's pause ; " the wretch has deceived his master, — he has betrayed my confidence like a vile robber ; he feared that I should live because I surpass him so much in science ; he wanted to inherit the laborious work I had nearly concluded ; he laid a trap for me, his master and benefactor! Oh Acharat!"

And gradually the old man's anger was aroused, his cheeks were dyed with a hectic tinge, his half-closed eyes seemed to glow with the gloomy brightness of those phosphorescent lights which sacrilegious children place in the cavities of a human skull. Then he cried : —

"Return, Acharat, return! Look to yourself! You know that I have conjurations which evoke fire and raise up supernatural spirits! I have evoked Satan, — him whom the Magi called Phegor, in the mountains of Gad, — and Satan was forced to leave his bottomless pit and appear before me! I have conferred with the seven angels who ministered to God's anger upon the same mountain where Moses received the ten commandments! By my will alone I have kindled the great tripod with its seven flames which Trajan stole from the Jews! Take care, Acharat, take care!"

But there was no reply.

Then his brain became more and more clouded.

"Do you not see, wretch," said he, in a choking voice, "that death is about to seize me as it would the meanest mortal ? Listen, Acharat! you may return ; I will do you no harm. Return: I renounce the fire ; you need not fear the evil spirit, nor the seven avenging angels. I renounce vengeance, and yet I could strike you with such terror that you would become an idiot and cold as marble, for I can stop the circulation of the blood. Come back, then, Acharat; I will do you no harm, but, on the contrary, I can do you much good. Acharat, instead of abandoning me, watch over my life, and you shall have all my treasures and all my secrets. Let me live, Acharat, that I may teach them to you. See, see!"

And with gleaming eyes and trembling fingers he pointed to the numerous objects, papers, and rolls scattered through the vast apartment. Then he waited, collecting all his fast-failing faculties to listen.

"Ah, you come not!" he cried. "You think I shall die thus, and by this murder — for you are murdering me — everything will belong to you! Madman! were you even capable of reading the manuscripts which I alone am able to decipher, — were the spirit even to grant you my wisdom for a lifetime of one, two, or three centuries, to make use of the materials I have gathered, — you shall not inherit them! No, no, a thousand times no! Return, Acharat, return for a moment, were it only to behold the ruin of this whole house, — were it only to contemplate the beautiful spectacle I am preparing for you! Acharat! Acharat! Acharat!"

There was no answer, for Balsamo was during this time replying to the accusation of the Five Masters by showing them the mutilated body of Lorenza. The cries of the deserted old man grew louder and louder; despair redoubled his strength, and his hoarse yellings, reverberating in the long corridors, spread terror afar, like the roaring of a tiger who has broken his chain or forced the bars of his cage.

"Ah, you do not come!" shrieked Althotas; "you despise me! you calculate upon my weakness! Well, you shall see! Fire! fire! fire!"

He articulated these cries with such vehemence, that Balsamo, now freed from his terrified visitors, was roused by them from the depth of his despair. He took Lorenza's corpse in his arms, reascended the staircase, laid the dead body upon the sofa where two hours previously it had reposed in sleep, and, mounting upon the trap, he suddenly appeared before Althotas.

"Ah! at last!" cried the old man, with savage joy. "You were afraid! you saw I could revenge myself, and you came! You did well to come, for in another moment I should have set this chamber on fire!"

Balsamo looked at him, shrugged his shoulders slightly, but did not deign to reply.

"I am athirst!" cried Althotas, "I am athirst! Give me drink, Acharat!"

Balsamo made no reply; he did not move; he looked at the dying man as if he would not lose an atom of his agony.

"Do you hear me?" howled Althotas; "do you hear me?"

The same silence, the same immobility on the part of the gloomy spectator.

"Do you hear me, Acharat?" vociferated the old man, almost tearing his throat in his efforts to give emphasis to this last burst of rage; "water! give me water!"

Althotas's features were rapidly decomposing.

There was no longer fire in his looks, but only an unearthly glare; the blood no longer coursed beneath his sunken and cadaverous cheek; motion and life were almost dead within him. His long sinewy arms, in which he had carried Lorenza like a child, were raised, but inert and powerless as the membranes of a polypus. His fury had worn out the feeble spark which despair had for a moment revived in him.

"Ah!" said he, "ah! you think I do not die quickly enough! You mean to make me die of thirst! You gloat over my treasures and my manuscripts with longing eyes! Ah! you think you have them already! Wait, wait!"

And, with an expiring effort, Althotas took a small bottle from beneath the cushions of the arm-chair and uncorked it. At the contact with the air, a liquid flame burst from the glass vessel, and Althotas, like some potent magician, shook this flame around him.

Instantly the manuscripts piled round the old man's armchair, the books scattered over the room, the rolls of paper disinterred with so much trouble from the pyramids of Cheops and the subterranean depths of Herculaneum, took fire with the rapidity of gunpowder. A sheet of flame overspread the marble slab, and seemed to Balsamo's eyes like one of those flaming circles of hell of which Dante sings.

Althotas no doubt expected that Balsamo would rush amidst the flames to save this valuable inheritance which the old man was annihilating along with himself, but he was mistaken. Balsamo did not stir, but stood calm and isolated upon the trap-door, so that the fire could not reach him.

The flames wrapped Althotas in their embrace, but, instead of terrifying him, it seemed as if the old man found himself once more in his proper element, and that, like the salamanders sculptured on our ancient castles, the fire caressed instead of consuming him.

Balsamo still stood gazing at him. The fire had reached the woodwork, and completely surrounded the old man; it roared around the feet of the massive oaken chair on which he was seated, and, what was most strange, though it was already consuming the lower part of his body, he did not seem to feel it.

On the contrary, at the contact with the seemingly purifying element, the dying man's muscles seemed gradually to distend, and an indescribable serenity overspread his features like a mask. Isolated from his body at this last hour, the old prophet on his car of fire seemed ready to wing his way aloft. The mind, all-powerful in its last moments, forgot its attendant matter, and, sure of having nothing more to expect below, it stretched ardently upwards to those higher spheres to which the fire seemed to bear it.

At this instant Althotas's eyes, which at the first reflection of the flames seemed to have been re-endowed with life, gazed vaguely and abstractedly at some point in space which was neither heaven nor earth. They looked as if they would pierce the horizon, calm and resigned, analysing all sensation, listening to all pain, while with his last breath on earth the old magician muttered, in a hollow voice, his adieus to power, to life, and to hope.

"Ah!" said he, "I die without regret. I have possessed everything on earth, and have known all; I have had all power which is granted to a human creature; I had almost reached immortality!"

Balsamo uttered a sardonic laugh, whose gloomy echo arrested the old man's attention. Through the flames which surrounded him as with a veil, he cast a look of savage majesty upon his pupil.

"You are right," said he; "one thing I had not foreseen, — God!"

Then, as if this mighty word had uprooted his whole soul, Althotas fell back upon his chair. He had given up to God the last breath, which he had hoped to wrest from him.

Balsamo heaved a sigh, and, without endeavouring to save anything from the precious pile upon which this second Zoroaster had stretched himself to die, he again descended to Lorenza, and touched the spring of the trap, which readjusted itself in the ceiling, veiling from his sight the immense furnace, which roared like the crater of a volcano.

During the whole night the fire roared above Balsamo's head like a whirlwind, without his making an effort either to extinguish it or to fly. Stretched beside Lorenza's body, he was insensible to all danger; but, contrary to his expectations, when the fire had devoured all, and laid bare the vaulted walls of stone, annihilating all the valuable contents, it extinguished itself, and Balsamo heard its last howlings, which, like those of Althotas, gradually died away in plaints and sighs.

## CHAPTER CXXXIII.

MONSIEUR le Duc de Richelieu was in his bedchamber, at his house in Versailles, where he was sipping chocolate, attended by Rafté, who was going over his accounts.  The duke was so engaged in contemplating his reflection in a distant mirror, that he bestowed very little attention on the calculations, more or less exact, of his secretary.

Suddenly the sound of creaking shoes was heard in an antechamber, betokening the presence of a caller; and the duke hastily despatched the rest of his chocolate, all the time watching the door uneasily.

There were times when Monsieur de Richelieu, like any other old courtier, did not care to receive callers.

The valet announced Monsieur de Taverney.  Doubtless the duke would have invented some excuse for deferring the call to another day, or at least to a later hour, but scarcely had the door opened before the impatient old man rushed into the room, grasped the end of one of the marshal's fingers as he passed him, and hastened to fling himself into an easy-chair, which shook, more from the shock caused by his haste in getting into it than from the weight of the old man.

As he glided by Richelieu, he appeared to him like one of those fantastic creations in which Hoffman has since made us believe.  He indeed heard the chair creak, and a deep sigh issue out of its depths; then, turning to his guest, —

"Eh, baron," said he, "what is the news?  You seem as sad as grim death."

"Sad," said Taverney, — "sad?"

"*Pardieu!* It seems to me that you certainly would not sigh were you happy."

The baron looked at the marshal with a meaning glance, which implied that, as long as Rafté was present, he would not divulge the significance of his sigh.

Rafté understood, without even turning his eyes in the direction of the baron, for, like his master, he too had been carefully watching the mirror all the time.

Having understood, he then wisely withdrew.

The baron's eyes followed his retreating figure, and scarcely had the door closed behind him when he said : —

"Do not call me sad, duke; rather designate me as uneasy, as mortally uneasy."

"Bah ! "

"In truth," cried Taverney, clasping his hands together, "you may well feign surprise; for the past month you have allured me with vague words such as these: 'I have not seen the king,' or again, 'The king has not yet seen me,' or 'The king treats me coldly.' *Cordieu!* duke, is that the way to talk to an old friend ? A month ! think of it ! it is an eternity."

Richelieu shrugged his shoulders.

"What the devil should I say to you baron ? " answered he.

"Eh ! tell me the truth."

"*Mordieu!* I have told you the truth, I have dinned it into your ears ; but you will not believe me, that is all."

"What, you a duke and peer, a marshal of France, do you think you can make me believe that you, — a gentleman of the bedchamber, who attends the levée every morning, — you do not see the king ? Come, come ! "

"I have told you once, and I tell you again. It may not seem probable, but it is only the truth. For three weeks I, a duke and peer, I, a marshal of France, I, a gentleman of the bedchamber, have attended the morning levée without missing a single day."

"And the king did not speak to you," broke in the baron

impatiently, "you did not speak to the king?  Do you
think me capable of swallowing such a falsehood as that?"

"Eh, baron, my dear, you are really getting impertinent.
You accuse me of lying, as you might were you forty years
younger, and still capable of wielding the small-sword."

"But it is maddening, duke!"

"Oh, that is another thing.  Get angry, if you like.  I
am angry myself."

"You are angry?"

"I have occasion to be.  When I tell you that, to this
day, the king ignores me; when I tell you that his Majesty
actually turned his back upon me, when I tell you every
time I have been preparing a pleasant smile with which to
greet him, he has looked at me with a wry face; in short,
you can readily see how weary I am of going to Versailles.
Under these circumstances what would you have me do?"

Taverney savagely bit his nails, while the marshal was
thus answering him.

"I do not understand it," said he at last.

"Nor I, baron."

"Really, the king seems to enjoy making you uneasy;
for, indeed—"

"Yes, that is exactly what I say to myself, baron.  In
short —"

"Come, duke, we must find some way out of these perplexities; we must discover the meaning of all this."

"Baron, baron," answered Richelieu, "it is a dangerous
thing to question the acts of a king."

"You think so?"

"Yes, would you like me to tell you something?"

"Speak on!"

"Well, I have my suspicions."

"What are they?" said the baron, haughtily.

"Ah! now you are getting angry."

"I have occasion, I think."

"Then we will speak no more about it."

"No, no, speak! explain yourself!"

"You are possessed with a devil, clamouring for your explanations. It is really a monomania with you. Be careful!"

"You are charming, duke. You see all our plans delayed, an unaccountable stagnation in the progress of my affairs, and you calmly tell me to wait."

"What stagnation? Tell me!"

"In the first place — Wait a moment!"

"A letter?"

"Yes, from my son."

"Ah! the colonel."

"A great colonel!"

"What! is he not already that?"

"Philip has been awaiting at Rheims nearly a month the appointment which the king promised him; it has not yet arrived, and the regiment leaves in two days."

"The devil! the regiment leaves!"

"Yes, for Strasbourg."

"So that, if Philip does not receive the appointment within two days —"

"Well?"

"In two days he will be here."

"Yes, I understand; the poor boy has been forgotten. It often happens in cabinets organised like those of the present ministry. Had I been minister the commission would have been sent."

"Hum!" replied Taverney.

"What do you say?"

"I say I do not believe a word of it."

"What?"

"Had you been minister, you would have consigned Philip to five hundred devils!"

"Oh!"

"And his father with him!"

"Oh! Oh!"

"And his sister farther away still!"

"It is a pleasure to chat with you, Taverney, you are so witty. But let us say no more about it."

"I ask nothing better. But my son requires something different; his present condition is intolerable. The king must be seen."

"That is exactly what I cannot do."

"Cannot speak to him?"

"Ah, my dear friend, one cannot speak to the king unless he is willing to talk."

"Make him do so."

"Ah, I am not the pope, myself."

"Then," said Taverney, "nothing remains for me to do but to speak to my daughter. There is something behind all this."

This remark worked like magic.

Richelieu had sounded Taverney; he knew that he was a *roué*, like his youthful friends, Monsieur Lafare or Monsieur de Nocé, whose reputation had been well preserved. He feared the alliance of father and daughter; he was afraid some hidden plan might bring disgrace upon himself.

"Well, do not get angry," said he; "I will try again. I must invent some excuse."

"You have an excuse already."

"I?"

"Certainly."

"What is it?"

"The king has made a promise."

"To whom?"

"To my daughter. And this promise —"

"Well?"

"Can be brought to his memory —"

"Truly, that is an expedient. Have you this letter?"

"Yes."

"Give it to me."

Taverney drew the letter from his pocket and handed it to the duke, counselling him to be both daring and wary.

"Fire and water!" said Richelieu; "come, we are talking wildly. No matter; the wine is drawn, we must drink."

He rang the bell.

"Bring my clothes, and order the carriage," said the duke.

Then, turning towards Taverney, —

"Will you stay while I dress?" asked he, in an uneasy manner.

Taverney understood that he would disoblige his friend by answering in the affirmative.

"No, my dear friend, impossible," said he; "I must take a turn about the city. Make an appointment with me for some other time."

"Well, at the château."

"So be it; at the château."

"You, too, must see his Majesty."

"Do you think so?" said Taverney, delighted.

"I insist upon it. I wish you to verify, yourself, the truth of what I have told you."

"I do not doubt your veracity; yet, since you wish it — "

"You are glad to?"

"Frankly, yes."

"Well, in the glass gallery, at eleven o'clock, while I am with his Majesty."

"So be it. Adieu!"

"Without bad feeling, dear baron," said Richelieu, who, even to the last, did not wish to make an enemy whose power he could not fathom.

Taverney climbed into his carriage and rolled away, busily occupied in thinking over the situation. He spent the intervening time in driving up and down the garden. Meanwhile, Richelieu, left to the care of his valet, made himself young again at his ease, — an important occupation, which never took the illustrious conqueror of Mahon less than two hours.

However, Taverney, in his own mind, had allowed him a much longer time, and was surprised, as he watched carefully, to see the carriage of the duke draw up before the door of the palace, at exactly eleven o'clock. He saw the officers salute Richelieu, while the hussars conducted him into the palace.

Taverney's heart beat rapidly. He left the drive·and slowly, much more slowly than his eager spirit would have willed, he went to the glass gallery, where a number of the less favoured courtiers, of officers bearing petitions, and of ambitious gentlemen, placed themselves like statuary on the slippery floor, a pedestal very appropriate for the favourites of fortune. Taverney, breathing excitedly, mingled in the crowd, taking care, however, to seize a corner near the door, through which he saw the marshal pass on his way to the presence of the king.

"Oh," murmured he, between his teeth, "to think that I should be condemned to mix with these country boors and dirty soldiers, I, who only a month ago dined with the king!" And his frowning brow indicated the presence of more than one infamous conjecture which would have made poor Andrée blush.

## CHAPTER CXXXIV.

### THE MEMORY OF KINGS.

RICHELIEU, as he had promised, boldly placed himself in his Majesty's line of vision, just as Monsieur de Condé had handed him his shirt.

When the king perceived the marshal, he turned around so suddenly that the shirt fell on the floor, and the prince drew back in surprise.

"Pardon, my cousin," said Louis XV., in order to show the prince that no personal affront was intended by this quick gesture.

Indeed, Richelieu readily comprehended that he was the cause of his anger. But, as he had already decided to arouse his anger should it be necessary, in order to have a serious explanation, he turned about, as at Fontenoy, and stationed himself on a spot which the king would have to pass on his way into his audience chamber.

The king, no longer seeing the marshal, began to talk freely and pleasantly. He dressed, and began to plan for a hunt at Marly, discussing it at length with his cousin; for the Condés always had the reputation of being great sportsmen.

But at the moment when he entered his audience chamber, when all around him had already gone away, he perceived Richelieu, gracefully bowing in a most pleasing manner, and this sight recalled to his memory Lauzun, who could bow so well.

Louis XV. stopped, disconcerted.

"Still here, Monsieur de Richelieu?" said he.

"At your Majesty's service; yes, sire."

"But are you not going to leave Versailles?"

"I have not left it during the last forty years, except to render some service to your Majesty."

The king stopped and looked at the marshal.

"Let's see," said he, "you wish something, do you not?"

"I, sire?" said Richelieu, "what can I wish?"

"But you are pursuing me, duke. *Morbleu!* such is plainly the case."

"Yes, sire, with my love and with my respect. Thank you, sire."

"Oh, you pretend that you do not hear me! Nevertheless, you understand me wonderfully well. Know then, duke, I have nothing to say to you."

"Nothing, sire?"

"Absolutely nothing."

Richelieu assumed a profound indifference.

"Sire," said he, "it has always been a satisfaction to me to know in my own heart that the assiduity with which I have served you has been wholly disinterested. It is a great thing, sire, since I have known you for forty years; and yet the most envious can never say that the king has ever bestowed personal favours on me. On that point, happily, my reputation is already secured."

"Eh, duke, if you need anything, ask for it, only ask quickly."

"Sire, I require absolutely nothing, and, for the present, I entreat your Majesty —"

"What?"

"To allow some one to enter your presence to thank you."

"Who, pray?"

"Sire, one who is under obligations to the king."

"But, in short —"

"Some one, sire, to whom your Majesty has accorded signal honours. You have granted him the honour of sitting at table with your Majesty, of tasting that delicious conversation, that charming gaiety, which makes your Majesty the most fascinating of dinner companions; for that reason, once admitted to that companionship, one never forgets, and eagerly longs to continue so pleasing a custom."

"You speak extravagantly, Monsieur de Richelieu."

"Oh, sire!"

"In short, of whom are you speaking?"

"Of my friend Taverney."

"Your friend?" cried the king.

"Pardon, sire."

"Taverney," repeated the king, evincing a kind of terror that astonished Richelieu.

"What then, sire,—an old comrade,"—he stopped a moment,—"a man who served under Villars with me." He stopped again.

"You know, sire, it is customary in society to designate by the title of friend all one's acquaintances who are not enemies. It is merely a polite term, which often means nothing."

"It is a dangerous expression, duke," replied the king curtly,—"an expression to be used with discrimination."

"Your Majesty's counsels are words of wisdom. Monsieur de Taverney, then—"

"Monsieur de Taverney is a bad man."

"Well, sire," said Richelieu, "on my word as a gentleman, I do not doubt the truth of that."

"A man without delicacy, Monsieur le Maréchal."

"As to his delicacy, sire, I shall not speak of that to your Majesty. I vouch only for what I know."

"What! you will not answer for the delicacy of your friend, of an old comrade, of a man who has served with you under Villars,—in short, of a man whom you have presented to me? Still you say you know him."

"I know him, certainly, sire; but I know nothing about his delicacy. Sully told your ancestor, Henry IV., that he saw his fever leave him, clothed in a green garment; but I humbly acknowledge, sire, that I should never have known how to clothe the delicacy of Monsieur de Taverney."

"In short, marshal, I tell you he is a bad man, and he has played a bad part."

"Oh, if your Majesty tells me that!"

"Yes, monsieur, I do tell you so."

"Well," replied Richelieu, "your Majesty relieves me by speaking in this way. No, I admit, Taverney is not a flower of delicacy, and I have indeed observed that such is the case. But, sire, until your Majesty condescended to let me know your opinion — "

"It is, that I detest him."

"Ah! the decree has gone forth, sire; fortunately for the wretch," continued Richelieu, "a powerful intercession pleads in his behalf with your Majesty."

"What do you mean?"

"If the father is so unfortunate as to be displeasing to the king — "

"And very much so!"

"I do not question it, sire."

"What, then, are you going to say?"

"I am going to say that a certain angel with blue eyes and blonde hair — "

"I do not understand you, duke."

"That may be, sire."

"Yes, I candidly confess I wish to know your meaning."

"An ordinary person like me, sire, trembles in raising the corner of the veil under which so many amorous and fascinating mysteries are concealed. I repeat it, sire, how much kindness Taverney must show to her who mitigates the indignation of the king against him. Oh, yes, Mademoiselle de Taverney must be an angel!"

"Mademoiselle de Taverney is a little monster physically, as her father is morally," cried the king.

"Bah!" cried Richelieu, completely stupefied, "are we then deceived, and that beautiful appearance — "

"Never again speak of that girl to me, duke; the very thought of her makes me shiver."

Richelieu hypocritically clasped his hands.

"Oh God!" said he, "appearances are deceitful! If your Majesty, the finest connoisseur in the kingdom — if your Majesty, infallibility personified — had not assured me of that, how could I have believed it? What, sire, so deformed?"

"More than that, monsieur,— marked by an illness, frightful, a hidden disease, duke. But not a word more about her,— you will kill me."

"Oh Heaven!" cried Richelieu, "I will not open my mouth again on the subject. Kill your Majesty! Oh, what a calamity! What a family! How unfortunate this poor boy is!"

"Of whom are you speaking now?"

"Oh, this time of a faithful, sincere, devoted servant of your Majesty. Indeed, sire, he is a model, and you have rightly judged him so. In this case, I will answer for it, your favours have been well bestowed."

"But who is the person under discussion? Speak, duke, I am in a hurry!"

"I am speaking," said Richelieu softly, "of the son of the one, the brother of the other. I am speaking of Philip de Taverney,— of that brave young man to whom your Majesty has given a regiment."

"I — I have given a regiment to some one?"

"Yes, sire; a regiment for which Philip de Taverney is still waiting, it is true, but you have indeed given it to him."

"I?"

"*Dame!* I believe so, sire."

"You are an idiot!"

"Bah!"

"I have given nothing at all, marshal."

"Truly?"

"But what the devil is it to you?"

"But, sire —"

"Does it concern you?"

"No, not the least in the world."

"You have, then, sworn to burn me by degrees at this fire of thorns."

"What then, sire? It seemed to me,— I now see that I was mistaken,— it seemed to me that your Majesty had promised."

"But this has nothing to do with me. I have my minister of war; I do not give away regiments. Ah! you are the advocate of this brood? I told you that you ought not to speak to me; and now you have sent all my blood in the wrong direction."

"Oh, sire!"

"Yes, all in the wrong direction. Though the devil himself were the advocate, I would not thus spend the whole day with him."

And thereupon the king turned his back upon the duke, and fled into his audience chamber, leaving Richelieu more unhappy than can be told.

"Ah! now," murmured the old marshal, "now I know where I stand."

And, brushing his clothes with his handkerchief, for in the excitement of his interview he had shaken powder all over himself, Richelieu turned his steps towards the gallery, in the corner of which his old friend was awaiting him consumed by impatience. With eager eyes, his heart in his mouth, and extended arms, he stood before him.

"Well, what is the news?" said he.

"Nothing, monsieur," replied Richelieu, with a disdainful sneer, and a hateful twitch of his shirt frill. "I beg you not to say another word to me."

Taverney looked at the duke with wide open eyes.

"Yes, you are very displeasing in the king's sight, and he who is displeasing to the king is offensive to me."

Taverney stood as if his feet were embedded in the marble, stunned and stupefied.

Still Richelieu kept on his way.

But when he had reached the door of the glass gallery, he ordered his valet to take him to Luciennes, and disappeared.

# CHAPTER CXXXV.

## ANDRÉE'S SWOONS.

WHEN Taverney had recovered his faculties, had meditated over this piece of bad luck, he decided that it was time to have a serious explanation with her who was the primary cause of all these troubles.

Consequently, burning with wrath and indignation, he started off in the direction of Andrée's residence.

The young girl had just completed her toilet, and stood with her rounded arms lifted, pinning into place behind her ear two rebellious curls.

Andrée heard her father's step in the antechamber at the very moment when, with a book under her arm, she was leaving her room.

"Ah, good-morning, Andrée," said Monsieur de Taverney, "are you going out?"

"Yes, father."

"Alone?"

"You can see for yourself."

"Are you always alone?"

"Since Nicole's disappearance I have not had a waiting-maid."

"But you should not wait upon yourself, Andrée; that is not proper. A woman that does so will not be thought well of at court. I would have advised you to do differently, Andrée."

"Excuse me, father, but the dauphiness is waiting for me."

"I assure you, Andrée," replied the baron, getting excited as he talked, "I assure you, mademoiselle, that this simplicity will end in making you seem ridiculous."

"Father!"

"Ridicule destroys everywhere, most of all at court."

"Monsieur, I will think it over. But now, Madame la Dauphine will be pleased to see me less carefully dressed, since it will merely be an indication of my desire to reach her all the sooner."

"Go, then, and return, I beg, as soon as you are at liberty. I wish to talk with you on a very important subject."

"Yes, father," said Andrée.

And she resumed her walk.

"Wait, wait," cried he; "do not go out in that condition; you have forgotten your rouge. You are shockingly pale."

"I, father?" said Andrée, stopping.

"But, indeed, when you look in your mirror, what can you be thinking of? Your cheeks are pale as wax, and you have dark rings under your eyes. You will frighten people if you go out like that."

"I have no time to change my toilet, father."

"It is disgusting, disgusting!" said the baron, shrugging his shoulders; "there is not another such woman in the world, and this one is my daughter. What a cruel fate! Andrée! Andrée!"

But Andrée was already at the bottom of the staircase; she turned around.

"At least," said the baron, "say you are ill; make yourself interesting, *mordieu!* since you will not try to be beautiful."

"Oh, for that matter, father, I can truthfully say that I am ill, for I am really suffering at this moment."

"Good!" grumbled the baron, "that will do for an excuse; ill!" but he added between his teeth, "Plague take the haughty prude!"

And he went back into her room, and carefully examined everything that might help him in his surmises, or give him any clew as to the real state of things.

All this time Andrée was walking across the square and along the flower beds. Often she raised her head to take deeper breaths of air, for the mingled perfumes of the flowers freshly blooming overpowered her and made her dizzy.

Thus, uncomfortable and overcome by the heat of the sun, seeking something by which to support herself, she reached the antechamber of Trianon, still struggling against this new, strange illness. Madame de Noailles, standing in the doorway of the cabinet, let her understand at once that it was time for her, and that they had been waiting for her. In fact, the abbé, reader to the princess, had breakfasted with the dauphiness, who often admitted those of whom she was fond to such privileges. The abbé was praising the rolls that the German housekeepers often placed so deftly around a cup of coffee and cream.

The abbé was talking instead of reading, and telling the dauphiness all the news of Vienna, which he had gathered from the journalists and the diplomatists. At this period, politics were freely discussed as well as the greatest secrets of the government officers, and it was not uncommon for the ministry to learn the news, that the gentlemen of the court had divined or perhaps invented.

Moreover, the abbé was discussing the latest rumours of a secret outbreak, caused by the sale of grain at a high price, which Monsieur de Sartines had quickly stifled, and had had five of the heaviest monopolizers sent to the Bastille.

Andrée entered. The dauphiness also had her days of caprice and headache. The abbé had been very entertaining. The thought of Andrée and her book tired her, after the abbé's conversation.

Consequently, she told her second reader that she ought to make a point of not being late, adding that punctuality was a good thing in itself, and above all when occasion called for it. Andrée, overwhelmed by this reprimand, and stung by its injustice, made no answer, although she

might have said that her father had delayed her, and,
being in pain, she had been obliged to walk slowly.

No, troubled and overcome, her head drooped, and, as if
already dead, her eyes closed, and she fell forward.   Had
it not been for Madame de Noailles, she would have fallen
to the floor.

"Have a little firmness, mademoiselle," murmured
Madame de Noailles.

Andrée did not answer.

"But, duchess, she is ill," cried the dauphiness, rising,
and going up to Andrée.

"No, no," replied Andrée, quickly, her eyes filling
with tears; "no, madame, I am all right, or rather I am
better."

"But she is as white as her handkerchief, duchess; look!
Indeed, it is my fault; I scolded her, poor child !  Sit down,
I wish it."

"Madame ! "

"I command it.   Give her your folding chair, abbé."

Andrée sat down, and under the soothing influence of
this kindness, little by little, her spirits revived, and the
colour came back into her cheeks.

"Well, mademoiselle, can you read now?" asked the
dauphiness.

"Yes, yes, certainly; at least, I hope so."

And Andrée opened her book at the place where she had
left off the day before, and in as intelligible and agreeable
a tone of voice as she could command she began to read.

Scarcely had her eyes traversed more than two or three
pages, before black specks flew in front of them, things
began to go round and round before her, and she could not
see to read.

Andrée again grew pale, a cold perspiration covered her
forehead, and the dark rings under her eyes, with which
Taverney had reproached her so bitterly, increased, so that
the dauphiness, who at Andrée's first hesitation had raised
her head, cried out, —

"Again. See, duchess, truly this child is ill; she is losing consciousness."

And this time the dauphiness herself ran with a bottle of salts, which she made her reader breathe in. Thus refreshed, she wished to try again to read, but in vain; her hands trembled so violently that for some moments she could not hold the book.

"Decidedly, duchess," said the dauphiness, "Andrée is suffering, and I will not have her illness increased by staying here."

"Then mademoiselle must go at once to her home," said the duchess.

"Why so?" said the dauphiness.

"Because," said the lady of honour, with a low bow, "this is the way in which small-pox begins."

"Small-pox?"

"Yes,— fainting fits, swoons, chills."

The abbé perceived himself exposed to the danger which Madame de Noailles pointed out, and rising cautiously, in the confusion caused by this woman's illness, he made his escape on tiptoe, and so cleverly that no one saw him go.

When Andrée realised that she was actually in the arms of the dauphiness, shame at so inconveniencing a person of such high rank summoned all her scattered strength, or rather her will power. She immediately went to the window to get the air.

"You should not stand in the draught, my dear girl," said the dauphiness. "Go home; I myself will go with you."

"Oh, I assure you, madame," said Andrée, "that I am fully recovered now. Since you kindly permit me to retire, I can go home alone."

"Yes, yes; and do not worry," said the dauphiness; "you shall not be scolded any more, since you are so sensitive, little sly one."

Andrée, touched by this kindness, which seemed so like that of a sister, kissed the hand of her protectress and went out of the room, while the dauphiness watched her anxiously.

When she had at last descended the stairs, the dauphiness called to her from the window, —

"Do not return at once. Walk around the garden, the sun will do you good."

"Oh, *mon Dieu!*" said Andrée, "how kind!"

"And please send the abbé back to me; he is taking a lesson in botany in that bed of Holland tulips."

Andrée was obliged to take a circuitous route in order to reach the abbé. She crossed the garden; she walked along with bowed head, a little dull still from the effects of the fainting fits, from which she had been suffering all the morning. She paid no attention to the birds, which flew, startled, over the hedges and beds of flowers, nor to the bees lingering near the thyme and lilacs. For the same reason she did not notice, twenty feet from her, two men, who were talking together, one of whom watched her with troubled and disturbed looks. They were Gilbert and Monsieur de Jussieu. The former, leaning on his spade, was listening to the wise professor, who was explaining to him the way to water delicate plants, so that the moisture might run down into the ground, and not stand on the plants. Gilbert seemed to be listening to this lecture with enthusiasm, and Monsieur de Jussieu deemed it only natural for one interested in this science; indeed, it was a lecture which drew applauses from the benches of students in the public courses. For a poor young gardener, was it not indeed a great piece of good luck to hear such a lecture, delivered in the very presence of nature?

"Here are, you see, my child," said Monsieur de Jussieu, "four different kinds of soil, and if I cared to take the time, I could find ten other kinds mingled with these four principal ingredients; but for a gardener's apprentice this distinction would be a little too fine. A florist should always taste the soil, as a gardener tastes his fruits. Do you follow me, Gilbert?"

"Yes, monsieur," answered Gilbert, his eyes fixed, his mouth half opened; for he had seen Andrée, and, standing where he was, he could continue to watch her without letting the professor suspect that his lecture was not being religiously listened to and comprehended.

"In order to taste the soil," said Monsieur de Jussieu, still deceived by Gilbert's absent-mindedness, "shut up a handful in a sieve, turn a few drops of water softly over it, and taste this water when it comes through, filtered by the earth placed in the sieve above it. Savours of salts, either acrid, or insipid, or flavoured with some natural essences, adapt themselves wonderfully to the juices of the plants which you wish to put in it. For in nature, as your old patron, Monsieur Rousseau, says, all is analogy, assimilation, a tendency to combine and form one substance."

"Oh, *mon Dieu!*" cried Gilbert, reaching out his arms before him.

"What is the matter?"

"She has fainted, monsieur! she has fainted!"

"What is that? Are you mad?"

"She, she!"

"She?"

"Yes," replied Gilbert, eagerly, "a lady." And his fright and pallor, added to his reply of "She," would have betrayed him had not Monsieur de Jussieu turned his eyes above, to follow the direction of Gilbert's hand.

Looking in that direction, Monsieur de Jussieu saw, indeed, Andrée, who had dragged herself behind a hedge, and had fallen upon a bench. There she lay, motionless, and almost unconscious. It was the time at which the king was accustomed to call on the dauphiness, and he had to cross the orchard on his way from the Great to the Little Trianon. He now suddenly appeared. He held a vermilion peach (a wonder of precocity), and, like the selfish king he was, was asking himself if it would not be better for the welfare of France for him to test this peach, rather than to allow Madame la Dauphine to enjoy its savour.

The sight of Monsieur de Jussieu's haste, as he ran towards Andrée, whom the short-sighted king could scarcely see, and whom he had not recognised at all, and the stifled cries of Gilbert, which indicated great terror, hastened the progress of the king.

"What is the matter? what has happened?" asked Louis XV, approaching the hedge, from which he had been separated only by the length of the walk.

"The king!" cried Monsieur de Jussieu, holding the young girl in his arms.

"The king!" murmured Andrée, and fainted.

"But what is it?" repeated Louis XV., "a woman? What has happened to this woman?"

"Sire, a swoon."

"Ah! let us see," said Louis XV.

"She is quite unconscious, sire," added Monsieur de Jussieu, pointing to the young girl, as she lay rigid and motionless on the bench, where he had placed her.

The king drew near, recognised Andrée, and cried, shuddering: —

"Again! Oh, this is frightful! she should stay at home, since she is subject to such ill turns. It is not proper to be dying like this all day long, in the presence of every one."

And Louis XV. retraced his steps towards the pavilion of the Little Trianon, muttering a thousand disagreeable remarks about poor Andrée. Monsieur de Jussieu, who did not know of the preceding events, remained stupefied; but, turning and seeing Gilbert ten feet distant, in an attitude of fear and anxiety, —

"Come here, Gilbert," he cried; "you are strong; you must carry Mademoiselle de Taverney home."

"I!" cried Gilbert, trembling, "I carry her, touch her? No, no; she would never forgive me!"

And he ran away, distracted, calling for aid.

## CHAPTER CXXXVI.

### DOCTOR LOUIS.

A few feet from the place where Andrée had fainted, two under gardeners were working. They rushed out at Gilbert's cries, and placing themselves under the command of Monsieur de Jussieu, carried Andrée into her room, while Gilbert followed at a distance with bowed head, slowly and sadly, like an assassin walking behind the body of his victim.

Monsieur de Jussieu, having reached one of the principal entrances, relieved the gardeners of their burden. Andrée had just opened her eyes.

The sound of voices, and the commotion caused by the accident, attracted Monsieur de Taverney, who came out of the room. He saw his daughter, still trembling, trying to regain sufficient strength for walking up the stairs, supported by Monsieur de Jussieu; he ran up, asking, as did the king, "What has happened? what is the matter?"

"Nothing, father," replied Andrée, feebly; "only a little ill turn."

"Is mademoiselle your daughter, monsieur?" said Monsieur de Jussieu, bowing to the baron.

"Yes, monsieur."

"Then I cannot leave her in better hands. But, in Heaven's name, consult a doctor!"

"Oh, it is nothing," said Andrée.

And Taverney repeated: —

"Surely, it is nothing."

"I certainly hope so," said Monsieur de Jussieu; "but mademoiselle was really very pale."

And thereupon, having conducted Andrée to the very top of the stairs, he took leave.

The father and daughter were alone.

Taverney, who during Andrée's absence had certainly had time enough for reflection, then took Andrée's hand as she stood, and, leading her to a couch, made her sit, and sat down beside her.

"Excuse me, monsieur," said Andrée; "will you kindly open the window? I need air."

"I wish to speak to you on a rather important matter, Andrée, and, in this cage in which you are placed, one cannot breathe without being heard on all sides. But no matter; I will talk in a low voice."

And he opened the window. Then, returning, and sitting down near his daughter, and inclining his head,—

"It must be admitted," said he, "that the king, who at first showed such an interest in you, exhibits very little gallantry in letting you live in such a den as this."

"Father," said Andrée, "there are no accommodations at Trianon; you know that is the great fault of that residence."

"Were there no accommodations for others," said Taverney, with an insinuating smile, "I should not be surprised; but for you, indeed, I do not understand it."

"You have too exalted an opinion of my merits," said Andrée, with a smile; "and, unfortunately, every one is not of your opinion."

"All who know you, my daughter, on the contrary agree with me."

Andrée bowed, as she would have done in expressing her thanks to a stranger; for these compliments, coming from her father, began to fill her with apprehensions.

"And," continued Taverney, in the same modulated voice, "and the king knows you, does he not?"

And as he spoke, he shot upon the young girl a look of intolerable inquisitiveness.

"The king barely knows me," replied Andrée, very

naturally. "I fancy I am of little consequence in his estimation."

These words aroused the baron.

"Of little consequence!" cried he ; "indeed, I do not understand your words, mademoiselle. Of little consequence! truly you set a low price on your person."

Andrée looked at her father in astonishment.

"Yes, yes," continued the baron, "I say it, and I repeat it. Your modesty even extends so far as to forget what is due to your own personal dignity."

"Oh, monsieur, you greatly exaggerate! The king has indeed taken an interest in our family misfortunes; the king has deigned to do something for us; but there are so many unfortunate people around his Majesty, so many bounties bestowed by his royal hands, that oblivion must necessarily surround us, after he has relieved us through his kindness."

Taverney observed his daughter carefully, and with a certain admiration for her reserve and her impenetrable discretion.

"Now," said he, drawing near her, "now, my dear Andrée, your father shall be the first solicitor to seek you, and in that capacity I hope you will not refuse me."

Andrée, in her turn, looked at her father, and, with all the curiosity of her sex, desired an explanation.

"Come," continued he, "we all ask it of you; do something for us, for your family."

"But why do you make that request of me? What would you have me do?" cried Andrée, bewildered at the tone, and the hidden meaning of his words.

"Are you disposed, yes or no, to ask for something for me and for your brother? Speak!"

"Monsieur," said Andrée, "I will do whatever you command me; but, in truth, are you not afraid we shall appear too eager? Already the king has presented me with a gift, worth more than a hundred thousand francs. His Majesty has, besides, promised my brother a regiment. We shall thus receive a large share of the favours bestowed by the court."

Taverney could not repress a burst of loud and derisive laughter.

"Do you not think all that is sufficiently paid for?"

"I know, monsieur, that your services are very valuable," replied Andrée.

"Eh!" cried Taverney, "what in the devil are you speaking of my services for?"

"Of what should I speak, then?"

"Indeed, you are mocking me with your foolish dissemblings."

"What have I to dissemble, *mon Dieu!*" exclaimed Andrée.

"But I know all, my daughter."

"You know?"

"All, I tell you!"

"All what, monsieur?"

And Andrée's face was suffused with a blush, called forth by this gross attack on the most delicate of consciences. The respect of a father for his child stopped Taverney suddenly in the rapid flow of these interrogations.

"Go on," said he, "as long as you please. You wish to be reticent and mysterious, it appears. So be it. Let your father and brother remain in the obscurity of oblivion. But remember my words. If one does not begin by wielding the sceptre, one may never have an opportunity of ruling later."

And Taverney turned about on his heel.

"I do not understand you, monsieur," said Andrée.

"Very well; but I understand myself," said Taverney.

"That does not count, since two of us are speaking."

"Well, then, I will be more explicit. Call to your aid all the diplomacy with which nature has endowed you, and which is a virtue of our family; do all you can, while you have the opportunity, for the good of your family and for your own advantage; and the first time you see the king,

tell him that your brother is awaiting his appointment,
and that you dwell in an apartment without air or a good
view. In a word, do not be silly enough to show too
much love and disinterestedness."

"But, monsieur — "

"Say that to the king this evening."

"But where do you wish me to see the king?"

"And add that it is not suitable for his Majesty to
come — "

At the very moment when Taverney would doubtless,
by more explicit words, have roused the tempest which
was gathering in Andrée's breast, and would have accorded
the explanation required for enlightening Andrée's mind,
steps were heard on the stairway.

The baron at once stopped talking, and hastened to the
baluster to ascertain who was coming to see his daughter.

Andrée, in surprise, saw her father step back against
the wall.

Almost at the same moment the dauphiness, followed by
a man clothed in black, and leaning on a long cane, entered
the little room.

"Your Highness," cried Andrée, summoning all her
strength, and advancing to greet the dauphiness.

"Yes, little invalid," answered the princess; "I bring
you comfort and a physician. Come, doctor! Ah!" continued the princess, perceiving the baron, "your daughter
is suffering, and you have not taken care of the poor
child."

"Madame," stammered Taverney.

"Come, doctor," said the dauphiness, with that charming
kindness which she alone possessed to perfection, "come,
feel this pulse, question these weary eyes, and tell me
what ails my *protégée*."

"Oh, madame, madame! how good you are!" murmured
the young girl; "how dare I receive your Highness?"

"In this kennel, you should add, dear child. So much
the worse for me, who have provided such poor accom-

modations for you. I will look after that. Now, child,
give Doctor Louis your hand; he is my physician. Take
care; he is a philosopher, who can divine, and at the same
time a wise man, who can see."

Andrée smilingly gave the doctor her hand. The latter,
still a young man, whose intelligent face evinced all that
the dauphiness had claimed for him, had not ceased, since
he entered the room, to take into his consideration, first,
the illness itself, then the locality, then this strange conduct on the part of the father, who manifested annoyance,
but no anxiety.

The wise man could see, the philosopher had perhaps
already guessed. Doctor Louis tested the pulse of the
young girl for some minutes, and then asked her to describe her symptoms.

"A deep distaste for all food," answered Andrée;
"sudden twinges of pain; fever that rushes suddenly to
my head; spasms, palpitations, fainting fits."

As Andrée described her symptoms, the doctor became
graver and graver. He ended by dropping her hand and
looking into her eyes.

"Well, doctor," said the princess to the physician,
"*quid?* as the consulting physicians say. "Is the child
in danger, and do you condemn her to death?"

The doctor looked at Andrée, and once more examined
her in silence.

"Madame," said he, "the illness of mademoiselle is quite
natural."

"And dangerous?"

"No, not usually," said the doctor, smiling.

"Ah, well," said the princess, breathing more freely,
"do not trouble her further."

"Oh, I shall not trouble her any more, at all."

"What! shall you leave her no prescription?"

"There is really nothing to do for mademoiselle's
illness."

"Really?"

"No, madame."

"Nothing?"

"Nothing."

And the doctor, as if to avoid further explanations, took leave of the princess, under pretext of having other patients who needed him.

"Doctor, doctor!" said the dauphiness, "if you have not told me this merely to reassure me, I am more ill than Mademoiselle de Taverney! So bring me, this evening, without fail, the sleeping draughts which you promised me."

"Madame, I will prepare them myself when I return home."

And he went out.

The dauphiness remained with her reader.

"Don't worry, my dear Andrée," said she, with a kind smile; "your illness is nothing serious, for Doctor Louis will not prescribe for you."

"So much the better, madame," replied Andrée, "for then nothing shall interfere to prevent my serving your Highness, and I feared that above all else. However, with all due deference to the wise doctor, I assure you, madame, I do suffer."

"It cannot be a serious illness, however, since the doctor smiles at it. Sleep now, my child. I will send some one to wait on you, for I see that you are alone. Will you come with me, Monsieur de Taverney?"

She gave Andrée her hand and went out, having given her the comfort which she had promised her.

## CHAPTER CXXXVII.

MONSIEUR DE RICHELIEU'S WORD-PLAY.

MONSIEUR DE RICHELIEU, as we have seen, proceeded to Luciennes with the hasty decision and the unfailing judgment which was characteristic of the ambassador of Vienna and the conqueror of Mahon. He reached his destination in a seemingly gay and careless mood; ran up the staircase like a boy; pulled Zamore's ears as he used, in the happy days of his earlier acquaintance with him; and, as it were, forced open the door of the famous blue satin boudoir, where poor Lorenza had seen Madame Dubarry getting ready for her expedition to the Rue Saint-Claude.

The countess, reclining on a couch, was just giving Monsieur d'Aiguillon her commands for the morning. Both looked around, hearing a noise, and seemed confused on recognising the marshal.

"Ah, monsieur the duke!" cried the countess.

"Ah, my uncle!" said Monsieur d'Aiguillon.

"Yes, yes, madame! you here, nephew?"

"What, is it indeed yourself?"

"It is truly myself in person."

"Better late than never," replied the countess.

"Madame," said the marshal, "capriciousness is characteristic of old age."

"Which means you have recovered for Luciennes —"

"A great love which only capriciousness would have made me lose. That is exactly the case, and you have fathomed my inmost thoughts."

"Hence you return —"

"Hence I return; that's just it," said Richelieu, seating himself in the most comfortable easy-chair, which he had seen at his first glance.

"Oh! oh!" said the countess, "perhaps there is still another reason which you have not mentioned. Caprice is not enough for a man of your calibre."

"Countess, you should not press me. I am really better than I am represented, and if I return, you understand, it is — "

"It is?" asked the countess.

"Because I wanted to come here."

Monsieur d'Aiguillon and the countess burst out laughing.

"How lucky we are," said the countess, "to have a little sense, which enables us to appreciate the humour with which you are so richly endowed!"

"What?"

"Yes, I give you my oath, people of less sense would not understand, would be completely in the dark, would seek elsewhere the reason of your return. Truly, on the faith of a Dubarry, you alone, dear duke, are capable of such exits and entrances; Molé, Molé himself, is a·wooden actor compared with you."

"Then you do not believe that my heart prompts my return," cried Richelieu. "Countess, countess, be careful! you will give me a poor opinion of you. Oh! you need not laugh, my nephew, or I shall call you Peter, and shall not build anything upon you."

"Not even a little ministry?" asked the countess.

And for the second time the countess burst out laughing, without making any attempt to stifle her mirth.

"Well, strike! strike!" said Richelieu, pretending to be offended; "I will not stop you. I am too old; I can no longer resist. Abuse me, countess, it is a safe pastime now."

"On the contrary, countess, be careful," said d'Aiguillon; "should my uncle again plead his weakness we should be lost. No, monsieur the duke, we will not attack you again; for, powerless as you are, or pretend to be, you will return our attack with interest. No; to tell you the truth, we are really very glad to see you here again."

"Yes," said the countess, joking, "and in honour of your return we will send off cannon, rockets; and you know, duke —"

"I know nothing," said the marshal, with childlike simplicity.

"Well, in fireworks there is always some wig burned by the sparks, some hat crushed by the rocket-sticks."

The duke felt of his wig and looked at his hat.

"That is it, that is it," said the countess; "but you have come back. So much the better. As to me, I am full of my jokes, as Monsieur d'Aiguillon has remarked. Do you know the cause of my gaiety?"

"Countess, countess, you are going to say something spiteful!"

"Yes, but it will be the last."

"Well, speak on."

"I am in good spirits because your return presages good weather."

Richelieu bowed.

"Yes," continued the countess, "you are like the birds of whom the poets write, who always precede a calm. What is the name of these birds, Monsieur d'Aiguillon, of whom you write in your poems?"

"Halcyons, madame."

"That is it. I hope you are not vexed, marshal, at my comparing you to a bird with such a pretty name."

"I shall be the less vexed, madame," said Richelieu, with a slight expression of complacency, — a complacency that with him always boded some great piece of maliciousness; "I shall be the less vexed because the comparison is true."

"There now!"

"I bring good, excellent news."

"Ah!" said the countess.

"What is it?" said d'Aiguillon.

"What the devil! my dear duke, you are very importunate," said the countess; "give the marshal time to tell his news."

"Devil, no; it makes no difference to me. I can tell it at once; it is already an old story."

"Marshal, if your news is so stale —"

"*Dame!*" said the marshal, "it is either take or refuse, countess."

"Well, be it so, let us take it."

"It seems, countess, the king has fallen into a trap."

"Into a trap?"

"Yes, completely."

"What kind of a trap?"

"That which you have sprung for him."

"I?" said the countess; "I have set a trap for him?"

"*Parbleu!* you know it well."

"No, on my word, I know nothing of the sort."

"Ah, countess, it is not kind to be so mysterious with me."

"Truly, marshal, I am not trying to be so; I beg you tell me what you mean?"

"Yes, uncle, enlighten us," said D'Aiguillon, who suspected that the old man's dubious smile veiled some evil plan. "Madame is quite uneasy at this suspense."

The old man turned toward his nephew.

"*Pardieu!*" said he; "it would be indeed droll for madame the countess not to have confided in you, my dear D'Aiguillon. In that case, affairs would be even more complicated than I imagined."

"I, my uncle?"

"He?"

"Of course 'you,' of course 'he.' To speak unreservedly, countess, have you not admitted him into your confidence in your intrigues against the king, — this poor duke, who has played so difficult a part?"

Madame Dubarry blushed. It being early in the morning, she had used neither her rouge nor her patches; hence her blushes could be seen. But it was dangerous to blush.

"You are both looking at me in open-eyed astonishment," said Richelieu. "Must I enlighten you on the subject of your own affairs?"

"Enlighten us, enlighten us!" said both together.

"Well, the king, with his wonderful discernment, has found out everything."

"What can he have found out? Tell me," said the countess; "I am dying of curiosity."

"But the understanding you have with my nephew here —"

D'Aiguillon turned pale, and his looks seemed to say to the countess, "See, I was sure there was some mischief behind all this."

In such cases women are braver than men. The countess rallied all her forces for a combat.

"Duke," said she, "I fear riddles in which you assume the *rôle* of sphinx, for then it seems as if sooner or later I should be devoured bodily. Relieve my uneasiness; it may be a joke, but I find it a very poor one."

"Poor countess! on the contrary, it is a capital one," cried Richelieu; "not mine, but yours, you know."

"I do not agree with you, marshal," said Madame Dubarry, biting her lips impatiently, and nervously tapping the floor with her little foot.

"Come, come, no pride, countess," continued Richelieu; "it is well. You feared that the king would conceive an attachment for Mademoiselle de Taverney. Oh, you need not dispute it; it has been infallibly proved to me."

"It is true; I make no attempt to conceal the fact."

"Well, fearing that, you wished also to play a similar game with his Majesty?"

"I do not deny it. Go on."

"We will proceed, countess, we will proceed. But to prick his Majesty, whose skin is rather thick, you needed a very sharp thorn. Well, well, I am speaking figuratively, you understand?"

And the marshal began to laugh, or rather, to pretend to be convulsed with laughter, that he might, while thus engaged, watch more closely the anxious faces of his two victims.

"How figuratively?" said D'Aiguillon, who was the first to recover his composure, and who even assumed a playful air.

"You did not understand me," said the marshal; "the figure was atrocious. I meant that madame the countess wished to arouse the king's jealousy, and that she selected a man of character and of wit; in short, one of nature's wonders, for that purpose."

"Who dares say that?" cried the countess, enraged as the powerful always are when proved to be in the wrong.

"Who dares say that? Why, every one, countess."

"Every one is no one, you know very well, duke."

"On the contrary, madame, every one includes a hundred thousand people in Versailles alone, six hundred thousand in Paris, twenty-five millions in France. And you see I do not include the Hague, Hamburg, Rotterdam, London, Berlin, where there are proportionately as many news-papers as in Paris."

"And they say at Versailles, at Paris, in the Hague, at Rotterdam, at London, and at Berlin?"

"Well, they say that you are the most spirited, charming woman in Europe; they say that, thanks to this ingenious stratagem of seeming to have taken a lover—"

"A lover! What grounds have they for such a foolish accusation?"

"Accusation! What are you saying, countess? Admiration! They know really that it is nothing; but they admire your stratagem. Upon what is this enthusiasm, this admiration grounded? It is grounded on the brilliant nature of your disposition, on your clever schemes, on the grounds of your pretending to have been alone on the night, you remember, when I, the king, and Monsieur d'Aiguillon were at your house,—the night when I left first, when the king left second, and Monsieur d'Aiguillon was the third."

"Well, go on."

"Upon your having pretended to stay alone with D'Aiguillon, as if he were your lover, of making him leave Luciennes quietly in the morning, still as if he were your lover, and in such a way that two or three foolish people, two or three gulls, like myself, for example, might see it and might proclaim it from the house-tops in such a way that the king might have heard of it, might have become alarmed, and might quickly have abandoned the little Taverney in his fear of losing you."

Madame Dubarry and D'Aiguillon could hardly keep their countenances.

Richelieu did not molest them either by his looks or his movements; indeed, he seemed wholly engrossed by his snuff-box and his shirt frill.

"And in fact," said Richelieu, still playing with his shirt frill, "it seems that he has really left the little one."

"Duke," replied Madame Dubarry, "I pass you my word, I do not in the least follow you in your vague ramblings; and I am positive that, should you speak to the king as you have to me, he would understand you still less."

"Really!" said the duke.

"Yes, really; you accredit me, the world accredits me, with more imaginative faculty than I possess. I should never have attempted to arouse the king's jealousy in the way you describe."

"Countess!"

"I would take my oath!"

"Countess, you are a perfect diplomatist; there are no better diplomatists than women; a perfect diplomatist never acknowledges that he has played a losing game. There is a well-known axiom among politicians which I often have heard in my capacity of ambassador: 'Do not tell any one the means which have once brought you success; they may bring you success twice.'"

"But, duke—"

"The means have succeeded, that is all. And the king is at variance with all the Taverneys."

"But, truly, duke," cried Madame Dubarry, "you have a way of arriving at conclusions peculiar to yourself."

"Ah! do you not believe the king is on bad terms with the Taverney family?" said Richelieu, desirous of avoiding a quarrel.

"I do not mean that."

Richelieu tried to take the countess's hand.

"You are a bird," said he.

"And you are a serpent."

"Oh, very well. Next time I will hurry to bring you news, if I am to be rewarded in this way."

"Uncle, do not be deceived," quickly said D'Aiguillon, who perceived the drift of this manœuvre of Richelieu; "no one has a higher opinion of you than madame the countess; she was praising you to me at the very moment when you were announced."

"The fact is," said the marshal, "that I love my friends; that is why I wished to be the first to assure you of your triumph, countess. Do you know the Taverney father actually wished to sell his daughter to the king?"

"But it has already been done, I think," said Madame Dubarry.

"Oh, countess, how clever that man is! He is a serpent. Just fancy, I was quieted by his professions of friendship, —he, my old companion on the battle-field. I am easily influenced by those I love and trust. And then how could I know or suspect that this Aristides had come directly from his country home to Paris, to try to cut the grass from under the feet of Jean Dubarry, the cleverest of men? My devotion to your interest, indeed, needed a little good sense and penetration. On my honour, I was blind."

"And what you have told me is accomplished?" asked Madame Dubarry.

"Oh, wholly done, I assure you. I have handled this worthy purveyor so roughly that he must have played his part by this time, and we are now in possession."

"But the king?"

"The king?"

"Yes."

"I have questioned his Majesty on three points."

"The first?"

"The father."

"The second?"

"The daughter."

"The third?"

"The son. Now his Majesty has kindly called the father a — pander; the daughter, an impertinent hussy; and as to the son, his Majesty has not given him any name, so completely has he forgotten him."

"Very well; then we are rid of the whole tribe?"

"I think so."

"Had we better send the fellow back to his hole?"

"I do not think it worth while: there are other devices."

"And what about the son, whom the king has promised a regiment?"

"Ah! your memory is better than the king's. It is true Monsieur Philip is a pretty enough boy, who has bestowed on you killing glances. *Dame!* He is neither colonel, captain, nor brother of the favourite; but he has been honoured by your remembering him."

By these words the old duke tried to awaken jealousy in his nephew's heart. But D'Aiguillon, by this time, was too preoccupied to heed the old man's remark. He was trying to account for the actions of the old marshal, and to find out the real motive of his return.

After thinking it over a little, he concluded that it was merely the wind of favour that had wafted Richelieu to Luciennes. He made a sign to Madame Dubarry, which the old duke saw reflected in a pier glass before which he was standing, adjusting his wig; and Madame Dubarry at once asked Richelieu to stay and drink chocolate with her.

D'Aiguillon took leave of his uncle with a hundred caresses, which the old man returned.   The latter remained alone with the countess, before the round table which Zamore had brought in.

The old marshal took in all the countess's scheming, murmuring in a low voice, —

"Were I twenty years old, I should be looking at the clock and saying, In an hour I shall be minister.   What a foolish thing life is!" continued he, still speaking to himself; "during the first part, one places one's body at the service of one's spirit; during the second part, the vanquished spirit becomes the servant of the body.   It is absurd."

"Dear marshal," said the countess, interrupting her guest's soliloquy, "now, since we are such good friends, and, moreover, since we two are here alone, tell me why you gave yourself so much trouble as to put that little piece of affectation into the king's bed?"

"Faith, countess," replied Richelieu, sipping his cup of chocolate through his lips, "I do not know.   I have often asked myself the same question."

## CHAPTER CXXXVIII.

### THE RETURN.

MONSIEUR DE RICHELIEU knew what course Philip would pursue, and he might safely have predicted his return; for that very morning, on his way from Versailles to Luciennes, he had met him on the highway, going towards Trianon, and he had passed near enough to him to have seen on his face all the symptoms of sadness and distress with which it was overshadowed.

Philip, forgotten at Rheims; Philip, at first overwhelmed with kindness, — a kindness which had gradually turned into indifference and neglect; Philip, at one time annoyed by the ostentatious attentions of his jealous fellow officers, and the favours bestowed upon him by his superiors in rank; Philip, as disfavour little by little tarnished with its breath his brilliant career, was disgusted to see friendship change to coldness, and confidences to rebuffs; and in his sensitive spirit sorrow had assumed all the characteristics of regret.

Philip longed for the days of his lieutenancy at Strasbourg, where he was stationed when the dauphiness entered France; he longed for his kind friends, his fellow officers, his comrades; above all, he longed for the calm and pure atmosphere of his paternal home, at whose fireside La Brie was high priest. All trouble finds consolation in silence and oblivion, — that refuge for restless souls; and the solitude of Taverney, which had witnessed the decline of things, as well as the downfall of its inhabitants, had something philosophical in its influences, which appealed with a powerful voice to the young man's heart. But what Philip most longed for was the companionship of his sister; her judgment, always so good,—a judgment derived from loftiness of soul, rather than from experience; for lofty souls have the eminent and remarkable characteristic of unconsciously soaring above mean and petty spirits. Placed by nature above the vulgar herd, they escape the snares, the wounds, and the rebuffs which vex more sordid natures, who, skilful as they may be in manœuvring and deceiving, cannot always avoid annoyances of that nature.

As soon as Philip felt this weariness of soul, this discouragement and unhappiness in his solitude, he could not help imagining that Andrée, a part of himself, could not be happy at Versailles, while he, a part of Andrée, was unhappy at Rheims. Then he wrote the letter of which we already know, telling of his approaching return.

This letter surprised no one, the baron least of all; he was more surprised that Philip had had the patience to wait so long, while he himself was burning with impatience, and for the last fortnight had begged Richelieu, every time he saw him, to hasten matters.

Philip set a certain limit to the length of the time during which he would wait for his commission. At the end of that period, his appointment not having arrived, he took leave of his officers without seeming to notice their sneers or their satirical remarks,— sneers and sarcasms veiled under a polite exterior, which at that epoch was one of the characteristic virtues of the French people; and which were somewhat restrained by the respect which a man of parts always inspires in those around him.

· Up to the last minute he had awaited his appointment with more fear than hope; he mounted his horse and began his journey to Paris.

The three days on the road seemed to him an eternity, and the nearer he came to his destination, the more his father's silence toward him, and above all that of Andrée,

who had promised to write to him twice a week, filled him
with vague apprehension.

As we have already said, Philip arrived at Versailles
about noon, just as Monsieur de Richelieu was going away
from there.  Philip had travelled part of the night, had
slept only a few hours at Melun; he was therefore so
drowsy that he did not see Monsieur de Richelieu in his
carriage, or even recognise his livery.

He directed his course to the gate of the park, where he
had taken leave of Andrée the day that he went away.  At
that time the young girl, without any occasion for sadness,
since the family affairs were then at the height of pros-
perity, felt herself surrounded by an atmosphere filled with
vague warnings of serious approaching troubles.

Philip himself also had shared, in a measure, Andrée's
superstitious fears; but gradually his spirits revived, his
judgment came to his aid in helping him to gain control
over himself, and now, alas! it was this same Philip
who, after all, from no cause whatever, had become a
victim to the same alarms, without finding any solace in
himself to help him overcome this depressing sadness,
which, having no real occasion, seemed to him to be a
presentiment.

When his horse stepped on the pavement, the clattering
of his hoofs attracted the attention of a person who came
out from behind the tall hedges.  It was Gilbert, holding
a pruning-knife in his hand.

The gardener recognised his former master; on his side,
Philip recognised him.

Gilbert had been wandering about for a month like a
soul in pain, which cannot find rest.  To-day, busily engaged in carrying out a plan he had resolved upon, he was
trying to find all the spots in the garden that commanded
either a view of the dwelling, or of Andrée's window, so
that he could at any time see the house without exciting
the attention of others, and could indulge in his emotion
unobserved.  With a knife in his hand, for the sake of

appearances, he ran along the copses and gardens, here breaking off sprays of flowers, pretending to prune them, there stripping off the bark from the young lindens, under pretext of getting resin or gum, all the time listening, looking, and wishing.

During the month that had just passed away, the young man had grown pale; his face had lost all the freshness of youth, excepting a strange fire in his eyes, joined to the dull and heavy pallor of his complexion. But his mouth, compressed by cunning, his sidelong glances, the trembling of the muscles of his face, belonged to the more sober years of ripe age.

Gilbert, as we have said, recognised Philip, and started as if to go back behind the hedge; but Philip urged his horse toward him, crying,—

"Gilbert! ho! Gilbert!"

Gilbert's first inclination was to run away; a second more, and the dizziness of terror, and that delirium which really cannot be accounted for, but which the ancients, who sought a reason for everything, attributed to the god Pan, would have impelled him to flee helplessly through the walks, the thickets, the hedgerows, even into the water itself.

Philip's kind, reassuring words were happily heard and understood by this poor youth.

"Don't you recognise me, Gilbert?" said Philip.

Gilbert realised that he was acting foolishly, and stopped short. Then he slowly and defiantly retraced his steps.

"No, Monsieur le Chevalier, I did not recognise you. I thought you were one of the guard, and, as I was not working, I was afraid you would report me for punishment."

Philip was satisfied with this explanation; he dismounted, passed the bridle of his horse over one arm, and, leaning with the other on Gilbert's shoulder, he noticed that he was trembling violently.

"What is the matter, Gilbert?" he said.

"Nothing, monsieur," said Gilbert.

Philip smiled sadly.

"You do not like us, Gilbert," said he.

The young man trembled again.

"Oh, I understand," continued Philip; "my father treated you harshly and unkindly. But I, Gilbert?"

"Oh, you," murmured the young man.

"I, I have always liked you, stood up for you."

"It is true."

"Then forget the bad for the good. My sister, too, has always been kind to you."

"Oh! no, no, it is not that!" replied the youth vehemently, with an incomprehensible expression; for it included an accusation against Andrée, and an excuse for himself. It flashed out in pride, and groaned in remorse.

"Yes, yes," said Philip, in his turn, "I understand; my sister is somewhat haughty, but she is kind at heart."

Then, for this conversation was only for the purpose of delaying an interview which he feared, with a superstitious dread, —

"Do you know where she is now, my good Andrée? Speak, Gilbert!"

This name smote sadly against Gilbert's heart; he answered, in a stifling voice, —

"Why, at home, I suppose. How should I know?"

"Alone, always alone and weary, my poor sister!" interrupted Philip.

"Alone now, yes, monsieur, according to her usual custom; for since Nicole ran away — "

"What! has Nicole run away?"

"Yes, monsieur, with her lover."

"With her lover?"

"At least, so I suppose," said Gilbert, who saw he had gone too far; "it is commonly reported so."

"But, in truth," said Philip, more and more uneasy, "I do not understand it, Gilbert; I have to drag the words from you. Be a little more obliging. You have wit, you are not wanting in a natural distinction of manner; do not spoil these good traits by an assumed rudeness, which is quite foreign to your nature, and which is very far from pleasing."

"But I do not know what you wish, monsieur; and if you think a moment, you will see that I cannot know. I work all day in the garden. *Dame!* I do not know what is going on in the palace."

"Gilbert, Gilbert, at least, you have eyes to see."

"I?"

"Yes; and you might be a little interested in all who bear my name; for, poor as was the hospitality at Taverney, you have shared it yourself."

"Indeed, Monsieur Philip, I am very much interested in you," said Gilbert, in a rough, hard voice; for Philip's gentleness, and another feeling which he could not divine, had softened this fierce heart. "Yes, I am fond of you, monsieur, and so I will tell you that your sister is quite ill."

"Quite ill! my sister!" cried Philip, violently. "Quite ill! my sister quite ill, and you did not tell me so at once!" And immediately abandoning his slow steps for quicker ones: "What is the matter with her, for God's sake?" asked he.

"*Dame!*" said Gilbert, "they don't know."

"But what then?"

"Only, she fainted three times to-day on the parterre, and at this very moment the physician of madame the dauphiness has paid her a visit, as has also the baron."

Philip waited to hear no more; his forebodings were realised, and in the presence of a real danger he regained all his courage. He left his horse with Gilbert and ran as fast as he could toward the offices.

As for Gilbert, left to himself, he hastened to the stables with the horse, and then fled, — like those wild and evil birds that never linger around the dwellings of man.

## CHAPTER CXXXIX.

PHILIP found his sister lying on the couch of which we have already had occasion to speak.

On entering the antechamber, the young man noticed that Andrée had carefully carried off all the flowers of which she was so fond; for since this illness the perfume of flowers was unbearable to her, and she attributed to this irritation of the cerebral fibres all the bad feelings she had experienced during the past fortnight.

At the moment of Philip's entering the room, Andrée was asleep, her beautiful forehead was clouded, and her eyes rolled painfully in their sockets. Her hands hung at her sides, and although the blood was running down into them, they were as white as those of a wax image. She was so perfectly still that she did not seem to be living, and one would have to listen to her breathing to be convinced that she was not dead.

Philip had rushed along rapidly ever since Gilbert had told him that Andrée was ill, and consequently he reached the bottom of the staircase quite out of breath. But there he stopped a moment to think; his good sense asserted itself, and he went up the stairs more calmly until he reached the threshold of the room. He carefully walked along without any more noise or motion than a sylph. He wished to see for himself, with that solicitude peculiar to people who are fond of each other, and to judge the nature of the illness by its symptoms; he knew Andrée was so kind and so tender, that, after having seen and heard him, she would guard every act and movement that he might not be frightened. He entered, then, so softly, pushing the door open gently, that Andrée did not hear him, and he was in the middle of the chamber before she stirred at all.

Philip had time to look at his sister, to note her pallor, her immobility, her stony aspect. He noticed the strange expression of her eyes, so sunken and hollow, and, more alarmed than he would have thought possible, it suddenly occurred to him that her sufferings were largely caused by an unhappy mind. This idea caused Philip to shudder with dread, and he could not repress a movement of alarm.

Andrée raised her eyes, and, crying aloud, jumped up from the couch like a dead person suddenly brought back to life, and, panting in her turn, clung to her brother's neck.

"You, you, Philip!" cried she.

And her strength left her before she could say any more. Besides, what else could she say, when that was her only thought.

"Yes, yes, yes," replied Philip, embracing and supporting her, for he felt her sinking in his arms; "I have come back, and to find you sick. What is the matter with you?"

Andrée began to laugh nervously, which, far from reassuring Philip, as the invalid wished, made him feel badly.

"You ask what ails me. Do I look so ill?" said she.

"Oh yes, Andrée! you are pale and trembling."

"But how can you see that, brother? I am not even indisposed. Who, then, has informed you so incorrectly? *Mon Dieu!* Who has been so foolish as to frighten you? But, indeed, I do not know what you mean. I am wonderfully well, except for these little fainting turns, which go away as quickly as they come."

"Oh! but you are so pale, Andrée."

"Have I usually much colour?"

"No; but you usually look like a living person; but to-day —"

"It is nothing."

"Wait, wait; a moment ago your hands were burning, now they are as cold as ice."

"That is easily explained, Philip. When I saw you come in —"

"Well?"

"I felt a thrill of joy, and the blood rushed to my heart, that is all."

"But you are tottering, Andrée; you are holding on to me."

"No, I am only embracing you, that is all. Don't you wish me to embrace you, Philip?"

"Oh, dear Andrée!"

And he pressed the young girl to his heart. At the same moment Andrée felt her strength failing her again. In vain she tried to cling to her brother's neck; her hand slipped, cold as death, and she fell back on the couch, whiter than the muslin curtains on which her lovely figure was outlined.

"See, see, you are deceiving me!" cried Philip. "Ah, dear sister, you are suffering, you are ill!"

"The flask, the flask!" murmured Andrée, forcing a smile, which he never forgot to his dying day.

And her eyes failing, her hand lifted with difficulty, she pointed out a flask on the little desk near the window.

Philip, still keeping his eyes on his sister, whom he hated to leave, went to the piece of furniture. Then, having opened the window, he placed the flask under the young girl's pinched nostrils.

"There, there," said she, breathing long breaths of air and of life, "see, I am all right again. Tell me, do you think me so ill, now?"

But Philip did not think of answering; he looked intently at his sister.

Andrée gradually recovered herself, sat up on the couch, took Philip's trembling hand between her moist hands; and, her face softening, the blood returning to her cheeks, she appeared more beautiful than ever.

"Ah, *mon Dieu!*" said she; "look, Philip, I am all right, and I am willing to wager that had you not, with the best intentions in the world, come upon me so suddenly, I should not have had this turn, and should have been well. But appearing so unexpectedly before me, Philip,— before me, who love you so deeply, —you, you who are the moving power, a part of my life, — it would have been enough to kill me had I been well."

"Yes, that is all very plain, very plausible, Andrée; but tell me, I beg you, to what cause do you attribute this illness?"

"How should I know, dear brother? It is the spring, the season of flowers. You know I am very nervous. Only yesterday the perfume of the Persian lilacs in the garden suffocated me. You know what enervating odours these magnificent bunches, swayed on the early spring breezes emit; well, yesterday — Oh heavens! wait, Philip, I will not think of it; I am afraid it will make me ill again."

"Yes, you are right; it may be that. Flowers are very dangerous. Don't you remember that when I was a child at Taverney I wished to have my bed turned around, so that I could see the lilac hedge? We both thought it would look so pretty, lying in bed. But the next day, you know, I did not awaken; the next day every one except you, who would not believe that I could die without saying good-bye to you,— every one, I say, thought I was dead. You were scarcely six years old at that time, and it was you alone who succeeded, by force of kisses and tears, in calling me back to life."

"And air, Philip, it is air which one needs at such times. I can't seem to get air enough."

"Ah, sister, sister, you have forgotten all about that; you have had flowers in your room."

"No, Philip; indeed, for the last fortnight there has been not even an Easter daisy here. How strange it is for me, who have always been so fond of flowers, to have suddenly taken this aversion for them! Then I have had

headache. Mademoiselle de Taverney has had the headache; and what a lucky person this Mademoiselle de
Taverney is! for — thanks to this headache, which has
caused her to faint — she has aroused the interest of the
court and the city in her condition."

"How so?"

"There is no doubt of it. The dauphiness herself has
had the kindness to visit me. Yes, Philip, what a charming protectress! what friend so charming as madame the
dauphiness! She has cared for me, nursed me, brought
her own physician to see me; and when this solemn person, whose opinion is infallible, had felt my pulse, looked
at my eyes and my tongue, do you realise the greatest piece
of good luck that has befallen me?"

"No."

"Well, he discovered purely and simply, that nothing
in the world ailed me, that Doctor Louis had no prescription to give me, — he who, it is said, cuts off every day
arms and legs, the very thought of which makes me
shudder. So, Philip, you see I am remarkably well.
Who, then, can have alarmed you?"

"It was that little idiot of a Gilbert, *pardieu!*"

"Gilbert?" said Andrée, with an undisguised movement
of impatience.

"Yes, he told me you were quite ill."

"And you believed the little simpleton, good for nothing
but to do or speak evil?"

"Andrée, Andrée!"

"Well?"

"You are growing pale again."

No; it is only Gilbert who rouses my ire. It is enough
to meet him on my path, I need not hear him spoken of
when he is not here."

"Wait, you are fainting again."

"Oh, yes, yes! *mon Dieu!* But it is as — " and Andrée's
lips grew white, and her voice stopped.

"How strange this is!" murmured Philip.

Andrée made an effort.

"No, it is nothing," said she; "don't think any more of these nervous feelings. Here I am on my feet; hold, if you can trust me, Philip, we will walk around together, and in ten minutes I shall be all right."

"I think you do not understand your own strength, Andrée."

"No. If Philip's return cannot restore me to health, I must be dying. Shall we go out, Philip?"

"All in good time, dear Andrée," said Philip, gently checking his sister. You have not yet wholly reassured me; wait a little."

"So be it."

Andrée fell back on the couch, drawing Philip beside her, and holding his hand clasped in hers.

"And why," continued she, "why do you appear here suddenly, without writing to tell us you were coming?"

"But answer me, dear Andrée, why did you stop writing to me?"

"Yes, I have not written to you during the last few days."

"For nearly two weeks, Andrée."

Andrée hung her head.

"It was negligence," said Philip, gently reproaching her.

"Oh, no; suffering, Philip! Wait, you are right; my illness came on the very day you ceased hearing from me. Since that time the things dearest to me have wearied me, even been distasteful to me."

"Indeed, I am pleased, in the midst of all this, with one thing you have said."

"What have I said?"

"You said you were happy. So much the better; for, while you have been loved and thought kindly of here, no one has done as much for me."

"For you?"

"Yes, for me, who have been completely forgotten down there, even by my own sister."

"Oh Philip!"

"Would you believe it, my dear Andrée, since my departure, which I was urged to make so hurriedly, not one word have I heard of the pretended regiment which I was to have received, and which the king promised me through Monsieur de Richelieu and my own father."

"Oh! I am not at all surprised at that," said Andrée.

"What! you are not surprised?"

"No. If you knew, Philip, Monsieur de Richelieu and my father are fickle men; they seem like two bodies without a soul. I cannot understand the ways of these people. In the morning my father went over to see his ' old friend,' as he calls him. He sends him to Versailles to see the king; then he returns here to wait, and passes the time asking me questions, whose meaning I do not understand. The day wears away; no news. Then Monsieur de Taverney gets very angry. The Duke de Richelieu drives him away, he says. The duke is a traitor. Whom does the duke betray? I ask you; for myself, I know nothing about it, and I acknowledge to you that I care little. Monsieur de Taverney lives like the damned in Purgatory, waiting for something that does not happen, for some one who does not come."

"But the king, Andreé, the king?"

"What! the king?"

"Yes, the king, so favourably inclined towards us."

Andrée looked timidly around her.

"What?"

"Listen! The king — speak low — I think the king is very capricious. His Majesty at first showed great interest in me, in you, in our father, in short, our whole family; but suddenly this interest grows cold, without my being able to guess why or how. The fact is, his Majesty no longer pays any attention to me, — turned his back upon me only yesterday, when I fainted in the garden."

"Oh I see! Gilbert was right; you did faint there."

"That miserable little Monsieur Gilbert has taken the

trouble of telling you that, of telling every one, perhaps. What does it matter to him whether I faint or not? I know very well," continued Andrée, laughing, "that it is not proper to faint in a palace; but, indeed, one does not faint at will, and I did not do it on purpose."

"But who blames you, my dear sister?"

"Eh! the king?"

"The king."

"Yes; his Majesty was going from the Great Trianon through the orchard just at the fatal moment. I was quite stupid and dazed, stretched out on a bench in the arms of that good Monsieur de Jussieu, who was doing the best he could, when the king perceived me. You know, Philip, fainting deprives one of all consciousness of what is going on around one. Well, when the king saw me, senseless as I was, I believe I saw him frown, look at me in anger, and grumble some unkind remarks between his teeth. Then his Majesty hurried off, shocked, I suppose, at my presumption in being ill in his garden. Indeed, dear Philip, it was not my fault."

"Poor child," said Philip, affectionately pressing his sister's hands, "I believe you, it was not your fault; and then — "

"That is all, my dear; and Monsieur Gilbert might have spared his remarks."

"Come, you are hard on the poor lad."

"Oh yes, defend him; he is a charming subject."

"Andrée, for mercy's sake, do not be so unkind towards this lad; you wound him, you treat him harshly. I have seen you do it. Oh, *mon Dieu!* what is the matter now?"

This time Andrée fell back on the sofa cushions without saying a word; this time the flask did not restore her. The swoon could not be overcome until the circulation was restored.

"Truly," murmured Philip, "you do suffer in a way to frighten people more courageous than I where your sufferings are concerned. You may say what you like, this trouble of yours should not be treated lightly."

"But indeed, Philip, since the doctor said — "

"The doctor does not convince me, and never will, until I have spoken to him myself. Where can this doctor be seen?"

"He comes every day to Trianon."

"But at what time every day? In the morning?"

"Morning and evening, when he is on duty."

"Is he on duty now?"

"Yes, my dear, at seven o'clock in the evening precisely, for he is very punctual, he will climb the staircase to the apartments of the dauphiness."

"Well," said Philip, more quietly, "I will wait here with you."

## CHAPTER CXL.

### A MISUNDERSTANDING.

PHILIP continued talking quite naturally, yet at the same time watching his sister out of the corner of his eye. Andrée, in her turn, was struggling to keep from fainting again.

Philip had a great deal to say about his disappointments, the neglect of the king, and Monsieur de Richelieu's inconsistency; and when the clock struck seven he left suddenly, taking little care to conceal from Andrée what he was going to do. He walked directly toward the queen's apartments, and stopped far enough away not to be questioned by the serving-men, and, at the same time, near enough to admit of no one's passing him without his recognising them. He had waited only about five minutes, when the doctor's stately and almost majestic figure approached; he recognised him from Andrée's description.

Although the day was fast declining, despite the difficulty of reading in the dim light, the doctor perused a pamphlet, recently published at Cologne, on the causes and effects of paralysis of the stomach. Gradually the darkness fell around him, and the doctor had just decided that he could no longer see to read, when a moving and opaque body intercepted the light before the eyes of the wise doctor. He raised his head, saw a man in front of him, and asked, —

"What is wanted?"

"Pardon me, monsieur," said Philip. "Have I the honour of addressing Monsieur the Doctor Louis?"

"Yes, monsieur," replied the doctor, closing his book.

"Then, monsieur, a word with you, if you please."

"Monsieur, pardon me, but my duty takes me to the dauphiness. It is time for me to be with her, and I cannot attend to you now."

"Monsieur," and Philip made a supplicating gesture, as if to prevent the doctor from going by him, "monsieur, the person in whose behalf I entreat your aid, is in the service of the dauphiness. She is suffering greatly, whereas the dauphiness is not ill at all."

"In the first place, of whom are you talking?" asked the doctor.

"Of a person into whose house the dauphiness herself conducted you."

"Ah! ah! perchance you are asking for Mademoiselle Andrée de Taverney?"

"Truly, monsieur."

"Ah! ah!" said the doctor, raising his head quickly, and looking keenly at the young man.

"You know how she suffers."

"Yes; she has spasms, has she not?"

"Frequent faintings, monsieur. She fainted to-day three or four times in the space of a few hours, and I caught her in my arms."

"The young lady is worse then?"

"Alas! I do not know; for you understand, doctor, when people love —"

"You love Mademoiselle de Taverney?"

"More than my life."

Philip spoke these words with such a lofty fraternal expression of affection, that the doctor was completely deceived as to their significance.

"Ah! ah! it is you then?"

The doctor hesitated.

"What do you mean, monsieur?" asked Philip.

"It is then you who are —"

"Who are what, monsieur?"

"Eh, *parbleu!* who are her lover," said the doctor, impatiently.

Philip retreated two steps, put his hand to his forehead, and became deathly pale.

"Monsieur, be careful, you are insulting my sister."

"Is Mademoiselle de Taverney your sister?"

"Yes, monsieur; and I should not have thought that my words could have caused such a misunderstanding in your thoughts."

"Excuse me, monsieur; the strangeness of the hour, the mysterious manner in which you have conversed with me, made me suspect that a more tender sentiment than a brother's —"

"Oh, monsieur, no lover or husband could ever love my sister more devotedly than I."

"Very well; under these circumstances I can easily see how my words must have hurt you, and I humbly ask your pardon. Allow me, monsieur —"

And the doctor made a movement, as if he were going in.

"Doctor," insisted Philip, "I entreat you, do not leave me without reassuring me as to my sister's condition."

"But why do you worry about her condition?"

"Why? *mon Dieu!* my own observations."

"Have you noticed any indications of her being ill?"

"Serious ones, doctor."

"That depends."

"Listen, doctor; there is something hidden in all this. It would seem that you dare not give me a definite answer to my inquiries."

"Rather, attribute my abruptness to my impatience in hastening to the dauphiness, who is awaiting me."

"Doctor, doctor," said Philip, wiping his steaming brow, "did you not speak of a lover in connection with Mademoiselle de Taverney?"

"Yes, but you have undeceived me on that point."

"Did you, then, think that Mademoiselle de Taverney had a lover?"

"Pardon, monsieur; I need not account to you for my thoughts."

"Doctor, have mercy on me! Doctor, you have dropped a word that has sunk into my heart, like the broken point of a dagger. Doctor, do not try to put me off. However delicate a subject this illness may be, tell me what is the nature of it, that you can explain it to a lover, but not to her own brother. Doctor, I beg you, answer me!"

"In return, I beg you to excuse me from replying, monsieur; for I perceive from the burden of what you have said, that you are no longer master of yourself."

"Oh Heaven! do you see, you doctor, that every word you say only pushes me nearer an abyss which I shrink from entering?"

"Monsieur!"

"Doctor," cried Philip, with renewed vehemence, "you have inferred that you have a revelation to make to me which will require all my fortitude and courage to meet calmly."

"But I do not know what revelation you can mean; I certainly have not implied anything of the sort."

"You do a hundred times more than say, — you make me imagine such things. Oh, it is not kind, doctor! You see how my very heart is being consumed before your eyes; you see how eagerly I beseech, I implore you. Speak, then, speak! I have courage, I have powers of endurance. This illness, perhaps disgrace — Oh, doctor, why don't you contradict me?"

"Monsieur de Taverney, I have not spoken of it either to the dauphiness, your father, or yourself. Ask no more of me."

"Yes, yes; but you see I can interpret your reticence; you see that I follow the hidden fatal path of your inmost thoughts. Stop me, if I am going astray."

"Adieu, monsieur," said the doctor sharply.

"Oh, do not go away without telling me either one thing or the other! I only ask one word from your lips."

The doctor stopped.

"Monsieur," said he, suddenly, "that would only take us back to my fatal mistake."

"Speak no more of that, doctor."

"On the contrary, let us discuss it. Just now, a little late, perhaps, you tell me that mademoiselle is your sister; but previously, so vehemently did you express your love for her, telling me she was dearer to you than life itself, that naturally I mistook your position."

"That is true."

"If you love your sister so dearly, she ought to give you a like affection in return."

"Ah, monsieur, Andrée loves me more than any one in the world."

"Well, then, go back to her, ask her the meaning of this mystery, which I cannot explain to you, and if her love for you is as great as yours for her she will tell you all. One tells many things to a friend that one conceals from one's physician. Then perhaps she will tell you this thing which I would sooner lose one of the fingers on my right hand than reveal to you. Adieu, monsieur."

And the doctor again turned toward the pavilion.

"Oh! no, no, monsieur," said Philip, his words choked by his tears, and mad with grief; "no, doctor, I have not heard aright; you cannot have said that!"

The doctor gently moved away; but his manner was full of compassion.

"Do as I advise you, monsieur, and believe it is the best thing to do."

"Oh, but think of it! If I believe you, I shall have to give up what I have believed in all my life, to accuse an angel, yes, to tempt Providence itself. If you insist on my believing you, at least prove the truth of your suspicions."

"Adieu, monsieur."

"Doctor!" cried Philip, desperately.

"Take care! If you speak thus violently, you will

reveal what I had decided to conceal from every one, and
what I would have wished to hide from you above all the
rest."

"Yes, yes, you are right, doctor," said Philip, so low
that he hardly seemed to breathe; "but even science occasionally is mistaken, as you must acknowledge you yourself are sometimes in the wrong."

"Rarely, monsieur," answered the doctor. "I never make
a statement with my lips until my eyes and my judgment
tell me, 'I have seen it, I know it, I am sure of it.' Yes,
truly, you are right. At times I may have made mistakes,
as I am only fallible after all; but this time, judging
from all the indications, I am right. Come, be calm; let
me go."

But Philip could not let the matter rest here; he placed
his hand on the doctor's arm in such a piteous way that
the latter stopped.

"One last, one supreme favour, monsieur," said he.
"You see how confused my mind is? I seem to be going
mad. It is a matter of life or death to me to prove the
truth of this calamity that threatens me. I am going to
my sister, but I shall not speak of this to her until you
have seen her again. Consider."

"You are the one to consider, monsieur; for myself, I
have nothing more to say."

"Monsieur, promise me, — it is a favour that the executioner would not refuse his victim, — promise me to visit
my sister again, after you leave her Highness the dauphiness! Doctor, in Heaven's name, promise me you will!"

"It is quite unnecessary, monsieur; yet, stop a bit, it is
my duty to do as you wish. After I have left the dauphiness, I will call and see your sister."

"Oh, thanks, thanks! Come, and then you will acknowledge to me that you were mistaken."

"I wish I might with all my heart; and should I be, I
will acknowledge it with pleasure. Adieu."

And the doctor, liberated, went away, leaving Philip on

the esplanade, — Philip, trembling with fever, bathed in a cold perspiration, and no longer knowing in his half mad condition, either where he was, or the man with whom he had been speaking, or the secret about to be revealed to him. Without seeing them, he looked at the sky, where the stars were coming out one by one, and at the pavilion, already lighted.

## CHAPTER CXLI.

### AN INVESTIGATION.

As soon as Philip's scattered senses had returned, and he had once more become master of himself, he turned his steps toward Andrée's apartments. But gradually, as he approached the house, the phantom of his unhappiness seemed to melt away, and he seemed to have been striving with a dream, and not with reality. The farther off the doctor went, the more incredible seemed his hints. Surely, science had made mistakes; but virtue had never failed.

Yet, when Philip met Andrée, he was so pale, so changed, so haggard, that she in her turn began to feel uneasy about her brother, and to ask him how it was possible for him to have changed so perceptibly in so short a time.

Only one thing could have caused this effect in her brother's appearance.

"Good heavens, brother!" said she, "am I, then, so ill?"

"Why?" asked Philip.

"Because your consultation with Doctor Louis seems to have alarmed you."

"No, my sister," said Philip; "as you told me, the doctor is not at all uneasy about you, and I had hard work to get him to come back."

"Is he coming back?" said Andrée.

"Yes, he is coming back. Do you care, Andrée?"

And Philip looked intently at the young girl as he spoke.

"Oh, no," said she, innocently, "if only this call may

reassure you a little; that is all I care for. But what has
made you so frightfully pale? It quite upsets me."

"Does it trouble you, Andrée?"

"How can you ask such a question of me?"

"Do you, then, love me sincerely, Andreé?"

"What did you say?" said the young girl.

"I ask you, Andrée, if you love me as dearly as you did
when we were children together."

"Oh Philip! Philip!"

"So I am one of the dearest persons in the world to
you?"

"The very dearest, the only one I love," said Andrée.
Then blushing in dismay, "Excuse me, Philip, I forgot—"
said she.

"Our father, — did you not, Andrée?"

"Yes."

Philip took his sister's hand, and looked at her affectionately.

"Andrée," said he, "you must not think that I would
blame you should your heart contain a love that was neither
for myself nor for my father." Then, sitting beside her, he
continued, "You have reached the age in which a young
girl's heart speaks more warmly than she would wish, and
you know God himself has said that a woman should
leave her father and her family to follow her husband."

Andrée gazed at Philip as if he were speaking to her
in an unknown tongue. Then beginning to laugh, with an
inexpressible frankness, —

"My husband," said she, "did you say husband, Philip?
He is still unborn, or at least I have never met him."

Philip, touched by Andrée's candid exclamation, drew
nearer to her, and, holding her hand in his own, answered:—

"Before one has a husband, one has a lover, a fiancé."

Andrée, completely bewildered, let the young man's gaze
sink into the lowest depths of her clear eyes, which reflected her very soul.

"Sister," said Philip, "ever since you were born, I

have been your best friend, and I have always considered you my only one; I never would leave you to play with the other boys. We have been much together and nothing has disturbed the implicit confidence we have always had in each other. Why is it, Andrée, that you have, for some little time, been so changed toward me?"

"Changed! I changed toward you, Philip! Do tell me what you mean. You have talked very strangely to me ever since you came back. I can't understand it."

"Yes, Andrée," said the young man, pressing her to his breast, "yes, my sweet sister, youthful passions have supplanted our childhood affection, and you do not think me good enough to confide to my care all the love that warms your heart."

"Brother," said Andrée, more and more astonished, "why do you speak to me in that way? What have I to do with love?"

"Andrée, first let me ask you a question which calls forth all my courage, and which is filled with dangers for you, with anguish for me. I know very well, that in asking, or rather compelling, your confidence now, I shall lose much of your esteem; I would rather, indeed, I hate to say it, — I would rather make you love me less, than leave you a victim to the frightful misfortunes which threaten you, Andrée, if you persist in this deplorable silence, of which I would not have thought you capable, towards a brother, or one whom you love."

"My brother, my dear," said Andrée, "I give you my oath, I do not know what you mean."

"Andrée, will you compel me to enlighten you?"

"Oh, yes! indeed, yes!"

"But then, if spurred on by you, I speak too plainly, if I cause a blush to overspread your face, shame to weigh down your heart, then blame only yourself for having forced me, by your lack of trust in me, to pierce to the very depths of your soul, and to draw forth your secret from its hiding-place."

"Truly, Philip, I assure you I shall not be offended."

Philip looked at his sister, rose and strode rapidly up and down the room. There was a strange incongruity between his suspicions and the composure of this young girl, and he did not know what to make of it.

Andrée, for her part, looked at her brother in bewilderment, and as she encountered this sternness so different from his usual fraternal gentleness, she gradually grew cold with apprehension.

Thus, before Philip began to speak, Andrée rose, went to him, and, slipping her arm through her brother's, looked at him with an indescribable tenderness. "Listen, Philip," said she, " look at me as I am looking at you."

"I could ask nothing better," said the young man, fixing his glowing eyes upon her, "what do you wish to say to me ? "

"I wish to say to you, Philip, that you have always been jealous of my affection. It is natural, as I myself have always been jealous of your care and love ; well, look at me as I told you to do."

The young girl smiled.

"Do you read any secret in my eyes ? " she continued.

"Yes, yes, I see one," said Philip. "Andrée, you love some one."

"I ! " cried the young girl, with an astonishment so unaffected, that the most skilful actress could never have imitated her tone as she spoke the word "I."

And she began to laugh.

"I love some one ? " said she.

"Some one loves you, then ? "

"My faith, so much the worse ; for as that unknown person has never met me, or told me of his love, it is certainly wasted."

Then, seeing his sister laugh and joke so unreservedly at his questions, looking at her eyes so clear and blue, her whole bearing, so pure, Philip, who felt Andrée's heart as it beat against his own so steadily, reflected that a

month's absence could never have changed this young
girl's character hitherto so blameless.  Andrée certainly
had been unworthily suspected; science had lied.  He
acknowledged that there was some excuse for Doctor Louis,
who did not not know the purity and delicacy of Andrée's
character, who thought her like other girls of high rank,
who, excited by the excessive ardor of corrupted blood, or
by the example of others, sold themselves without regret,
or even ambition.  Philip looked again at Andrée and
realized how fallacious their theory had been.  He was so
happy at her exoneration that he embraced her with the
enthusiasm of the martyrs who gladly met death confessing their belief in the purity of the Virgin Mary and in
her Divine Son.

Just at the time of the change in Philip's feelings, a
step was heard on the stairs.  It was Doctor Louis, who,
faithful to his promise, had come to fulfil it.  Andrée
trembled.  In her present condition, everything startled
her.

" Who is coming ? " said she.

"Doctor Louis, probably," said Philip.

At the same moment the door opened, and the doctor,
so anxiously awaited by Philip, appeared in the room.

As we have said, he was one of those serious, earnest
men for whom science is a sacred thing, and who study its
mysteries religiously.

In this material age, it was a rare thing to find a man
like Doctor Louis who sought to discover diseases of the
soul under those of the body.  He pursued his course
openly, caring little for popular comment or obstacles in
his path, making the most of his time, the heritage of the
industrious, with an avarice which made him rude with
the idle and the talkative.  That is the reason of his curt-
ness toward Philip on their first encounter.  He took
him for one of those fops of the court who often fawn
upon a doctor, that they may draw compliments from him
in their conquests in love, and are proud to have a secret

to pay for. But as soon as the medallion was turned, and the doctor perceived the sad, threatening form of a brother, where he was looking only for a more or less amorous lover, — as soon as, in place of an offence, he had seen a misfortune, — the philosophical doctor, the kind-hearted man, was moved to pity; and after Philip's last words he said to himself, "Not only may I have been mistaken, I actually hope I have been deceived." Consequently he would have visited Andrée again had Philip not begged him to do so, in order to satisfy himself, by a more positive examination, that his first opinion had been correct.

He entered, and his first look — that comprehensive look peculiar to his profession — fell upon Andrée and remained fixed on her.

Indeed, whether from the excitement of the doctor's visit or from natural causes, Andrée was immediately seized by one of the attacks so alarming to Philip; she trembled, with difficulty carrying her handkerchief to her lips.

Philip, busily engaged in greeting the doctor, did not notice her.

"Doctor," said he, "be kind enough to forgive my rude manner toward you when I first met you, an hour ago. I was then as excited as I am now calm."

The doctor looked from Andrée to the young man, whose smile and effusiveness he tried to fathom.

"Have you talked with your sister, as I advised you to do?" he said.

"Yes, doctor, yes."

"And you are reassured?"

"I have more of heaven and less of hell in my heart."

The doctor took Andrée's hand and felt her pulse, for a long time.

Philip looked at him and seemed to imply, "Go on, doctor, I no longer fear a doctor's opinion."

"Well, monsieur?" said he triumphantly.

"Monsieur le Chevalier," answered Doctor Louis, "leave me alone with your sister."

These words, simply pronounced, shook the young man's confidence.

"What, still more?" said he.

The doctor made a sign.

"Very well, I will leave you," replied Philip sadly.

Then to his sister, "Andrée, be true and open with the doctor."

The young girl shrugged her shoulders, as if she did not understand his meaning.

Philip replied, "Well, while he is asking you about the state of your health, I will take a turn in the park. The time for which I ordered my horse has not yet arrived, so I may see you again before I go, and talk a moment with you."

And he pressed Andrée's hand, trying to force a smile.

But the young girl saw that his smile and his manner of clasping her hand were forced and convulsive.

The doctor gravely led Philip to the door and closed it.

After that he sat down beside Andrée on the couch.

## CHAPTER CXLII.

### THE CONSULTATION.

THE deepest silence reigned without. Not a breath of wind was stirring, no voice was heard; all nature was at rest.

On the other side, all the service at Trianon was over for the day. The servants had gone to their rooms. The little court was deserted.

Andrée in the depths of her heart felt somewhat disturbed at the importance Philip and the doctor attached to her illness.

She wondered at the doctor's return, since that very morning he had made light of her illness, and had not even prescribed for her; but, thanks to her native purity, the clear mirror of her soul was not in the least dulled by all these suspicions.

Suddenly the doctor, who had continued to look at her attentively, after having turned the light of the lamp full upon her, took her hand, more as a friend or confessor than as a doctor, merely feeling her pulse.

This unexpected movement so surprised Andrée, that she was on the point of withdrawing her hand.

"Mademoiselle," said the doctor, "did you yourself wish to see me, or am I only here at your brother's desire?"

"Monsieur," replied Andrée, "my brother came back to tell me that you were coming here again; for after your having told me this morning that my illness was not in the least serious, I certainly should not have presumed to send for you again."

The doctor bowed.

" Your brother," continued he, " seems to be very jealous of his honor, even unreasonably so, and doubtless that is why you have not confided in him ? "

Andrée looked at the doctor, as she had looked at Philip.

" You, too ? " said she haughtily.

" Pardon me, mademoiselle, let me conclude."

Andrée made a gesture of patience, or rather of resignation.

" It is quite natural," continued the doctor, " that, on perceiving the grief and the wrath that possessed the young man, you should have obstinately guarded your secret ; but with me, mademoiselle, with me, who am more interested in the maladies of the souls of my patients than of the ills of the bodies, with me, who see and who know, with me, who consequently can meet you on the difficult path of confession, you certainly should be more open."

" Monsieur," answered Andrée, " had I not seen my brother's face assume a serious, and indeed a sad expression, had I not seen your dignified form and known your reputation for sobriety, I should certainly believe that you were both acting a comedy for my amusement, to make me take some disagreeable dose of medicine after you had finished and had succeeded in frightening me."

The doctor frowned. " I entreat you," said he, " to put an end to this dissimulation."

" Dissimulation ! " cried Andrée.

" Shall I call it hypocrisy ? "

" But, monsieur," cried the young girl, " you really are becoming very disagreeable ! "

" Say rather that I have found you out."

" Monsieur ! "

Andrée rose ; but the doctor gently pushed her down again.

" No," continued he, " my child, I do not insult you ; I serve you, and, if I convince you, I save you. So neither your angry words nor your pretended indignation can turn me."

"But what do you wish?  What will you have?"

"Confess, or on my honor, I shall have a very poor opinion of you."

"Monsieur, once again, my brother is not here to defend me.  I tell you that you are insulting me, and that I do not understand you.  I demand from you a clear and concise explanation of this pretended illness."

"For the last time, mademoiselle," replied the astonished physician, "will you not spare me the pain of making you blush?"

"I do not understand! I do not understand! I do not understand!" replied Andrée; looking at the doctor with eyes sparkling with interrogation, defiance, even menace.

"Well, I understand you, mademoiselle; you doubt science, you hope to conceal your condition from every one; but do not be deluded; with one word I can overthrow all your pride: you are *enceinte!*"

Andrée shrieked aloud and fell back on the sofa.

This cry was followed by the noise of a door, violently pushed open, and Philip leaped into the room, sword in hand, with angry eyes and trembling lips.

"Miserable creature," he said to the doctor, "you lie."

The doctor looked slowly toward the young man, still retaining Andrée's pulse, which beat as if she were half dead.

"What I have said, I have said, monsieur," replied the doctor, looking at Philip in scorn, "and I do not fear your sword; drawn or in its sheath, it will not make me say what is false."

"Doctor," murmured Philip, letting his sword fall.

"You wished me to verify by a second examination my first opinion.  I have done so.  Now that its certainty is established, nothing can make me doubt its truth.  I am extremely sorry such is the case, my young friend, for my sympathy for you is equalled only by my contempt for your sister, whose obstinate lying has filled me with scorn."

Andrée remained motionless; but Philip made a gesture of protestation.

"I am a family man, monsieur," continued the doctor, "and I know all you may, all you must suffer. I extend to you my services and promise secrecy. My word is sacred, monsieur, and every one will tell you that I esteem it more highly than my life."

"Oh, monsieur, it is impossible."

"I do not know about its being impossible; it is true. Adieu, Monsieur de Taverney."

And the doctor turned in his slow, calm way, and walked out, after having looked affectionately at the young man, who, as soon as the door was closed, sank down in grief into an arm-chair, about two feet away from Andrée.

When the doctor had gone, Philip arose, closed the door into the corridor, that of the room, and the windows, and approaching Andrée, who was watching these mysterious proceedings in a bewildered condition,—

"You have cowardly and stupidly deceived me," said he, folding his arms; "cowardly, because I am your brother, because I have been weak enough to love and esteem you above all others, and this confidence should have called forth yours, had your love for me ceased; stupidly, because to-day the infamous secret of our dishonour is shared by a third person; because, despite your discretion, it may already have been discovered by others; because, in short, had you in the first place confided your condition to me, I might have saved you from shame, if not through affection for you, at least through my self-respect; for I should have saved myself in saving you. This is the way in which you have utterly failed. Your honour, while you are not married, belongs to those who bear your name, which name you have defiled. See, now, I am no longer your brother, since you have denied me that right. I am now a man, eager to snatch your whole secret from you, by all available means, so that from this knowledge I may make some reparation for myself. I come to you, then, filled with grief and indignation, and I say to you, ' Since you have been cowardly enough to resort to lies, you shall receive the punishment of liars.' Acknowledge, then, your sin, or — "

"Threats!" cried Andrée; "threats to a woman!"

"Yes, threats; not to a woman, to a creature devoid of honour and of good faith."

"Threats!" cried Andrée, becoming gradually exasperated, "threats to me, who know nothing, who understand nothing, who regard you both as sanguinary madmen in league to kill me with grief, if not shame!"

"Well, then," cried Philip, "die then! die, if you will not confess! die this very moment! God judges you, and I will deal the blow."

And the young man grasped his sword convulsively, and, quick as lightning, put the point against his sister's breast.

"Well, well, kill me!" cried she, without shrinking from the flash of his sword, or trying to escape the pain of a wound.

And, half mad, she threw herself forward, filled with grief. Her movement was so sudden that the sword would have pierced her breast had not Philip's sudden terror at the sight of a few drops of blood that stained the muslin around the young girl's neck made him draw back.

The young man's strength and grief failed him; he dropped the iron from his hands, and, falling on his knees in tears, he clasped the young girl in his arms.

"Andrée! Andrée!" cried he, "no, it is I who should die! You love me no longer, you know me no more; I have nothing to live for. Oh Andrée! you love another so much that you would die rather than confide in me! Oh Andrée! I am the one to die, rather than you!"

He started to flee, but Andrée had already seized him by the neck, beside herself, covering him with kisses and bathing him in tears.

"No, no," said she; "you were right at first. Kill me,

Philip, for I am already condemned! But you, so pure,
so noble, so good, — you, whom no one accuses, — live and
pity me, instead of cursing me!"

"Oh, my sister," replied the young man, "in the name
of Heaven, in the name of the love we once bore each other,
come, fear nothing, either for yourself or for him whom
you love! Whoever he may be, he shall be sacred to me,
were he my bitterest enemy, were he the vilest of men.
But I have not an enemy, Andreé; you, who are so noble
in heart and thought, must have chosen your lover wisely.
Whoever you may have selected, I will go to him, I will
call him brother. You say nothing. Is a marriage between
you impossible? Do you mean that? Well, so be it, I
will be resigned; I will keep my grief to myself; I will
stifle this imperious voice of honour which demands his
blood. I exact nothing from you, not even this man's
name. If he is dear to you, he shall be pleasing to me.
Only, we will leave France, we will flee together. The
king has given you a valuable necklace; we will sell it.
We will give my father part of the price, then, with the
rest, we will live in obscurity. I truly care for no one;
you see I am wholly devoted to you; I shall be all yours,
and you all mine, Andrée. Andrée, you know my plans,
you see to what extent you can rely on my love for you.
Will you still refuse me your confidence, after what I have
told you? Come, come, will you not call me brother?"

Andrée had heard in silence all the distracted young
man's words. Only the beating of her heart showed that
she was still living; only her expression denoted that she
was still conscious.

"Philip," said she, after a long silence, "you thought I
no longer loved you; poor brother! you thought that I
loved another man; you thought that I had forgotten the
law of honour; I, who am of noble lineage, and who understand the full significance of that fact. My dear one, I
forgive you. Yes, yes, in vain have you called me infamous; in vain have you called me coward. Yes, yes, I

forgive you; but I will not forgive you if you can believe me wretched enough to swear falsely to you.  I swear to you, Philip, by God who hears me, by the spirit of my mother, who, it seems, can no longer protect me, — I swear to you, by my ardent love for you, that no thought of love has ever disturbed me, that no man has ever said to me, 'I love you,' that no kiss has ever touched my hand, that I am pure in heart, virgin in desire, as on the day of my birth.  Now, Philip, as God holds my soul, you hold my body in your power."

"It is well," said Philip, after a long silence; "it is well, I thank you.  Now I look into the depths of your soul.  Yes, you are pure, innocent, dear victim; but there are magic drinks, poisoned philtres.  Some one has set an infamous trap for you.  What they could have taken from you living only with your life itself, they have rudely snatched from you while you slept.  You have fallen into a snare, Andrée; but now we are united, consequently, now we are strong.  You trust to me your honour, and the means of avenging it?"

"Oh yes, yes!" said Andrée, vehemently; "for if you avenge me it will be for a crime."

"Well," continued Philip, "come, help me, sustain me.  Let us seek together.  Go over, hour by hour, all the days that have passed.  Let us follow the helping thread of memory, and at the first clew —"

"Oh, I wish it, I wish it!  Let us look!"

"Well, have you noticed any one following you, watching you?"

"No."

"No one has written to you?"

"No one."

"Not a man has told you he loves you?"

"Not one."

"Women have wonderful insight in these affairs, in default of letters, of avowals of love; have you never noticed any one who seemed to desire you?"

"I never noticed anything of the kind."

"Dear sister, think over all the events of your life, all the smallest details."

"Direct me."

"Have you never walked alone?"

"Never, in my remembrance, except to go to see the dauphiness."

"When you went into the park, into the woods?"

"Nicole always went with me."

"Speaking of Nicole, has she left you?"

"Yes."

"What day?"

"The very day you went away, I believe."

"She was a girl of questionable character. Do you know the particulars of her flight? Think carefully."

"No; I only know that she went away with a young man whom she loved."

"What were your last relations with that girl?"

"Oh, *mon Dieu!* about nine o'clock she came in as usual to my room, undressed me, fixed my glass of water, and went out."

"Did you notice whether she mixed anything in the water?"

"No; besides, this circumstance would not have aroused my suspicions, for I remember that when I raised the glass to my lips I experienced a peculiar sensation."

"What kind of one?"

"The same I once felt at Taverney."

"At Taverney?"

"Yes; when that stranger came there."

"What stranger?"

"The Count de Balsamo."

"The Count de Balsamo? And what kind of a sensation?"

"Oh, something like dizziness, like fainting; then the loss of all my faculties."

"And you say you experienced that sensation at Taverney?"

"Yes."

"Under what circumstances?"

"I was at the piano, I felt myself fainting. I looked in front of me, and saw the count in a mirror. From that time, I remember nothing, except that, when I awoke, I was still at the piano, without knowing how long I had slept."

"Is that the only time you experienced that sensation?"

"Once again, on the day, or rather the night, of the fireworks, I was dragged along by the crowd, on the point of being crushed, destroyed. I summoned all my strength for the struggle. All at once my arms relaxed, a cloud passed over my eyes; but across the cloud I could still see this man."

"The Count de Balsamo?"

"Yes."

"And you slept?"

"I slept or fainted, I cannot tell which. You know how he carried me away, and took me home to my father's house."

"Yes, yes. This night, the night of Nicole's departure, did you awaken?"

"No; but I experienced all my former sensations, — the same strange feeling, the same nervous faintings, the same torpor, the same sleep."

"The same sleep?"

"Yes; sleep full of vertigos, in which, still struggling, I experienced strange influences, to which I had yielded."

"Great Heavens!" cried Philip; "go on, go on!"

"I went to sleep."

"Where, pray?"

"On my bed, I am sure of it; and I found myself on the floor, on the carpet, alone, suffering and cold as a dead person just coming back to life. On awaking, I called for Nicole, but in vain; she had disappeared."

"And was this the same kind of slumber?"

"Yes."

"The same as at Taverney? The same as on the day of the *fête?*"

"Yes, yes."

"The two first times before you fell you saw this Joseph Balsamo, this Count de Fenix?"

"Truly."

"And the third time you did not see him?"

"No," said Andrée, in terror, for she began to understand; "but I felt his presence."

"Well," cried Philip, "now do not be alarmed, be reassured, be proud, Andrée; I know your secret. Thanks, dear sister, thanks; now we are safe."

Philip took Andrée in his arms, pressed her fondly to his heart, and, carried away by the ardour of his resolution, he rushed out of the room, not waiting for any further explanations. He ran to the stable, saddled his horse, leaped on his back, and hastily started on the road to Paris.

# CHAPTER CXLIII.

## GILBERT'S CONSCIENCE.

ALL these scenes which we have just described smote most painfully on Gilbert's consciousness.

The ill-balanced susceptibility characteristic of him had been put to a very severe trial, as, hidden in a corner of the garden which he had sought out for himself, he daily saw the progress of Andrée's illness on her face and her bearing when the pallor which had alarmed him the previous evening appeared so much more marked and reproachful the next morning, and the rays of the sun shone in upon her at her window. Then, whoever had taken the trouble to look carefully at Gilbert's face, would have seen engraven upon it lines of remorse, such as the old masters so often depicted on the countenances of penitents in their paintings.

Gilbert at the same time both loved and hated Andrée's refulgent beauty, which, added to her other superior charms, only drew a sharper line of distinction between them; at the same time it attracted him like a treasure which he longed to acquire. Such were the reasons for his love and his hatred, his longing and his contempt. But from the time when her good looks began to fade, when Andrée's face revealed her shame and her suffering, — from the time, in short, when it was becoming dangerous for Andrée, dangerous for Gilbert, — the situation took on a new aspect, and Gilbert, who was eminently just, adapted his views to this changed condition of affairs. His first feeling was one of deep sadness; he could not see his mistress losing her health and her beauty without pain. He experienced the delicious pride of pitying this woman, so overbearing, so disdainful toward himself, and felt much sympathy for her, as he foresaw the scorn by which she would soon be overwhelmed.

We do not pretend to excuse Gilbert; pride justifies nothing. Also, pride was not the only sentiment that controlled his feelings when he contemplated the condition of affairs. Every time he saw Andrée, pale, suffering, bowed under the weight of her illness, appearing like a phantom before his eyes, he experienced a leaping of the heart, the blood rushed through his eyelids like tears, and he pressed an uneasy, clinched hand against his heart, to stifle the revolt of his conscience.

"It is through my crime that she is lost," murmured he.

And after having thrown an eager, longing look upon her, he would flee, seeming in his fear to see her always before him, and to hear her moaning. With this remorse in his heart, he experienced one of the most painful feelings that agitate man; with this raging love in his breast, he needed some solace; and he would have gladly given his own life for the right of falling on his knees before her, of taking her hand, of comforting her, of calling her back to consciousness when she fainted. His helplessness on those occasions was a punishment which brought more torture than words can express.

Gilbert endured this martyrdom for three days. From the first he had noticed the change, the almost imperceptible indications of Andrée's condition. Where no one else had noticed anything unusual, he, the accomplice, had seen and understood the situation; moreover, he had made a study of the evil, and knew the exact time when the crisis would arrive.

The day of Andrée's fainting turns he spent in trances, in agitations, in wandering wildly about, — all sure indications of a conscience at bay. All these goings and comings, all these pretences of indifference or haste, these sympathetic or sarcastic outbursts, which Gilbert considered wonders of dissimulation and of tact, the very lowest of the clerks of the châtelets, or the door-keepers of Saint-Lazare, would have readily understood, and interpreted as easily as the ferret of Monsieur de Sartines could read in cipher. When a man runs rapidly until he is out of breath, stops suddenly, sometimes making inarticulate sounds, and again preserving the deepest silence; when he is seen paying no attention to whatever sound there may be around him, digging in the ground, or wildly hacking at the trunks of trees, one naturally thinks to one's self, "If that man is not a criminal, he must be a fool."

After the first twinges of remorse, Gilbert had passed from a state of pity to one of self-interest. He saw that Andrée's fainting fits could not continue without a reason for them being sought; for every one would not consider them natural and of no account. Gilbert recalled to mind all the brutal and hasty forms of justice, which seek by questionings, by searchings, and by a course of reasoning unknown to other people, to obtain information, and which put on the criminal's track those bloodhounds full of resources who are called "instructors," the worst kind of robbery by which dishonour is brought on a man.

Again, what Gilbert had done appeared to him, from a moral standpoint, most repulsive, and deserving of punishment. He began to tremble, indeed; for he feared Andrée's sufferings would soon invite an investigation.

Then, like the criminal in the famous painting, whom an angel of remorse pursues by the faint light of a torch, Gilbert never ceased casting frightened glances on all around him. Every sound, every whisper, aroused his suspicions. Every remark, however insignificant, made in his presence, seemed to him to have some relation either to himself or to Mademoiselle de Taverney. He saw Monsieur de Taverney go from the king's apartments to those of his daughter. The house on that day assumed to him an air of defiance and conspiracy quite foreign to its usual appearance.

The mystery increased when he saw the doctor and madame the dauphiness go towards Andrée's room.

Gilbert was one of those sceptics who believe in nothing; he cared little for God or man. But he had taken science for his deity, and believed in its omnipotence.

At certain times Gilbert questioned the unfailing penetration of the Supreme Being, but he never doubted the physician's powers of insight. Doctor Louis's arrival at Andrée's apartments was a blow from which Gilbert's mind could not recover. He ran to his room, stopping abruptly in his work, quite regardless of the orders of those over him. Having arrived there behind the meagre curtain, which he had arranged in such a way that he could easily observe the opposite apartments, he exerted all his powers that he might gather from a stray look or movement the result of this conference.

Nothing happened to enlighten him. Once only he saw the dauphiness approach the window looking out upon a part of the court which she probably never had noticed before. He also could distinguish the figure of Doctor Louis as he opened the window to let some fresh air into the room. As to hearing what he said, or seeing the play of his features, he was quite unable to do either; a thick curtain, which hung the length of the window, prevented any knowledge of what was going on within.

The young man's anguish can readily be imagined. The lynx-eyed physician had already discovered the cause of the illness. A declaration must be made, but not at once, as Gilbert very wisely imagined, for the presence of the dauphiness would prevent that; yet soon, after the two strangers had gone, it must take place between the father and his daughter.

Gilbert, wild with grief and impatience, beat his head against the walls of his attic. He saw Monsieur de Taverney go out with the dauphiness; the doctor had already gone. "The explanation will take place between the dauphiness and the baron," he thought.

The baron did not return to his daughter. Andrée remained alone on the sofa, and spent the time, partly in the reading which her spasms and headache had forced her to suspend, partly in meditations so profound and so strange, that Gilbert, seeing her occasionally through a gap that the wind made in the curtain, took them for a kind of ecstasy.

At last, Andrée, overpowered by grief and emotion, slept. Gilbert took advantage of this respite to go out, in order to gather any reports or remarks that were being circulated.

This time was precious to him, since it gave him a chance to reflect. Danger was so imminent, that he made a sudden heroic resolution for contending against it. This was the first support on which this restless spirit, compelled to be wary, leaned and found a little rest.

But what resolution could he make? Any change, under such circumstances, would attract attention. Flight? Yes, flight with youthful energy, with the vigour of despair and of fear, which double one's natural strength until one becomes equal to a whole army,—to hide by day, to travel by night, and finally arrive—

Where?

And in what place could he be so safely hidden that the revengeful arm of the king's justice could not drag him forth? Gilbert knew the ways of the country. What would be thought in a place almost savage, almost deserted? — for he did not think of the city,— what would be thought in a small town, a hamlet, of a stranger coming to beg his bread from day to day, or else be accused of stealing it?

And then Gilbert knew himself well: an unusual countenance — a countenance which henceforth would carry the indelible imprint of a dreadful secret — would attract the attention of the first person who looked at him.

Flight was already dangerous, for discovery would be disgrace. Flight might stamp Gilbert as guilty; he repelled that idea, and as his mind had only strength enough to form one plan, the unfortunate one, since he must give up all idea of flight, saw nothing left him but death.

It was the first time this idea had occurred to him; indeed, the apparition of this lugubrious phantom could only be evoked by extreme fear.

"It will still be time," said he to himself, "to think of death when everything else fails; besides, it is cowardly to take one's life, as Monsieur Rousseau has said. It is more noble to suffer."

Upborne by this paradoxical thought, Gilbert began to walk through the garden.

This new glimmer of security had only just shone upon him when Philip's unforeseen arrival, which we have related above, overturned all his ideas, and called forth a new series of perplexities. The brother! the brother sent for! It was then conclusively proved. The family had kept it quiet; but would make all the investigations, all the minutest details, which, for Gilbert, meant the torture of the Conciergerie, of the Châtelet, and of La Tournelle. He would then be dragged into Andrée's presence, forced to kneel before her, and in this attitude to confess his crime; and he would be killed like a dog, by a blow or a knife, — a lawful vengeance already justified by numerous precedents.

King Louis XV. was very obliging to the nobility in such cases.

Then, Philip was the most redoubtable champion that Andrée could summon. Philip, the only one of the family who had ever treated Gilbert like a man, — indeed almost like an equal, — Philip might destroy the guilty wretch as surely by a single remark as by a sword thrust, if this remark were, "You have eaten our bread, and you bring dishonour upon us."

We have seen how Gilbert ran away at first sight of Philip, and how, in coming back, he was only following an instinct of not accusing himself; and from that time he concentrated all his strength in one mighty effort, — that of resistance. He followed Philip, saw him go to Andrée's room, saw him conversing with Doctor Louis. He observed all, passed his judgment on all, and understood the cause of Philip's despair. He saw his grief rise and increase; the terrible scene with Andrée he divined from their shadows on the curtains.

"I am lost," he thought.

And immediately, his reason wandered. He held a knife in his hand, prepared to kill Philip as soon as he should appear in the doorway, and then, if necessary, to kill himself.

Quite unexpectedly, he saw Philip and his sister becoming reconciled. Gilbert saw him on his knees, kissing Andrée's hands. Here was a new hope, a gate of safety. If Philip no longer showed anger, it must be because Andrée had told him that she did not know the name of the guilty person. If she, the only witness, the only accuser, did not know, then no one need ever know. If Andrée, foolish hope, knew and would not divulge it, then it meant for him more than safety, it meant good luck, it meant triumph. From this moment Gilbert rose to the occasion. Nothing arrested his progress, now that he clearly understood the situation.

"If Mademoiselle de Taverney does not accuse me," he said, "where are there to be found any evidences? And, fool that I am, would she accuse me of the crime itself, or of its result? Indeed, she has never reproached me for the crime; nothing during these last three weeks has pointed out either that she dislikes me or seeks to avoid me more than formerly. If, then, she does not know the cause, there is nothing in its effect to implicate me, more than any one else. I myself saw the king in Mademoiselle's room. I could testify to the fact before her brother, and, despite his Majesty's denials, I should be believed. Ah! but that would be a dangerous game to play; the king has too many means of asserting his innocence, or of removing my testimony. I had better keep

quiet.  But, putting the king out of the question, whose
name cannot be mentioned in this connection, without fear
of imprisonment for life, or even death, is there not that
unknown man who, on that very night, made Mademoiselle de Taverney go down into the garden ?  But he, how
will he defend himself ?  How will they know him ?  How
will they find him if they discover his complicity ?  He is
only an ordinary man like myself.  I am as smart as he, I
can defend myself against him.  Beside, no one would suspect me.  God alone saw me," added he in his thoughts,
laughing bitterly.  " But this God, who has seen my tears
so many times and my griefs, without making any sign, —
why should He be unjust enough to reveal my hidden
guilt on this occasion, the first time that happiness has
been within my grasp.  Moreover, if there is any crime,
it is His, not mine; Voltaire has proved conclusively that
there is no such thing as miracles.  I am safe, I am at
peace, my secret is mine alone.  The future is mine."

After these reflections, or rather, after this compromise
with his conscience, Gilbert locked up his tools, and went
out to spend the evening with his companions.  He was
gay, careless, free.  He had been remorseful, he had been
afraid, — a twofold weakness which a man, a philosopher,
would hasten to forget.  Only he did not reckon on his
conscience, he did not sleep.

# CHAPTER CXLIV.

## TWO GRIEFS.

GILBERT had rightly understood the situation when he said to himself, on the remembrance of this unknown man, whom he had surprised in the garden on the evening so fatal to Mademoiselle de Taverney, —

" Will he come back ? "

In fact, Philip was utterly ignorant of the place where Joseph Balsamo, Count de Fenix, lived.

But he remembered that high-born lady, that Marquise de Saverny, at whose house on the 31st of May Andrée had been carried for the care she needed.

It was not late enough for him to call on this lady, who lived in the Rue Saint-Honoré. Philip repressed all the agitation in his mind and his feelings. He went to the lady's house ; and the lady's maid gave him at once, without any hesitation, Balsamo's address, Rue Saint-Claude, au Marais.

Philip immediately started for the above-named street.

But it was not without deep emotion that he took hold of the knocker of this suspicious house, where, as he thought, were forever buried poor Andrée's peace of mind and honour. But, summoning all his will power, he repressed his indignation and emotions, that he might hold all his powers in reserve in case of need.

He then knocked at the entrance with a firm hand, and, according to the habits of the house, the gate was opened.

Philip entered the court-yard, holding his horse by the bridle. But he had not taken four steps, when Fritz, going out from the vestibule and standing at the top of the staircase, stopped him with the question, —

"What does monsieur want ? "

Philip trembled as if he had encountered some unforeseen obstacle. He scowled upon the German, as if Fritz had over-stepped his duties as servant.

"I wish," said he, "to speak to the master of the house, to the Count de Fenix," passing his horse's bridle through a ring, and walking toward the house, which he entered.

"Monsieur is not at home," said Fritz, letting Philip pass him, with the politeness of a well-trained servant.

Strangely enough, Philip seemed to have foreseen everything, except this simple reply.

"Where shall I find him ? " said he.

"I do not know, monsieur."

"You should know, however."

"I beg your pardon, my master does not confide in me."

"My good fellow," said Philip, "I must speak to your master this evening."

"I doubt if it would be possible for you to do so."

"I must; it is on a matter of the greatest importance.

Fritz bowed, without making any response.

"Has he gone out ? " said Philip.

"Yes, monsieur."

"He will come back soon ? "

"I do not think so, monsieur."

"Ah, you do not think so ? "

"No."

"Well," said Philip, getting feverishly impatient, " while I wait, go, tell your master — "

"But I have the honour of informing you that monsieur is not here," replied Fritz calmly.

"I know the importance of orders, my good fellow, and particularly of yours; but they cannot, indeed, apply to me, whose call your master could not have foreseen, as I have come here unexpectedly."

"The order is for every one, monsieur," replied Fritz, blundering.

"Then, since he gives you an order," said Philip, "the Count de Fenix must be here."

"Well, what then ?" said Fritz, in his turn getting out of patience at this continued insistence.

"Very well, I will wait for him here."

"Monsieur is not here, I tell you," said he ; "there has been a fire in the house, and ever since it has not been habitable."

"You are living here, however," said Philip, blundering in his turn.

"I am here to guard the house."

Philip shrugged his shoulders, with the air of a man who does not believe what is told him.

Fritz began to get angry.

"Moreover," said he, "whether monsieur the count is here or not, either in his absence or his presence, it is not the custom for people to get into his house by force. And if you do not conform to his rules I shall be obliged—"

Fritz stopped.

"To what ?" demanded Philip.

"To put you out," replied Fritz calmly.

"You !" cried Philip, with gleaming eyes.

"I," replied Fritz, assuming, as is characteristic of his nation, all those cold-blooded appearances so irritating to others.

And he took a step towards the young man, who, exasperated, beside himself, grasped his sword in his hand.

Fritz without showing any emotion at the sight of the sword, without calling for assistance, — perhaps, indeed he was alone, — Fritz seized from an armoury a kind of stake, armed with a short blade, and throwing himself upon Philip, like a cudgel player, rather than a fencer, broke into pieces the little sword of the other.

Philip gave a cry of rage, and, rushing to the armoury in his turn, tried to seize a weapon.

At this moment a secret door in the corridor was opened, and, emerging from its gloomy shadows, the count appeared.

"What is going on, Fritz ?" asked he.

"Nothing, monsieur," answered the servant, putting

down his stick, and placing himself, like a barrier, in front
of his master, who, standing on the steps of the staircase,
towered above him by half his height.

"Monsieur the Count de Fenix," said Philip, "is it the
custom of people, in your country, to have their servants
receive them sword in hand, or is the custom peculiar to
your house?"

Fritz put down his spear, and, upon a signal from his
master, placed it in a corner of the corridor.

"Who are you, monsieur?" asked the count, who could
hardly see Philip by the dim light of his lantern.

"Some one who will see you and talk with you."

"Who WILL?"

"Yes."

"That word is sufficient excuse for Fritz, monsieur, for I
will speak to no one, and while I am in my own house I
do not recognise the right of any one to compel me to
speak. You, then, are guilty of a wrong against me; but,"
added Balsamo, with a sigh, "I forgive you on condition
that you trouble me no further."

"It comes well from you to ask me not to trouble you,
when you have caused me so much trouble."

"I, — I caused you trouble?" demanded the count.

"I am Philip de Taverney," cried the young man, thinking that with the count's conscience that name would
reveal all.

"Philip de Taverney? Monsieur," said the count, "I
have received hospitality from your father; you are welcome to mine."

"Ah! you are very good!" murmured Philip.

"Kindly follow me, monsieur."

Balsamo stealthily closed the door of the staircase,
and, walking in front of Philip, he took him to the room
where we have in the course of our narrative necessarily
seen some scenes enacted, and, last of all, that in which
the Five Masters called upon Balsamo. The salon was
lighted as if some one was expected, but it was evident
that this was one of the luxurious customs of the house.

"Good evening, Monsieur de Taverney," said Balsamo' in so gentle and suppressed a tone of voice, that Philip was constrained to look at him. But when he saw Balsamo he stepped back.

The count indeed was but the shadow of his former self; his sunken eyes emitted no light, his cheeks in growing thin had encircled his mouth in two folds, and the angles of his face stood out bare and bony as a skull.

Philip stopped, spellbound. Balsamo saw his amazement, and a smile of mortal sadness flitted over his lips.

"Monsieur," said he, "I must ask you to pardon my servant; but, in truth, he was merely obeying his orders, and if you will excuse my saying so, it is you, allow me to remark, who have been in the wrong in forcing an entrance into my house."

"Monsieur," said Philip, "there are times in one's life that call for extreme measures. Such is my present situation."

Balsamo made no answer.

"I wished to see you," continued Philip. "I wished to speak to you; I would have faced death itself to reach you."

Balsamo continued to keep silence, and seemed to wait for the young man to enlighten him, without having strength or curiosity to ask him to do so.

"I have you now," continued Philip, "I have you now, and will explain to you, if you will allow me. But, first, will you dismiss this man ?"

And with his finger Philip pointed at Fritz, who had just drawn the portière as if asking his master's orders in regard to the importunate caller.

Balsamo looked at Philip, as if to discover his intentions, and found himself face to face with a man his equal in rank and position, for Philip had regained his usual composure and force. He was impenetrable.

Then Balsamo, with a simple movement of his head, or rather of his eyebrows, sent Fritz away; and both men sat down opposite each other, Philip with his back to the fireplace, Balsamo with his elbow resting on a small table.

"Speak quickly and to the point if you please, monsieur," said Balsamo, "for I listen to you only through kindness, and I warn you I get fatigued very easily."

"I shall speak as I must, monsieur, and as is convenient to me," said Philip. "And with your permission I will begin by asking you a question."

At this remark a frightful frown came over Balsamo's eyebrows, and his eyes emitted an electric flash. It had awakened in him such memories, that Philip would have trembled had he seen the powerful emotions that were stirring in the depths of Balsamo's heart. However, after spending a few moments in gaining control over his feelings, —

"Question," said Balsamo.

"Monsieur," replied Philip, "you have never accounted to me for the way you passed your time on the famous night of the 31st of May, when you carried my sister away from the dead and the dying, who were crowded together in the Place Louis XV."

"What of that?" demanded Balsamo.

"It signifies that your conduct, on that night, Monsieur le Comte, has been, and is now more than ever, a subject of suspicion to me."

"Suspicion?"

"Yes, and in all probability, it was not that of a man of honour."

"Monsieur," said Balsamo, "I do not understand you. You must see that my head is tired, weak, and this weakness naturally makes me impatient."

"Monsieur!" cried Philip, in his turn irritated by the tone, at once calm and haughty, in which Balsamo addressed him.

"Monsieur," continued Balsamo in the same voice, "since I have had the honour of seeing you, I have experienced a great misfortune. My house has been partly burned, and various precious things, very precious, you hear me, have been lost to me. In consequence of this trouble, I am somewhat confused. Be more explicit, then, or I shall take leave of you at once."

"Oh! not a step, monsieur," said Philip, "not a step; you cannot take leave of me as easily as you imagine. I will respect your trouble, if you will show a little compassion for mine. To me also, monsieur, a great misfortune has come, — greater than yours, I am sure."

Balsamo smiled the most despairing smile that ever was seen on human lips.

"Yes, monsieur," cried Philip, "I have lost the honour of my family."

"Well, monsieur," replied Balsamo, "what can I do to alleviate your misfortune?"

"What can you do?" said Philip, with flashing eyes.

"Certainly."

"You can restore to me what I have lost, monsieur."

"Oh, you are mad, monsieur!" cried Balsamo, and he reached his hand toward the bell.

But he made this movement so slowly, and with so little anger, that Philip's arm stopped him at once.

"I mad?" cried Philip, in an angry tone. "But do you not know what happened to my sister? my sister, who fainted in your arms the 31st of May? my sister, whom you took to a house which you called respectable, I call infamous? my sister, in a word, whose honour I ask of you, sword in hand?"

Balsamo shrugged his shoulders.

"Oh, *mon Dieu!* what a roundabout way of getting at such a simple thing!"

"Wretch!" cried Philip.

"What a deplorable voice you have, monsieur!" cried Balsamo, with the same sad impatience. "You stun me. What! have you come here to accuse me of having insulted your sister?"

"Yes, coward!"

"Another useless exclamation and insult, monsieur. Who the devil told you I had insulted your sister?"

Philip hesitated. The tone with which Balsamo pronounced these words bewildered him. It was either the height of impudence, or the cry of a pure conscience.

"Would you like to know who told me?" replied the young man."

"Yes, I demand it of you."

"My sister herself, monsieur."

"Well, monsieur, your sister —"

"You were going to say —" cried Philip, with a threatening gesture.

"I was going to say, monsieur, that you have given me a very poor idea of yourself and your sister. The speculation that some women make on their dishonour is one of the most deplorable things in the world. Either you have come, with threats on your tongue, like one of the fierce brothers in the Italian play, to force me, sword in hand, to marry your sister, or, since you know that I make gold, you are after my money. Well, monsieur, you will fail in both points; you shall not have my money, and your sister shall remain a maiden."

"Then if you have any blood in your veins, I will have it now," cried Philip.

"No, not even that, monsieur."

"What?"

"I shall keep what blood I have; for were I to lose it, I should have wished a more worthy occasion than the present. So, monsieur, oblige me by going away quietly; and if you make a noise, as a noise gives me a headache, I shall summon Fritz. Fritz will come, and, on a gesture from me, he will break you in two like a reed. Go."

This time Balsamo rang, and, as Philip tried to prevent him, he opened an ebony cabinet on the table, and took from it a double-barrelled pistol.

"Well, I prefer that," cried Philip; "kill me!"

"Why should I kill you?"

"Because you have dishonoured me."

The young man in his turn pronounced these words with such a sincere accent, that Balsamo looked at him with an expression full of gentleness.

"Can it be possible," said he, "that you are speaking to me in good faith?"

"Do you doubt it? Do you doubt the word of a gentleman?"

"And," continued Balsamo, "can Mademoiselle de Taverney have conceived and given utterance to such a preposterous idea? Well, let me give you satisfaction. I swear to you, on my honour, that my conduct toward mademoiselle, your sister, on the night of May 31st, was irreproachable; no point of honour, no human tribunal, no divine justice could discover that it was anything but that of an honourable man; do you believe me?"

"Monsieur," said the young man, astonished.

"You know that I do not fear a duel; you can see it in my eyes, can you not? As to my weakness, do not be mistaken on that point; it is only on the surface. It is true, I have little colour in my face; but my muscles have lost none of their strength. Will you prove it? See—"

And Balsamo, with one hand raised an immense bronze vase placed on a stand of Boule's without any difficulty.

"Well, so be it, monsieur," said Philip. "I believe you as to the 31st of May; but it is only a subterfuge of yours. You base your assertion on a mistake in the date; you have seen my sister again since then."

Balsamo hesitated in his turn.

"It is true," said he; "I have seen her."

And his forehead, light for a moment, grew fearfully dark.

"Ah, you see!" said Philip.

"Well, if I did see your sister again; what does that prove against me?"

"It proves that you have thrown her into one of those mysterious slumbers of which already three times, on your approach, she has felt the symptoms, and that you have

taken advantage of her condition to cover the secret of
your crime."

"Again, I ask you, who has told you that?" cried
Balsamo in his turn.

"My sister."

"How does she know, if she was asleep?"

"Ah, you confess, then, that she was asleep."

"More, monsieur; I will go so far as to tell you that I
put her to sleep myself."

"Put her to sleep?"

"Yes."

"And for what reason, if not to dishonour her?"

"For what reason? Alas!" said Balsamo, letting his
head fall forward on his breast.

"Speak, speak, then!"

"For the reason that I wished to make her reveal a
secret dearer to me than my life."

"Oh ruse! Oh subterfuge!"

"And on that evening," continued Balsamo, pursuing
his own train of thought, rather than answering Philip's
exclamation, "and on that evening your sister —"

"Was dishonoured; yes, monsieur."

"Dishonoured?"

"My sister is a mother."

Balsamo cried out.

"Oh, it is true, it is true!" said he; "I remember, I
left her without awakening her."

"You confess, you confess!" cried Philip.

"Yes; and what villain during that dreadful night —
oh! that night so dreadful for all of us, monsieur — what
villain could have taken advantage of her slumber?"

"What! you mock me, monsieur?"

"No; I wish to convince you."

"It would be difficult to do so."

"Where is your sister now?"

"Where you found her so easily."

"At Trianon?"

"Yes."

"I will go to Trianon with you."

Philip was dumb with amazement.

"I have been guilty of an error," said Balsamo, "but I am innocent of any crime. I left this child in a magnetic slumber. Well, to compensate for this fault, I will find out for you the name of the guilty wretch."

"Tell it! tell it!"

"I do not know it myself," said Balsamo.

"Who does know it, then?"

"Your sister."

"But she has refused to tell it to me."

"Perhaps; but she will tell me."

"My sister?"

"If your sister accuses some one, you would believe her?"

"Yes; for my sister is an angel of purity."

Balsamo rang.

"Fritz, a carriage!" said he, when the German appeared.

Philip paced the room like a madman.

"The guilty one," said he, "the guilty one, — you promised to tell me his name."

"Monsieur," said Balsamo, "your sword has been broken in the fray; let me offer you another one."

And he took from an armchair a magnificent sword, with hilt of silver-gilt, which he placed in Philip's belt.

"But you?" said the young man.

"I, monsieur, need no weapons," replied Balsamo; "my defence is at Trianon, and you yourself shall be my defender, when your sister shall have spoken."

A quarter of an hour afterward they got into a carriage, and Fritz, at full gallop, started them on the road to Versailles.

## CHAPTER CXLV.

### THE RIDE TO TRIANON.

ALL these trips, and all this explanation had taken time, so that it was nearly two o'clock in the morning when they went out from the Rue Saint-Claude. It took an hour and a quarter to reach Versailles, and ten minutes to go from Versailles to Trianon. It was, accordingly, half past three when the two men reached their destination.

During the second part of the drive the dawn began to sprinkle with its rosy light the fresh green woods and the hillsides of the Sèvres. As if a veil had slowly been drawn from before their eyes, the ponds of Ville-d'Avray and the more distant ones of Buc were lit up like mirrors. Then, at last, the colonnades and roofs of Versailles appeared, already reddened by the still invisible sun. From time to time a window glistened in the violet light of the morning mist, which was reflected back in sparkles. On arriving at the end of the avenue that led from Versailles to Trianon, Philip had the carriage stopped, and, addressing his companion, who, during the whole drive, had kept a sad silence, —

"Monsieur," said he, "it is so early, I am afraid we shall have to wait here for some time. The gates of Trianon are never opened before five o'clock in the morning, and I am afraid that, if we tried to get in earlier, we might arouse the suspicions of the watchmen and the guard."

Balsamo made no answer, but evinced, by a bow of his head, his willingness to comply with Philip's suggestion.

"Beside, monsieur, this delay will give me time," continued Philip, "to communicate to you some reflections that have occurred to me on the way."

Balsamo bestowed upon Philip a vacant expression of weariness and indifference.

"As you please, monsieur," said he; "speak, I am listening."

"You told me, monsieur," replied Philip, "that during the night of the 31st of May you carried my sister to the residence of Madame la Marquise de Saverny."

"You assured yourself of that fact, monsieur," said Balsamo, "for you called and thanked this lady yourself."

"You then added that, after one of the servants of the king's stable had accompanied you from the house of the marquise to my house in Rue Coq-Heron, you were not alone with her; I have believed you on your word of honour."

"And you have done well, monsieur."

"But, in thinking over the later, more recent circumstances, I am forced to believe that the night when you passed through the garden at Trianon you must have entered my sister's chamber."

"I have never been in your sister's chamber at Trianon, monsieur."

"Listen, now. Before we see Andrée, some things must be cleared up."

"Clear up these things, Monsieur le Chevalier; I ask nothing better, for we have come for that purpose."

"Well, that evening — answer me carefully, for what I am going to say is positive, I have it from my sister's lips — that evening, I say, my sister went to bed early; did you find her in bed?"

Balsamo shook his head in denial.

"You deny it. Take care," said Philip.

"I do not deny it, monsieur. You question me; I answer."

"Well, I shall continue questioning you; continue answering."

Balsamo evinced no irritation, but, on the contrary, signed to Philip that he was waiting for him.

"When you went up to my sister's apartment," continued Philip, getting more and more excited, "when you surprised her, and put her to sleep by your infernal power, Andrée had retired: she was reading; she experienced those drowsy sensations which your presence has always called forth in her, and she lost consciousness. Well, you say that you were only questioning her; but you add, you went away without awakening her; yet," added Philip, seizing Balsamo's arm, and clasping it convulsively, "yet, when she recovered consciousness the next day, she was no longer on the bed, but at the foot of the sofa, half naked. Reply to this accusation, monsieur; do not evade it."

During this appeal, Balsamo, like a man awakening from sleep, chased away, one by one, the dark reveries that clouded his spirits.

"Truly, monsieur," said he, "you ought not to have reverted to this subject, and seek thus to provoke me to a constant quarrel. I came here as a favour to you, and for your own good; it seems to me you are rapidly forgetting that fact. You are young; you are an officer; you are accustomed to speaking loud, with your hand on the hilt of your sword; all that makes you draw false conclusions, under serious circumstances. I did more for you down there than I ought to have done to convince you, and to set your mind at rest. You are beginning again; take care, for, if you weary me, I shall lose myself in the depths of my sorrows, in comparison to which yours are but mere trifles; and when I sleep, monsieur, woe to him who wakes me. I never entered your sister's chamber, I can assure you of that. Your sister, of her own accord, although in obedience to my will, came to me in the garden."

Philip made a movement, but Balsamo stopped him.

"I promised you a proof," continued he, "and I will give you one. Will you have it immediately? So be it. Let us enter Trianon instead of thus wasting our time. Do you prefer to wait? Then let us wait quietly and calmly, if you please."

Having said this, and in the way our readers know was so peculiarly his own, Balsamo, the light fading from his eyes, relapsed into meditation.

Philip uttered a low growl, like a savage beast ready to bite; then suddenly changing his attitude and his thought, —

"To overcome this man," said he, "one must use either persuasion or some kind of a superiority. As yet, I have found no way either of persuading or overcoming him. Let me try to be patient."

But as it was impossible for him to be patient near Balsamo, he jumped from the vehicle and began pacing the verdant driveway in which the carriage had stopped.

At the end of ten minutes, Philip found that he could wait no longer. At the risk of arousing suspicion, he preferred to have the gate opened before the time.

"Besides," murmured Philip, entertaining an idea which several times already had occurred to his mind, "what suspicions could the Swiss have if I tell him that I am so anxious about my sister's health that I have been to Paris to get a physician, and have brought him here before daybreak?"

Adopting this suggestion, which, from constantly dwelling upon it in his mind, had lessened his fears, he ran to the carriage.

"Yes, monsieur," said he, "you are right; there is no sense in waiting any longer. Come! Come!"

But he had to repeat this appeal. Only at the second time did Balsamo lay off his shawl in which he was enveloped; he fastened his great-coat with its burnished steel buttons, and left the carriage.

Philip took a path which led by a short cut to the gate of the park.

"Walk fast," said he to Balsamo.

And his steps became so rapid, that Balsamo could barely keep up with him. The gate was opened, Philip proffered his explanation to the guard, and they both went through.

When the gate was closed behind them, Philip stopped once more.

"Monsieur," said he, "one last word: we are now at the end; I do not know what questions you will ask my sister; spare her at least the horrible scenes that may have taken place during her slumber; spare the purity of her soul, although she may have lost that of her body."

"Monsieur," replied Balsamo, "listen to what I tell you here. I never penetrated the park beyond the clump of trees you see yonder, opposite the building where your sister lives; consequently, as I have already had the honour of telling you, I have never gone into Mademoiselle de Taverney's room. As to the scene, the effects of which you fear on your sister's spirits, these effects will be produced on you alone, and one who is asleep, since, from this moment, without taking another step, I will order mademoiselle, your sister, to fall into a magnetic slumber."

Balsamo stopped abruptly, crossed his arms, turned toward the house in which Andrée dwelt, and remained perfectly still for a moment, his eyebrows knitted, and an expression of great will power overspreading his whole countenance.

"Hold!" said he, letting his arms fall; "Mademoiselle Andrée must be asleep by this time."

Philip's face expressed the doubts he felt.

"Ah! you do not believe me?" replied Balsamo. "Well, then, wait. In order to prove to you that I need not enter her room, I will order her, all asleep as she is, to come down here to us, to the very spot where I spoke with her at our last interview."

"So be it," said Philip; "when I see, I shall believe. Let us go into this walk and wait behind the hedge."

Philip and Balsamo went to the appointed place. Balsamo reached out his arms toward Andrée's apartments.

But scarcely had he made this movement, when a slight sound was heard in the neighbouring hedge.

"A man!" said Balsamo; "take care!"

"Where, then?" said Philip, looking around for him whom the count had noticed.

"There, in the coppice to the left," said the latter.

"Oh yes," said Philip; "it is Gilbert, a former servant of ours."

"Have you anything to fear from this young man?"

"No, I believe not; but no matter. Stop, monsieur; if Gilbert is up, there may be others about, too."

All this time Gilbert was going away, frightened; for, seeing Philip and Balsamo together, he felt instinctively that he was lost.

"Well, monsieur," said Balsamo, "what are you going to do?"

"Monsieur," said Philip, experiencing, despite himself, a kind of magnetic charm that this man diffused around him, "monsieur, if really your power is great enough to lead Mademoiselle de Taverney to us, show this power by some kind of a sign, but do not bring my sister to so public a place as this, or the first comer may hear your questions and her answers."

"It is time," said Balsamo, seizing the young man by the arm, and showing, him at the window of the main corridor, Andrée, white and stiff. She had left her room, and, obedient to Balsamo's order, was preparing to descend the staircase.

"Stop her, stop her!" said Philip, dazed and frightened at the same time.

"So be it," said Balsamo.

The count reached out his arm in the direction of Mademoiselle de Taverney, who stopped at once.

Then, like a statue on its way to a banquet of stones, after stopping a moment, she wheeled about abruptly, and went back into her room.

Philip hastened after her; Balsamo followed him. Philip

entered the room at almost the same time as Andrée herself, and, seizing the young girl in his arms, he made her
sit down.   Balsamo entered a few moments after Philip,
and closed the door behind him.

But, short as had been the interval between these entrances, a third person had had time to slip in between
the two men, and to go into Nicole's closet, where he hid,
realising that his life might hang on this interview.

This third person was Gilbert.

## CHAPTER CXLVI.

### THE REVELATION.

BALSAMO closed the door behind him, and appeared on the threshold just as Philip was looking at his sister with terror mingled with curiosity.

"Are you ready, chevalier?" demanded he.

"Yes, monsieur, yes," stammered Philip, trembling.

"We can begin to question your sister, then?"

"If you please," said Philip, trying to relieve his breathing from the weight that seemed to press on his breast.

"But, first," said Balsamo, "look at your sister."

"I see her, monsieur."

"You believe that she is asleep, do you not?"

"Yes."

"And that, consequently, she has no consciousness of what is going on around her?"

Philip did not answer, he only made a gesture of doubt.

Then Balsamo went to the fireplace and lit a candle, which he passed before Andrée's eyes without causing her to move an eyelid.

"Yes, yes, she sleeps; but what a strange sleep! *Mon Dieu!*" said Philip.

"Well, I will question her, or rather, since you have expressed a fear that I may ask her some unpleasant question, you may interrogate her yourself, chevalier."

"But I have already spoken, I have touched her, in fact; she did not seem to hear me or to feel my touch."

"It is because you are not in sympathy with her. I will make you so."

Whereupon Balsamo took Philip's hand and placed it in Andrée's. At once the young girl smiled and murmured, —

"Ah! it is you, brother?"

"You see," said Balsamo, "she recognises you now."

"Yes; how strange it is!"

"Question her; she will answer."

"But if she could not remember when she was awake, how can she now that she is asleep?"

"It is one of the mysteries of science."

And Balsamo, sighing, sat down in an arm-chair in the corner.

Philip remained immovable, his hand still holding Andrée's. How could he begin his questions, which would probably result in the revelation of her dishonour, the name of the wretch on whom he might not be able to wreak his vengeance?

As to Andrée, she was in a sort of ecstatic calmness, and her face expressed a sensation of repose, rather than any emotion.

Trembling from head to foot, he nevertheless, in obedience to a glance from Balsamo enforcing him to begin, prepared to question his sister.

But the more he meditated on this misfortune, and the more serious his face became, that of Andrée in the same way became clouded, and she herself opened the conversation.

" Yes, you are right, brother; this great trouble affects the whole family."

Andrée thus gave utterance to the thought in Philip's mind.

Philip waited no longer after this beginning; he trembled as he spoke.

"What trouble?" answered he, without realising what he was saying.

" You know very well, brother."

"Make her tell; she will tell."

"How am I to make her?"

"Will her to speak, that is all."

Philip looked at his sister, with this wish in his mind. Andrée blushed.

"Oh," said the young girl, "how wrong it was of you to think Andrée had deceived you."

"You love no one then?" asked Philip.

"No one."

"Then it is not an accomplice. It is a villain with whom I must deal."

"I do not understand you, brother."

Philip looked at the count for his advice.

"Urge her on," said Balsamo.

"How shall I urge her?"

"Question her freely."

"Without regard for the child's modesty?"

"Oh! do not worry, when she awakes she will not remember anything about it."

"But can she answer my questions?"

"Do you see?" demanded Balsamo of Andrée.

Andrée trembled at the sound of this voice; she turned her dull eyes toward Balsamo.

"Not so clearly as if you were questioning me yourself; still I see."

"Well," demanded Philip, "if you see, sister, describe to me minutely what took place the night that you fainted."

"Do not begin with this night of the 31st of May. It seems to me your suspicions date farther back than that. Now is the time for you to be enlightened once for all."

"No, monsieur," replied Philip, "it is unnecessary, and from this moment I believe what you tell me. He who has such power as you possess does not use it for any ordinary purpose. Sister," repeated Philip, "tell me all that took place on the night in which you fainted."

"I do not remember," said Andrée.

"You hear, count?"

"She must remember, she must tell; order her to do so."

"But if she was asleep?"

"Her mind was awake."

Then he rose, extended his hand toward Andrée, and with a frowning brow which indicated a doubling of his will power, —

"Remember," said he, " I will it."

"I remember," said Andrée.

"Oh!" said Philip, wiping his forehead.

"What do you want to know?"

"Everything."

"From what time?"

"From the time you went to bed."

"Do you see yourself?" said Balsamo.

"Oh, yes, I see myself. I am holding the glass Nicole prepared for me in my hand. Oh Heaven!"

"What? what is the matter?"

"Oh, wretched girl!"

"Explain, sister, explain."

"This glass contains a drink that has been drugged. Should I drink it, I would be lost."

"A drink that has been drugged?" cried Philip; "for what purpose?"

"Wait, wait."

"First the drug."

"I was carrying it to my lips; but at that moment—"

"Well?"

"The count called me."

"What count?"

"He," said Andrée, pointing toward Balsamo.

"And then?"

"Then I put down the glass, and went to sleep."

"After that? after that?" cried Philip.

"I got up and went to join him."

"Where was the count?"

"Under the lime-trees opposite my window."

"Did the count not enter your room at all, sister?"

"Never."

Balsamo looked at Philip, and seemed to say, —

"You see now whether I was deceiving you."

"And you said that you went to join the count?"

"Yes, I obeyed him when he called me."

"What did the count want of you?"

Andrée hesitated.

"Tell, tell," cried Balṣamo; "I shall not listen."

And he fell back on the chair, burying his head in his hands, to prevent hearing Andrée's words.

"Tell me what the count wanted," repeated Philip.

"He wanted to ask me about —"

She hesitated again; one would have said that she feared she would hurt the count's feelings.

"Go on, sister, go on," said Philip.

"About a person who had escaped from his house and —" Andrée lowered her voice, — "and has since died."

Low as Andrée had spoken, Balsamo either heard or imagined he heard these words, and he groaned aloud.

Philip stopped; there was a moment's silence.

"Keep on, keep on," said Balsamo, "your brother wishes to know all; he must know all. After this man had gained the desired information, what did he do?"

"He hastened away," said Andrée.

"Leaving you in the garden?" asked Philip.

"Yes."

"What did you do then?"

"As he went away, and as the power by which I was sustained went away with him, I fell."

"Fainted?"

"No, still asleep, but a very deep slumber."

"Can you remember what happened to you during this slumber?"

"I will try."

"Well, what was it? Tell us."

"A man came from out the hedge, took me in his arms, and carried me away."

"Where?"

"Here, into my rooms."

" Ah ! — and this man, can you see him ? "

" Wait, yes, yes. Oh ! " continued Andrée with a weary, disgusted look, " it is that little Gilbert again."

" Gilbert ? "

" Yes."

" What did he do ? "

" He put me on my sofa."

" After that ? "

" Wait — "

" See, see," said Balsamo, " I will it."

" He listens, he goes into the other room, he shrinks back alarmed, — he enters Nicole's closet — *Mon Dieu! mon Dieu! "*

" What! "

" A man follows him, and I, who cannot get up, cannot defend myself, still asleep — "

" Who is this man ? "

" Brother! brother! "

And Andrée's face expressed the deepest trouble.

" Tell me who this man is," ordered Balsamo, " I will it."

" The king," murmured Andrée, " it is the king."

Philip shuddered.

" Ah," murmured Balsamo, " I feared it."

" He comes up to me," continued Andrée, " he speaks to me, he takes me in his arms, he embraces me. Oh my brother! my brother! "

Great tears filled Philip's eyes, and his hand grasped the sword Balsamo had given him.

" Speak, speak! " said the count in a more commanding tone than ever.

" Oh what good luck! He is troubled — he stops — he looks at me — he is afraid — he flees. Andrée is saved! "

Philip breathed again, hanging on every word that fell from Andrée's lips.

" Saved! Andrée saved! " repeated he mechanically.

" Wait, brother, wait."

And the young girl sought Philip's arm as if for support.

"Afterward, afterward?" said Philip.

"I had forgotten."

"What?"

"There, there, in Nicole's closet, a knife in his hand; I see him, pale as death!"

"Who?"

"Gilbert."

Philip held his breath.

"He follows the king," continued Andrée; "he closes the door behind him, he places his foot on the candle, which is burning a hole in the carpet; he comes toward me! Oh!—" The young girl lifted herself in her brother's arms. Every muscle in her body grew stiff, as if ready to break. "Oh, the vile wretch!" said she at last, and she fell back, powerless.

"My God!" said Philip, not daring to interrupt her.

"It is he! it is he!" murmured the young girl. But reaching up to her brother's ear, with flashing eyes and trembling voice, "You will kill him, Philip, will you not?"

"Oh, yes!" cried the young man, leaping up; and he hit and overturned a table covered with pieces of china. They were all broken to bits.

In the confusion of this noise, another sound, mingled with the shaking of the partitions, was heard; but a cry from Andrée rose above all the rest.

"What is that?" said Balsamo; "a door has been opened."

"Have we been overheard?" cried Philip, sword in hand.

"It was he, he!" cried Andrée, "still he!"

"Who, then, is 'he'?" cried the young man.

"Gilbert, still Gilbert! Ah! you will kill him, Philip, you will kill him?"

"Yes, yes, yes!" cried the young man.

And he rushed into the antechamber, sword in hand, while Andrée fell back upon the sofa.

Balsamo hastened to the young man and seized him by the arm.

"Careful, careful, monsieur; you do not wish your secret to become public. It is day now, and the echoes in a palace reach far."

"Oh Gilbert! Gilbert!" cried Philip; "and he was in hiding all the time; he heard us. I could kill him! May misfortune attend the wretch!"

"Yes, but silence; you will find the young man. You must think of your sister. See, she begins to feel fatigued, after experiencing so many emotions."

"Oh yes, I understand her sufferings by the force of my own; this frightful, irreparable misfortune! Oh monsieur, monsieur! I shall die from its effects!"

"On the contrary, monsieur; you shall live for her, for she needs you, she loves you, only. Love her, pity her, keep her carefully. And now," continued he, after a few moments' silence, "you need me no longer, do you?"

"No, monsieur; forgive my suspicions, forgive my offences; still, all this trouble was indirectly caused by you."

"I make no excuses for myself; but you forget what your sister told you."

"What did she say? I have lost my head."

"Had I not come, she would have taken the drugged drink that Nicole prepared for her, and then it would have been the king. Would that misfortune have been greater?"

"No, monsieur, it would have been the same in any case. I see plainly that we are fated. Awaken my sister, monsieur."

"But she would see me; she would perhaps imagine what has happened. It would be better for me to awaken her, as I put her to sleep, at a distance."

"Thanks! thanks!"

"Then I will say adieu, monsieur."

"One word more. You are a man of honour?"

"Oh, you wish it kept secret?"

"Count!"

"That is quite an unnecessary injunction, monsieur. First, because I am a man of honour; next, having made up my mind to have nothing more to do with people, I shall at once forget them and their secrets. At the same time, monsieur, count on me, if I can ever be of service to you. But no, no, I am of no use to any one; I am not needed in the world any longer. Adieu, monsieur, adieu."

And bowing to Philip, Balsamo cast one more glance at Andrée, whose head had fallen back with all the symptoms of grief and weariness.

"Oh science!" murmured he, "what victims are sacrificed on your altars for naught?"

And he disappeared.

As he went away, Andrée gradually recovered her senses.

She raised her head, heavy as if made of lead, and, looking at her brother, in perplexity, —

"Oh Philip!" murmured she, "what has been going on?"

Philip choked back his tears, and, smiling bravely, —

"Nothing, sister," said he.

"Nothing?"

"No."

"And yet I seem to have been mad, and to have dreamed."

"Dreamed? and what have you dreamed, my dear, good Andrée?"

"Oh! Doctor Louis, Doctor Louis, brother!"

"Andrée," cried Philip, pressing her hand, "you are pure as the day; but everything accuses you, everything is against you; a dreadful secret is laid on us two. I will go and hunt up Doctor Louis, and get him to tell the dauphiness that you are attacked by a fit of homesickness, and that only a visit at Taverney will overcome it; and then we will go to Taverney rather than anywhere else.

Then we two down there, all by ourselves, loving each other, consoling each other — "

"Yet, brother," said Andrée, "if I am as pure as you say — "

"Dear Andrée, I will explain all that; in the mean time, get ready for our departure."

"But my father?"

"My father?" said Philip, soberly, "my father? That is my affair; I will prepare him."

"He will go with us, then?"

"Father? Oh, impossible, impossible! Just we two, Andrée, by ourselves, I say."

"Oh! how you frighten me, my dear! how you alarm me, brother! how I suffer, Philip!"

"God is everywhere, Andrée," said the young man, "so take heart. I will run and find the doctor. As for you, Andrée, it is grief because you have left Taverney, grief which you would conceal from madame the dauphiness, which has caused your illness. Come, come, sister, be brave; our honour is at stake."

And Philip hastened to embrace his sister, for he himself was choking with suppressed emotion.

Then he picked up his sword, which he had let fall, placed it in its sheath with trembling hands, and rushed out on to the landing.

A quarter of an hour later he knocked at the door of Doctor Louis, who, while the court was at Trianon, lived at Versailles.

## CHAPTER CXLVII.

### DOCTOR LOUIS'S LITTLE GARDEN.

DOCTOR LOUIS, at whose door we have left Philip, was walking in a little garden enclosed between four high walls, which formed part of the dependencies of an old convent of the Ursulines, transformed into a storehouse for the dragoons of the king's household.

Doctor Louis was reading, as he walked, the proofs of a new book which he was in process of publishing, stooping from time to time to pull up the weeds from the path in which he was walking, or from the garden on either side; for he had a fine instinct of symmetry and order.

A single servant, a little surly, like all servants of busy men, who do not like to be disturbed, took charge of the doctor's house. At the noise which the brass knocker, ringing under Philip's hand, made, she went to the door and partly opened it.

But the young man, instead of stopping to parley with the servant, pushed open the door and went in. Once within the passage, he perceived the garden, and in the garden the doctor.

Then, paying no attention to the words or the cries of the watchful guardian, he rushed into the garden.

At the sound of his steps, the doctor raised his head.

" Ah ! " said he, " is it you? "

" Pardon me, doctor, for having forced an entrance, and invaded your solitude; but the time you foresaw has arrived; I need you, and I come to claim your assistance."

" I promised it to you, monsieur," said the doctor, " and I will keep my promise."

Philip bowed, too agitated to trust his voice.

Doctor Louis took in the situation.

"How is the invalid?" he asked, uneasy at Philip's pallor, and fearing some catastrophe would end this drama.

"Very well, thank God, doctor; and my sister is so good, and so pure a girl, that indeed God will not be unjust enough to send to her suffering and danger."

The doctor looked at Philip as if to question him; his words seemed a continuation of his denials of the evening before.

"Is she, then, the victim of some surprise, or of some plot?"

"Yes, doctor, victim of an infamous plot."

The practitioner clasped his hands and raised his eyes toward heaven.

"Alas!" said he, "we live in frightful times in this respect, and the nations need a physician as well as the individuals."

"Yes," said Philip, "let them come. No one would be more rejoiced to see them than I; but in the mean time —"

And Philip made a gesture of sadness.

"Ah!" said the doctor, "I see you are one of those who think crime can be revenged by violence and murder."

"Yes, doctor," calmly replied Philip, "I am one of those."

"A duel," sighed the doctor, "which, even should you kill the offender, would not restore your sister's honour to her, and which, should you be killed, would only plunge her into despair. Ah! monsieur, I believed you to be a just man; I thought you had an intelligent heart. It seems to me that I heard you express the desire of keeping this thing secret."

Philip placed his hand on the doctor's arm.

"Monsieur," said he, "you are strangely mistaken in me; I have well balanced reasoning powers, since they spring from deep convictions and a pure conscience. I do not wish to avenge myself, but to fight for the right; I do not wish to expose her to abandonment and death by getting myself killed, but to avenge her by killing the guilty wretch."

"Would you, a gentleman, kill him? become an assassin?"

"Monsieur, had I seen him ten minutes before the crime, gliding like a robber into that chamber, into which his low station allowed him not even the right of placing his foot, and had I killed him then, every one would have said that I did right. Why, then, should I spare him now? Has his crime made him sacred?"

"So this sanguinary plot is embedded in your mind, placed firmly in your heart?"

"Embedded, placed firmly! I shall certainly find him some day, wherever he may hide, and on that day I tell you, monsieur, I shall kill him like a dog, without pity and without remorse."

"Then," said Doctor Louis, "then you would commit a crime as odious as the one he committed himself, or perhaps even more so; for one never knows to what lengths an imprudent word or a coquettish movement, escaping from a woman, may impel the desire and the inclination of a man. Assassinate him! when other reparations are possible, when a marriage — "

Philip raised his head.

"Are you not aware, monsieur, that the Taverney-Rouges date from the Crusades, and that my sister is of as high rank by birth as an infanta or an archduchess?"

"Yes, I understand, and the criminal is not in the same position; he is low-born, — a clodhopper, as you men of high rank would call him. Yes, yes," continued he, with a bitter smile, "God has made men of a certain inferior clay, that they may be killed by other men more delicately organised. Yes, you are right, monsieur; kill him, kill him."

And the doctor turned his back upon Philip, and began to pull up the weeds here and there in his garden."

Philip folded his arms.

"Doctor, listen to me," he said; "this is no question of a seducer, to whom a flirt has given more or less encouragement; this is no question of a man tempted and lured on as you describe him. The guilty man is a miserable dependent of ours, who, after having eaten the bread we gave him of our compassion, that night, taking advantage of a factitious slumber, of a fainting fit, of death, as it were, has traitorously, cowardly defiled the purest, holiest of women, whom by daylight he would not have dared look in the face. Before a tribunal, this wretch would certainly be doomed to death. Well, I myself will judge him as impartially as a court of justice, and I will kill him. Now, doctor, will you, who are considered so generous, so great, make me pay for a service I ask of you, or impose a condition upon me? In rendering it to me, will you do like those who seek to oblige, and at the same time help themselves in serving others? If such is the case, doctor, you are not the upright man I have respected; you are only an ordinary man, and, despite the contempt in which you now hold me, I am superior to you,— I who, without reserve or regret, have confided my whole secret to you."

"You say," replied the doctor thoughtfully, "you say the culprit has fled?"

"Yes, doctor; doubtless he had divined that the revelation would soon take place. He heard himself accused, and immediately took to flight."

"Well, now what do you wish of me, monsieur?" said the doctor.

"Your assistance in getting my sister away from Versailles, that we may envelop in a still darker, more silent shadow this dreadful secret, whose revelation would bring such dishonour upon us."

"I will impose upon you one condition only."

Philip drew back.

"Listen," continued the physician, with a gesture that imposed silence; "hear me! A Christian philosopher, of

whom you have made a confessor, is obliged to impose
upon you, not a condition in return for service rendered,
but one required by the rights of moral obligations.
Humanity is a duty, monsieur, it is not a virtue. You
speak to me of killing a man; it is my duty to prevent
you by all the means in my power, as I would have prevented the execution of the crime that has been committed
against your sister. So, monsieur, I beg you to give me
your oath."

"Oh! never, never!"

"You will do it?" cried Doctor Louis, vehemently,
"you will do it, man of blood? See above all the hand of
God, and do not attempt to direct the blow yourself. You
say the culprit was in your power?"

"Yes, doctor; by opening a door, could I have known
he was there, I should have encountered him face to face."

"Well, he has fled, he is afraid; his punishment has
begun. Ah! you laugh; what God does seems weak to
you. Remorse is inadequate, in your opinion. Wait,
wait! you shall remain with your sister, you shall not
pursue the culprit! If you encounter him, — that is to
say, if God places him in your power, well, I also am a
man, — in that case you will see."

"Monsieur, monsieur, will he not always fly from me?"

"Who knows? eh, *mon Dieu!* An assassin flees, an
assassin seeks a hiding-place, an assassin fears the scaffold; and yet, as if he were magnetised, the sword of
justice draws the guilty one, who finally falls under the
hand of the executioner. Besides, it is not a question now
of giving up all that you have undertaken so painfully.
Should you kill this man, you would merely succeed in
arousing the curiosity of all the inquisitive gossips with
whom the circle in which you move is filled, and whom
you could never convince of your sister's innocence. Such
an act on your part would only result in a public avowal
of the crime, and in a scandalous report of its punishment.
No, no, have confidence in my judgment, keep silence,
conceal this misfortune."

"But when I have killed this wretch, who will know that I have killed him in behalf of my sister?"

"A cause for the murder would be sought for."

"Well, so be it, doctor. I will obey, I will not pursue the culprit; but God will be just. Oh yes, God uses impunity as a bait; God will restore him to my sight."

"Then God will have condemned him. Give me your hand, monsieur."

"There it is."

"What must we do for Mademoiselle de Taverney? Tell me?"

"We must seek to excuse her to the dauphiness, on the plea of homesickness, the air, the court."

"That can easily be done."

"Yes; that will be your duty, and I intrust it to you. Then I will take her to some distant part of France, to Taverney, perhaps, far from all eyes, from all suspicions."

"No, no, monsieur, that would be impossible. The poor child needs constant care and consolation; she will require all the help of science. Let me find a place for her near here, in a small village I know, — a retreat a hundred-fold better concealed, a hundred-fold safer, than the wild country whither you would take her."

"Oh, doctor, do you think so?"

"Yes, I think so, and with reason. Suspicion always moves away from the centre, as the circles made by a stone thrown into the water increase in size; yet the stone does not move away, and when its undulations cease, no one thinks of hunting for it, buried as it is under the depth of the water."

"Well, doctor, begin your part of the work."

"From to-day, monsieur."

"Forewarn the dauphiness."

"This very morning."

"And about the rest?"

"Within twenty-four hours you shall have my answer."

"Oh thanks! doctor; you are a perfect Godsend!"

"Well, young man, now that all is arranged between us, do your part; return to your sister, comfort her, protect her."

And the doctor, after having followed Philip's retreating figure with his eyes until he was out of sight, resumed his walking, his proofs, and his clearing of his little garden.

## CHAPTER CXLVIII.

### THE FATHER AND SON.

WHEN Philip returned to his sister, he found her very much agitated,—much excited.

"Dear one," said she to him, "I have been thinking, during your absence, of everything that has happened to me since that dreadful time; it is a gulf that will swallow up all that is left of my reason. Let me see, you have seen Doctor Louis?"

"I have just been to his house, Andrée."

"That man brings a terrible accusation against me; is it true?"

"He is not wrong, my sister."

Andrée turned pale, and her white, tapering fingers twitched nervously.

"The name," she then said, "the name of the coward who has wronged me?"

"My sister, you must forever be ignorant of it."

"Oh Philip! you do not speak honestly; Philip, you do not act as your conscience dictates. The name! I must find it out, so that, feeble as I am, with nothing left for me but prayer, I may call down on the criminal all the wrath of God! The name of that man, Philip!"

"My sister, let us never speak of that."

Andrée took hold of his hand and looked him in the face.

"Oh!" she said, "that is the way you answer me, you who wear a sword—"

Philip paled at this exhibition of anger, and then repressed his own indignation.

"Andrée," he said, "I am unable to tell you that; I do

THE FATHER AND SON. 441

not know myself. Secrecy is ordered me by the destiny that weighs us down; this secret, if exposed, would compromise our family honour, — a last gift of God which we should carefully guard."

"But this man, Philip, this man who mocks at us, this man who defies us! — Oh, my God! this man who laughs fiendishly at us, perhaps, in his obscure hiding-place!"

Philip wrung his hands and, looking up to heaven, did not reply a word.

"That man," cried Andrée, redoubling her anger and indignation, "perhaps I know that man. In a word, Philip, let me describe him to you; I have already described his strange influence over me; I believe you have already sought him."

"That man is innocent; I have seen him, I have proved it. So seek no further, Andrée, seek no further."

"Philip, let us ascend still higher than this man, will you not? Let us go even to the highest ranks of powerful men of this kingdom; let us mount even to the king!"

Philip put his arms around the poor child, sublime in her ignorance and her indignation.

"Well," he said, "both of those you have named while awake you have named when asleep; both of those that you accused with the ferocity of virtue, you justified when you saw the crime committed, so to speak."

"Then I have named the guilty one?" said she, with flaming eyes.

"No," replied Philip, "no, do not question me more; imitate me, submit to destiny; the misfortune is irreparable; it is doubled by the impunity of the criminal. But hope, hope! God is above all, God reserves for the oppressed a mournful joy which is called vengeance."

"Vengeance!" murmured she, frightened by the terrible emphasis Philip gave to the word.

"In the mean time calm yourself, my sister; shake off the grief and shame my foolish curiosity has aroused in you. If I had known! oh if I had known!"

And he buried his head in his hands in deep despair.
Then he suddenly looked up.

"What have I to complain of?" said he, with a smile.
"My sister is pure, she loves me; she has never betrayed
my confidence or affection. My sister is young, like myself, kind, as I am; we will live together, we will grow
old together. United, we will boldly face the whole
world!"

In proportion as the young man talked consolingly,
Andrée grew gloomy; she bowed her pale face, and assumed
an attitude of fixed despair, which Philip tried bravely to
overcome.

"You always speak of just us two," she said, fixing her
blue eye penetratingly on her brother's calm face.

"Of whom do you wish me to speak, Andrée?" keeping
his same expression.

"But—we have a father; how will he treat his daughter?"

"I have told you this evening," replied Philip coldly,
"to forget all grief and fear, to cast aside, as the wind
blows away the mists of early morning, all remembrances
and all affection except that which I give you. In short,
my dear Andrée, you are loved only by me in this world,
and I only by you. Poor, forsaken orphans, why should
we submit to the yoke of gratitude or of relationship?
Have we received either favours or protection from our
father? Oh!" added he, with a bitter smile, "you know
my inmost thoughts, the feelings of my heart. If we ought
to love him of whom you speak, I would say to you, 'Love
him!' I am silent, Andrée; refrain from saying more."

"Then, brother, what am I to think?"

"Sister, in great misfortunes we often remember words
spoken to us when we were too young to understand them:
'Fear God!' Oh yes, we are cruelly reminded of God:
'Respect your father.' Oh sister, the strongest proof of
the respect we can give each other is to efface him from
our memory."

"That is true," murmured Andreé sadly, and sank back
in the easy-chair.

"My dear, we will not waste time in idle words; collect all your possessions. Doctor Louis has gone to find madame the dauphiness, and to warn her of our departure. You already know the reason he will assign, — the need of a change of air, — your inexplicable illness. Get everything together, I repeat, for our departure."

Andrée rose.

"The furniture?" she said.

"Oh, no; linen, clothes, jewelry."

Andrée obeyed.

First she placed the boxes in the closet in order; arranged the clothes in the wardrobe, where Gilbert had hidden; then she took some jewel-cases, which she was preparing to put in the principal box.

"What is that?" said Philip.

"It is the casket of jewels sent to me by the king for my presentation at court, at Trianon.

Philip grew pale on realising the richness of the gift.

"With these jewels, only," said Andrée, "we can live in affluence anywhere. I have been told that the pearls alone are worth one hundred thousand francs."

Philip closed the case.

"They are very valuable indeed," said he; and, taking the case from Andrée's hands, "I think there are some other jewels, sister," he added.

"Oh, my dear, they cannot be compared to these; they adorned, however, the toilet of our good mother, fifteen years ago. The watch, the bracelets, the ear-rings, are set with brilliants. There is also the portrait. Father wished to sell them all, because, he said, they were no longer fashionable."

"Still, they are all that we have left to us now," said Philip; "our only resource. Sister, we will melt the gold and sell the jewels around the portrait; we shall thus have twenty thousand francs, which is quite enough for the unhappy."

"But — this case of pearls is mine," said Andrée.

"Never touch the pearls, Andrée; they would burn you. Every one of these pearls is of such a kind that it would scar any forehead it touches."

Andrée shuddered.

"I will take charge of the case, and give it to the one to whom it belongs. I tell you truly it is not ours, and we certainly do not wish to pretend it is, do we, Andrée?"

"As you will, brother," said Andrée, trembling with shame.

"Dear sister, dress yourself for your last visit to madame the dauphiness; show yourself calm, respectful, affected, at leaving such a kind protectress."

"Oh, yes, I am indeed affected," murmured Andrée, much moved; "it is one of the bitterest griefs caused by my misfortune."

"For myself, I am going to Paris, sister, and I will come back here towards evening; as soon as I return, I will take you away. Pay all that you owe here."

"Nothing, nothing. There was Nicole; she has fled. Ah, I forgot little Gilbert!"

Philip shook, and his eyes flashed.

"You owe Gilbert?" he cried.

"Yes," said Andrée, innocently; "he has furnished me with flowers ever since the beginning of the season. Besides, as you have told me yourself, often I have been unjust and harsh toward this lad, who, after all, has always been polite. I will recompense him differently."

"Do not seek Gilbert," murmured Philip.

"Why not? He must be in the garden. I will send for him there."

"No, no, you would only be wasting precious time. But I, as I go along the drives, will come across him. I will speak to him, I will pay him."

"Then that will be settled all right."

"Yes; adieu until evening."

Philip kissed the hand of the young girl, who sprang into his arms. He felt her heart beating against his in this sweet embrace, and without any further delay he started for Paris, where the carriage left him before the door of the little house in the Rue Coq-Heron.

Philip knew he would find his father here. The old man, since his strange disagreement with Richelieu, found life at Versailles insupportable; and he sought, like all people of superabundant spirits, to beguile mental torpor by the excitement of moving about from place to place. In fact the baron, when Philip rang at the entrance of the court-yard, was pacing the little garden and the adjoining court, swearing frightfully. He started at the sound of the bell, and ran to open the gate himself. As he expected no one, this unforeseen visit filled him with hope; the unhappy man in his fall caught at every branch. He received Philip, therefore, with a feeling of disappointment mixed with curiosity. But he had no sooner seen his interlocutor's face than its baneful pallor, its rigid lines and compressed lips, froze the reservoir of questions with which he was prepared to deluge him.

"You?" said he, simply; "and by what chance?"

"I shall have the honour of explaining that to you, monsieur," said Philip.

"Good! Is it a serious matter?"

"Serious enough; yes, monsieur."

"This boy has always a ceremonious way enough to disturb any one. Is it misfortune or good luck that brings you here?"

"It is misfortune," said Philip, soberly.

The baron trembled.

"Are we wholly alone?" demanded Philip.

"Yes, certainly."

"Are you willing to have us go into the house, monsieur?"

"Why not out in the open air, under these trees?"

"Because there are certain things that cannot be spoken of under the open sky."

The baron looked at his son, obeyed a silent gesture from

him, and, affecting to be unmoved, even smiling, he followed him into the salon on the ground floor, whose door Philip had already opened. When the doors were carefully closed, Philip awaited a gesture from his father before commencing the conversation, and when the baron had comfortably settled himself in the best arm-chair in the room, —

"Monsieur," said Philip, "my sister and myself are going to take leave of you."

"How is that?" said the baron, greatly surprised. "You — you go away! And the service ?"

"There is no more service for me, monsieur; as you know, the king's promises have not been fulfilled, happily."

"That is a *happily* that I do not understand."

"Monsieur!"

"Explain it to me! How can you be happy at not being colonel of a fine regiment? You carry your philosophy to an extreme."

"I would carry it far enough not to prefer dishonour to fortune; that is all. But let us not enter, if you please, monsieur, into considerations of this kind."

"Enter there, *pardieu !*"

"I entreat you," replied Philip, with a firmness that signified, "I will not do so."

The baron frowned.

"And your sister? Is she likewise oblivious of her duty? her attendance on madame?"

"These are the very duties that must give way to others, monsieur."

"Of what nature, if you please?"

"Of the most imperative necessity."

The baron rose.

"Only foolish people make enigmas," grumbled he.

"Is what I have told you indeed an enigma to you?"

"Absolutely," replied the baron, with a coolness that astonished Philip.

"I will explain, then: my sister has gone away because she was obliged to flee to escape dishonour."

The baron burst out laughing.

"*Mon Dieu!* what model children I have!" said he. "The son gives up all hope of a regiment because he fears dishonour; the daughter gives up an assured position because she fears dishonour.  Truly, I have returned to the days of Brutus and Lucretia!  In my time, — a miserable time, doubtless, and not equal to these fine days of philosophy, — when a man saw dishonour in the distance, and when, like you, he carried a sword, and had taken lessons from two masters and three provost-marshals, he avenged the first dishonour at the point of his sword."

Philip shrugged his shoulders.

"Yes, it is hardly the thing to speak in this way to a philanthropist, who does not like to see blood flow; but officers are not born exactly to be philanthropists."

"Monsieur, I know as well as you the necessity that a point of honour imposes upon us; but the shedding of blood will not redeem."

"Phrases, mere phrases of philosophy!" cried the old man, becoming actually majestic in his irritation.   "I believe I was going to say, of a coward."

"You did well not to say so," replied Philip, pale and trembling.  .

The baron proudly met the implacable and menacing look of his son.

"I said," replied he, "and my logic is not so bad as they would make me believe, — I said that all the dishonour in this world comes, not from an action, but from what is said of the action.  Ah! it is thus: commit a crime before the blind, the deaf, or the dumb, and would you be dishonoured?  You will answer me by the absurd quotation, 'The crime, not the scaffold, makes the disgrace.'  It is very well to talk to children, or women, in that way, but to a man, *mordieu!* one speaks a different language.  For the sake of argument, allow me this supposition. If the blind man has seen, the deaf has heard, the dumb man has spoken, you seize your sword, and you tear out the eyes of the one, the tympanum of another, and you cut out the tongue of the third; that is the way for a gentleman of the house of Taverney-Rouge to reply to an attack of dishonour."

"A gentleman of that name knows that the first of the things he ought not to do is to commit a dishonourable action, that is why I will not reply to your arguments. Only it occasionally happens that opprobrium originates from an inevitable piece of misfortune; that is the situation in which my sister and myself are placed."

"I proceed to your sister. If, according to my way of reasoning, man ought never to flee from a thing which he can combat and overcome, a woman also ought to keep firm. Of what worth is virtue, monsieur and philosopher, except for repulsing the attacks of vice?"

And Taverney began to laugh.

"Mademoiselle de Taverney is afraid, is she not? She feels very weak."

Then Philip suddenly drew nearer.

"Monsieur," said he, "Mademoiselle de Taverney has not been weak; she has been overcome; she has succumbed; she has fallen into a trap."

"Into a trap?"

"Yes. Keep, I beg you, a little of that heat which animated you just now, to blast those wretches who have so cowardly plotted the ruin of that spotless honour."

"I do not understand you."

"You soon will understand. A coward, I tell you, has shown some one into Mademoiselle de Taverney's chamber."

The baron grew pale.

"A coward," continued Philip, "has willed that the name of Taverney — mine, yours, monsieur — should be marred by an indelible stain. Come, where is your youthful sword, to shed a little blood? Is not the thing worth the trouble?"

"Monsieur Philip!"

"Ah, do not fear! I accuse no one; I know no one. The crime was plotted in the dark, executed in the dark; its result shall be hidden in darkness, too. I will it; I, who interpret in my own way the glory of our house."

"But how do you know?" cried the baron, recovering from his stupor by the allurement of a shameful ambition, of an ignoble hope. "By what token have you conceived this?"

"No one who shall see my poor sister in a few months will ask for any further tokens?"

"Then, Philip," cried the old man, his eyes full of joy, "then the good luck and glory of our house have not departed; then we shall triumph."

"Then — you are indeed the man I believed you," said Philip, with supreme disgust; "you have betrayed yourself, and you have failed in intelligence from the standpoint of a judge, as you have failed in heart, from that of your son."

"Insolent!"

"Enough," replied Philip. "Fear to evoke by speaking so loud the ghost of my mother, too unconscious of all this, alas! in her present state; she who, had she lived, would have watched over her daughter."

The baron lowered his eyes before the dazzling fire which shone in those of his son.

"My daughter," replied he, after a moment, "will never leave me against my will."

"My sister," said Philip, "will never see you again, father."

"Has she said so?"

"She herself sent me to tell you so."

The baron wiped his whitened, moist lips with trembling hands.

"So be it," said he.

Then, shrugging his shoulders, —

"I have been unfortunate in my children," said he; "a fool and a brute."

Philip made no answer.

"Good, good," continued Taverney.    "I need you no longer; go, if your essay is recited."

"I have still two things to say to you, monsieur."

"Speak!"

"The first is this: the king has given you a case of pearls."

"To your sister, monsieur."

"To you, monsieur.    Besides, it matters little, my sister does not wear such jewels.    Mademoiselle de Taverney is no prostitute; she begs you to return the case to the donor. Or, as you fear to offend his Majesty, who has done so much for our family, to keep the case yourself."

Philip handed the casket to his father.    The latter took it, opened it, looked at the pearls, and put it on the chiffonier.

"Next?" said he.

"Then, monsieur, as we are not rich, since you have either pledged or perhaps spent, our mother's property,— for which I do not reproach you, God forbid!—"

"It would be better," said the baron, grinding his teeth.

"But, in short, as we have only Taverney left of this moderate inheritance, we beseech you to choose between Taverney and this little establishment in which we are sitting.    Dwell in one, and we will take the other."

The baron rumpled his lace frill with rage, which was shown only by the moving of his fingers, the moisture on his forehead, the trembling of his lips.    Philip himself did not notice this agitation; he had turned away his face.

"I prefer Taverney," replied the baron.

"Then we will take the hotel."

"When shall you leave?"

"This very evening.    No, immediately."

Philip bowed.

"At Taverney," continued the baron, "one can be a king with three thousand francs.    I shall be twice king."

He reached his hand toward the chiffonier, took the

casket, and put it in his pocket; then he went toward the door. Suddenly, turning back with an evil leer, —

"Philip," said he, "I will allow you to sign our name to the first treatise on philosophy you may publish. As to Andrée, for her first production, advise her to call it Louis or Louise; it is an honourable name," and he went out, sneering.

Philip, with bloodshot eyes, with burning brow, grasped the hilt of his sword, murmuring, —

"Oh God, give me patience! help me to forget!"

## CHAPTER CXLIX.

### A CASE OF CONSCIENCE.

AFTER having written, with the scrupulous care characteristic of him, a few pages of his "Rêveries d'un Promeneur Solitaire," Rousseau finished his frugal breakfast.

Although a retreat in the delightful garden of Ermenonville had been offered him by Monsieur de Girardin, Rousseau, hesitating to submit to the slavery of the great, as he called it, in his mania of misanthropy, still dwelt in the little apartment house in the Rue Plastrière that we know already.

As for Thérèse, having put her little house in order, she was just going to market with her basket.

It was nine o'clock in the morning. The housekeeper, in accordance with her usual custom, had asked Rousseau what he would like for dinner that day.

Rousseau emerged from his reverie, slowly turned his head, and looked at Thérèse like a man only half awake.

"Whatever you please," said he, "provided there are cherries and flowers."

"Perhaps," said Thérèse, "if they are not too expensive."

"Very well," said Rousseau.

"For in short," continued Thérèse, "I do not know whether what you do is no longer of any value; but it seems to me you do not receive as much in payment for it as you used."

"You are mistaken, Thérèse. I am paid the same price; but I get tired, and work less, and then my bookseller is in arrears, to the extent of half a volume, with me."

"You will see that this one will make you a bankrupt again."

"We will trust not; he is an honest man."

"An honest man, an honest man! You think that, when you have said that, you have said all?"

"At least I have said much," replied Rousseau, smiling; "for I could not say that of every one."

"That is not strange: you are so cross!"

"Thérèse, we are wandering from the question."

"Yes, you wish cherries, gourmand; you want flowers, sybarite."

"What would you have, my good housewife?" replied Rousseau, with angelic patience; "my heart and head are so bad that, as I cannot go out, I would like at least to enjoy the bounties that God so freely distributes over the fields."

Truly, Rousseau was pale and exhausted, his listless hands turned over the leaves of a book, which he was not even reading.

Thérèse shook her head.

"All right, all right," said she. "I am going out for an hour; don't forget that I have put the key under the door-mat, and that if you want anything —"

"Oh, I shall not go out," said Rousseau.

"I know very well that you will not go out, since you can hardly stand up; but I mention it that you may know where to find it in case any one calls during my absence, for should you hear the bell ring, you must unlock the door. You know I never ring."

"Thanks, good Thérèse, thanks. Now, start along."

The housewife went out grumbling, as usual; but the noise of her heavy, slow steps was heard on the staircase for some time.

No sooner was the gate safely closed, than Rousseau took advantage of his solitude to stretch himself luxuriously on his chair; he watched the birds, which were pecking at a little piece of bread on the window seat, and drew in long draughts of the sunshine, which streamed in between the chimneys of the neighbouring houses. His young and lively thoughts were no sooner set at liberty than they spread their wings, like the sparrows after their joyful repast.

Suddenly the gate creaked on its hinges, and interrupted the sweet reverie of the philosopher.

"What," said he, "back already! Can I have slept while only thinking that I was indulging in day dreams?"

The door of his study opened gently in its turn.

Rousseau was sitting with his back toward the door; convinced that it was Thérèse who had entered, he did not change his position. There was a moment's silence. Then, in the midst of this silence, —

"Pardon, monsieur," said a voice, which made the philosopher start.

Rousseau turned quickly around.

"Gilbert!" said he.

"Yes, Gilbert; once more I crave your pardon."

It was Gilbert, indeed.

But Gilbert, pale, his hair dishevelled, scarcely concealing under his disordered clothes his thin and trembling limbs; Gilbert, in a word, whose appearance made Rousseau tremble, and drew from him an expression of pity, which closely bordered on uneasiness. Gilbert had the fixed and gleaming eyes of hungry birds of prey; a smile of affected timidity contrasted with this look, as would the upper part of the eagle's solemn head with the lower portion of the cunning head of a wolf or a fox.

"Why do you come here?" cried Rousseau vehemently, for he did not like untidiness, and considered it in others an indication of an evil purpose.

"Monsieur," replied Gilbert, "I am hungry."

Rousseau shuddered on hearing the sound of this voice, uttering the most terrible word in human speech.

"And how did you get in here?" he said; "the door was shut."

"Monsieur, I know that Madame Thérèse is in the habit of leaving the key under the door-mat; I waited for Madame Thérèse to go out, for she does not like me, and would perhaps have refused to receive me, or to let me come near you; then, knowing that you were here alone, I came up. I took the key from its hiding-place, and here I am."

Rousseau raised himself on the arms of his chair.

"Hear me," said Gilbert, "one moment, only one moment! I give you my oath I deserve to be heard."

"Let me see," said Rousseau, stupefied at the sight of this face, which no longer bore any expression of the feelings common to most people.

"I ought to begin by telling you that I am driven to such an extremity that I do not know whether to steal, to kill myself, or to do something still worse. Oh! do not fear me, my master and protector," said Gilbert, with a voice full of gentleness; "for I believe, on further reflection, that I shall die without having to kill myself. During the last week, in which I have been flying from Trianon, I have traversed the woods and the plains without eating anything, except raw vegetables or the wild fruit in the woods. I am completely exhausted; I am ready to fall from fatigue and lack of vitality. As for stealing, I certainly should not attempt anything of the sort in your house; I love it too well, monsieur. As to the third thing, oh! in order to accomplish that — "

"Well?" said Rousseau.

"Well, it needs resolution, which I have come here to seek."

"Are you mad?" cried Rousseau.

"No, monsieur; but I am very unfortunate, much discouraged, and I should have drowned myself in the Seine this morning, had not a reflection prevented me."

"What was it?"

"Something you yourself have written: 'Suicide is a robbery committed on the human race.'"

Rousseau looked at the young man as if to say to him, "Are you so conceited as to think I had you in mind in writing that?"

"Oh, I understand," murmured Gilbert.

"I do not believe so," said Rousseau.

"You mean to say, ' Would your death, you, a miserable wretch, who are nobody, who possess nothing, who do nothing, be an event?' "

"I am not thinking of that," said Rousseau, ashamed of being understood so well; "but you are hungry, I believe?"

"Yes, so I have said."

"Well, then, you, who know so well where the door is, know also where the bread is kept; go to the cupboard, take some bread, and go away."

Gilbert did not move.

"If you do not wish bread, if you seek money,—I do not believe you would be wicked enough to maltreat an old man who was your protector in the very house in which you have taken refuge,—be satisfied with this little."

And, feeling in his pocket, he drew out some pieces of money and offered them to him.

Gilbert repulsed his hand.

"Oh!" said he, with bitter grief, "it is not a question of either money or bread; you did not understand what I meant when I spoke of killing myself. If I do not take my life, it is because now my life may be of use to some one; it is because my death would rob some one, monsieur. You, who know so well all the social laws, all natural obligations, I appeal to you, monsieur, is there in this world any tie which can bind a man who wishes to die to life again?"

"There are many of them," said Rousseau.

"Is one of these ties that of being a father?" murmured Gilbert. "Look at me when you answer me, Monsieur Rousseau, that I may read your reply in your eyes."

"Yes," stammered Rousseau, "yes, certainly; but why do you ask such a question?"

"Monsieur, your words shall be a law to me," said Gilbert. "Weigh them carefully, I entreat you, monsieur. I am so unfortunate that I would like to take my life; but—but I have a child."

Rousseau started from his chair in astonishment.

"Oh! do not jeer at me, monsieur," said Gilbert, humbly. "You may think your words would only prick my heart, but in reality they would wound it like so many sword thrusts. I tell you again, I have a child."

Rousseau looked at him without replying.

"But for that, I should be dead already," continued Gilbert. "In this perplexity I said to myself that you would advise me wisely, and I came to you."

"But," demanded Rousseau, "why should I advise you, I? Did you come to me when you committed the fault?"

"Monsieur, this fault," and Gilbert, with a strange expression, drew nearer to Rousseau.

"Well?" said he.

"This fault," said Gilbert, "there are people who call it a crime."

"A crime! All the more reason, then, for your not speaking about it to me. I am a man, like yourself, and not a father confessor. Besides, what you tell me does not surprise me in the least; I have always foreseen that you would turn out badly. You have a corrupt nature."

"No, monsieur," replied Gilbert, shaking his head sadly; "no, monsieur, you are mistaken. My mind is unnatural, or rather perverted. I have read many books which have expatiated on the equality of castes, the pride of spirit, the dignity of instincts. These books, monsieur, were signed by such illustrious names that a poor countryman like me might well be led astray. I am lost."

"Ah! I see the drift of your conversation, Monsieur Gilbert."

"What?"

"You blame my teaching. Have you not free will?"

"I do not blame it, monsieur; I told you what I had read. I blame my own credulity. I believed; I fell. There are two causes for my crime ; you are the first, and I come first to you. I shall next go to the second, but in its turn, all in good time."

"Well, what do you wish me to do?"

"I ask for neither gift, shelter, nor bread, although I am an outcast and hungry; no, I seek moral support; I ask the sanction of your teachings; I ask you to restore to me, by a word, all my strength, which is broken, not by inanition in my legs and my arms, but by doubt in my soul. Monsieur, I adjure you tell me if it is the pain of hunger in the muscles of my stomach which I have experienced for the last week, or the torture of remorse in the functions of my mind. In perpetrating this crime, monsieur, I have caused a child to be born. Now, tell me, must I tear my hair out in my bitter despair, and roll in the dust, crying, 'Forgive,' or must I utter the words of the woman in the Scriptures, 'I have but done as all the rest; let him that is better than I cast the first stone." In a word, Monsieur Rousseau, you, who must have felt as I feel, consider this question. Tell me, is it in accordance with nature's laws for a father to desert his child?"

No sooner had Gilbert uttered that word than Rousseau became paler than Gilbert himself, and his features worked convulsively.

"What right have you to speak thus to me?" he stammered.

"Because, being at your house, Monsieur Rousseau, under this roof whose hospitality you have given to me, I have read what you have written on this subject; because you have declared that children born in shame belong to the State, which ought to take care of them. In a word, because you have always been regarded as an upright man, although you have abandoned the children who have been born to you."

"Wretch," cried Rousseau, "you have read my book, and you use such language in speaking to me!"

"Well, what then?" said Gilbert.

"Then you have a bad spirit joined to a bad heart."

"Monsieur Rousseau!"

"You have misunderstood my book as you have also

comprehended life and its questions amiss; you have skimmed only the surface of the pages, as you have beheld only the exterior of my face. Ah! you expect to make me an accomplice in your crime, by quoting to me from the books that I have written, by saying to me, 'You confess you too have done this, therefore I can do it.' But, monsieur, what you do not know, what you have not read in my books, what you have not even guessed at in them, is the fact that the whole life of him whom you have taken for a model, this life of pain and sorrow, I could exchange for an existence of joy, frivolity, and ease. Have I less talent than Monsieur Voltaire? could I not produce as much as he? Even working less hard than I have done, could I not sell my books at as high a price as he, and make the money run into my coffers, keeping always part of my wealth for the use of my publishers? Do you not know that gold attracts gold? I might have kept a carriage and taken a young and beautiful mistress to drive in it, and this luxury, you may be sure, would not have exhausted the reservoirs of poetry in my soul. Have I no passions? Speak! Search my eyes, in which, although my years number sixty, the fire of youth and ambition still glows. You, who have read or copied my books, consider, call to your mind the fact, that despite declining years, despite most real and serious misfortunes, my heart, still young, seems to have inherited all the strength of the other parts of my constitution, that I might the better endure life's hardships. Burdened with infirmities which keep me from walking, I still feel more vigour and vitality for enduring sorrow than in the flower of my life I ever experienced in the enjoyment of the rare pleasures which God has given me."

" I know all that, monsieur," said Gilbert, "I have been with you and I have realised the truth of what you tell me."

" Then, if you have been with me, if you have understood so well, has not my life a meaning to you that others cannot perceive ?　Does not this strange self-denial, which is not natural to me, explain to you that I wished to expiate — ? "

"Expiate! " murmured Gilbert.

"Have you not understood," continued the philosopher, "that, having been forced by this misery to make an extreme determination at first, I have never since found any other excuse for this resolution than disinterestedness and a continuance in my unhappy condition.　Have you not seen that I have punished my spirit by humiliating it ? For my spirit was to blame ; my spirit, which could find refuge only in contradictions for its justification ; while, on the other hand, I punished my soul by an unending remorse."

"Ah! " cried Gilbert, " this is the way you answer me. You, philosophers, who fling your precepts at the rest of the world, you drive us to despair, and then blame us if we are angry with you.　Eh! what avails your humiliation to me, while it is secret, — your remorse, as long as you conceal it ? Oh woe, woe to you, monsieur !　May the crimes committed in your name descend again upon your own head ! "

"Upon my head, you say !　Curses and punishment at the same time, for you forget the punishment ; oh! that would be too much.　Would you, who have sinned like me, condemn yourself as severely as you have me ? "

" Even more severely," said Gilbert, " for my own punishment will be terrible ; for now I have no longer any faith in anything.　I shall let my adversary, or rather my enemy, kill me ; a suicide which my unhappiness counsels, my conscience forgives ; for now my death is no longer a robbery committed on humanity, as you wrote in a sentence which you yourself do not believe."

" Stop, wretch ! " said Rousseau, " stop.　Have you not already done evil enough in your foolish credulity ?　Must you do still more by stupid scepticism ?　You mentioned a child to me ? you told me that you were, or rather were going to become, a father ? "

"I said so," reiterated Gilbert.

"Do you know what it is," murmured Rousseau in a low voice, "to drag with you, not to death but to shame, creatures born to inhale the free pure air of virtue, which God bestows as a dowry upon every one at his birth? Now, hear all the shocking details of my condition. When I forsook my children, it was because I thought that society, always jealous of any superiority in its members, would fling this wrong in my face as an infamous reproach. Then I sought justification for myself in contradictions. I, who had not known what it was to be a father, spent ten years of my life in advising mothers how to bring up their children. I, who had been weak and corrupt, wrote treatises for my country on good citizenship. Then one day the executioner, who avenges society, the country, and orphans, unable to reach me, seized my book and burned it as a living shame to the country whose atmosphere it had poisoned. Come, decide, judge, seek out. Have I done right? have I given bad advice? You do not answer, God, who himself holds the unfailing scales of right and wrong, would be perplexed to decide it. But I myself find an answer, deep in the heart that beats in my breast: 'Woe to you, unnatural father, who have forsaken your children. Woe to you if you meet a young prostitute who mocks you with her light laugh at the street corners, for perchance she may be your own daughter, whom hunger has impelled to this shameful life. Woe to you if you meet the thief who has just been arrested with his guilt fresh upon him, for perhaps he is the son you abandoned, whom hunger has driven to crime.' "

After these words, Rousseau, who had arisen, fell back in his chair.

"And yet," continued he in a broken voice which had an accent of prayer, "I have not been as guilty as they think. I have seen a mother without any compassion, an accomplice in my sin, forget, even as animals forget, and I have said to myself, 'God lets the mother forget, it must be right for her to forget.' Well, I was in error then, and you, who have heard me say to you what I have never said to any other person, to-day, you must not be left in error."

"That is to say," continued the young man knitting his brows, "you would never have forsaken your children had you had the means of supporting them ?"

"Only rigid necessity; no, never, I give you my oath, never!" And Rousseau solemnly raised his trembling hands toward heaven.

"Is twenty thousand francs," said Gilbert, "enough to support a child ?"

" Yes, it is enough," said Rousseau.

"Well," said Gilbert, "I thank you, monsieur; I know now what to do."

"And in any case, young as you are," said Rousseau, "you can support your child by your labour. But you spoke of a crime; you will be sought, pursued, perhaps — "

"Yes, monsieur."

"Well, hide yourself, my child. The little room in the attic is always open to you."

"I love you, my dear master," said Gilbert, "and your offer fills me with joy. I ask only a temporary shelter from you. As to my food, I shall earn it. You know I am not an idler."

"Well," said Rousseau with an uneasy air, "if the thing is settled, go up to your room. Only Madame Rousseau must not see you here. She never goes up to the attic; for, since you left us, we never lock up anything. Your pallet is still there. Arrange it as best you can."

"Thanks, monsieur; under these circumstances I shall be much happier than I deserve."

"Now, is that all you wish ?" said Rousseau, looking toward the door.

"No, monsieur, one word more, if you please."

" Speak !"

"At Luciennes you accused me once of having betrayed you. I would betray no one, monsieur; I was following my love."

"Speak no more of that. Is that all?"

"Yes. Now, monsieur, when one does not know the address of some one living in Paris, can one obtain it?"

"Doubtless, if the person is well known."

"He of whom I am speaking is well known."

"His name?"

"Monsieur the Count Joseph Balsamo."

Rousseau shuddered, he had not forgotten the meeting in the Rue Plastrière.

"What do you wish of this man?" asked he.

"Quite a simple thing. I accused you, my master, of being the moral cause of this crime, since I thought I was only obeying a natural law."

"And I have undeceived you?" cried Rousseau, trembling at the thought of his responsibility.

"You have at least enlightened me."

"Well, what do you mean?"

"That my crime had a physical, as well as a moral cause."

"And is the Count of Balsamo the physical cause?"

"Yes, I have imitated examples; I have seized an occasion; and in doing so have acted like a wild animal rather than a man. You are the example; Monsieur the Count Balsamo is the occasion. Do you know his address?"

"Yes."

"Give it to me, then."

"Rue Saint-Claude, au Marais."

"Thanks, I will go first to him."

"Take care, child," cried Rousseau, holding him back, "he is a deep, powerful man."

"Do not fear, Monsieur Rousseau, I have made up my mind, and you have taught me to restrain myself."

"Quick, quick, go up-stairs. I hear the door of the court-yard opening. It is doubtless Madame Rousseau coming back. Hide yourself in the attic until she has come in here again, then go out."

"Where is the key, please?"

"On the nail in the kitchen, as usual."

"Adieu, monsieur, adieu."

"Take some bread, I will get you some work to do this evening."

"Thanks!"

And Gilbert slipped out so quickly that he reached the attic before Thérèse had climbed the first flight of stairs.

Provided with the precious address which Rousseau had given him, Gilbert was not long in carrying out his plan.

Indeed, Thérèse had no sooner closed the door than the young man, who from his attic door had observed all her movements, descended the stairs with as much speed as if he had not been already so weakened by his long fast. His head was filled with hopeful plans, vengeance dominating and overshadowing all other emotions, with its complainings and accusations.

He arrived at the Rue Saint-Claude in a condition hard to describe.

As he entered the court-yard of the hotel, Balsamo was just escorting the Prince de Rohan thither, who was paying his generous alchemist a visit. As the prince was rendering his last words of thanks to Balsamo, the poor, ragged fellow slid in like a dog, not daring to look around him, for fear of being dazzled.

The carriage of Prince Rohan was awaiting him at the boulevard. The prelate slowly crossed the court-yard that separated him from his carriage, and drove rapidly away as soon as its door was closed upon him. Balsamo had followed him with a melancholy look, and, when the carriage had disappeared, he turned toward the steps. Upon the stairs was a kind of beggar in an attitude of supplication. Balsamo went up to him; although his lips were silent, his expressive face questioned him.

"A quarter of an hour's audience, please, count," said the young man in ragged clothes.

"Who are you, friend?" said Balsamo, with the greatest gentleness.

"Do you not recognise me?" asked Gilbert.

"No; but it makes no difference. Come in," replied Balsamo, not at all disturbed either by the strange appearance of the suppliant, or by his clothing or his importunity.

Going before him, he took him into the first room they encountered, where, after they had seated themselves, without any change either in his voice or his expression, he said, —

"Did you ask if I recognised you?"

"Yes, Monsieur le Comte."

"Indeed, it seems to me as if I had seen you somewhere."

"At Taverney, monsieur, when you came there, the evening of the day before the arrival of the dauphiness."

"What were you doing at Taverney?"

"I was living there."

"As a family servant?"

"No; as a member of the family."

"You have left Taverney?"

"Yes, monsieur, nearly three years ago."

"And you came —?"

"To Paris, where at first I studied with Monsieur Rousseau at his house; after which I had a situation in the Trianon gardens as an assistant florist-gardener, under the protection of Monsieur de Jussieu."

"You quote two well-known names. What do you want of me?"

"I will tell you." And, making a pause, he looked steadily at Balsamo.

"Do you remember," continued he, "of having been at Trianon the day of the great storm, six weeks ago next Friday?"

Serious as he already was, Balsamo became even more sober.

"Yes, I remember," said he; "did you, by chance, see me there?"

"I saw you."

"Then you have come here to be paid for the secret?" said Balsamo, in a threatening tone.

"No, monsieur; it is more for my interest to keep the secret than for yours."

"Then you are he named Gilbert?" said Balsamo.

"Yes, monsieur."

Balsamo fixed a long and penetrating look on the young man, whose name recalled so terrible an accusation. He was surprised, he who knew men so well, at the composure of his bearing and the dignity of his words.

Gilbert stood before a table, without leaning against it or deriving any support from it; one of his tapering hands, white despite his rural labour, was hidden in his breast, the other fell gracefully at his side.

"I read in your face," said Balsamo, "what your object was in coming here. You know that a dreadful charge has been made against you by Mademoiselle de Taverney, that, by the aid of science, I have compelled her to tell the truth. You are going to reproach me for this testimony, are you not? this calling forth of a secret, which, but for me, would have been shrouded in the darkness of the grave?"

Gilbert merely shook his head.

"Yet you would have been wrong," continued Balsamo; "for, even admitting that I had any desire of denouncing you without being forced by my own interest to do so, — I, who was accused of the wrong myself, — admitting that I would have betrayed you like an enemy, that I had attacked you, while I might have been satisfied only to have defended myself, — admitting all this, you have no right to say a word, for you have committed a cowardly deed."

Gilbert tore his breast with his nails, but made no reply.

"If you are imprudent enough to walk in the streets of Paris, as you are now doing," replied Balsamo, "the brother will pursue you, the sister will have you killed."

"Oh! as to that, it is of little consequence," said Gilbert.

"What! of little consequence to you?"

"Yes. I loved Mademoiselle Andrée, — I loved her as she will never again be loved; but she despised me, — me, who have always thought of her so respectfully; she despised me, — me, who have twice held her in my arms, without daring even to kiss the hem of her dress."

"So that is the case, and that is the respect you have paid her. You have avenged yourself for her scorn by what? by a secret attack."

"Oh, no, no! I did not plan this attack! An occasion for committing the crime was provided for me."

"By whom?"

"By you."

Balsamo drew back as if a serpent had stung him.

"By me?" he cried.

"By you; yes, monsieur, by you!" repeated Gilbert. "Monsieur, you put Mademoiselle Andrée to sleep, and then you fled. In proportion to the distance between her and you, as you went away, her limbs failed her. Finally, her strength deserted her entirely, and she fell. I then took her in my arms, to carry her back to her room; I felt her body touching mine; a statue had become alive. I, who loved her, I yielded to my love. Am I, then, as wicked as I am thought to be? I ask you, — you, the cause of my misfortune."

Balsamo conveyed a look, filled with pity and sadness, upon Gilbert.

"You are right," said he; "I am the cause of your crime, and this young girl's misfortune."

"And, instead of trying to repair it, you, who are so great that you should also be good, — you have increased the unhappiness of this young girl, you have exposed the culprit to death."

"It is true," replied Balsamo; "you speak wisely. For some time, you see, I have been an unfortunate man, and all my schemes, on leaving my brain, have become threatening and injurious. That is true of misfortunes which I also have undergone, and which you do not comprehend. At the same time, that is no reason why I should make others suffer. What can I do for you? Tell me."

"I ask some means of reparation from you, Monsieur le Comte, for all this crime and trouble."

"You love this young girl?"

"Oh yes!"

"There are many kinds of love. What is the nature of yours?"

"Before possessing her, I loved her distractedly; now, I love her passionately. I should die of grief if she received me in anger; I should die of joy would she let me only kiss her feet."

"She is of noble birth, yet she is poor," said Balsamo, reflectively.

"Yes."

"Still, her brother is a fine man, who is little affected by the empty privilege of high birth. What would happen if you asked of him his sister's hand in marriage?"

"He would kill me," replied Gilbert, coldly; "yet, as I desire death more than I fear it, if you advise me to make this demand, I will do so."

Balsamo reflected.

"You are a man of spirit," said he, "and you may still be considered a man of spirit, although your deeds, apart from my complicity, are truly criminal. Well, go, and seek, not Monsieur Taverney the son, but Monsieur le Baron Taverney, his father, and tell him, tell him — listen attentively — that the day on which he will allow you to marry his daughter you will bring her a dowry."

"I cannot say that, monsieur; I have nothing."

"And I, I tell you that you shall bestow upon her a dowry of a hundred thousand crowns, which I will give you in reparation for the trouble and the crime for which you blame me."

"He would not believe me; he knows that I am poor."

"Well, then, if he should not believe you, you shall show him these bank-notes, and he will doubt no longer."

As he said these words, Balsamo opened the table drawer and counted out thirty bank-notes, each worth ten thousand francs. Then he passed them to Gilbert.

"And is that money?" asked the young man.

"Read."

Gilbert looked eagerly over the writing on the bills he held in his hands, and realised that Balsamo had spoken truly. A joyful light shone in his eyes.

"It might be possible," cried he; "but no, such generosity would be too sublime."

"You are distrustful," said Balsamo. "It is quite natural; but learn to discriminate among the objects of your mistrust. Take this hundred thousand crowns and go to Monsieur de Taverney."

"Monsieur," said Gilbert, "such a sum to be given simply on my word? I cannot believe in the reality of this gift."

Balsamo took a pen and wrote: —

"I give as dowry to Gilbert, the day on which he shall sign the marriage contract with Mademoiselle Andrée de Taverney, the sum of one hundred thousand crowns, which I have intrusted to him in advance in the hope of a happy transaction.

"JOSEPH BALSAMO."

"Take this paper, go, doubt no longer."

Gilbert received the paper with trembling hands.

"Monsieur," said he, "I owe such good fortune to you that henceforth you shall be a God on earth to me."

"There is only one God whom we should worship," replied Balsamo, gravely; "and it is not I. Go, friend."

"One last favour, monsieur."

"What is it?"

"Give me fifty francs."

"You ask me for fifty francs, while you hold three hundred thousand in your hand?"

"These three hundred thousand will not be mine," said Gilbert, "until the day on which Mademoiselle Taverney consents to marry me."

"And what will you do with fifty francs?"

"I will buy a decent coat, in which to present myself at the baron's."

"Wait, my friend, here it is," said Balsamo; and he gave him the fifty francs for which he had asked.

Upon this he dismissed Gilbert with a bow, and with the same slow, sad step he went back into his apartments.

## CHAPTER CL.

### GILBERT'S PROJECTS.

ONCE in the street, Gilbert's feverish imagination cooled somewhat; for during the latter part of the count's conversation his fancy had carried him into the realm of the probable, and even beyond that, into that of the possible.

Once in the Rue Pastourel, he sat down on a milestone, and, looking around him to assure himself that no one was watching him, he drew the bank-notes from his pocket, quite crumpled from the pressure of his hand.

Then a dreadful thought passed through his mind, and even made the perspiration come on his forehead.

"Well," said he, looking at the bank-notes, "if this man has not deceived me, if he has not laid a snare for me, if he does not send me to certain death, under the pretext of procuring unfailing happiness for me, if he has not treated me as sheep are treated, in luring them to the slaughter with a bunch of flowering herbs. I have heard that there are a great many counterfeit bank-notes in circulation, by the aid of which *roués* of the court deceive the opera girls. Let me see if the count has tried to dupe me." And he took one of the ten thousand franc notes from the bundle; then, going to a merchant's and showing him the bill, asked him for the address of a banker who would change it for him, as his master, he said, had told him to do so.

The merchant turned it over and over, greatly admiring it, for the sum was immense, and his shop quite small. Then he told him that the banker whose services he required lived in the Rue Sainte-Avoie.

So the note was good.

Gilbert, happy and beside himself with joy, immediately gave the reins to his imagination, and tied the bundle of notes tightly in his handkerchief; and seeing in the Rue Sainte-Avoie the shop of a dealer in second-hand clothes, he went there and made a purchase with twenty-five francs, — that is to say, with one of the two louis that Balsamo had given him. He selected an entire suit of maroon cloth, whose fitness pleased him, a pair of black silk stockings, a little faded, and a pair of shoes with bright buckles. A tolerably fine shirt completed the outfit, which was neat rather than expensive, and Gilbert cast an admiring glance at his reflection in the clothier's mirror. Then, leaving his old clothes in addition to the twenty-five francs, he put the precious handkerchief in his pocket, and passed from the old-clothes dealer's shop to that of the hairdresser, who, in less than a quarter of an hour, succeeded in making Balsamo's *protégé's* head stylish, and even handsome in appearance.

At last, when all these operations were completed, Gilbert went into a baker's shop, near the Place Louis XV., and bought two sous' worth of bread, which he ate hastily on his way to Versailles. At the fountain of the Conférence he stopped to take a drink of water. Then he resumed his journey, refusing the importunities of the coachmen, who could not see why a young man so well attired should wish to save fifteen sous at the expense of his shoe polish. What would they have said, had they known that this young man, who was thus travelling on foot, was carrying three hundred thousand francs in his pocket.

But Gilbert had his own reasons for travelling on foot. In the first place, because he had firmly resolved not to spend a sou more than was absolutely necessary; also the need he felt of being alone, that he might the more easily indulge in reverie and soliloquy.

God only knows what happy dreams filled the head of the lad during the two hours and a half which he spent on the road. In this time he had travelled more than four leagues, without realising the distance, or feeling at all tired, so powerful was his organisation. He formed all his plans, and decided to begin the conversation something · after this fashion. To approach Taverney, the father, with lofty words; then, when he should have obtained the baron's sanction, to interview Mademoiselle Andrée with such eloquence that not only would she forgive him, but also she would at once conceive a great respect and affection for the author of the pathetic discourse that he had prepared.

As he dwelt upon all this in his thoughts, his hopes gradually surmounted all his fears, and it seemed impossible to Gilbert that a girl in Andrée's condition would hesitate to accept the reparation offered by love; more particularly as the love was accompanied by a dowry of a hundred thousand crowns.

Gilbert, in building all these castles in Spain, was as innocent and simple as any child of the primitive races. He forgot all the wrong that he had done, — he who was perhaps, after all, more honourable than he had been considered. All his forces ready, he arrived at the grounds of Trianon with his heart in his mouth. Once there, he was ready for anything; for Philip's first outbreak of wrath, which he trusted his generous offer would soon dispel; of Andrée's scorn, at first, which his love would soon overcome; for the cold haughtiness of the baron, which his gold must dissolve.

Indeed, Gilbert, although he had grown up in the country, far from people and the customs of society, intuitively perceived that three hundred thousand francs in one's pocket would be a sure armour against all weapons. He feared Andrée's sufferings most of all; he mistrusted his own weakness in the face of this misfortune, — a weakness that would take from him a part of the means necessary for his success.

He entered, then, into the gardens, looking about him,

not without a pride that became him well, at the gardeners, yesterday his companions, to-day below him in the social scale.

His first question was about the Baron de Taverney. He addressed, naturally, the servant on duty at the offices.

"The baron is not at Trianon," answered he.

Gilbert hesitated a moment.

"And Monsieur Philip?" asked he.

"Oh! Monsieur Philip has gone away with Mademoiselle Andrée."

"Gone away?" cried Gilbert, in dismay.

"Yes."

"Then Mademoiselle Andrée has gone away?"

"Five days ago."

"To Paris?"

The servant made a gesture which signified, "I don't know anything about it."

"What! do you know nothing about it?" cried Gilbert. "Mademoiselle Andrée has gone without letting it be known where she went? She must have had some reason for going."

"How foolish!" said the servant, evincing little respect for Gilbert's maroon coat. "Of course, she would not have gone without some reason for doing so."

"Why did she go, then?"

"For a change of air."

"For a change of air?" repeated Gilbert.

"Yes; it seemed that the climate of Trianon did not agree with her, and the doctor ordered her to go away."

It was useless to question further; it was evident that the servant on duty had told him all he himself knew about Mademoiselle de Taverney.

Still, Gilbert, stupefied, could not believe his own ears. He hastened to Andrée's room, and found the door closed. Bits of glass, pieces of straw and of hay, threads from the mattress on the floor, everything spoke of a departure.

Gilbert went into his old room, which he found just as

he had left it. Andrée's window was open to admit the air, and he could see into the antechamber. The apartment was quite empty.

Gilbert gave way to a paroxysm of grief. He beat his head against the wall, wrung his hands, and rolled on the floor. Then, like a madman, he rushed out from the garret and down the staircase, flying along as if he had wings; he pushed his way into the woods, his hands clutching his hair, and with screams and oaths he flung himself down behind the hedge, cursing his life and those who had bestowed it upon him.

"Oh, it is all over!" murmured he; "God will not let me find her again. God will let me die of remorse, despair, and love; thus I shall expiate my crime, and avenge her whom I have injured. Where can she be? At Taverney? Oh! I will go there, I will go there! I will go to the ends of the earth! I will climb to the clouds if needs be! Oh! I will find some trace of her, and I will follow it, should I fall on the road from hunger and fatigue."

After a while he resumed his journey, and entered Paris at about seven o'clock in the evening. That is the hour at which the crowd in Paris go out to walk up and down the paths in the Champs Élysées, between the early evening fogs and the artificial light, which makes the days in that city twenty-four hours in length.

The young man, in compliance with the resolution he had made, boldly went at once to the Rue Coq-Héron, and knocked without a moment's hesitation.

Silence, only, answered him. He redoubled his blows with the knocker, but to no effect.

Then, as this last resource on which he had counted failed, filled with rage, he beat his body, which suffered much less than his mind, with his hands, and turned abruptly at the street corner, pushed the spring of Rousseau's door, and went up the stairs. The handkerchief which contained the thirty bank-notes had also the attic key tied in it. Gilbert jumped into the room as he would have plunged into the Seine had it been flowing along in that place.

Then, as the evening was beautiful, and fleecy clouds were floating in the blue sky, as the fragrance from the lime and chestnut trees was wafted to his senses, as the bats beat noiselessly against the panes of the little windows, Gilbert, restored to a consciousness of life and its blessings by all these softening influences, approached the window, and, seeing through the trees the pavilion of the garden where he had found Andrée, whom once he thought forever lost to him, felt as if his heart would break, and fell almost fainting against the edge of the gutter, his eyes dimmed with vague and stupid contemplation.

## CHAPTER CLI.

A VAIN STRUGGLE, IN WHICH GILBERT FINDS THAT IT IS
EASIER TO COMMIT A CRIME THAN TO OVERCOME A
PREJUDICE.

IN proportion as Gilbert's grief diminished, his plans
became more definite and decisive. In the mean time, the
increasing darkness prevented his distinguishing any of the
objects around him. Then an overwhelming longing possessed him to see the trees, the house, the paths, now
indistinguishably massed together in the dim light, while
over all the air hung as over an abyss.

He remembered how one evening, in happier times,
when he had wished to find out about Andrée, to see her,
to hear her speak, even at the risk of his life, as he had
not at that time recovered from his illness following the
31st of May, he had glided down the length of the gutter,
from the upper floor to the ground, until he reached the
blessed garden itself.

At that time he had run great danger in penetrating into
that house where the baron dwelt, where Andrée was so
well protected; and yet, despite the peril, Gilbert recalled
to his mind the sweetness of the situation, and the joy
with which his heart beat, at the sound of her dear voice.

"Suppose I try it again," he thought; "for a last time
travel the sanded paths on my knees, and search for the
footprints of my dear mistress."

This word, which would have caused such frightful
results had it been overheard, Gilbert pronounced almost
aloud, taking a strange pleasure in speaking it. Gilbert
interrupted his monologue to look intently at the place

where he thought the pavilion must be. Then, after a moment's silence and contemplation, he resumed: —

"There is nothing to denote that any one else is occupying the pavilion, — no lights, no sounds, no open door. I will go and see."

Gilbert had at least one merit. After he had resolved to do a thing, he lost no time in executing his plans. He opened the garret door, descended on tiptoe, like a sylph, passed Rousseau's door, and, having reached the second floor, slid down the gutter pipe to the ground, at the risk of making old trousers of those he had bought new in the morning.

Arrived at the foot of the trellis, he experienced anew all the sensations of his first visit to the pavilion. The gravel creaked under his feet, and he recognised the little gate by which Nicole had let in Monsieur de Beausire. Then he went toward the stairs to press his lips against the brass button of the shutter, saying to himself that doubtless Andrée's hand had often touched it. Gilbert's crime had made his love seem to him a kind of religion. Suddenly a sound from the interior, soft and subdued, like that of a light footstep on the floor, made Gilbert tremble. He drew back; his face became livid; and at the same time, so unbalanced was his mind, owing to his distress of the eight or ten days, that when he perceived a ray of light across the door he believed that superstition, the daughter of ignorance and remorse, was flashing before his vision one of its evil torches, and that it was this torch that shone through the slats of the blinds. He fancied that his terrified soul had called forth another soul, and it was indeed time for one of those hallucinations engendered by wild and unbounded passions.

Moreover, the step and the light came nearer. Gilbert saw and heard, still doubting the evidence of his senses; but as the window suddenly opened at the very moment when Gilbert was going up to it to look through the blinds, he was thrown violently backward by the shock, against the side of the wall, and, screaming aloud, he fell on both knees. What he had seen had overcome him more than the blow he had received; for in this house, which he had thought deserted, at the very door at which he had knocked for admittance in vain, Andrée herself appeared before his eyes. The young girl, for it was in fact she, and not her ghost, cried aloud, as Gilbert had done. Then, less frightened, for doubtless she was waiting for some one, —

"Who is there?" said she. "Who are you? What do you want?"

"Oh, pardon, pardon!" cried Gilbert, his eyes humbly fixed on the ground.

"Gilbert! Gilbert, you here!" cried Andrée, in surprise, quite unmixed with fear or anger. "Gilbert in the garden! What are you doing here, friend?"

This last appellation smote the young man to the very depths of his heart.

"Oh!" cried he, stifled with emotion, "do not overwhelm me, mademoiselle, be pitiful; I have suffered so much!"

Andrée looked at him in amazement, as if she could not understand the meaning of this humility.

"First," said she, "get up and tell me how you happen to be here."

"Oh mademoiselle!" cried Gilbert, "I shall never arise until you have forgiven me."

"What have you done against me that you plead my forgiveness? Speak, explain yourself. In any case," continued she, with a sad smile, "as the offence cannot be very serious, it will be easy to forgive it. Did Philip send you the key?"

"The key?"

"Of course. He arranged for me to open the door to no one in his absence, and as you have come in, and as you cannot have climbed over the walls, he must have given you the facilities for entering."

"Your brother, Monsieur Philip?" stammered Gilbert.

"No, no, he did not give it to me; but let us not stop to talk about him. You have not gone away then, Mademoiselle? You have not left France? Oh happiness! unhoped for happiness!"

Gilbert raised himself on one knee, and with outstretched arms returned thanks to Heaven, with strange fervour. Andrée leaned toward him, and, looking uneasily at him, said: —

"You talk foolishly, Monsieur Gilbert, and you will tear my dress. Let go of my dress, I entreat you, and put an end to this farce."

Gilbert arose. "You are angry," said he, "but I ought not to complain of that, for I deserve your wrath. I know that I ought not to have come here in this way. But I did not know that the pavilion was inhabited. I thought it empty, deserted. I came here only to awaken memories of you. That is all, chance alone. — Indeed, I do not know what I am saying. Excuse me, I had intended to speak to your father, but he had disappeared."

Andrée moved uneasily. "My father?" said she, "why my father?"

Gilbert mistook this reply. "Oh! because I fear you too much," said he. "And yet I know very well that it would be better for all arrangements to be made between you and me; it would be the surest means of reparation."

"Reparation! what do you mean by that?" said Andrée. "What reparation is called for? Tell me."

Gilbert looked at her humbly and lovingly. "Oh, do not be angry," he said, "it is indeed a great boldness on my part, I know very well. It is presumptuous for one in my humble position to aspire so high; but the evil is done."

Andrée made a movement.

"The crime, if you call it so," continued Gilbert; "yes, the crime, for truly it was a great crime. Well, blame fate, not my heart, for this crime."

"Your heart! your crime! fate!" cried she. "You are insane, Gilbert, and I am afraid of you."

"Oh! it is impossible that with such respectfulness, such remorse, that with bowed head and clasped hands I thus placed before you could inspire in you any other feeling than that of pity. Mademoiselle, hear my words: I make a solemn vow, here before God and men, I will consecrate my whole life to the expiation of this mistake of a moment. I will make your happiness so great that it will blot out all remembrance of past grief. Mademoiselle — "

Gilbert hesitated.

"Mademoiselle, consent to a marriage, which will sanctify a criminal union."

Andrée took a step backward.

"No, no," said Gilbert. "I am not a madman. Do not try to flee from me, do not draw away from my embrace; in mercy, in pity, consent to be my wife."

"Your wife?" cried Andrée, believing that she herself must be mad.

"Oh!" continued Gilbert, tears streaming down his face, "oh! tell me that you forgive me for that dreadful night. Tell me that my deed fills you with horror, but tell me also that my penitence evokes forgiveness from you. Tell me that my love, so long repressed, justified my crime."

"Wretch!" cried Andrée in a frenzy of rage, "it was you then? Oh my God! my God!"

And Andrée seized her head with both hands, and clasped it tightly, as if to prevent herself from pursuing this disgusting thought.

Gilbert drew back, silent and petrified, in the presence of this beautiful, pale Medusa's face, which expressed at the same time fear and wonder.

"Have you kept me for this wretchedness, my God!" cried Andrée, with growing excitement, "to see my name doubly dishonoured, dishonoured by crime, dishonoured by the criminal? Answer, coward! Answer, wretch! Was it indeed you?"

"She did not know it!" murmured Gilbert in dismay.

"Help! help!" cried Andrée, going back into the house.
"Philip, come to me, Philip!"

Gilbert, who had followed her, sad and hopeless, looked
about him, either to find a place where he might gloriously
fall under the blows he expected, or to find some weapon
of defence.

But no one answered Andrée's call. She was alone in
the house.

"Alone, alone!" cried she, bursting forth in wrath. "Go
out from here, scoundrel! do not tempt God's anger
further."

Gilbert gently raised his head.

"Your wrath," murmured he, "is the anger I dread
most in this world. Do not crush me under its weight.
Have pity on me." And he clasped his hands, entreatingly.

"Assassin! assassin! assassin!" screamed the young
girl.

"But will you not listen to me?" said he. "Listen to
me first, and then kill me if you will."

"To listen to you would but add to my punishment.
What can you say? Go on."

"What I just said, that I have done wrong; yet whoever
could read my heart would find it possible to excuse me.
Besides, I bring the means of reparation with me."

"Oh!" cried Andrée, "then that is the meaning of the
word that filled me with horror, even before I understood the
situation; a marriage! — I believe you said a marriage?"

"Mademoiselle!" stammered Gilbert.

"A marriage," continued the young girl with increasing
haughtiness. "Oh! it is not anger I feel toward you so
much as contempt and hatred. Such contempt, a feeling
at the same time so deep and so terrible, that I wonder
you can endure the looks I cast upon you and live."

Gilbert grew pale. Two tears of anger shone in his
eyes: his lips were pinched and blanched like two threads
of pearl.

"Mademoiselle," said he, shaking with rage, "I am not

so mean that I cannot make full reparation for the loss of your honour."

Andrée drew herself up.

"If it is a question of lost honour, it is yours that is affected and not mine, monsieur. In my position my honour still remains unstained, but should I marry you, I should dishonour myself."

"I should not think," replied Gilbert, in a cold, curt tone, "that a woman, after she has become a mother, ought to consider anything at all but the future of her child."

"And I, I should not suppose you would dare concern yourself about that, monsieur," said Andrée, with flashing eyes.

"On the contrary, I do concern myself about it, mademoiselle," replied Gilbert, beginning to rise from under the furious foot that had trampled him; "I concern myself about it, for I do not wish this child to die of hunger, as often happens in the houses of the nobility, where girls have their own ideas of honour.. All men are equal; men who are themselves superior to others have proclaimed this maxim. I can understand why you do not like me, for you cannot read my heart; still more, why you despise me, for you do not know my thoughts; but I shall never understand how you can deny me the right of caring for the welfare of my child. Alas! in wishing to marry you, I was not seeking to gratify any desire, passion, or ambition; I would merely be fulfilling a duty. I should condemn myself to a condition of servitude; I should give you my life. *Mon Dieu!* you need never have borne my name; indeed, had you wished, you might have continued to treat me like Gilbert the gardener; it would be right. But you have no right to sacrifice your child. Here are three hundred thousand francs, given to me as a marriage portion by a generous patron, who has judged me quite differently from you. If I marry you, the money will be mine. In fact, as far as I am concerned, if I live, I need only a little air to breathe; if I die, a trench in the ground to contain my body. All else that I can claim as my own I shall give to my child. Wait, see; here are the three hundred thousand francs."

He placed the three hundred thousand francs on the table in a pile, almost under Andreé's hand.

"Monsieur," said she, "you are labouring under a great delusion; you have no child."

"I?"

"Of what child are you speaking?" said Andrée.

"Why, of the one whose mother you are. Have you not confessed it before two witnesses? before your brother Philip, in the presence of the Count Balsamo? Have you not acknowledged that you are *enceinte*, and that it was I, —I, unhappy one!"

"Ah! you overheard me?" cried Andrée. "Well, so much the better! so much the better! You took me by force, like a coward, while I was asleep. It was a crime on your part. I am a mother, it is true, but my child has only a mother. Do you hear? You have violated me, it is true, but you are not the father of my child."

And, seizing the bank-notes, she threw them scornfully out of the room, in such a way that they touched the unhappy Gilbert's pallid face in their flight. Then he felt so deep an anger stirring within him, that Andrée's good angel might well have trembled once more for her safety. But this wrath was restrained by its own violence, and the young man passed before Andrée, without a word.

He had hardly crossed the threshold before she hastened behind him, and closed doors, blinds, windows, and shutters, as if she wished by this action to place the universe between the present and the past.

# CHAPTER CLII.

## RESOLUTION.

How Gilbert went safely home, how he could, without dying of grief and rage, sustain the anguish of that night, how he even arose in the morning without at least having become gray-headed, all this we cannot pretend to be able to explain to our readers.

When day at last came, Gilbert was seized with a violent desire to write to Andrée,— to attack her with all the convincing, strong arguments that had passed through his mind during the night. But so many times had he proved the inflexible disposition of this young girl, that he no longer felt any hope. Writing, besides, would be a concession repugnant to his pride. Reflecting that his letter might be crumpled and thrown away, without even being read,— also fearing that it might be the means of bringing on his track a number of furious, unreasoning enemies, — these considerations prevented him from writing.

It then occurred to Gilbert that Andrée's father, noted for his avarice and his ambition, might view his offer more favourably. As for her brother, he was good-hearted, and only his first impulse need be dreaded.

"But," said he, "of what use to me is it to be upheld by Monsieur de Taverney and by Philip, while Andrée continues saying, ' I do not know you '? Well," added he to himself, "nothing binds me to this woman; she herself has taken care to break all the links which might have united us."

He was musing thus as he tossed on his mattress in grief, recalling angrily every change of Andrée's voice and expression; at the same time, he was enduring inexpressible tortures, for he loved her to distraction.

When the sun, already high above the horizon, penetrated Gilbert's attic, he arose, trembling at the hope of seeing his enemy in the garden or the pavilion.

It would be joy mingled with sorrow. But suddenly a bitter flood of hatred, of remorse, of wrath, checked this desire. He remembered all the contempt and scorn which this young girl had heaped upon him; and, stopping short in his garret, by a sudden force of mind over matter, —

"No," said he, "no. You shall not go and look out of the window; you shall not sip the poison, which would only kill you. She is cruel; she, who never has cared when you have humbled yourself before her; she, who has never spoken a word of consolation or kindness to you; she who has taken pleasure in piercing your heart, full of innocent and chaste love. She is wholly without honour or religion; she, who would deny a father the right of caring for his child, and would condemn the poor little creature to oblivion, to misery, to death perhaps, provided this child bring disgrace on the bosom in which it was conceived. No, Gilbert, criminal as you may be, loving and base as you are, I forbid you to approach that window, or bestow one glance on that pavilion. I forbid you to pity her condition, to weaken your mental faculties by constantly brooding over the past. Live like the brutes, working and satisfying the wants of your body. Make use of the time, which glides away so rapidly, while you are wasting it in anger and revenge; and remember always that the only way of preserving your self-respect, of rising above these haughty aristocrats, is to be more noble than they."

Pale, trembling, longing to approach the window, still he obeyed the commands of his mind. He might be seen, little by little, slowly, as if his feet had taken root in this room, walking, a step at a time, to the staircase. At last he emerged on his way to seek Balsamo.

But, suddenly returning, —

"Fool!" said he, "miserable idiot that I am! I spoke, I planned vengeance, and what vengeance should I accomplish? Kill the woman? No, she would fall, only too happy to brand me with another crime. Disgrace her publicly? No, that would be cowardly. Is there no sensitive spot in this woman's soul where a prick of the needle would wound her as effectively as a sword-thrust? She needs to be humiliated; yes, for she is even prouder than I myself. But to humiliate her, — how? I have nothing, I am nobody; and doubtless she will soon disappear in some obscure hiding-place. Truly, my presence, sudden appearances, a look of scorn or of defiance, would punish her severely. I know that a mother without pity must be a heartless sister, and would send her brother to kill me. But what prevents my learning how to kill a man, as I learned how to reason or to write? What prevents me from throwing Philip on the ground, disarming him, and laughing in the face of the avenger, as well as in that of the injured person herself? No, no; this way would be absurd. He who does not reckon on the intervention of God or of chance relies in vain on his own prowess and ability. I, I alone, with my naked arm, with my reason purged from fancy, with strength of muscles given by nature and discretion, I will thwart the plans of these unhappy ones. What does Andrée wish? What does she possess? What weapons can she forge for her defence and my overthrow? Let me think."

Then, sitting on a projection of the wall, he concentrated all his mental forces.

"What pleases Andrée," said he, "I must detest. Must I destroy, then, all that I detest? Destroy? Oh no! My revenge must never drive me to evil; it must never compel me to use fire or sword. What, then, is left me? I have it. I must seek the cause of Andrée's superiority; I must see by what chain she will restrain at the same time my heart and my arms. Oh! never to see her more! Never to be seen by her! To pass within two steps of that woman when, smiling in her insolent beauty, she holds her child by the hand, — her child, who will never know me. Heaven and earth!"

And Gilbert punctuated this sentence with a furious blow of his fist against the wall, and a still more frightful oath, which arose to the sky.

"Her child!" That was the secret of all this perturbation. "She must never possess this child, whom she would bring up to curse the name of its father; she must learn, on the contrary, that this child will grow up to despise the name of Andrée. In a word, this child, whom she would never love, whom she would perhaps torture, for she has a bad heart, — this child, by whom I might be continually lashed, Andrée must never see, and she must experience on losing it the pangs of a lioness on being robbed of her young."

Gilbert arose, overflowing with wrath and fiendish joy.

"That is the way," said he, pointing his hand toward Andrée's pavilion. "You have condemned me to shame, to loneliness, to remorse, and to love; I will condemn you to unavailing sorrow, to loneliness, to shame, to terror, to hatred, without means of vengeance. You shall seek me; I shall have fled. You will cry for your child, if only to tear it to pieces when you shall have found it; but at least this furor of longing shall have been kindled in your soul by me; it will be a blade without a hilt that I shall have plunged into your heart. Yes, yes, the child, — I shall have the child! Not your child, as you called it, but mine, Gilbert's. Gilbert shall have his child! aristocrat through his mother. My child! my child!"

And gradually he became filled with wild transports of joy.

"Now," said he, "it is no longer a question of weak revenge or boorish laments; I have conceived a serious, complicated plot. I need no longer order myself not to look out at the pavilion; but I must concentrate all my powers, all my mind, in looking after the success of my undertaking. I will watch Andrée," said he, solemnly; going to the window, "day and night. You shall not make a movement that I shall not espy; you shall not utter a cry of grief that I shall not promise you a more bitter one; you shall not wear a smile that I shall not answer it by a malignant, insulting laugh. You are my prey, Andrée; a part of yourself is my prey. I am watching; I am watching."

Gilbert then went to the window and saw that the shutters of the pavilion had been opened; then Andrée's shadow glided across the curtains and the ceiling of the room, reflected doubtless from some mirror. Presently Philip, who had risen somewhat earlier, and had been at work in his own room, which was just back of Andrée's, came in and greeted his sister.

Gilbert observed that a very animated conversation was being carried on by them both. Of course they must be speaking of him, and of the events of the preceding night. Philip was pacing back and forth in evident perplexity. Perhaps Gilbert's advent had necessitated a change in their first plans; perhaps they would seek peace, obscurity and oblivion elsewhere. At this thought, Gilbert's eyes glowed so brightly that it seemed as if their light might penetrate beyond the pavilion, even into the middle of the earth.

But almost at the same time, a young waiting-maid entered by the garden gate, she bore some kind of a recommendation. Andrée received her favourably, for she at once took her little bundle of clothes into the room formerly occupied by Nicole. Then certain purchases of furniture, recently made, various household supplies and utensils, strengthened Gilbert's conviction of the fact that the brother and sister were going to remain quietly in this' house.

Philip examined carefully the lock of the garden door, and had some one else look at it. What more than anything else convinced Gilbert that they suspected him of having used a false key given him by Nicole, was the fact that the locksmith, in Philip's presence, changed the wards of the locks. This was the first joy amidst all these events that Gilbert had experienced. He smiled ironically.

"Poor people," murmured he, "they are not so dangerous. They have changed the lock, but they have not suspected that I had the daring to climb the wall. They have a very mean opinion of you, Gilbert. So much the better. Yes, proud Andrée," added he, "despite the locks on the doors, if I wish to enter your house I can do so. But at last I am the fortunate one; I despise you, and unless caprice—" He pirouetted on his heels in imitation of the *roués* of the court. "But no," continued he bitterly, "this is not worthy of me. I will have nothing more to do with you. . . . Sleep in peace. I have what is better than the possession of you,—I have the means of torturing you at my ease. Sleep!"

He left the window, and, after having glanced quickly over his clothes, hastened to see Balsamo.

## CHAPTER CLIII.

THE FIFTEENTH OF DECEMBER.

GILBERT did not have any difficulty in inducing Fritz to usher him into Balsamo's presence.

The count was lying on a sofa, like a rich and idle man, resting from the fatigue of a night's repose; at least that was what Gilbert thought, on seeing him thus extended at such an hour. Doubtless he had ordered his servant to admit Gilbert as soon as he should present an appearance, for he was not obliged to speak his name or say a word. At his entrance Balsamo leaped lightly from his couch, and closed his book, which he was holding opened without reading it.

"Oh, oh!" said he. "Here is a lad who is going to be married."

Gilbert made no answer.

"Good!" said the count, resuming his attitude of indifference, "you are happy and you are almost grateful. You have come to thank me. That is unnecessary. Keep that, Gilbert, for new occasions. Thanks are a kind of currency which please many people, particularly when accompanied by a smile. There, my friend, there."

There was something at once of such deep sadness and yet of gentleness in Balsamo's words and his manner of speaking them that they seemed to Gilbert a reproach, and at the same time a revelation.

"No," said he, "you are mistaken. I am not going to be married."

"Ah!" said the count, "what then? What has happened?"

"I have been rejected," replied Gilbert.

The count turned around suddenly.

"You did not understand, my friend."

"Not at all, monsieur. At least I do not believe so."

"Who has rejected you?"

"The young lady."

"Of course. Why did n't you speak to her father?"

"Because fate decreed otherwise."

"Ah! you are a fatalist?"

"I have no capacity for believing."

Balsamo frowned and looked at Gilbert with a kind of curiosity.

"Do not speak so of things of which you are ignorant," said he. "In men it is stupidity, in children presumption. I am perfectly willing for you to be proud, but not foolish; tell me you have no capacity for being an idiot, and I will agree with you. But to resume, what have you been doing?"

"Well, I wished, like the poets, to spend my time in dreaming, not doing. I wished to walk in the paths where I had enjoyed amorous reveries, and suddenly the reality came before me, all unprepared for it. The reality killed me on the spot."

"It serves you right, Gilbert. For you are like the scouts of an army, who have to march with a musket in their right hand, and a dark lantern in their left."

"In short, monsieur, I have failed. Mademoiselle Andrée has called me 'scoundrel,' 'assassin,' and wishes to have me killed."

"Good! But her child?"

"She told me that the child was hers, not mine."

"Then?"

"Then I went away."

"Ah!"

Gilbert raised his head.

"What would you have done?" said he.

"I do not yet know. Tell me what you wish to do."

"To punish her who has made me undergo such humiliations."

"Mere talk."

"No, monsieur, I have solemnly resolved."

"But — did she wrest your secret or your money from you?"

"My secret is my own. No one shall take it from me. The money is yours, and I bring it back to you."

And Gilbert opened his vest, and drew from it the thirty bank-notes, which he counted out one by one, on Balsamo's table. The count took them, folded them, all the time closely watching Gilbert, whose face did not betray the slightest emotion.

"He is honest, he is not avaricious. He has spirit, strength of character. He is a man," thought he.

"Now, Monsieur le Comte," said Gilbert, "I must render you an account of the two louis which you gave me."

"Do not overdo it," replied Balsamo; "it was right to give back the hundred thousand crowns, but it is childish to think of returning forty-eight francs."

"I did not wish to return them. I only desired to let you know how I spent them, that you might realise that I need more."

"That is a different thing. You ask then for — ?"

"I ask —"

"Why?"

"To do something of which you have just spoken."

"So be it. You wish to be avenged?"

"Nobly, I think."

"I do not doubt it; but cruelly, too?"

"Yes, cruelly."

"How much do you need?"

"I need twenty thousand francs."

"And you will not touch this young woman?" said he, expecting to check Gilbert by this question.

"I shall not touch her."

"Her brother?"

"No more than herself, nor her father."

"You will not calumniate her?"

"I shall never open my mouth to pronounce her name."

"Very well, I understand. But it amounts to the same thing in the end, to attack a woman with the sword, or to kill her by constant insults. You will oppress her by presenting yourself before her, by following her, by overwhelming her with smiles filled with insult and hatred."

"I have so little inclination to do the things you mention that I intend to ask you, in case I should wish to leave France, for the means of crossing the ocean, without expense to myself."

Balsamo cried out.

"Master Gilbert," said he, in a voice at once sad and affectionate, yet containing neither grief nor joy, "Master Gilbert, it seems to me you are not consistently playing your rôle of disinterestedness. You ask me for twenty thousand francs; yet it cannot possibly cost you a thousand for your passage."

"No, monsieur; for two reasons."

"What are they?"

"First, because the day I set sail I shall not have a farthing; for, hear me carefully, Monsieur le Comte, I do not ask this money for myself. I ask for it only in reparation of the fault which you helped me to commit."

"Ah, you are tenacious," said Balsamo, with compressed lips.

"Because I am right. I ask the money for reparation, I tell you, not for means of subsistence or consolation to myself. Not a sou of the twenty thousand francs shall go into my pocket; they have their destination."

"Your child, I see."

"My child, yes, monsieur," said Gilbert with a certain pride.

"But you, yourself?"

"I, I am strong, free, and intelligent. I can always get a living, I shall live."

"Oh! you will live! God never implanted so strong a desire for life in souls doomed to an early death. God clothes warmly the plants which must endure the winter's cold. He gives a steel armour to hearts which must endure hard blows. But, I believe, you have spoken of two motives for not keeping the thousand francs. The first, delicacy."

"The second, prudence. The day on which I shall leave France I shall be obliged to conceal myself. I cannot go to a port and find a captain, show him my money, as is commonly done I believe, and, in trying to sell myself, succeed in keeping my whereabout hidden."

"Then you think I can help you to disappear?"

"I know that you can."

"Who has told you so?"

"Oh! you have too many supernatural means at your disposal not to have also a whole storehouse of quite natural resources. A sorcerer is never so sure of himself that he has not some safe retreat."

"Gilbert," suddenly said Balsamo, stretching out his hand toward the young man, "you have an adventurous, bold spirit; you are made up of good and evil, like a woman; you are stoical and unaffectedly good. I will make a great man of you. Stay here, I assure you this hotel is a safe asylum; besides, I shall leave Europe in a few months, I will take you with me."

Gilbert listened. "In a few months," he said, "I would not answer no. But to-day I must say to you, 'Thanks, monsieur, your proposition is dazzling to an unfortunate man, still — I refuse it.'"

"For the vengeance of a moment is it worth while to risk a future of fifty years, perchance?"

"Monsieur, my fancy or my caprice is always worth more to me than anything else in the world at the time. Besides, apart from revenge, I have a duty to perform."

"Here are your twenty thousand francs," replied Balsamo, without the least hesitation.

Gilbert took the bank-notes, and, looking at his benefactor, said, "You give like a king."

"Oh! better, I hope," said Balsamo, "for I do not ask even to be remembered."

"Well, I am tenacious, as you just said, and, when my task shall be fulfilled, I will repay you this twenty thousand francs."

"How ? "

"In placing myself at your service for as many years as are required for a servant to repay his master twenty thousand francs."

"You are illogical this time, Gilbert. You said to me only a moment ago, ' I ask you for twenty thousand francs which you owe me.' "

"That is true, but you have gained my heart."

"I am very glad," said Balsamo without any expression of pleasure. "Then you will be mine if I will it ? "

"Yes."

"What can you do ? "

"Nothing ; but I can learn to do anything."

"That is true."

"But I would like to have in my pocket the means of leaving France in two hours, if it be necessary."

"Ah ! then you would leave my service ? "

"But I could return to you."

"And I could easily find you. Well let us make an end of it. Talking at such length tires me. Bring up the table."

"Here it is."

Balsamo took the papers, and read, half aloud, the following lines, on one of the papers covered with three signatures, or rather three strange names in cipher : —

"The 15th December, on the Havre, for Boston, P. J. L'Adonis."

"What do you think of America, Gilbert ? "

"That it is not France ; that it would be very pleasant

for me to go by sea, at a certain time, into some country that is not France."

" Well, — towards the 15th of December : is not that the certain time of which you spoke ? "

Gilbert counted on his fingers, reflectively.

" Exactly," said he.

Balsamo took a pen, and wrote two lines only on a piece of white paper : —

" Receive on L'Adonis a passenger.
                    " JOSEPH BALSAMO."

" But this paper is dangerous," said Gilbert, " and I, who seek a shelter, may find the Bastille."

" From having too much imagination, one becomes foolish," said Balsamo. " L'Adonis, my dear Gilbert, is a merchant ship in which I am the principal owner."

" Pardon me, Monsieur le Comte," said Gilbert, bowing, " I am, indeed, a poor fellow, whose head is easily turned sometimes, but never twice in succession ; excuse me, and believe in my gratitude."

" Go, friend,"

" Adieu, Monsieur le Comte."

" Au revoir," said Balsamo, turning away.

## CHAPTER CLIV.

### THE LAST AUDIENCE.

In November, that is to say, several months after the above events, Philip de Taverney emerged from the house where he and his sister dwelt, at an hour which for that time of year may be considered early.  Already all the small shops of the busy Parisians were displaying their wares, although it was still too dark to see without lights.  There were the hot cakes which the poor traders from the country districts ate with all the relish and avidity of epicures, trucks loaded with vegetables, carts full of fish and oysters going to market, and yet in all this bustle there was a certain quietness which the poor observed, in deference to the slumber of the rich.  Philip hastened to cross the thronged populous district in which he dwelt, and proceeded to the Champs Élysées, now completely deserted.

The leaves were turning red on the tops of the trees, already strewing the beaten paths of the Cours la Reine, and the bowling-greens, devoid of people at this early hour, were covered by a thick carpet of rustling leaves.

The young man was dressed like the rich middle class of Parisians, in a coat with long skirts, in breeches and silk stockings.  He carried a sword; his carefully arranged hair would indicate that he must have spent a long time before daybreak with the hair-dresser, that indispensable personage for the adornment of the age.

As Philip perceived the morning wind rumpling his hair and scattering the powder right and left, he hastened along, scowling with vexation, to ascertain if the public vehicles, usually standing around, were yet out.

He did not have to wait long. A carriage, faded, battered, and used up generally, drawn by a lean dun mare, came jolting along. The driver, with a watchful dejected expression of countenance, was looking to the right and the left among the trees for a passenger, as eagerly as Æneas watched the Tyrrhenian Sea for his ships.

On catching a glimpse of Philip, he whipped up his horse, and the carriage soon overtook its passenger.

"If you can manage to get me to Versailles at nine o'clock precisely, I will give you half a crown," said Philip.

In fact, Philip had made one of those morning appointments which the dauphiness had just begun to grant. Active and breaking loose from every rule of etiquette, the princess herself was in the habit of inspecting, every morning, the repairs she had started at Trianon; and when she encountered suppliants to whom she had promised an interview, she would quickly hear and dismiss them, with an affable air, not devoid of dignity, yet at the same time with haughtiness, if she perceived her manner was misconstrued. At first, Philip had planned to make his trip on foot, for he was reduced to the strictest economy; but his self-respect, or perhaps merely a feeling which a military man never loses, of wishing to present a creditable appearance in the eyes of a superior, had made him throw economy to the winds, that he might reach Versailles in a manner worthy of his rank.

Philip had decided to return on foot. Thus the patrician Philip and the plebeian Gilbert, starting from opposite extremes, had met on the same step of the ladder.

Philip saw again with aching heart all this fairy-like Versailles, where so many bright, cherished dreams had allured him with their promises. Sadly he looked around on the well known scenes, which now recalled only memories of his misfortune and shame. At nine o'clock, pre-

cisely, he loitered, armed with his letter of audience, in the
garden, near the pavilion. He perceived, about one hundred feet away, the dauphiness talking with the architect.
She was enveloped in marten furs, although the weather
was not yet very cold.

The young dauphiness, in a hat like those worn by Wat-
teau's ladies, was outlined against the evergreen hedges.
Sometimes the vibrations of her silvery, clear voice reached
Philip's ears, and awakened in him feelings that usually
dispel grief from wounded hearts.

Several people, to whom, as to Philip, hearings had
been promised, appeared one after another at the entrance
of the pavilion, in an antechamber of which a guard came
to seek them in order. Placed along the passages, every
time Marie Antoinette returned with Mique following her,
they received a word from her, and sometimes the special
favour of exchanging a few words, spoken privately.

Then the princess awaited the arrival of the next
visitor.

Philip was the last. He had already seen the eyes of
the dauphiness turned upon him, as if she sought to recognise him. He blushed, and tried to preserve a modest,
patient attitude.

The usher at last went up to him, and asked him if he
too would not like to be presented to the dauphiness.
Otherwise, she would quickly re-enter the house, and once
within would see no one.

Philip accordingly walked along. The dauphiness did
not once lose sight of him while he was traversing the
space of the one hundred feet that separated them, and he
chose the most favourable time for making his respectful
salutation.

The dauphiness turned toward the usher.

" The name of the person who just bowed to me ? "
said she.

The usher consulted his list : —

" Monsieur Philip de Taverney, madame," replied he.

"Indeed," said the princess.

And she looked longer and more inquisitively than before at the young man. Philip stood, slightly bowing.

"Good day, Monsieur de Taverney," said Marie Antoinette. "How is Mademoiselle Andrée?"

"Quite ill, madame," replied the young man, "but my sister will be pleased at your condescension in expressing an interest in her."

The dauphiness did not answer. She read in the sad, pale lines of Philip's face the record of much suffering. She could with difficulty recognise in this man, modestly arrayed in citizen's clothes, the fine young officer who had been the first to greet her when she stepped upon French soil.

"Monsieur Mique," said she, turning toward the architect, "we have already decided about the ornamentation of the ball-room; the grove near by is already settled. Pardon me for having kept you out in the cold so long."

It was a dismissal. Mique bowed and went away.

The dauphiness at the same time bowed to all the people who were waiting a little way apart, and they at once withdrew. Philip thought this gesture was intended for him as well as the others, and his heart began to sink, when the dauphiness, passing before him said, "You were telling me that your sister is ill?"

"If not exactly ill, madame," Philip hastily replied, "at least languid."

"Languid!" exclaimed the dauphiness, all interest, — "one so healthy as she?"

Philip bowed. The young princess looked at him in a penetrating way, which, were she a man, one would call an eagle's glance.

Then, after a pause, "Let me walk a little," said she, "the wind is cold."

She took a few steps. Philip stood still.

"What, will you not follow me?" said Marie Antoinette, turning round.

Philip made two bounds and was by her side.

"Why did you not acquaint me sooner of Andrée's condition? I was so interested in her welfare."

"Alas!" said Philip, "your Highness has just spoken the word. Your Highness was interested in my sister; but now—"

"I am still interested, monsieur. Yet it seems to me she left my service too soon."

"Necessity, madame," said Philip, in a low voice.

"What! it is a frightful expression. Necessity! Explain what you mean, monsieur."

Philip made no answer.

"Doctor Louis," continued the dauphiness, "told me that the air of Versailles was detrimental to Mademoiselle de Taverney's health; that staying in her home at Taverney would re-establish it once more. That is all I have been told; in fact, your sister only called once on me before her departure. She was pale; she was sad; I must say that she evinced much devotion to me in that last interview, for she wept freely."

"Sincere tears, madame," said Philip, whose own heart was beating violently; "their source is not yet exhausted."

"It seemed to me," pursued the princess, "that your father might have compelled his daughter to come to the court, and that doubtless this child longed for her country home; some attachment—"

"Madame," Philip hastened to reply, "my sister longs for your Highness only."

"And she suffers. A strange malady, that the country air should alleviate, and yet it only increases it."

"I will no longer deceive your Highness," said Philip. "My sister's illness is a deep grief, which borders on despair. Mademoiselle de Taverney loves no one in the world except your Highness and myself; but she is beginning to prefer Divine love to all earthly affections, and it is in regard to this desire of my sister that I have entreated an interview with you."

The dauphiness raised her head.

"She wishes to enter the religious life, does she not?"

"Yes, madame."

"And would you, who love her so dearly, allow that?"

"I believe I rightly understand her situation, madame, and I myself advise her to adopt this course. Yet I love my sister too much to make this advice seem suspicious, or to be accused of avarice; and the world at large will not view my conduct in this light. I should gain nothing by having Andrée retire to a convent, for we neither of us possess anything."

The dauphiness reflected, stealthily observing Philip: —

"That is what I just said, monsieur, when you failed to grasp my meaning. You are not rich?"

"Your Highness!"

"No false shame, monsieur; we are considering this poor girl's welfare. Answer me sincerely, like the truthful man I am sure you are."

With shining, honest eyes, Philip met the gaze of the dauphiness, and did not cringe.

"I will answer, madame," said he.

"Well, does necessity compel your sister to withdraw from the world? Let her speak. Good God! How unfortunate princes are! God has given them a heart full of sympathy for the unhappy, but he has denied them the clairvoyant power of divining misfortune that is hidden behind a veil of discretion. Answer, then, frankly. Is it necessity?"

"No, madame," replied Philip firmly; "no, it is not. Nevertheless, my sister wishes to enter the convent of Saint-Denis, and we possess only a third of the entrance money."

"The entrance money is sixty thousand francs," exclaimed the princess, "and you have only twenty thousand?"

"Scarcely that, madame; but we know that your Highness can, by a single word, without opening your purse, cause them to admit one of your *protégées*."

"Truly, I can do so."

"That, then, is the only favour which I dare ask of your Highness, unless you have promised to intercede for some one with Madame Louise de France."

"Colonel, you surprise me strangely," said Marie Antoinette. "To think of there being such unhappiness near me, and I so unconscious of it! Ah, colonel, it is not right!"

"I am not colonel, madame," replied Philip; "I am your Royal Highness's devoted servant."

"Not colonel, you say? Since when?"

"I have never been one, madame."

"The king promised you a regiment in my presence."

"The appointment of which has not been consummated."

"But you had a rank —"

"Which I have given up, having fallen into disfavour with the king."

"Why?"

"I do not know."

"Oh!" said the dauphiness, deeply moved. "Oh the court!"

Then Philip smiled sadly.

"You are an angel from heaven, madame," said he; "and I regret that I do not serve the house of France, that I might have an opportunity of dying for you."

Such a bright, shining light gleamed from the eyes of the dauphiness, that Philip buried his face in his hands. The princess made no effort to console him, or to banish the thought that possessed him at that moment.

Silent, and breathing heavily, she tore to pieces some Bengal roses, plucked from their stem by her restless, nervous hand.

Philip controlled himself.

"Pardon me, madame," said he.

Marie Antoinette made no reply to these words.

"Your sister shall enter Saint-Denis to-morrow if she wishes," she said, with feverish rapidity. "And you, in a month you shall be at the head of a regiment; I wish it."

"Madame," replied Philip, "will you crown your kindness by hearing my final explanations? My sister will accept the kindness of your Royal Highness; I must refuse it."

" You refuse it?"

"Yes, madame; I have received an insult from the court. The enemies who have inflicted it upon me would only find a way of wounding me still more should they see me thus elevated."

"What! under my protection?"

"Rather because of your gracious protection, madame," said Philip, firmly.

"It is true," murmured the princess, turning pale.

"And then, madame — No, I forget, I forget, while I am speaking to you, that there is no longer any happiness on earth for me; I forget that, having gone back into the dark, I must remain there. In the dark a courageous man prays and remembers."

Philip pronounced these words in a way that made the dauphiness tremble.

"A day will come," said she, "when I can say with impunity what now I can only think. Monsieur, your sister can enter Saint-Denis whenever she pleases."

"Thanks, madame, thanks!"

"As to you, I wish you would ask something of me."

"But, madame —"

"I wish it."

Philip saw the gloved hand of the princess lowered toward him. This hand remained held out, as if in expectation; it may have·expressed only a demand. The young man knelt, took the hand, and slowly, with palpitating heart, pressed it to his lips.

"Ask, come, ask!" said the dauphiness, so moved that she did not draw back her hand.

Philip bowed his head; a flood of bitter thoughts engulfed him, like a ship in a storm. He remained some seconds still and motionless. Then, looking up, pale, and with flashing eyes, —

"A passport to leave France," he said, "the day my sister enters Saint-Denis."

The dauphiness drew back as if terrified; then, seeing all the grief, which doubtless she comprehended, which perhaps she shared, she could only answer by these almost unintelligible words: —

"Very well."

And she vanished in a cypress path, the only one that had preserved its never-falling leaves, a mantle of the tomb.

## CHAPTER CLV.

### THE CHILD WITHOUT A FATHER.

THE day of pain, the day of shame, drew near. Andrée, despite the more and more frequent visits of the good Doctor Louis, despite Philip's tender care and sympathy, grew sad from hour to hour, like the condemned, as their last hour approaches. Her unhappy brother sometimes found her dreamy and trembling. Her eyes were dry; for whole days at a time she would not speak a word; then, suddenly, she would start up, walk rapidly across her room several times, trying, like Dido, to escape herself, — that is to say, to escape the sorrow that was killing her.

At last, one evening, seeing her paler, more restless, more nervous than usual, Philip sent for the doctor to come that very night. It was the 29th of November. Philip had succeeded in keeping Andrée up until a late hour; he had conversed with her on the saddest, most personal topics, — those which the young girl dreaded, as a wounded man dreads the touch of a harsh, heavy hand that would hurt him. He was sitting near the fire: the servant, on going to Versailles for the doctor, had forgotten to close the shutters, so that the reflection of the light, and even of the fire, softly illuminated the carpet of snow thrown on the gravel of the garden by the first winter frosts.

Philip waited until his sister seemed composed, then he said, without any preamble, —

"Dear sister, have you taken your final resolution?"

"On what subject?" said Andrée, with a sad sigh.

"On the subject of your child, sister."

Andrée trembled.

"The time is drawing near," said Philip.

"My God!"

"And I should not be surprised if to-morrow —"

"To-morrow?"

"To-day even, dear sister."

Andrée became so pale, that Philip, alarmed, seized and kissed her hand.

Andrée at once resumed the conversation.

"Brother," said she, "I shall not treat you with the hypocrisy of base souls. Expectation of good is confused in my mind with that of evil. Since I have lost confidence in the good, I cannot discern the bad. So judge me as you would judge a foolish person; perhaps you will prefer to take the philosophy which I am going to expound to you, seriously. It is, I give you my oath, the complete expression of the sentiments which I have gathered from my experience."

"Whatever you may say, Andrée, whatever you may do, you will always be to me the woman I love and respect above all others."

"Thanks, my only friend. I am bold enough to say that I am not unworthy of your promise. I am a mother, but it is God's will — at least, so I believe," added she, blushing — "that maternity should be in a creature analogous to fructification in a plant. The fruit comes only after the flower. In the flowering, the plant is made ready, — transformed; for flowering, it seems to me, is love."

"You are right, Andrée."

"For myself," replied the young girl, quickly, " I have experienced neither preparation nor transformation. I am an anomaly; I have not loved; I have not desired; my heart and my mind are those of a maiden, as is my body. And yet, sad prodigy! what I have not wished, what I have not even dreamed of, God sends to me,—He who never gave fruit to a tree created sterile. What longings, instincts, have I in that direction? What resources even? The mother, even in the pain of childbirth, knows and rejoices in her lot. I,—I know nothing about it; I tremble even in thinking of it; I am approaching this last day in the same way in which I would draw near the scaffold. Philip, I am accursed!"

"Andrée, my sister."

"Philip," replied she, with inexpressible vehemence, "do I not well perceive that I hate this child? Oh, yes, I hate it! I shall remember all my life, if I live, Philip, the day when I first felt this mortal enemy I am bearing stir within me; I shudder when I recall the movement, so sweet to mothers, of this little innocent creature, and how it kindled in my blood a fever of rage, and called curses to my lips, until then so pure. Philip, I am a wicked mother; I am accursed!"

"In the name of Heaven, good Andrée, be calm! Let not your mind inflame your heart. This child is a part of yourself; I love it, for it is yours."

"You love it!" exclaimed she, frenzied and livid. "You dare tell me that you love my dishonour and your own! You dare declare to me that you love this souvenir of a crime, this emblem of a cowardly rascal! Well, Philip, I have expressed my thoughts. I am not cowardly, I am not hypocritical. I hate the child because it is not my child, and I have not so considered it. I execrate it, because it will perhaps resemble its father. Its father! Oh! I shall die some day in speaking that hateful word! My God!" said she, throwing herself on her knees on the floor, "I cannot kill this child at birth, for you have made it breathe. I could not kill myself while I was bearing it, for you have forbidden suicide as well as murder. But, I pray you, I beseech you, I entreat you, if you are just, if you pity the wretched, if you have not decreed that I should die of despair, after having lived in opprobrium and in tears, my God, take this child back again! My God, take this child's life! My God, deliver me, avenge me!"

Terrible in rage, and supreme in her agitation, she beat her forehead against the marble chimney-piece, despite the efforts of Philip, who held her in his arms.

Suddenly the door opened; the servant ushered in the doctor, who took in the situation at a glance.

"Madame," said he, with the tranquillising effect which a doctor always imposes, "madame, do not add to your approaching pains. You," said he to the servant, "prepare the things of which I spoke to you as we drove along; you," said he to Philip, "be more reasonable than madame, and instead of sharing her fears and weaknesses, join your remonstrances to mine."

Andrée arose almost ashamed. Philip put her in an easy-chair.

The patient then turned red, and threw herself back in the chair in a convulsion of pain. Her clinched hands clutched the fringe on her chair, and the first cry issued from her violet lips.

"This anger, this fall, this excitement, have all hastened the crisis. Retire to your room, Monsieur de Taverney, and courage!"

Philip, his heart beating wildly, rushed toward Andrée, who had heard, who was trembling, and who, springing up despite her pain, hung by both arms to her brother's neck. She embraced him wildly, kissed his cold cheek, and said to him, in a low voice, —

"Adieu! adieu! adieu!"

"Doctor! doctor!" exclaimed Philip, desperately, "do you hear?"

Louis separated the two unhappy ones with gentle firmness, replaced Andrée in the arm-chair, led Philip into his room, locked the door which led into Andrée's room; then, drawing the curtains, and closing the doors, he thus shrouded the scene which was to take place between the physician and the woman, — between God and both.

At three o'clock in the morning, the doctor opened the door, behind which Philip was weeping and imploring.

"Your sister has a son," he said.

Philip clasped his hands.

"Do not go in," said the doctor; "she is sleeping."

"She is sleeping!  Oh doctor, is it really true that she is asleep?"

"If it were otherwise, monsieur, I should say to you, 'Your sister has brought forth a son, but this son has lost his mother!'  Besides, look!"

Philip craned his neck.

"Hear her breathing."

"Yes, yes, yes!" cried Philip, embracing the doctor.

"Now, you know we have engaged a nurse.  As I passed the Point du Jour, where she lives, I stopped and warned her to hold herself in readiness.  But you only can conduct her here; you only must be seen.  Take advantage of the invalid's slumber, and go in the carriage that brought me here."

"But you, doctor? you?"

"I?  I have a very sick patient in the Place Royale, — a case of pleurisy.  I must spend to-night by his bed, that I may watch the workings and the result of my medicines."

"The cold, doctor?"

"I have my shawl."

"The town is not very safe."

"Twenty times, in as many years, I have been stopped in the night; I have always answered, 'Friend, I am a doctor, and I am on my way to a patient.  Do you wish my cloak?  Take it; but do not kill me, for without me my patient would die.'  And see, monsieur, this cloak has had twenty years of service.  The thieves have always left me."

"Good, doctor.  To-morrow, then?"

"I will be here to-morrow at eight o'clock.  Adieu."

The doctor instructed the servant to watch the invalid carefully, and told her what to do for her.  He wished the

child to be placed beside its mother.   Philip begged him
to remove it, recalling his sister's last words.

Louis then himself put the child into the waiting-maid's
room, and then departed by way of the Rue Montorgueil,
while the carriage bore Philip in the direction of Roule.

The maid slept in the arm-chair, near her mistress.

# CHAPTER CLVI.

## THE ABDUCTION.

In the intervals of that recuperative slumber which always follows great prostration, the soul seems to gain a double victory over the body; the power of appreciating the comfort of the situation, and the power of watching over the weary body overcome by a death-like exhaustion.

Andrée, restored to life and consciousness, opened her eyes and saw her maid near her sleeping. She heard the joyful crackling of the fire, and wondered at the restful silence of the room, in which everything seemed to partake of the repose she herself was enjoying. She heard and saw as in a dream, and at the same time realized that she was awake. She luxuriated in this gentle tranquillity, and collected her ideas slowly one by one, as if she feared the return of complete realisation of the situation.

Suddenly, a weak, faint cry, far away apparently, reached her ear, through the thickness of the partition. This sound produced anew in Andrée all the tremblings which she had so often experienced. All the hatred which had so long disturbed her tranquillity, and had banished her natural sweetness of character, returned suddenly as a shock causes commotion in the liquid of vases where dregs are quietly lying, and the limpid water becomes clouded. From this moment sleep and repose fled from Andrée. She remembered; she was filled with hatred. But the force of sensations is usually proportioned to the physical strength of the body. Andrée no longer felt the energy which had sustained her in her interview with Philip.

The infant's cry seemed to her first a grief, then an annoyance. She began to question Philip's natural delicacy, which had prompted him to remove the child, until it seemed to her that it was positively a cruel thing for him to do. The thought of the ill-will we bear toward a person is not as repulsive to us as the sight of it when revealed to our vision. Andrée, who had loathed this child while invisible, who had even longed for its death, was actually hurt by its unhappy cries. "He is suffering," she thought.

Then she began to reason with herself: "Why should I care for its sufferings, — I, the most unfortunate of human beings?"

The child uttered a cry somewhat louder and more plaintive.

Then Andrée perceived that its voice seemed to awaken an answering chord in her soul, and felt her heart drawn as by an invisible cord toward the poor forsaken little being. She now at last realised that of which before she had vaguely felt the want. Nature had achieved one of its purposes.

Physical suffering, that powerful bond, had connected the mother's heart with the slightest movement of the child.

"It shall not be," thought Andrée, "that this poor orphan's cry shall evoke the wrath of Heaven against me. God has given his tiniest creatures, hardly born, the most eloquent of voices. One may kill them, that is, put them out of suffering, but one has no right to inflict pain upon them. Were such the case, God would never have allowed them to cry so pitifully."

Andrée raised her head and tried to call the maid. But the robust peasant could not be aroused by her weak voice; already the baby had stopped crying. "Doubtless," thought Andrée, "the nurse has come. I heard the outer door open. Yes, some one is walking about in the next room, — and the little thing is no longer crying. An unknown protection is already encompassing it and reassures its imperfect intelli-

gence. Oh! should not the mother take care of her child?
For a few crowns, the child born of my body, will find
a mother, and by and by, when it will pass by me, its
mother, who have suffered so much for it, who have given
it life from my life, and will not even look at me and will
say 'Mother!' to a hireling, more generous in her venal
love than I in my just resentment. It shall not be. I
have suffered, I have paid for the privilege of looking this
little being in the face, I have a right to make it love me
for my care, respect me for my sacrifice and my sorrows."

She made a more determined effort, summoned all her
strength, and called, "Marguerite! Marguerite!"

The maid slowly awoke, without moving in her chair,
where she lay still heavy with sleep.

"Do you hear me?" said Andrée.

"Yes, madame, yes," said Marguerite, regaining her wits.
And she drew near the bed.

"Does madame wish to drink?"

"No."

"Madame wishes to know the time?"

"No — no," her eyes never once leaving the door that
led into the next room.

"Ah! I understand. Madame wishes to know whether
her brother has returned?"

Andrée seemed to struggle against her desire, with all
the weakness of a haughty spirit and all the strength of
a warm, noble heart.

"I wish," uttered she slowly, "I wish — Open that door,
Marguerite."

"Yes, madame. How cold it is out there! The wind
— what a draught, madame!"

In fact, the wind rushed into Andrée's chamber with
such violence that it blew the flame of the candle and of
the night lamp.

"It is the nurse, who must have left a door or a window
open. Look, Marguerite, look! That — baby must be
cold."

Marguerite turned toward the next room.

" I will cover it," she said.

" No, — no,"murmured Andrée in a weak, broken voice,
" bring it to me."

Marguerite stopped in the middle of the room.

"Madame," said she gently, "Monsieur Philip was very
particular about having the child left in there, — for fear,
doubtless, of vexing madame, or of causing her some
emotion."

" Bring me my baby! " cried the young mother, with
heart-broken vehemence ; for her eyes, which had been dry
even in her acutest suffering, now were overflowing with
tears, which must have brought loving smiles to the faces
of the angels in heaven, who watch over little children.

Marguerite hastened into the room.   As soon as she had
gone out, Andrée buried her face in her hands.

The maid re-entered immediately, a blank look on her face.

" Well ? " said Andrée.

" Well — madame — has any one been here ? "

" What — any one, who ? "

"Madame, the baby is not there."

"Indeed, I just heard a noise," said Andrée, " of footsteps.   The nurse must have come while you were asleep.
She did not wish to awaken you.   But where is my
brother.   Look in his room."

Marguerite ran to Philip's chamber.   " No one ! "

" That is strange," said Andrée, her heart beating painfully ; " would he so soon have gone out without seeking
me ? "

" Ah ! madame ! " cried the maid, suddenly.

"What is it ? "

" The street door has just been opened.   Monsieur Philip
has come back.   Come in, monsieur, come in."

Philip had truly returned.   Behind him, a country-
woman, enveloped in a shawl of striped wool, was smiling
the complacent smile with which the hireling always greets
his patron.

"Sister, sister, I am here," said Philip, coming into the room.

"Good brother. What trouble, what annoyance, I cause you. Ah! here is the nurse. I was afraid she had left."

"Left! she has only just arrived."

"She has come back, you mean? No, I heard her just now, softly as she stepped."

"I do not know what you mean, sister. No one — "

"Oh! I thank you, Philip," said Andrée, drawing him to her, and accenting every one of her words. "I thank you for having understood me so well, that you did not wish to have this child carried off until I had seen it, caressed it. Philip, you knew my heart. Yes, yes, do not worry, I shall love my child."

Philip seized Andrée's hand and covered it with kisses.

"Tell the nurse to bring it here," added the young mother.

"But, monsieur," said the maid, "you know the child is not there."

"What? What are you saying?" said Philip.

Andrée looked at her brother in alarm.

The young man rushed to the maid's couch, hunted through it, and, finding nothing, uttered an alarmed cry.

Andrée watched him in the mirror; she saw him turn pale, his arms falling helplessly; she partially comprehended the truth, and, echoing his cry, she fell back unconscious on her pillow. Philip forgot himself in this new misfortune, this added grief. He summoned all his courage, and by dint of caresses, comfortings, and tears he recalled Andrée to life.

"My baby," murmured Andrée, "my baby!"

"We must save the mother," said Philip to himself. "Sister, my good sister, how foolish we are all of us! We forget that the good doctor has taken it away."

"The doctor!" cried Andrée, with the pain of doubt and the joy of hope.

"Yes, yes, we are losing our wits."

"Philip, you swear to me?"

"Dear sister, you have as good sense as I. Otherwise, how could the child have disappeared?"

And he forced a laugh, which deceived both nurse and maid.

Andrée recovered her spirits.

"Yet I heard —" said she.

"What?"

"Steps."

Philip shuddered.

"Impossible! You were sleeping."

"No, no, I was wide awake. I heard! I heard!"

"Well, you heard the kind doctor, who, fearing for the child's welfare, came back after I had gone and decided to take it away himself. Besides, he spoke to me about it."

"You are trying to reassure me."

"Why should I not reassure you? It is very simple."

"But then, I," objected the nurse, "what am I to do here?"

"Very true. The doctor is waiting at your house for you."

"Oh!"

"Go to him, then. You see this Marguerite slept so soundly that she either did not hear what the doctor said to her, or he had nothing to tell her."

Andrée fell back as calm as she could be after this frightful shock. Philip dismissed the nurse, and gave some instructions to the maid. Then, taking a light, he carefully examined the door of the next room, found the door of the garden open, saw foot-prints on the snow. He tracked them to the garden gate, where they were obliterated.

"A man's steps," said he. "The child has been abducted. Woe! Woe!"

## CHAPTER CLVII.

### THE VILLAGE OF HARAMONT.

THESE footprints on the snow were Gilbert's, who, since his last interview with Balsamo, had been fulfilling his task of watching and planning his revenge.

He had spared no pains. He had succeeded, by dint of pleasant words and little acts of kindness, in winning the affection of Madame Rousseau herself. His plan was simple. Of the thirty sous a day which Rousseau allowed his copyist, he had set aside a franc three times a week, which he spent in buying presents for Thérèse.

Sometimes a ribbon for her bonnet, sometimes a delicacy for the table, or a bottle of wine. The good woman, susceptible to anything that appealed to her taste or to her petty pride, was pleased with the praise at table that Gilbert bestowed on her culinary achievements.

For the Genevan philosopher had succeeded in gaining admittance for his young *protégé* to the family table, and during the last two months Gilbert, thus favoured, had added two louis to the treasure that reposed under his mattress, beside Balsamo's twenty thousand francs.

But what a life! What adherence to the line of conduct he had drawn for himself! Rising at daybreak, Gilbert would begin to discover for himself Andrée's condition, with infallible eye, that he might perceive the slightest change that would take place in the sober, regular life of the recluse. Nothing escaped his attention; neither the gravel of the garden walks on which his piercing sight measured the imprints of Andrée's foot, nor the folds of

the curtains, more or less carefully drawn, the openings
of which indicated to Gilbert Andrée's state of mind; for
on her sad days she would deprive herself even of the
light of day. In this way Gilbert knew what was taking
place in her heart and in her house.

He had likewise found a correct solution for all Philip's
movements; and, reckoning as he knew how to do, without error either as to the reason of his going out or his
object in coming back.

He even went so far as to follow Philip one evening
when the latter was on his way to Versailles to seek Doctor
Louis. This visit to Versailles had rather perplexed the
vigilant Gilbert. But when he saw the doctor two days
afterward secretly crossing the garden in the Rue Coq-
Héron, he understood that which had been a mystery to
him the preceding evening.

Gilbert had computed the time, and was aware of the
fact that the moment for the realisation of all his hopes
was fast approaching. Moreover, he had taken all the
precautions necessary for the successful fulfilment of an
enterprise surrounded by difficulties. This was his plan
of action.

The two louis would serve for the hiring of a cabriolet
with two horses, in the Faubourg Saint-Denis. This
carriage must be in readiness any day when it should be
wanted.

In addition, Gilbert had explored the suburbs of Paris in a
vacation of three or four days which he had taken. He had
visited a little town of Soissonnais, lying eighteen leagues
from Paris, and surrounded by a forest. This little town
was called Villers-Cotterets. Once there he had sought
out the only notary in the place, called Maître Niquet.

Gilbert presented himself to him as the son of a great
nobleman's steward. This nobleman, wishing to do a kindness to the child of one of his peasants, had intrusted
Gilbert with the commission of finding a nurse for it.

In all probability the nobleman's generosity would not

be confined to three months of nursing, and he would deposit, in addition, into Maître Niquet's own hand a certain sum for the child.

Then Maître Niquet, who had three fine sons of his own, had pointed out to him in a little village called Haramont, bordering on Villers-Cotterets, the daughter of the woman who had nursed his three sons; who, after having been legitimately married in his office, was continuing in her mother's occupation. This good woman was named Madeleine Pitou, and herself rejoiced in a son four years old, who seemed a very healthy lad. Besides, she had recently been confined, and consequently would be ready for Gilbert any day he should be pleased to bring or have the child sent to her.

After these arrangements had all been completed, Gilbert, with his usual punctuality, returned to Paris two hours before the expiration of his vacation. Now it may be asked why Gilbert had chosen the little village of Villers-Cotterets in preference to all the other suburbs.

In this selection, as in many others, Gilbert had been guided by Rousseau. Rousseau had one day spoken of the forest of Villers-Cotterets as one of the richest in vegetation in the world, and had added that in the deepest centres of its luxuriance three or four villages were hidden. In fact, it would be impossible for Gilbert's child to be discovered in one of these villages.

Above all, Haramont had struck Rousseau's fancy, — Rousseau, the misanthrope, the solitary, the hermit, who burst out every few moments in the following exclamations : —

"Haramont is the end of the world; Haramont is a desert. One could live and die there like a bird; on a branch while he is yet alive, under its leaves when he is dead."

Gilbert had even heard the philosopher describe the interior of a cottage, and with the fire of a genius recount in glowing terms every minutest detail, from the smile on the nurse's face to the bleating of the goat; from the appetis-

ing, thick vegetable soup to the perfume of the wild mul-
berry and the violet-coloured heather.

"I shall go there," said Gilbert to himself.  "My child
shall grow up under the shades where my master has
breathed his sighs and his aspirations." To Gilbert a
whim was an inexorable law, particularly when it assumed
the appearance of a moral necessity.

His joy was great, therefore, when Maître Niquet, fore-
stalling his desire, designated Haramont as the very place
for him.

On returning to Paris, Gilbert made inquiries concerning
the cabriolet.  He found one that was not handsome, but
it was in good repair, which was all that was necessary.
The horses were of heavy build; the driver was a dull fellow from the stables.  Gilbert was very anxious to attain
his end, without awakening any suspicion.  His story to
Maître Niquet had been received in good faith.  In fact, he
presented a suitable appearance in his new clothes for the
son of a steward of a fine establishment, or the valet in
disguise of a duke or peer.  His proposition awakened
no suspicion in the mind of the owner of the cabriolet.
At that time, confidences were often exchanged between
gentlemen and the people.  Money was confidentially received, and no embarrassing questions were asked.

Besides, at that time two louis were equal to four in
these days, and four louis will always insure the success
of an undertaking of this nature.

The proprietor engaged, therefore, to have his cabriolet
in readiness for Gilbert any time, at two hours' notice in
advance.

This enterprise possessed for the young man all the
attractions lent by philosophers and poets — two beings
very differently arrayed — to good actions and good resolu-
tions.  To take the child away from a cruel mother, that is
to say, to sow shame and disaster in an enemy's camp, and
then, with a change of front, to place it in a cottage among
peasants as virtuous as Rousseau had pictured them, and

to deposit on a child's cradle a large sum of money; to be regarded as a tutelary divinity by these poor people; to pass for a person of consequence; — that was what he wanted for the satisfaction of his pride, his resentment, his love for his neighbours, and his hatred for his enemies.

The fatal day at last arrived. It followed ten other days which Gilbert had passed in anguish, — ten nights which he had passed in sleeplessness. Despite the extreme cold, he slept with his window open; and every movement of Andrée or Philip was repeated in his ear, as the bell responds to the hand that draws its cord.

On the day of which we are speaking, he saw Andrée and Philip talking earnestly together by the fireplace. He saw the servant hastily depart for Versailles, without stopping to close the shutters. Immediately he ran and notified the owner of the cabriolet, standing in front of the stable all the time they were harnessing the horses, biting his hands and stamping on the pavement in his efforts to restrain his impatience. At last the postilion mounted his horse. Gilbert leaped into the cabriolet, which he ordered the man to stop at the corner of a street little frequented, near the market.

Then he returned to Rousseau's house, wrote a letter of farewell to the kind philosopher, of thanks to Thérèse, announcing that a little bequest called him to the South, that he would return, — all stated in a vague way. Then, his money in his pocket, a long knife in his sleeve, he was about to slide down the gutter-pipe into the garden, when an idea stopped him. The snow, — Gilbert, absorbed for the last three days, had not thought of that. Upon the snow his footmarks would be seen. These foot-marks would stop at Rousseau's house, would instigate an investigation on the part of Philip and Andrée, and, Gilbert's disappearance being coincident with the abduction, the whole secret would be discovered.

It was absolutely necessary, under these circumstances, to go around through the Rue Coq-Héron, enter by the little door of the garden, a thing he could easily do, as he had carried a pass-key to it around with him for the past month. From this entrance, a well-trodden path, on which his footsteps would make no impression, led to the house.

He did not lose a minute, and arrived at the house just as the carriage which brought Doctor Louis stopped before the main entrance of the little hotel.

Gilbert opened the door softly, saw no one, and hastened to hide in the corner of the pavilion near the summer house. It was a dreadful night. He could hear everything, — groans, cries of torture; he even heard the first wail of the son that was born to him.

Meanwhile, supported by the naked wall, he received without realising its presence all the snow which was falling thick and heavy from the clouded sky. His heart beat against the handle of his knife, which he pressed desperately against his breast. His eyes were fixed and bloodshot, flashing fire.

At last the Doctor went away; at last Philip exchanged his final words with the doctor.

Then Gilbert drew near the blind, leaving a track on the carpet of snow, now ankle deep, that crunched under his tread. He saw Andrée sleeping in her bed, Marguerite dozing in the arm-chair; and, looking for the child by its mother's side, he could not discover it.

He at once took in the situation, and went toward the entrance door; he opened it, not without a noise which alarmed him somewhat, and, penetrating even to the bed which had been Nicole's, he felt around until his icy fingers encountered the poor baby's face, and called forth the cries that Andrée had heard.

Then, wrapping the newly born child in a woollen blanket, he carried it off, leaving the door half open, lest, by attempting to close it, he should again make a noise.

A minute afterward, he had gained the street through the garden; he ran to seek his cabriolet, aroused the postilion, who had gone to sleep, and, drawing the curtain of the cab while the man was remounting, cried out, " Half a louis to you, if, in a quarter of an hour, we shall have passed the city limits."

The horses, sharpened for the ice, started off at a gallop.

## CHAPTER CLVIII.

### THE PITOU FAMILY.

ON the way, everything frightened Gilbert. The rumble of the carriages he met, or that passed his own, the soughing of the wind through the bare trees, seemed to his terrified imagination like an organised pursuit, or the cries of those from whom the child had been taken.

Yet nothing threatened him. The postilion bravely did his part, and the two horses arrived steaming at Dammartin, at the time Gilbert had arranged, that is, before the first streaks of the dawn.

Gilbert gave his half louis, changed horses and postilion, and resumed his journey. During all the first half of the drive, the child, carefully sheltered by its covering, and shielded by Gilbert himself, did not feel the cold nor utter a single cry. As soon as day dawned, seeing the country all around him, Gilbert felt more courageous, and, that he might drown the cries which the child was beginning to give forth, he started one of those endless songs such as he had often heard the huntsmen sing at Taverney on returning from the chase. The creaking of the axle-tree and the traces, the clatter of all the iron on the carriage, the sound of the bells on the horses, made a diabolical accompaniment to his song, which was increased by the postilion's breaking forth into the strains of a Bourbonnaise of rather a seditious character.

The result was that this last driver did not even suspect Gilbert of having a child with him. He stopped his horses at Villers-Cotterets, received the price already agreed upon, — a crown and six francs, — and Gilbert, taking his bundle, carefully wrapped in the folds of the covering, singing his song in the most serious manner possible, went rapidly away, jumped a ditch, and disappeared by a path covered with leaves that led to the little village of Haramont.

The weather had become very cold. The snow had ceased falling during the past few hours; the ground was hard, and bristling with underbrush and thorny bushes. Above could be descried the outlines of the trees of the forest, bare and gloomy, through whose branches the pale blue of the sky shone. The fresh air, the fragrance of the oaks, the icy pearls suspended from the ends of the branches, — all this freedom, this poetry, aroused the young man's lively imagination.

He walked rapidly and proudly through the little ravine, without once stumbling or looking around him; for in the midst of the clusters of trees he took for a landmark the steeple of the hamlet, and the blue smoke from the chimneys, which could be seen through the gray lattice-work of the branches. At the end of a short half-hour, he crossed a brook bordered with ivy and yellow cresses, and asked the children of a workman, at the first cottage he encountered, to guide him to Madeleine Pitou's house.

Silent and attentive, rather than stupid and lazy, like most peasants' children, the children rose, and, carefully studying the stranger's face, conducted him, holding each other's hands, to a somewhat large, well-built cottage, situated beside a brook that ran in front of most of the houses in the village. This brook was running merrily along, its limpid waters somewhat swollen from the early snow-storms. A wooden bridge — in other words, a plank — crossed the stream, and connected the road with the steps of earth leading to the house.

One of the children acting as guides bowed his head to Gilbert, indicating that they had reached the residence of Madeleine Pitou.

"There?" repeated Gilbert.

The child nodded his head without saying a word.

"Madeleine Pitou?" Gilbert again asked the child.

And, the latter having reiterated his former gesture of affirmation, Gilbert cleared the bridge and hastened to push open the cottage door, while the children, again joining hands, watched with all their might to see what this fine gentleman in brown coat and buckled shoes was going to do at Madeleine Pitou's house.

For the rest, Gilbert had seen no living soul in the village, except these children. Haramont was indeed the longed-for desert.

As soon as the door was opened, a sight full of charm for the world in general, and for a young philosopher in particular, met Gilbert's gaze.

A stout peasant woman was nursing a fine child a few months old, while kneeling in front of her another child — a vigorous boy of four or five years — was saying his prayers in a loud voice.

In a corner of the chimney-place, near a window, — or rather a hole cut in the wall and enclosed in glass, — another peasant woman, about thirty-five or thirty-six years of age, was spinning flax, her wheel on her right, a wooden stool under her feet, a large dog crouching by this stool.

The dog, perceiving Gilbert, barked in a hospitable and polite manner, just enough to show his vigilance.

Gilbert introduced the conversation by smiling at the nurse.

"Good Madame Madeleine," he said, "I greet you."

The peasant woman started.

"You know my name, monsieur?" she said.

"As you see; but do not let me interrupt you, I beg. Instead of one nursling that you have now, you will have two of them."

And he placed in the homely cradle of the country child the little city child he had brought.

"Oh, how pretty it is!" cried the peasant woman who was spinning.

"Yes, sister Angélique, very pretty," said Madeleine.

"Madame is your sister?" asked Gilbert, pointing to the spinner.

"My sister? Yes, monsieur," replied Madeleine, "my husband's sister."

"Yes, my aunt, Aunt Gélique," murmured the little fellow, in a low voice, who took part in the conversation without getting up from his knees.

"Be still, Ange; be still," said the mother. "You are interrupting monsieur."

"The proposition I am going to make to you, my good woman, is very simple. The child you see here is the son of one of my master's farmers, — a ruined farmer. My master, godfather to this child, wishes him to be brought up in the country, that he may become a good labourer, with good health, with good manners. Will you take care of this child?"

"But, monsieur —"

"He was born yesterday, and he has received no nourishment," interrupted Gilbert. "Besides, he is the nursling of whom the notary, Maître Niquet, of Villers-Cotterets, has already spoken to you."

Madeleine immediately snatched up the baby and gave him the breast with a generous impetuosity, which deeply touched Gilbert.

"I have not been deceived," he said. "You are a good woman. I intrust this child to your care, in my master's name; I see that he will be happy here, and I hope he will bring into this cottage a dream of happiness in exchange for what he receives here. How much did you receive per month for the children of Maître Niquet?"

"Twelve francs, monsieur. But Maître Niquet was rich, and he added a few francs occasionally for sugar and maintenance."

"Mother Madeleine," said Gilbert, proudly, "the child here will pay you twenty francs per month, which makes two hundred and forty francs per year."

"Jesus!" cried Madeleine. "Thanks, monsieur."

"Here is the first year's pay," said Gilbert, spreading upon the table ten bright louis, which made the women open their eyes in amazement, and over which little Pitou stretched a devastating hand.

"But, monsieur, if the child should not live?" timidly objected the nurse.

"It would be a great misfortune, — a misfortune that shall not occur," said Gilbert. "Here, then, is the agreed sum for the month's nursing; are you content?"

"Oh! yes, monsieur."

"Let us now agree upon an allowance for the other years."

"The child will remain with us?"

"Probably."

"In that case, monsieur, shall we be father and mother to it?"

Gilbert turned pale.

"Yes," said he, in a stifled voice.

"Then, monsieur, is the poor baby forsaken?"

Gilbert was not expecting such emotion,— such questions. Still, he resumed the conversation.

"I have not told you all," he said. "The poor father died of grief."

The two good women clasped their hands expressively.

"And the mother?" asked Angélique.

"Oh, the mother, the mother," replied Gilbert, breathing painfully, "no child, born or unborn, can depend on her."

They had reached this stage of the conversation, when the father Pitou came in from the fields, his demeanour calm and joyful. His was one of those honest, dull natures, full of gentleness and health, which Greuze has painted so truly. A few words explained to him the situation, or, at least, if he did not wholly understand it, his pride did not allow him to acknowledge the fact. Gilbert explained that the allowance of the child would be paid until he was fully grown, and able to support himself by the aid of his brain and his arms.

"So be it," said Pitou. "I believe we shall love this child, for he is very pretty."

"He, too," said Angélique to Madeleine, "he agrees with us in our opinion of the child."

"Then, I beg you, come with me to the notary, Maître Niquet; I will leave the necessary amount of money with him, that you may be satisfied, and the child may be happy."

"Immediately, monsieur," replied Pitou, the father.

And he arose.

Then Gilbert took leave of the kind women, and approached the crib in which the new arrival had been deposited, in place of the child of the family. He cast a sad glance on this cradle, and, for the first time looking in his son's face, perceived a marked resemblance to Andrée. This sight pierced his heart; he had to bury his nails into his flesh to keep back the tears which his wounded heart sent to his eyes.

He pressed a trembling, timid kiss on the cheek of the newly born child, and drew back trembling.

Father Pitou was already on the threshold, a stout stick in his hand, his best clothes on. Gilbert gave half a louis to the chubby Ange Pitou, who crawled between his legs, and the two women begged the honour of embracing him with the touching familiarity of country people.

This young father of eighteen had been weighed down by so many emotions, that a little more and he would have given way entirely. Pale, nervous, he began to lose control of himself.

"Let us leave," said he to Pitou.

Suddenly Madeleine cried, —

"Monsieur! Monsieur!"

"What is it?" said Gilbert.

"His name! his name! What shall we call him?"

"His name is Gilbert," said the young man, with manly pride.

## ˙CHAPTER CLIX.

### THE DEPARTURE.

THE business at the notary's was quickly despatched. Gilbert deposited in his name a sum of twenty thousand minus a few francs, designed to defray the expenses of educating and bringing up the child. He also reckoned on there being enough to start him in some business when he should arrive at manhood. Gilbert estimated the cost of educating and bringing up the child at five hundred francs a year, for a period of fifteen years. The rest of the money might be expended, either as a means in beginning business, or in purchasing some land for farming purposes.

Having thus looked after his child's welfare, Gilbert turned his attention to that of the people to whose care he was intrusting him; he wished to have his child present to the Pitous the sum of two thousand four hundred francs on his eighteenth birthday. Up to that time Maître Niquet was to give them only the stated sum of five hundred francs annually.

Maître Niquet was to receive the interest of the money in compensation for his guardianship.

Gilbert had a receipt legally drawn up by Niquet for the money, by Pitou for the child; Pitou having signed his signature regarding the money intrusted to Niquet, Niquet, on the other hand, witnessing to the fact that the child had been intrusted to Pitou. So speedily was all this accomplished, that about noonday Gilbert was ready to go, leaving Niquet lost in admiration of his business sagacity, and Pitou overwhelmed with joy at his rapidly acquired fortune.

On leaving the village of Haramont, Gilbert felt as if he had retired from the world. There was nothing left to him, either in the present or the future. He had left behind him his youth and its bright days free from care, when he had committed the act which might be considered criminal by men, and punished severely by God.

At the same time, confident in his own strength of mind and of body, Gilbert had courage enough to tear himself from the arms of Maître Niquet, who had conceived a great admiration and liking for him, and allured him by a thousand tempting promises.

But the mind is capricious; human nature is fickle. The more will power and spontaneity of action a man has, the more quickly he rushes from one enterprise to another, until suddenly he realises the leaps he has made, the distance he has travelled, and even the most courageous falter, and say to themselves, like Cæsar of old, "Have I acted wisely in crossing the Rubicon?"

Gilbert, finding himself on the edge of the forest, again gazed at the brown tops of the trees, which hid from his view all Haramont, except the steeple. This picture, so charming and peaceful, awoke in his breast sensations of sadness and of delight.

"Fool that I am," said he, "where am I going? Will not God in highest heaven turn away in wrath? What! I have an idea. A circumstance favours its execution. A man impelled by God to cause the evil I have done promised to make reparation for this evil, and to-day I am in possession of my child and of the treasure he gave me. With ten thousand francs — the other ten being set aside for my child — I can live as a happy farmer among these good villagers, in the bosom of this grand, bountiful nature. I can rest forever in the sweet happiness of work and of thought, forgetting the world, and making it forget me; I can — happy lot! — myself bring up this infant, and rejoice

in my own work. Why not? Are not all these good opportunities but compensations for my sufferings in the past?
Oh, yes, I can live thus; I can share in the division of
money with that child, beside bringing him up myself,
saving money that would otherwise be given to hirelings.
I can confess to Maître Niquet that I am his father. All
this is feasible."

And his heart slowly drank in a joy and hope such as he
had never before tasted in his happiest dreams. Suddenly,
the worm that nestled at the core of this delicious fruit
awoke and revealed its ugly head. It was remorse, it was
shame, it was misfortune.

"I cannot do it," said Gilbert, turning pale at the
thought, "I have stolen the child from that woman, as I
have stolen her honour. I have stolen money from that
man, in reparation of the evil. I have no right to reap
any benefits from it for myself. I have no right to protect this child, since I have deprived her of that privilege.
Either it belongs to both of us or to neither."

Upon uttering these words, painful as wounds, Gilbert
rose in despair; his face exhibited the saddest, most hei-
nous of passions. "So be it," said he, "so be it; I shall
suffer. Very well, everything and everybody shall fail me.
In place of sharing my goods, I have only evil to divide. Henceforth vengeance and unhappiness shall be my
heritage. Do not fear, Andrée, I will share it with you,
faithfully."

He turned toward the right, and, after a moment's reflection as to which way he should go, he plunged into the
woods, through which he walked all day, hoping to reach
Normandy, which he had supposed he might gain by a
four days' walk.

He had with him nine francs and a few sous. His bearing was honest, his face calm and peaceful. A book under
his arm gave him the appearance of a student returning
home to his father's house. He accustomed himself to
walking along the highway at night, and to sleeping by

day in the fields, under the sun's rays. Twice only, the wind disturbed him so much that he was obliged to enter a cottage, where, in a chair by the fireplace, he slept to his heart's content, without noticing the approach of night. He had always an excuse and a destination ready.

"I am going to Rouen," said he, " to my uncle's, and I came from Villers-Cotterets. I wished, like other young men, to make the journey on foot, for my own amusement."

No suspicion on the part of the countrymen ; the book always elicited respect. If Gilbert perceived any flitting doubt on some more compressed lips, he began to talk about his academy, where he was being educated, and the evil thoughts were at once dissipated.

For a week Gilbert lived thus like a countryman, spending ten sous a day and walking ten leagues. He at last reached Rouen, where he no longer had to ask his way.

The book he was carrying was a copy of " La Nouvelle Héloïse," richly bound. Rousseau had given it to him and written his name on a fly leaf. Gilbert, reduced to four francs ten sous, tore out this page, which he carefully preserved, and sold the book to a publisher for three francs. Three days after he beheld Havre in the distance, and caught a glimpse of the sea just as the sun was setting.

His shoes were in a condition not at all suitable for a young man jauntily attired in silk stockings ; but Gilbert had a bright thought. He sold his silk stockings, or rather exchanged them for a pair of shoes of irreproachable stoutness. As to their beauty, we will however say nothing about it.

This last night he spent in Harfleur, where he was lodged and boarded for sixteen sous. He ate oysters for the first time in his life. "A dish of the rich," said he, " for the poorest of men. Thus God does all things well, while man does only evil, as Rousseau has truly said."

At ten o'clock in the morning of the thirteenth of December, Gilbert entered Havre, and the first thing that caught his view was L'Adonis, a fine brig of three hundred tons, lying in a dock.

The pier was deserted. Gilbert boarded the ship by a gang plank. A cabin boy approached to question him.

"The captain ? " demanded Gilbert.

The boy pointed to the companion-way, and at the same time a voice from below shouted, " Have him come down."

Gilbert descended. He was conducted to a little room finished in mahogany and furnished with great simplicity.

A man of thirty, pale, nervous, with restless eyes, was reading a paper on the table of mahogany that matched the panels.

"What does monsieur wish ? " said he.

Gilbert indicated by a gesture that he wished the cabin boy sent away, and the latter immediately vanished.

"You are the captain of L'Adonis, monsieur ? " said Gilbert immediately.

" Yes, monsieur."

"Then this paper is addressed to you ? " And he handed the captain Balsamo's note.

Scarcely had he seen the hand-writing when he started up and said abruptly to Gilbert, " You too, so young ? Well ! well ! "

Gilbert merely bowed.

" You are going — ? " said he.

" To America."

" You leave — ? "

" When you yourself leave."

" Well, in a week then."

" What shall I do all this time, captain ? "

" Have you a passport ? "

" No."

"Then you must come on board to-night, after having walked all day outside the town, — in Sainte-Adresse, for instance. Speak to no one."

" I must eat. I have no more money."

"You shall dine here, you shall sup this evening."

"And after?"

"Once on board, you must not return to land again. You must stay here in hiding. You must leave without again looking at the sky. Once on the water, twenty leagues out to sea, you shall be as free as you will."

"Good."

"Do to-day whatever you have left to do."

"I have a letter to write."

"Write it."

"Where?"

"On that table. Here are pen, ink, and paper. The post-office is in the faubourg; the cabin boy will take you to it."

"Thanks, captain."

Gilbert, left to himself, wrote a short letter, with this superscription: —

"Mademoiselle Andrée de Taverney, Paris, Rue Coq-Héron, 9, — the first door beyond the Rue Plastrière."

Then he put the letter in his pocket, ate what the captain himself placed before him, followed the cabin boy, who conducted him to the post-office, where he mailed his letter.

All day long Gilbert watched the sea from the top of the cliffs. At night he returned. The captain was watching for him, and brought him on board the vessel.

## CHAPTER CLX.

### GILBERT'S LAST FAREWELL.

PHILIP had passed a dreadful night. Those foot-prints in the snow indicated without doubt that some one had entered the house and carried off the child. But whom should he accuse? There was no other indication of the offender.

Philip understood his father so well, that he at once implicated him in the transaction. Monsieur de Taverney believed Louis XV. to be the father of this child. He must, therefore, attach great value to keeping this living witness of the king's infidelity to Madame Dubarry. The baron must likewise believe that sooner or later Andrée would be restored to favour, and would purchase her future fortune at any price.

These reflections, based on the recent revelations of his father's character, consoled Philip somewhat, and he thought that very possibly, since he knew who had taken the child, he could compel them to surrender it.

He was on hand, therefore, at eight o'clock, to greet Doctor Louis, with whom he walked up and down the street for a long time relating the events of the past night. The doctor was a man of good judgment; he examined the marks in the garden, and, after reflection, agreed with Philip in his theory of the case.

"I know the baron well enough," said he, "to believe him capable of this evil deed. In the mean time cannot some other interest, even more immediate, have planned the abduction of this infant?"

"What interest, doctor?"

"That of its own father."

"Oh!" exclaimed Philip, "I did think of him for a moment, but the wretch cannot feed even himself. He is a mad visionary, now a fugitive, who must be afraid of my very shadow. Do not let us be deceived, monsieur. The miserable creature committed the crime on the provocation of the occasion; but now, far from wishing to vent my anger on him, although I hate him, the scoundrel, yet I believe I should avoid meeting him for fear of killing him. I think the remorse he is undergoing must be a severe punishment; I believe that hunger and exile will avenge me as effectively as my sword."

"Let us talk no more about it, monsieur," said the doctor.

"Only, will you be so kind, my dear good friend, as to consent to a last falsehood? For, above all else, Andrée must be reassured. Tell her that yesterday, feeling anxious about the child's health, you came back in the night and carried it to its nurse. It was the first fiction that occurred to my mind, and I invented it to allay her fears."

"I will tell her that; still, you will seek for the child?"

"I have a plan for finding it. I have decided to leave France; Andrée will enter the convent of Saint-Denis. Then I will seek Monsieur de Taverney. I will tell him that I know all; I will force him to reveal the hiding-place of the child. I will overcome his opposition, by threatening a public revelation, by threatening the intervention of madame the dauphiness."

"And what will you do with the child, if your sister is in the convent?"

"I will take it to some nurse that you shall recommend to me. Then to school, and when he shall be grown, I will take him with me, if he lives."

"And do you think that his mother will be willing either to give him over to you, or to abandon him herself?"

"In the future, Andrée will be guided by my wishes. She knows that I have asked and obtained the promise of madame the dauphiness to allow her to enter the convent. She would not háve me fail in respect to our protectress."

"I beg you, monsieur," said the doctor, "to come with me to the poor mother."

And they returned to Andrée, who, soothed by Philip's thoughtfulness, was sleeping sweetly.

Her first word was to question the doctor, who answered with smiling face.

After that, Andrée was blessed with the perfect calmness so necessary to the restoration of health, and convalesced so rapidly, that in ten days she was up and could walk in the conservatory, when the sun was shining upon the glass.

The very day of her first walk, Philip, who had been away for a few days, returned to the house in the Rue Coq-Héron with so solemn a face that the doctor, who happened to be there at the time, and who admitted him, felt a presentiment of a great misfortune.

"What is the matter?" asked he; "has your father refused to give up the child?"

"My father," said Philip, "has been seized by an attack of fever, which sent him to bed three days after he left Paris; and when I arrived he was very much prostrated. I mistook all his illness for a ruse, a subterfuge, for a proof even of his participation in the abduction. I insisted, I threatened. Monsieur de Taverney swore to me on the crucifix, that he understood nothing of what I meant."

"And you have returned with no tidings?"

"Yes, doctor."

"Convinced of the baron's veracity?"

"Almost convinced."

"More artful than you, he has not disclosed his secret."

"I threatened to interview the dauphiness, and the baron

turned pale. ' Destroy me if you will,' he said, ' dishonour your father and yourself; it will only be a wild piece of madness with no result. I do not know anything about it.' "

"As a result of which?"

"As a result of which, I return in despair."

At this moment Philip distinguished Andrée's voice calling, —

"Was that not Philip who came in?"

"Great God! here she is! What am I to tell her?"

"Silence!" said the doctor.

Andrée entered the room, and embraced the young man with a joyful tenderness that froze his heart.

"Well," said she, "whence do you come?"

"I have been to see Monsieur de Taverney, as I told you I was planning to do."

"Is the baron well?"

"Well? yes, Andrée; but I have made other visits. I have also interviewed several persons relative to your entrance to Saint-Denis. Thank God! everything now is ready; once safely there, you need think of your future only with calmness and security."

Andrée drew near her brother, sighing tenderly.

"Dear one," said she, "I no longer worry about my future. The future of my child is my only care, and I shall consecrate my life to the son God has given me. Such is my irrevocable resolution, since, now that I am once more strong, I no longer doubt my own powers. Living for my child, living in penury, working even if necessary, but never leaving him, day or night, such is my plan for the future. No more convent, no more selfishness. I belong to some one; God no longer needs me."

The doctor looked at Philip as if to say to him, "Well, did I not predict aright?"

"Sister," cried the young man, "sister, what do you say?"

"Do not blame me, Philip. It is no capricious wish of a

weak, empty woman. I will not trouble you; I will not impose anything on you."

"But — but, Andrée, I cannot stay in France; I must leave everything; I have no longer any fortune, or any future. I might consent to abandon you at the foot of an altar, but in the world, at work — Andrée, take care!"

"I have foreseen everything. I love you sincerely, Philip, but if you leave me I shall swallow my tears and seek refuge by my baby's cradle."

The doctor approached.

"This is sheer madness," he said.

"Ah, doctor, what would you have? To be a mother is intoxicating; but God has made me one. While my child needs me, I shall continue in this resolution."

Philip and the doctor exchanged a sudden glance.

"My child," said the doctor, "I do not claim to be an eloquent preacher, but I think I remember that God forbids us to make idols of those we love."

"Yes, sister," added Philip.

"God does not forbid a mother to love her child devotedly, I think, doctor?"

"Forgive me, my child; as philosopher, as physician, as preacher, I will try to penetrate the abyss of human passions with you. God has a moral, and at the same time a material, cause for all the commands He has given us. God forbids a mother's excessive love toward her child, because a child is such a fragile, delicate flower, subject to so many mishaps and sufferings, that to love it excessively is only to expose one's self to possible anguish."

"Doctor," murmured Andrée, "why are you saying such things to me? And you, Philip, why do you look at me with so much pity and such pallor?"

"Dear Andrée," interrupted the young man, "follow my loving advice. Your health is restored; enter the convent of Saint-Denis as soon as possible."

"I? I told you I would never leave my son."

"As long as he needed you," said the doctor, gently.

"My God!" cried Andrée, "what has happened?  Speak!
Something sad, — something cruel?"

"Take care," whispered the doctor to Philip; "she is
too weak for a sudden shock."

"Brother, you do not answer.  Explain yourself."

"Dear sister, you know on my journey I passed through
Point du Jour, where your son is being nursed."

"Yes.  Well?"

"Well, the child is a little ill."

"Ill? — the dear child!  Quick, Marguerite!  Marguerite, a carriage!  I will go and see my baby."

"Impossible!" cried the doctor.  "You are not able to
go out, or to get into a carriage."

"You told me this morning that it was quite possible;
you told me that to-morrow, on Philip's return, I might
go and see the little one."

"I thought you would be better."

"You were deceiving me?"

The doctor was silent.

"Marguerite," cried Andrée, "I will be obeyed!  A
carriage!"

"But you will die," said Philip.

"Well, let me die, then; I do not cling so closely to
life."

Marguerite waited, looking first at her mistress, then
the doctor, then Philip.

"What!  When I order!" cried Andrée, whose cheeks
were suddenly covered with a hectic flush.

"Dear sister!"

"I will not listen, and, if I am refused a carriage, I shall
go on foot."

"Andrée," suddenly said Philip, taking her in his arms,
"you shall not go; no, there is no need of your going
there."

"My child is dead!" said the young girl, coldly, letting
her arms fall on the side of the arm-chair to which the
doctor and Philip had guided her.

Philip answered only by kissing her cold, lifeless hands. Gradually Andrée lost her rigidity, her head fell on her bosom, and her tears flowed freely.

"It is God's will," said Philip; "we must submit to this new calamity. God, who is so great, so good; God, who has planned different things for you from what we have done; God, who doubtless thought the presence of this child, misinterpreted by others, would be an undeserved punishment for you."

"But why, then," murmured the poor mother, "why should God have made this innocent baby suffer?"

"God did not make it suffer, my child," said the physician. "It died the very night of its birth. Think of it only as a shadow, that came and then vanished."

"The cries that I heard?"

"Were its farewell to life."

Andrée hid her face in her hands, while the two men, their thoughts meeting in an eloquent look, congratulated each other on their pious lie.

Suddenly Marguerite entered, bearing a letter. This letter was addressed to Andrée. The superscription read: —

"Mademoiselle Andrée de Taverney, Paris, Rue Coq-Héron, 9, — the first door beyond the Rue Plastrière."

Philip showed it to the doctor over Andrée's head, who, no longer weeping, was still overwhelmed with grief.

"Who can have written this?" thought Philip. "No one knows her address, and it is not my father's handwriting."

"Here, Andrée," said Philip, "a letter for you."

Without reflecting, without resisting, without wondering, Andrée tore open the envelope, and, wiping her eyes, unfolded the paper to read it. But scarcely had she perused the first three lines of the letter when she cried aloud, and, rising like a mad woman, with terrible contortions of her arms and feet, fell like a statue into Marguerite's arms, who happened to be beside her.

Philip opened the letter and read: —

"On the Sea, December 15, 17—.

"I am leaving, driven away by you, and you will never see me again. But I carry away my child, who shall never call you mother.

"Gilbert."

Philip crushed the paper in a frenzy of wrath.

"Oh!" said he, grinding his teeth, "I had almost forgiven the rascal for his crime, committed on the spur of the moment; but this premeditated crime shall be punished. On your lifeless head, Andrée, I swear to kill the wretch at my first opportunity. God wills me to meet him, for he has filled the measure to the brim. Doctor, will Andrée come out of this safely?"

"Yes, yes."

"Doctor, to-morrow Andrée must enter the convent of Saint-Denis. By the day after to-morrow I must be at the nearest port. The coward has fled. I shall follow him. Besides, I must have this child. Doctor, what is the nearest seaport?"

"Havre."

"I shall be at Havre in thirty-six hours," replied Philip.

## CHAPTER CLXI.

FROM that moment, Andrée's house was sad and silent as a tomb. The knowledge that her son was dead would perhaps have killed Andrée. It would have been one of those heavy, abiding griefs that perpetually undermine. Gilbert's letter was so sudden a shock, that it revived in Andrée's generous soul all the aggressive forces and feelings that still remained there. Recovering consciousness, and looking about her, she met her brother's eyes, and read in them a wrath that inspired in her a new spring of courage.

She waited until she might regain sufficient strength for keeping her voice steady. Then, taking Philip's hand, "My dear," she said, "did you not mention the convent of Saint-Denis this morning, to which the dauphiness has promised me an entrance?"

"Yes, Andrée."

"Please take me to it, to-day."

"Thanks, sister."

"As for you, doctor," resumed Andrée, "mere thanks would be a poor return for all your kindness, devotion, and forbearance. Your reward, doctor, cannot be found on this earth."

She went up to him and embraced him. "This little medallion," she said, "encloses a portrait of me which my mother had taken when I was two years old. It ought to resemble my son; keep it, doctor, for it may sometimes speak to you of the child whom you have brought into the world, and of the mother whose life your care has saved."

Having said this, without allowing herself to give way to emotion, Andrée hastened to prepare for her journey, and, at six o'clock in the evening, she passed through the wicket door of the parlour of Saint-Denis, at whose gate Philip, unable to control his feeling, had taken what he said to himself may have been an eternal farewell.

Suddenly poor Andrée's strength deserted her. She returned to her brother, running with open arms, and held out her hands to him. He grasped them tightly, and despite the cold iron gate their burning cheeks touched and their tears were mingled.

"Adieu! Adieu!" murmured Andrée, whose grief burst forth in sobs.

"Adieu," replied Philip, stifling his anguish.

"If you ever find my son," said Andrée very low, "do not let me die without having embraced him."

"Be at rest. Adieu! adieu!"

Andrée detached herself from her brother's arms, and, supported by a lay sister, walked away, looking back constantly in the shadow cast by the convent walls.

As long as he could see her, he made a sign of recognition with his head, then he waved his handkerchief. At last, he received a final farewell, which she threw him from the depths of the dark path. Then an iron door closed behind her with a mournful sound, and all was ended.

Philip took the post at Saint-Denis. With his portmanteau behind him, he hastened on all that night and the following day, and reached Havre in the evening. He slept at the first inn he came to, and the next morning at daybreak started out to the piers to ascertain when the first boats were going to America.

He was told that the brig L'Adonis was ready to start for New York that very day. Philip sought the captain, who was finishing his final preparations, and on paying the passage money became one of the passengers. Then, having written for the last time to the dauphiness, to testify to her his respectful devotion and that she might know of his movements, he sent his baggage on board, and he himself embarked at the time of high tide.

Four o'clock was striking from the tower of François I.

when L'Adonis left the channel with spreading sails. The
sea was dark blue, the sky red along the horizon. Philip,
leaning on the railing after having saluted the few passengers, his fellow voyagers, looked at the French shore that
shone through the violet vapour, as the brig letting out more
sail and turning quickly to the right, passed La Hève and
gained the open sea. Soon the French shore, the sea, and
the other passengers, all vanished from Philip's sight. Dark
night spread her wings over all.

Philip went and shut himself into his state-room, that
he might again peruse the copy of the letter he had written
to the dauphiness, which might as well pass for a prayer
addressed to the Creator as for a farewell to a fellow
creature.

"Madame," he had written, "a man without hope and
without supports withdraws himself from you, regretting
that he has done so little for your future Majesty. This
man braves the tempests and storms of the sea, while you
remain among the dangers and intrigues of the government.
Young, beautiful, adored, surrounded by respectful friends
and idolising servants, you will forget him whom your
royal hand has deigned to elevate above the crowd. But I,
I shall never forget you; as I go to the new world, I shall
study the most efficacious means of serving you on your
throne. I leave to you my sister, poor forsaken flower,
who will have no other sunlight but that of your countenance. Deign sometimes to condescend to her, and in the
midst of your joy, of your sovereign power, in the chorus
of unanimous voices, I implore you, listen to the blessing
of an exile who will never hear you or perchance see you
more."

After reading this letter, Philip's heart ached. The
melancholy creaking of the ship, the rush of the waves as
they broke against the prow, combined, made a dismal sound
that would have saddened far happier feelings.

The night was long and sad to the young man. A visit
from the captain in the morning did not tend to lighten his
gloom. This officer told him that the greater part of the

passengers feared the sea and were staying in their rooms ; that the passage promised to be short, but unpleasant, owing to the high winds.

Philip fell into the habit of dining with the captain, and taking his breakfast alone in his state-room. And not finding himself hardened against the inconveniences of a sea voyage, he spent part of his time reclining on the deck, wrapped in his large military cloak. The rest of the time he spent in making plans for his future conduct. He kept up his spirits by diligent reading. Sometimes he encountered some of his fellow voyagers. There were two ladies who were on their way to claim some property left them in North America, and four men, one of whom, somewhat old, had his two sons with him. Such were the first-cabin passengers. On the other side Philip noticed several men of ordinary carriage, and more common appearance ; he did not find them particularly interesting.

As Philip became used to his sufferings they diminished somewhat, and he gradually recovered his serenity. Now and then fine days, bright and without storms, announced to the passengers the approach of the temperate latitudes. Then they remained longer on deck; and even in the night-time Philip, who had made a rule not to talk with any one, and who had concealed his name from the captain himself that he might avoid conversation on any painful subject, Philip could hear from his room, a few feet above his head, the voice of the captain as he walked to and fro, doubtless with some passenger. This was sufficient reason for him not to go up on deck. He then opened his port-hole for a little fresh air, and awaited the day.

Once only in the night, hearing neither talking nor walking, he went up on deck. The night was warm, the sky overcast, and in the wake of the vessel, springing up in whirls, thousands of phosphorescent atoms might be seen. This night, it seemed, was too dark and too stormy for the passengers, for Philip saw no one in the stern. Only on the forward deck, leaning against the mast of the bowsprit, a dark figure, which Philip could with diffi-

culty discern among the shadows, was either sleeping or
lost in reverie. Some second-cabin passenger, doubtless;
some poor exile looking forward, longing for the American
coast, as Philip was regretting the French shore.

Philip looked long and earnestly at this figure, immovable in its contemplation; then, as the morning cold struck
him unpleasantly, he hastened back to his room. Yet the
passenger in front still kept his gaze on the sky, which
was already beginning to grow lighter. Philip heard the
captain coming up behind him, and turned to greet him.

"Are you taking the fresh air, captain?" said he.

"Monsieur, I have just arisen."

"You are preceded by your passengers, as you see."

"By you, yes. But the officers, like the sailors, are
early birds."

"Not by me alone," said Philip. "See that man down
there, lost in dreams. He is also one of your passengers,
is he not?"

The captain looked, and appeared surprised.

"Who is that man?" asked Philip.

"A merchant," said the captain, somewhat embarrassed.

"Who is pursuing fortune?" murmured Philip. "This
brig goes too slowly for him."

The captain, instead of answering, went forward to seek
this passenger, spoke a few words to him, and Philip saw
the latter disappear down the companion-way.

"You have disturbed his reverie," said Philip to the
captain, who had rejoined him. "Moreover, he was not
annoying me."

"No, monsieur. I simply told him that the early morning cold was dangerous in these latitudes. Second-cabin
passengers are not furnished with good warm cloaks like
yours."

"Where are we now, captain?"

"Monsieur, to-morrow we shall see the Azores, where
we shall stop for fresh water, as it is getting so warm
now."

## CHAPTER CLXII.

### THE AZORES.

At the time the captain had foretold, they saw in front of the ship, shining in the sunlight far ahead, the shores of some islands, situated to the northeast. They were the Azores.

The wind was fresh, and the barque sped along. At about three o'clock in the afternoon, the islands stood out in full view. Philip saw the high peaks of the hills assuming strange forms; rocks, blackened by volcanic eruptions, cut in sharp points, overhanging deep chasms.

When they had approached within cannon shot of the first of these islands, the brig brought up to the wind, and preparations were begun for disembarking, and for taking in some fresh water, as the captain had notified them. All the passengers were anticipating with pleasure the thought of an excursion to the land. To place foot on firm ground, after twenty days and twenty nights of disagreeable sailing, is a kind of delight that only those who have made long sea voyages can appreciate.

"Gentlemen," said the captain to the passengers, whom he thought seemed undecided, "you have five hours to spend on land; take advantage of this opportunity. You will find, in this little, thickly settled island, springs of ice water for you who are naturalists; rabbits and red partridges for you who are sportsmen."

Philip took his gun and ammunition.

"But you, captain?" said he. "Why don't you come with us?"

"Because down there," replied the officer, pointing over the sea, "comes a ship of suspicious appearance, that has been following us for nearly four days. An ill-looking ship, so to speak, and I wish to watch and see what it intends to do."

Philip, satisfied with this explanation, embarked with the third load of passengers, and started for the shore.

The ladies, a few of the passengers fore and aft, either did not dare to descend, or were awaiting their turn.

The two boats then moved away, carrying joyful sailors, and still more joyful passengers.

The captain's last mandate was, —

"At eight o'clock, gentlemen, the last boat will go for you; be ready for the summons. Those late will be left behind."

When all, huntsmen and naturalists, had landed, the sailors entered at once a cave, situated a hundred feet from the shore, which turned sharply from the entrance, as if to avoid the rays of the sun.

A fresh spring of beautiful blue water glided under the mossy rocks, and was lost in fine sand within the cavern. The sailors stopped there, as we have already said, and filled their casks, which they rolled to the edge of the sea.

Philip watched them as they worked. He admired the bluish shadows of this cavern, the freshness, the sweet sound of the water, as it flowed along from cascade to cascade. He was surprised at finding at first dense darkness and extreme cold, while in a few moments the air seemed soft and balmy, and the shade filled with mysterious rays of light. Then, with arms outstretched, and knocking against the rocky sides of the cavern, he proceeded. He had begun by following the sailors without seeing them, but, little by little, every face, every feature, was visible and clear to him. And Philip preferred, as to clearness, the light of this cave to that of the sky, so glaring and harsh in full day in these climates. Meanwhile he heard the voices of the sailors dying away in the distance. One or two gun-shots resounded from the hill; then the noise ceased, and Philip was alone.

The sailors, for their part, had accomplished their task, and would not return to the cavern.

Philip gradually gave way to the enjoyment of this charming solitude and to his own varied emotions. He stretched himself on the soft, fine sand, leaned his back against the rocks covered with sweet-scented herbs, and lay buried in reverie.

The hours glided away; he had forgotten the world. Beside him his unloaded gun lay on a rock, and, that he might rest the more comfortably, he had taken his pistols, which he always carried with him, and laid them on the ground. All his past life recurred to his mind, slowly, solemnly, like a warning or a reproach; all that the future held in store for him flitted past him, like a timid bird that one may touch with a look, but never with a hand.

While Philip thus mused, doubtless others not a hundred feet away were dreaming, laughing, or hoping. He had a vague feeling of some one being near; and more than once fancied he heard the dip of the oars of the boats, as they approached the shore or carried back the passengers; some weary from the day's pleasure, others longing to resume their voyage.

But his meditations still remained undisturbed, either because the entrance of the cave had escaped the attention of some, or because others, having seen it, had not cared to enter it.

Suddenly a shadow, timid, undecided, halted on the very threshold of the cavern. Philip saw some one coming in, with outstretched hands, and head inclined toward the murmuring water. This person, more than once, knocked against the rocks, his foot having slipped on the herbs.

Then Philip arose and extended his hand to help the man back to the path. In this courteous movement his fingers touched the hand of the traveller in the shadows.

"This way," said he, pleasantly. "Monsieur, the water is here."

At the sound of this voice, the unknown hastily raised his head, and prepared to answer, revealing his face in the blue twilight of the grotto. But Philip, suddenly uttering a horrified cry, leaped back. The unknown, on his side, screamed in terror, and recoiled from Philip.

"Gilbert!"

"Philip!"

These two words clashed together, like subterranean thunder.

Then only the sound of a struggle of some sort was heard. Philip had clutched his enemy by the throat, and had dragged him deeper into the cave.

Gilbert let himself go without a word. Pushed against the rocky wall, he could draw back no farther.

"Wretch! I have you at last," raged Philip. "God has given you into my hands. God is just."

Gilbert was livid, and could not move; he let his arms fall by his sides.

"Oh, coward and scoundrel!" said Philip, "he has not even the beast's instinct of self-defence."

But Gilbert answered in a voice full of gentleness: —

"Defend myself. Why?"

"It is true, you know very well that you are in my power; that you deserve the most horrible punishment. All your crimes are proved. You have loaded a woman with shame, and you have killed her by cruelty. It was not enough for you to dishonour her, you tried to assassinate a mother."

Gilbert made no answer. Philip, who gradually became furious, lashed on by his own wrath, again seized Gilbert with angry violence. The young man made no resistance.

"Are you not a man?" said Philip, shaking him in rage. "Have you not a man's face? What! not even struggle? But I am strangling you; you perceive it, resist. Defend yourself. Coward! coward! assassin!"

Gilbert felt the pointed fingers of his enemy penetrating his throat; he turned around, shook himself, and, strong as a lion, threw Philip from him with one movement of his shoulders. Then he folded his arms.

"See," said he, "whether I cannot defend myself, if I wish. But why should I? There, take your gun. I would rather be killed by a single shot than torn to pieces by finger nails, and my body shamefully scratched."

Philip had, indeed, seized his gun, but at these words he dropped it.

"No," he murmured.

Then, rather louder,—

"Where are you going? How came you here?"

"I embarked on L'Adonis."

"You were in hiding, then? You did not see me?"

"I did not even know that you were on board."

"You lie."

"I do not lie."

"How does it happen that I did not see you?"

"Because I left my room only at night."

"So you were hiding?"

"Doubtless."

"From me?"

"No, I tell you. I am going to America on a mission, and I must not be seen. The captain has lodged me apart for this reason."

"You are in hiding, I tell you, to conceal from me your presence, and that of the infant you have stolen."

"The infant?" said Gilbert.

"Yes; you have stolen and carried away this child, to make it serve your purpose at some future day. Wretch!"

Gilbert shook his head.

"I have taken the child," said he, "so that he may not be taught to despise or deny his father."

Philip stopped a moment for breath.

"If that were true," said he, "if I could believe it, you would be less of a scoundrel than I thought you. But you have robbed me; why should you not lie to me?"

"Robbed! I robbed you?"

"You have stolen the child."

"He is my child; he is mine. One does not steal, monsieur, when one takes his own property."

"Listen!" said Philip, shaking with rage. "Just now I made up my mind to kill you. I had sworn it; I had the right to do it."

Gilbert did not answer.

"Now God enlightens me. God has thrown you in my way, as if to say to me, ' Vengeance is useless. Vengeance is right only when one is abandoned by God.' I shall not kill you; I shall only pull down the unfortunate edifice which you have built. This child is your resource for the future. You shall at once return him to me."

"But I have not got him here," said Gilbert. "One does not carry a two weeks old baby across the ocean."

"You must have found a nurse for him. Why could you not take the nurse with you?"

"I tell you that I have not taken the child with me."

"Then you have left him in France. At what place have you left him?"

Gilbert was silent.

"Answer! where have you left him to be brought up, and what resources had you?'

Gilbert was silent.

"Ah! wretch! you defy me," said Philip. "You do not fear to awaken my anger? Will you tell me where my sister's child is? Will you give me this child?"

"My child is my own," murmured Gilbert.

"Rascal! So you wish to die?"

"I do not wish to give up my child."

"Gilbert, listen, I speak gently. Gilbert, I will try to forget the past, I will try to forgive you. Gilbert, do you not understand my generosity? I forgive you. I forgive you all the shame and misfortune which you have brought on my family. It is a great sacrifice. Give me back the child. Will you have more? Do you wish me to try to vanquish Andrée's natural, legitimate repugnances? Shall I inter-

cede for you ?   Well, I will do so.   Give me back that child.
One   word   more.   Andrée   loves   her   son,   your   son,
ecstatically.   She will be moved by your repentance.   I
promise you so, I will answer for it.   But only give me
back this child, Gilbert, — give it to me."

Gilbert folded his arms, looking steadfastly at Philip
with eyes full of sadness.

"You have not believed me," he said; "I do not believe
you.   Not because you are not an honourable man, but because I have fathomed the deepest abyss of the prejudices
of rank.   There is no longer any return nor any forgiveness
possible.   We are mortal enemies.   You are the stronger.
Be the victor.   I do not ask you for your weapon.   Do not
ask me for mine."

"You acknowledge then that it is a weapon ? "

"Against scorn ?   Yes.   Against ingratitude ?   Yes.
Against insults ?   Yes."

"Once more, Gilbert," said Philip, his lip curling with
scorn, " will you ? "

" No."

" Take care."

"No."

"I do not wish to murder you.   I only wish to give you
an opportunity of killing Andrée's brother.   One crime
more.   Ah! it is a temptation.   Take this pistol; here is
another ; let us each count three and fire."

And he threw both pistols at Gilbert's feet.

The young man did not move.

" A duel," said he, " I have a right to refuse."

"You prefer me to kill you ! " cried Philip, mad with
rage and disappointment.

"I would rather be killed by you."

"Reflect.   I have lost control of myself."

"I have reflected."

"I am right.   God must absolve me."

"I know it.   Kill me."

"For the last time, will you fight ? "

"No."

"You decline to defend yourself ? "

"Yes."

"Well, then, die like a scoundrel, from whom I purge the earth, die like a heathen, die like a thief, die like a dog ! "

And Philip discharged his pistol at Gilbert, almost touching him with the muzzle. The latter stretched out his arms, swayed first backward, then forward, and fell on his face, without uttering a cry. Philip saw the sand under his feet, dyed in the bloody stream; his wits forsook him, and he rushed out of the cavern.

Before him was the shore; a boat was waiting. The time for starting had been appointed for eight o'clock, and it was now a few minutes after eight.

"Ah! here you are, monsieur," said the sailors. "You are the last; every one else is on board. What have you killed? "

Philip, on hearing that word, lost consciousness. They took him on board the ship, which was unfurling its sails.

"Every one has returned? " said the captain.

"We are bringing back the last passenger with us," said the sailors. "He must have had a fall, for he has fainted."

The captain gave the necessary orders, and the brig sailed rapidly away from the Azores at the same time that the unknown vessel which had annoyed them so long sailed into the harbour, under the American flag.

The captain exchanged signals, and, apparently reassured, sailed away into the shades of night.

It was not until the next day that they discovered that one passenger was missing.

## EPILOGUE.

### THE NINTH OF MAY.

On the ninth of May, 1774, at eight o'clock in the evening, Versailles presented a most curious and interesting spectacle.

From the first day of the month King Louis XV., attacked with a malady the serious nature of which his physicians at first dared not confess to him, kept his couch, and now began anxiously to consult the countenances of those who surrounded him to discover in them some reflection of the truth, or some ray of hope.

The physician Bordeu had pronounced the king suffering from an attack of small-pox of the most malignant nature, and the physician La Martinière, who had agreed with his colleague as to the nature of the king's complaint, gave it as his opinion that his Majesty should be informed of the real state of the case "in order that, both spiritually and temporally, as a king and as a Christian, he should take measures for his own safety and that of his kingdom."

"His most Christian Majesty," said he, "should have extreme unction administered to him."

La Martinière represented the party of the dauphin, — the opposition. Bordeu asserted that the bare mention of the serious nature of the disease would kill the king, and said that for his part he would not be a party to such regicide.

Bordeu represented Madame Dubarry's party.

In fact, to call in the aid of the Church to the king was
to expel the favourite.   When religion enters at one door,
it is full time for Satan to make his exit by the other.

In the mean time, during all these intestine divisions of
the faculty, of the royal family, and of the different parties
of the court, the disease took quiet possession of the aged,
corrupt, and worn-out frame of the king, and set up such
a strong position that neither remedies nor prescriptions
could dislodge it.

From the first symptoms of the attack, Louis beheld his
couch surrounded by his two daughters, the favourite, and
the courtiers whom he especially delighted to honour.
They still laughed and stood firm by each other.

All at once the austere and ominous countenance of
Madame Louise of France appeared at Versailles.   She
had quitted her cell to give to her father, in her turn, the
cares and consolations he so much required.

She entered, pale and stern as a statue of Fate; she
was no longer a daughter to a father, a sister to her
fellow sisters; she rather resembled those ancient proph-
etesses who in the evil day of adversity poured in the
startled ears of kings the boding cry, "Woe! Woe! Woe!"
She fell upon Versailles like a thunder-shock at the very
hour when it was Madame Dubarry's custom to visit the
king, who kissed her white hands, and pressed them like
some healing medicament to his aching brow and burning
cheeks.

At her sight all fled.   The sisters, trembling, sought
refuge in a neighbouring apartment.   Madame Dubarry
bent the knee, and hastened to those which she occupied;
the privileged courtiers retreated in disorder to the antechambers; the two physicians alone remained standing by
the fireside.

"My daughter!" murmured the king, opening his eyes,
heavy with pain and fever.

"Yes, sire," said the princess, "your daughter."

"And you come —"

"To remind you of God!"

The king raised himself in an upright posture and attempted to smile.

"For you have forgotten God," resumed Madame Louise.

"I!"

"And I wish to recall Him to your thoughts."

"My daughter! I am not so near death, I trust, that your exhortations need be so very urgent. My illness is very slight, — a slow fever, attended with some inflammation."

"Your malady, sire," interrupted the princess, "is that which, according to etiquette, should summon around your Majesty's couch all the great prelates of the kingdom. When a member of the royal family is attacked with small-pox, the rites of the Church should be administered without loss of time."

"Madame!" exclaimed the king, greatly agitated, and becoming deadly pale, "what is that you say?"

"Madame!" broke in the terrified physicians.

"I repeat," continued the princess, "that your Majesty is attacked with the small-pox."

The king uttered a cry.

"The physicians did not tell me so," replied he.

"They had not the courage. But I look forward to another kingdom for your Majesty than the kingdom of France. Draw near to God, sire, and solemnly review your past life."

"The small-pox!" muttered Louis; "a fatal disease! — Bordeu! La Martinière! can it be true?"

The two practitioners hung their heads.

"Then I am lost!" said the king, more and more terrified.

"All diseases can be cured, sire," said Bordeu, taking the initiative, "especially when the patient preserves his composure of mind."

"God gives peace to the mind and health to the body," replied the princess.

"Madame," said Bordeu, boldly, although in a low voice, "you are killing the king!"

The princess deigned no reply; she approached the sick monarch, and, taking his hand, which she covered with kisses, —

"Break with the past, sire," said she, "and give an example to your people. No one warned you; you ran the risk of perishing eternally. Promise solemnly to live a Christian life if you are spared, — die like a Christian, if God calls you hence!"

As she concluded, she imprinted a second kiss on the royal hand, and with slow step took her way through the antechambers. There she let her long, black veil fall over her face, descended the staircase with a grave and majestic air, and entered her carriage, leaving behind her a stupefaction and terror which cannot be described.

The king could not rouse his spirits, except by dint of questioning his physicians, who replied in terms of courtly flattery.

"I do not wish," said he, "that the scene of Metz with the Duchess de Châteauroux should be re-enacted here. Send for Madame d'Aiguillon, and request her to take Madame Dubarry with her to Rueil."

This order was equivalent to an expulsion. Bordeu attempted to remonstrate, but the king ordered him to be silent. Bordeu, moreover, saw his colleague ready to report all that passed to the dauphin, and, well aware what would be the issue of the king's malady, he did not persist; but, quitting the royal chamber, he proceeded to acquaint Madame Dubarry with the blow which had just fallen on her fortunes.

The countess, terrified at the ominous and insulting expression which she saw already pictured on every face around her, hastened to withdraw. In an hour she was without the walls of Versailles, seated beside the Duchess d'Aiguillon, who, like a trustworthy and grateful friend, was taking the disgraced favourite to her château

of Rueil, which had descended to her from the great Richelieu.

Bordeu, on his side, shut the door of the king's chamber against all the royal family, under pretext of contagion. Louis's apartment was thenceforward walled up: no one might enter but Religion and Death.

The king had the last rites of the Church administered to him that same day, and this news soon spread through Paris, where the disgrace of the favourite was already known, and circulated from mouth to mouth.

All the court hastened to pay their respects to the dauphin, who closed his doors and refused to see any one.

But the following day the king was better, and sent the Duke d'Aiguillon to carry his compliments to Madame Dubarry. This day was the ninth of May, 1774.

The court deserted the pavilion occupied by the dauphin, and flocked in such crowds to Rueil, where the favourite was residing, that since the banishment of Monsieur de Choiseul to Chanteloup such a string of carriages had never been witnessed.

Things were in this position, therefore: Would the king live, and Madame Dubarry still remain queen? or would the king die, and Madame Dubarry sink to the condition of an infamous and execrable courtesan?

This was why Versailles, on the evening of the ninth of May, in the year 1774, presented such a curious and interesting spectacle.

On the Place d'Armes, before the palace, several groups had formed in front of the railing, who, with sympathetic air, seemed most anxious to hear the news.

They were citizens of Versailles or Paris, and every now and then, with all the politeness imaginable, they questioned the *gardes du corps*, who were pacing slowly up and down the Court of Honour with their hands behind their backs, respecting the king's health.

Gradually these groups dispersed. The inhabitants of

Paris took their seats in the *pataches* or stage-coaches to return peaceably to their own homes; whilst those of Versailles, sure of having the earliest news from the fountain-head, also retired to their several dwellings.

No one was to be seen in the streets but the patrols of the watch, who performed their duty a little more quietly than usual, and that gigantic world called the Palace of Versailles became by degrees shrouded in darkness and silence, like that greater world which contained it.

At the angle of the street bordered with trees which extends in front of the palace, a man advanced in years was seated on a stone bench overshadowed by the already leafy boughs of the horse-chestnuts, with his expressive and poetic features turned towards the château, leaning with both hands on his cane, and supporting his chin on his hands.

He was nevertheless an old man, bent by age and ill-health, but his eye still sparkled with something of its youthful fire, and his thoughts glowed even more brightly than his eyes.

He was absorbed in melancholy contemplation, and did not perceive a second personage, who, after peeping curiously through the iron railing, and questioning the *gardes du corps*, crossed the esplanade in a diagonal direction, and advanced straight towards the bench, with the intention of seating himself upon it.

This personage was a young man with projecting cheekbones, low forehead, aquiline nose slightly bent to one side, and a sardonic smile. Whilst advancing towards the stone bench he chuckled sneeringly, although alone, seeming to reply by this manifestation to some secret thought.

When within three paces of the bench, he perceived the old man, and paused, scanning him with his oblique and stealthy glance, although evidently fearing to let his purpose be seen.

"You are enjoying the fresh air, I presume, monsieur?" said he, approaching him with an abrupt movement.

The old man raised his head.

"Ha!" exclaimed the new-comer, "it is my illustrious master!"

"And you are my young practitioner?" said the old man.

"Will you permit me to take a seat beside you, monsieur?"

"Most willingly." And the old man made room on the bench beside him.

"It appears that the king is doing better?" said the young man. "The people rejoice." And he burst a second time into his sneering laugh.

The old man made no reply.

"The whole day long the carriages have been rolling from Paris to Rueil, and from Rueil to Versailles. The Countess Dubarry will marry the king as soon as his health is re-established." And he burst into a louder laugh than before.

Again the old man made no reply.

"Pardon me if I laugh at fate," continued the young man, with a gesture of nervous impatience, "but every good Frenchman, look you, loves his king, and my king is better to-day."

"Do not jest thus on such a subject, monsieur," said the old man, gently. "The death of a man is always a misfortune for some one, and the death of a king is frequently a great misfortune for all."

"Even the death of Louis XV.?" interrupted the young man, in a tone of irony. "Oh, my dear master, a distinguished philosopher like you to sustain such a proposition! I know all the energy and skill of your paradoxes, but I cannot compliment you on this one."

The old man shook his head.

"And, besides," added the new-comer, "why think of the king's death? Who speaks of such an event? The

king has the small-pox; well, we all know that complaint.
The king has beside him Bordeu and La Martinière, who
are skilful men. Oh, I will wager a trifle, my dear master,
that Louis the Well-Beloved will escape this turn! Only
this time the French people do not suffocate themselves in
churches, putting up vows for him, as on the occasion of
his former illness. Mark me, everything grows antiquated
and is abandoned!"

"Silence!" said the old man, shuddering; "silence! for
I tell you you are speaking of a man over whom at this
moment the destroying angel of God hovers."

His young companion, surprised at this strange language,
looked at the speaker, whose eyes had never quitted the
*façade* of the château.

"Then you have more positive intelligence?" inquired
he.

"Look!" said the old man, pointing with his finger to
one of the windows of the palace; "what do you behold
yonder?"

"A window lighted up, — is that what you mean?"

"Yes; but lighted in what manner?"

"By a wax candle placed in a little lantern."

"Precisely."

"Well?"

"Well, young man, do you know what the flame of that
wax-light represents?"

"No, monsieur."

"It represents the life of the king."

The young man looked more fixedly at his aged companion, as if to be certain that he was in his perfect
senses.

A friend of mine, Monsieur de Jussieu," continued the
old man, "has placed that wax-light there, which will burn
as long as the king is alive."

"It is a signal, then?"

"A signal which Louis XV.'s successor devours with his
eyes from behind some neighbouring curtain. This signal,

which shall warn the ambitious of the dawn of a new reign, informs a poor philosopher like myself of the instant when the breath of the Almighty sweeps away, at the same moment, an age and a human existence."

The young man shuddered in his turn, and moved closer to his companion.

"Oh," said the aged philosopher, "mark well this night, young man! Behold what clouds and tempests it bears in its murky bosom! The morning which will succeed it I shall witness, no doubt, for I am not yet old enough to abandon hope of seeing the morrow; but a reign will commence on that morrow which you will see to its close, and which contains mysteries which I cannot hope to be a spectator of. It is not, therefore, without interest that I watch yonder trembling flame, whose signification I have just explained to you."

"True, my master," murmured the young man, "most true."

"Louis XIV. reigned seventy-three years," continued the old man. "How many will Louis XVI. reign?"

"Ah!" exclaimed the younger of the two, pointing to the window, which had just become shrouded in darkness.

"The king is dead!" said the old man, rising, with a sort of terror.

And both kept silence for some minutes.

Suddenly a chariot, drawn by eight fiery horses, started at full gallop from the court-yard of the palace. Two outriders preceded it, each holding a torch in his hand.

In the chariot were the dauphin, Marie Antoinette, and Madame Elizabeth, the sister of the king. The flame of the torches threw a gloomy light on their pale features. The carriage passed close to the two men, within ten paces of the bench from which they had risen.

"Long live King Louis XVI! Long live the queen!" shouted the young man, in a loud, harsh voice, as if he meant to insult this new-born majesty instead of saluting it.

The dauphin bowed; the queen showed her face at the window, sad and severe. The carriage dashed on and disappeared.

"My dear Monsieur Rousseau," said the younger of the two spectators, "then is our friend Mademoiselle Dubarry a widow?"

"To-morrow she will be exiled," said his aged companion. "Adieu, Monsieur Marat!"

THE END.